"RIVETING, TERRIFYING, AND JUST ABSOLUTELY GREAT...

Readers of Mr. McDowell's previous two novels will have no cause to be disappointed with GILDED NEEDLES. . . . It's a wonderfully complete and textured novel. McDowell is in perfect control from that creepy epigram right up to the book's last terrifying sentence. . . . To say that GILDED NEEDLES is a great read and that it offers the deep pleasure of going along for the ride with a novelist who is coming to the height of his powers, is to say two-thirds of it. The rest is the simple fact that Michael McDowell must now be regarded as the finest writer of paperback originals in America."

Stephen King

"Readers of weak constitution should beware."

Publishers Weekly

Other Avon Books by
Michael McDowell

THE AMULET
COLD MOON OVER BABYLON

MICHAEL McDOWELL

GILDED NEEDLES

AVON
PUBLISHERS OF BARD, CAMELOT AND DISCUS BOOKS

GILDED NEEDLES is an original publication of Avon Books. This work has never before appeared in book form.

AVON BOOKS
A division of
The Hearst Corporation
959 Eighth Avenue
New York, New York 10019

First Avon Printing, November, 1980

AVON TRADEMARK REG. U.S. PAT. OFF. AND IN
OTHER COUNTRIES, MARCA REGISTRADA, HECHO EN
U.S.A.

Printed in the U.S.A.

For Laurence

Revenge is a dish best eaten cold.
                              —Old Spanish proverb

Prologue
At Midnight

⊙⊙⊙⊙⊙⊙⊙⊙⊙⊙⊙⊙⊙⊙⊙⊙⊙⊙⊙⊙⊙⊙⊙⊙⊙⊙⊙⊙⊙⊙⊙⊙⊙⊙⊙⊙

ON a dark winter's night, seven children huddled around a grate on Mulberry Street. Each in turn, for the space of a minute or so, sat directly upon the iron grid to enjoy the warmth of the steam escaping from the underground furnace that heated the headquarters of the New York police. Barely clothed in filthy, formless rags and with faces and exposed skin dark with grime, they seemed only rickety shadows in the unlighted street, a coven of degenerate goblins. A shrill argument arose among the children whether a girl, who carried a wheezing infant in her arms, ought to be allotted a longer time upon the grate, but before the squabblers could come to any decision, their debate was drowned out by the sudden tolling of all the bells in the city.

The Year of Grace 1881 had become the Year of Grace 1882.

Not far away, in the cellar of a rotting building on Grand Street stood a stale-beer shop, a place so low that it was not even distinguished by a name. Impoverished, fallen, criminal, and diseased men and women there consumed flat beer that had been discarded by Bowery saloon keepers the night before as no longer fit to serve. The customers drank uncomplaining until they were insensible to the cold without and their misery within. The shop was run by a mute black man, who dispensed beer all night long into pottery mugs that had never been washed. In this close room, where a small coal fire served to fill the place with choking smoke without warming anyone, men raved against God, the women who had betrayed them, the authorities who had imprisoned them, the Democratic machine which had failed to set them free, and whomever else could be brought to enfeebled mind. The women, most of them mercifully unconscious, had folded themselves up into the dark corners, or sat with their heads pressed against the cold sweating walls. The purchase of two draughts at a cent each allowed them the privilege of remaining in the room until dawn. Ragged children fought beneath the tables, and the monkey of the consumptive organ grinder swung from the enraged to the stupefied without prejudice, and added his piercing chatter to the welter of incomprehensible voices.

Two sullen men, only that morning released from Blackwell's Island, sat gambling near the door of the shop. A slight pause in the turn of their greasy cards when the church bells began to ring was all the notice that was accorded the New Year in that unhappy place.

Not far away, in the cellar of a house on Mott Street, three young women wearing striped dresses and ecstatic smiles initiated a shy friend into the mysteries of opium-smoking. The giggling novice placed the tarlike bolus on the flattened end of the *yen hock,* which she had mistaken at first for a knitting needle, and turned it in the flame of the green fairy lamp. She glanced around her at the impassive dreamers, only half of them Chinese, and nervously whispered to her companions, "You cert that we're safe here?" When the New Year's bells penetrated that crowded, smoky, silent room, they were incorporated into a hundred lassitudinous dreams, a hundred visions of gray and blue.

A quarter of an hour before—on the other side of police headquarters from heathen Mott Street—a hansom cab had drawn up before an unobtrusive brick facade on West Houston Street and a veiled face framed with raven-black hair had peered anxiously out. The driver confirmed the address for his passenger, but drove away before her timid knock had gained her entrance into the house.

"Maggie sent me," she whispered to the severely dressed, severely featured woman who had opened the door. The veiled lady was an actress who half an hour before had received great applause for her portrayal of the titular heroine of *Ada the Girl Scout of the Sierras* at the National Theatre on the Bowery.

At the foot of the darkened stairs, the actress hesitated. Then, another young woman, prettily blond and in a gay red dress, appeared on the landing above and, waving a candle, beckoned her with soothing reassurances. "You're Dollie!" she exclaimed. "Oh such beautiful hair, such beautiful hair!"

Now the actress lay on a narrow iron bed in a tiny room on the fourth floor of the quiet house. She grasped and twisted the thin coverlet in agitation. Blithely humming, the pretty blond woman drew the thin curtains across the window and poured more coal upon the small fire in the grate. She turned gracefully with a smile, and in a cheery voice asked the actress if the laudanum had yet taken effect.

The actress's reply to the abortionist was lost amid the New Year's bells.

Not so very far from the quiet house where the pretty blond woman in the red dress pursued her lucrative trade was the Bowery, nearly impassible with revelers, though their number this Saturday night seemed not much greater than upon any other. Vendors of pasties and hot corn and fresh oysters screamed louder than those celebrating, and new tunes pounded out on spavined pianos poured from every other doorway. Rollicking music from the German bands alternated with the pop-pop of the shooting galleries and the rasping cries of the crippled and blind beggars who lined the walks. Boys who worked in bookshops for eight dollars a week kept festive company with young milliners. but were snubbed by the clerks who made a thousand dollars a year, boarded in houses in the west Twenties, and had come to the Bowery with their landladies' daughters. Italian families promenaded with stately pride along the lower Bowery and turned around only when they met their German counterparts walking south. Newsboys and bootblacks, never sufficiently protected against the cold, often frail and just as frequently found with cigars in their mouths, lounged on corners,

raced through the street in pursuit of some fight supposed
to be taking place a couple of streets away, or thronged
the entrances to the variety theaters. When the New
Year bells rang, the music, the hundreds of cries and
shoutings, the thousand boisterous happy conversations
on the Bowery blended and welled into one monstrous
cheer for the passing of the old year and the beginning of
the new.

Half a mile west of the Bowery, in front of the recently constructed New York Hospital on Fifteenth Street,
a young woman in drab demure attire walked arm-in-arm
with her sister, a schoolgirl dressed in a bright green frock,
a red jacket with fur trim, and a round fur hat with felt
ribbons streaming down the back. Just when they had
come within sight of the lamps of Satan's Circus—Sixth
Avenue—they unlinked. The older girl dropped into a
brick recess of the building on the corner and the schoolgirl stepped into the harsh light of the busy avenue and
stared about her tentatively. She scanned the faces of
passersby for a few moments and at last pulled on the
sleeve of one middle-aged gentleman whose pace had
slowed as he approached her.

"Please mister," she said, in a high plaintive voice,
"I've been separated from my sister. Can you help me to
find her again?"

The New Year's bells began to ring, but before they
had left off the schoolgirl and the middle-aged gentleman
were proceeding to a furnished chamber on Greenwich
Avenue where the child thought it possible that the elder
sister was waiting. The woman in drab attire emerged
from her hiding place and continued her monotonous circuit alone.

Only just beyond earshot of the traffic along Satan's
Circus, in rooms on the first floor of an old mansion, two
men stood with their backs to the fire in a carved marble
hearth, talking in low voices. The older man was tall and
imposing, with white hair and piercing blue eyes. His
companion was young and handsome, with short brown
hair and a thick brown beard. They were father- and
son-in-law and had spent the last evening of the year in
this club patronized by Republican lawyers and judges.
The clock on the mantel behind them chimed midnight;
they turned to look at it, and in the moment of turning

the bells of the church across the street began their celebratory peal. The two men shook hands with one another and then moved to the center of the room. The other dozen Republicans there laid aside their papers and their conversations and stood. They all shook hands, engineered small smiles, and wished their fellows the best for the coming year. The old man, at the end of a brief speech, expressed the certainty that 1882 would see the Democrats hounded from office and deprived of all influence in the city.

Along Fifth Avenue and around the fashionable squares uptown, where men and their wives still strolled about, the bells rang with particular beauty and clarity in the cold night. Everyone paused and smiled graciously to strangers who happened to be near. After the gentlemen had tipped their hats and the ladies had murmured well-bred wishes for the coming year, they all passed on toward home.

In the Fifth Avenue Hotel, the management had laid on a special supper. At half past eleven, when the doors to the dining room were opened, three hundred–odd guests charged through and were seated as they might at the thirty tables laid for twelve. An English duchess found herself beside a gentleman who boasted of having killed seventeen Seminoles on the shore of Lake Okeechobee, and across from a female advocate of free love. The duchess's titled son conversed with a confidence man whose right eye had been shot out by the Mexican police. At midnight thirty waiters appeared, each bearing a platter with a steaming roasted pig atop it. A United States senator toasted the new year with champagne and he was seconded in a babel of languages and accents.

A few streets away, in a second-floor window of a little slice of a house on gray and dreary Gramercy Park, stood a robed lady, her face harshly illumined by a guttering candle on the sill. One arm was raised and she impatiently fingered the drapery. She stared at the men who passed on the walk below, as if watching for one in particular.

Just as the bells of the Episcopal church on Fourth Avenue pealed the New Year, a young smooth-shaven man carrying a large black leather bag hurried up from the direction of Third Avenue. He glanced up at the window, signaled to the lady there, and expeditiously mounted the steps. The woman disappeared from the window and only a few moments later opened the door to admit the eagerly awaited hairdresser.

For the Irish woman wandering the Battery, whose infant had just perished in her arms; for the Italian merchant who had just sold his last morsel of tainted horse meat to the squatters living in shacks on the hilly wasteland above Eightieth Street; and for all those in between: for the poor whose poverty was such that they would soon die of it, for the criminals whose criminality was no final guarantee against the poverty they tried to escape, for the mildly prosperous and moderately respectable, for the moderately prosperous and very respectable, and for the very rich whose needn't trouble themselves with respectability, the year of Our Lord 1882 was begun.

Part I

The Black Triangle

Chapter 1

On a narrow short bed in a narrow short room lay a young woman whose freckled skin was pale and blotched, whose unrefined features were slack and heavy, whose long red hair spread tangled and disordered over the thin coverlet. Two children of eight years, each with a penny taper in a tin holder, approached the bed cautiously. The light flickering across their faces showed identical features and only the barest differentiation of sex.

The little girl, who was called Ella, poked a sharp finger into the ribs of the red-haired woman to make sure that she was dead. Ella nodded to Rob, her twin brother, and they set their candles, identical as themselves, on a rickety table by the head of the bed.

While Ella struggled to remove the coarse woolen skirt of the dead woman, Rob fetched a sharp pair of scissors from the dresser that stood near the hearth. He lifted the corpse's head, twisted the wiry red hair around his fist, and then snipped the tresses free, close to the scalp. Ella, plucking gingerly at the blood-drenched undergarments, breathily chanted: "No 'rings, no watch, no jew-la-ry . . ."

"No 'rings, no watch, no jew-la-ry," echoed her brother in an identical accent, and sharply turning aside the heavy head with his elbow, he cut the last thick strand of hair

9

from behind the ear. The woman's shorn head dropped back onto the pillow, and the filmed eyes flew open as if in outrage at the indignity.

Rob loosely twisted the hair and carried it to the dresser, well away from the candle flames. Then he assisted Ella in stripping the dead woman naked. Her clothes they folded and placed in a shallow basket, pulled from beneath the bed.

As her brother stretched and rolled the checkered cotton stockings, Ella went off briefly and came back with two wetted rags with which the children methodically wiped the corpse, paying particular attention to the clotted blood that colored the inside of her thighs. In a wandering melodic counterpoint, Rob and Ella Shanks continued their refrain: "No 'rings, no watch, no jew-la-ry . . ."

When finished, they undressed themselves, stacking their garments neatly upon the dresser. From a wooden box in the corner of the room, they took filthy, vermin-infested tatters of cloth and hung them upon their bodies in some mockery of attire. Then at the grate, where a small fire of coals burned smokily, Ella scraped the walls of the hearth with a poker to dislodge soot. After the children had smeared their faces and hands with the ashes, they appeared indistinguishable from any two street Arabs perishing of cold that night on the streets of New York.

Taking one another's hands, they pulled aside a corner of the curtain over the room's single window and peered out into the night but could see nothing more than the cold bright stars, the flat angular expanses of smoke-darkened brick, and the rotting fences that enclosed the blasted yard behind the house.

As they turned around again, a tall angular woman with harsh set features slipped noiselessly into the room. She had dark skin, black eyes set wide apart in a flat face, and a low beetling brow with greasy black hair crimped severely down over it. Louisa Shanks's dress was of heavily starched yellow bombazine and shone metallically in the scant firelight.

She approached the bed, bent forward from the waist, and passed one of the children's candles slowly up the length of the corpse. She eyed the dead woman with more of a critical than a moral or religious interest. She righted herself, turned to the children, and nodded her approval.

At this signal from their aunt, Ella unlatched the door that opened into the tiny yard in the back of the house. A blast of frigid air blew out the candles. The little girl ran out into the yard and pulled a low two-wheeled cart up to the door. A ribbon of bells running from one post to another across the back jingled merrily. Ella strapped herself into the harness of the small vehicle and stood patiently in the cold.

Inside, Louisa Shanks and her nephew Rob pulled a burlap bag over the corpse of the young woman on the bed, tied the top loosely, and then carried the body to the cart just outside. They concealed the burlap bag beneath a pile of rags.

Rob then ran to the end of the yard, quietly pulled open a wide picket gate, and scampered along a foul narrow passage to King Street. In a moment, Ella and Louisa heard his low-pitched whistle. Ella pulled the cart forward into the alleyway, which was only inches wider than the cart itself; she trembled with the cold. Louisa closed the gate behind her niece, and retreated into the house with the ribbon of bells she had removed from the cart so that the children's progress would be silent.

Crouching at the end of the alleyway, Rob waved his sister cautiously on and Ella pulled the cart out into the narrow street, dark but for the pallid yellow light that spilled from ground- and second-floor windows. All along the street men and women reeled in drunken boisterousness from one low hall to the next; muffled music grew suddenly louder whenever a street door was flung open. However, no one took any notice of the ragpickers who shambled up the middle of the street, silent and weary and slow, dark spots of cold misery in the midst of the New Year's revelry.

On busy, well-lighted MacDougal Street, they narrowly dodged two carriages whose drunken drivers were racing one another to City Hall Park on a bet, and went northward until they reached Bleecker Street—that strange compromise avenue where impoverished gentility shared lodgings with wealthy criminals in hiding, where married women met gentlemen who were not their husbands, and where well-bred octoroons entertained philanthropists and politicians. Rob dashed ahead of his trudging sister, an unconcerned beggar swinging around lampposts and staring doltishly in lighted shop windows.

But at a certain number, while his sister trailed wearily behind, harnessed to the cart, Rob leapt up the steps and through the unsecured entrance of a small brick house. He dashed down a greasy unlighted hallway and knocked at a door behind which was the loud uncontrolled laughter of several men and the stench of cheap tobacco.

A young man wearing ill-fitting trousers and a striped shirt opened the door and stared down at Rob. His laughter, evidently occasioned by some joke told by one of the several men who lounged about in the smoke-filled room behind him, died away, but a sharp sarcastic smile took its place. "Yes?" he said mockingly to Rob, "and to whom do I owe the honor of this first visit of the New Year? Sir? Have you a card to present?"

The four other young men in the room, laughing anew, pressed forward to examine the urchin in the doorway.

"Please, mister," whispered Rob, "I have something for you in my cart outside."

"Lettuce!" cried the young man, "you have brought me lettuce! As a New Year's gift!"

Rob shook his head bewildered.

"Or my sister," the young man cried. "You have brought my sister on a visit! John, come here, you have always said you wished to meet my sister. Well this young man, evidently an agent of the Pennsylvania Railway, has brought her to us on his cart. Sir," he said to Rob severely, "why have you left my sister in the cold? Bring her in! Bring her in!"

"Please, mister," said Rob, "maybe it is your sister on my cart. But if it is, then I'm sorry to tell you she's dead."

The man who had answered the door then waved his cigar in Rob's face as if it had been a candle by which he might observe the boy's features. "I've seen you before, haven't I?" he said soberly.

"Twice, sir."

"A young girl?"

Rob nodded.

"How did she die?" The four men behind the questioner listened intently to the exchange.

"Don't know, but she's dead."

"How much do you want?"

"Seven dollars."

The medical student nodded. "She's on your cart?"

"Yes, sir. Just outside. My sister's there. She's wrapped in burlap."

The medical student turned to his friends and called for a collection. The seven dollars was quickly made up in change and gold. While counting it over, he said, "John, you and Dick, go out there and bring it in. And for God's sake, don't let yourselves be seen!" Two of the men slipped into the passageway, and hastened toward the street door.

The medical student poured the money from one hand into the other while he waited for his friends to return. Rob stood patiently by.

In another moment the two friends appeared again in the doorway, furtively supporting the burlap bag between them. Once inside they hurried down the hallway and into the medical student's chamber. One of them loosened the string at the top of the bag and the shorn head of the dead girl flopped out onto the threadbare carpet.

The coins dropped into Rob's outstretched hands and in another second, he was gone. The door of the medical student's room closed softly, and the key was turned in the lock.

Chapter 2

❦❦❦❦❦❦❦❦❦❦❦❦❦❦❦❦❦❦❦❦❦❦❦❦❦❦❦❦❦❦❦

In the first hour of the new year, Lena Shanks sat alone in the parlor of the house on West Houston Street. Occasionally someone passing along the brick walk outside rapped an insolent greeting on the glass of the barred windows, but the thick layers of drapery were always closed to prevent the curious from peering in. The parlor was sumptuously but curiously decorated. All the fine furniture, all the upholstery, all the papering and paint and decoration were but a single color: gold.

The walls were covered in flocked gold paper, and the moldings and the plasterwork in the ceiling had been painted in gold leaf. The draperies and hangings, the lambrequins and the pillows, the hearth and the hardware were all the same color. The carpet on the floor was a dull gold wool squared with thin black lines, with funereal rosettes of black flowers in each gold square. The furniture had been painted gold and covered in gold-and-white striped damask. The ornaments on the mantel were of gold, and the paintings that hung upon the walls were encased in ornate gold frames. One of a pair of gold-painted curio cabinets contained books with gold-tooled leather bindings and the other displayed a motley collection of gold plate, jewelry, and gimcracks. The mirror above the mantel and the pier glass between the two windows had been sprayed with a fine layer of gold, so that the little in the room that was not gold was reflected in the one pervasive color. The furnishing of the oppressive chamber had not only an identity of hue, but of origin as well—everything had been stolen.

Lena Shanks sat bolt upright on a small gold chair drawn up before the gold-tiled hearth, with a basket of fine linens in her lap. By the light of the fire she worked with a pair of delicate scissors, pricking out the monogram that had been stitched into the corner of each piece.

Lena Shanks was five feet three inches tall and weighed about two hundred pounds. She possessed a face that was wide, common, and obviously Germanic. Her large nose was flat, her dull eyes were heavy-lidded, her wide lips were dull brown, cracked and generally parted—for the drawing of breath in so large a woman was ever a difficulty. Her fine brown hair was always pulled tight into a dense bun at the nape of her neck. This was to conceal the fact that she was missing her left ear, which had been bitten off in 1869 during a fight with Gallus Meg of the Hole-in-the-Wall; that ear was still to be seen, preserved with several others, in a jar of alcohol behind the bar of that low-down but flourishing establishment.

Lena wore dark voluminous skirts, white blouses, and tight black jackets with black lace edging. She was slow-moving, deliberate, and always walked with the help of a cane, which on occasion doubled as a weapon. The neighborhood knew her as "Black Lena," because of her jackets, but sometimes—more poetically—she was called "My Female Uncle," for "uncle" denoted a pawnbroker, and "pawnbroker" was a transparent euphemism for a receiver of stolen property, her primary occupation.

When the gold clock upon the golden lambrequin that covered the painted mantel chimed one o'clock, her daughter Daisy appeared in the doorway of the room.

"Girl and boy ought to be back," said Lena. Her German-accented voice was slow and thick and she did not look up from her work.

"Well, I hope they ain't been stopped!" cried their mother from the doorway. "How do you think Ella would explain the girl in her cart?" she laughed.

The girl whose corpse was tumbled in the corner of

the medical student's single room, awaiting a sober dissection by the five friends, was one of Daisy Shanks's rare failures. For Daisy, a careful abortionist, there was rarely the necessity to dispose of a corpse, whether by depositing it on Bleecker Street, in the rooms of a succession of medical students, or in the cold lap of the North River. The unfortunate young woman had been a waiter-girl at a saloon on Bayard Street; she had died in the fourth-story chamber where the actress now slept fitfully.

It was Lena Shanks who had established the abortion trade on West Houston Street in 1874, when her younger daughter was fourteen. Daisy had quickly found out everything there was to know of the methods of arresting a pregnancy, and her manner with the understandably nervous clients was so fetching and reassuring that in five years Lena entrusted the entire practice to her daughter and gratefully retired to the more congenial occupation of fencing stolen merchandise.

Daisy Shanks was twenty-two years old, a pretty young woman with a full figure that was always heavily trussed. She had flaxen hair, flaxen brows, but shamelessly dark eyes. Her lips were thin and colorless and needed paint to be seen at all. Daisy was bustling and energetic and wore a perpetual smile. Nothing cast her down, nothing could rouse her anger beyond a brief breathy petulance, and nothing could mitigate the love she bore her stern mother and her mute sister Louisa. She tended to dress in clothes that were certainly too tight and not very short of gaudy. But since she had expressed no interest in any man since the policeman—dead in an anarchist bombing —who had fathered Rob and Ella, her finery was evidently assumed only to please herself. Daisy was affectionately fond of her twins, but had never interfered with the strict upbringing and careful education of the pair by their aunt and their grandmother.

Daisy was adept in her illegal craft. She was always successful in aborting the unborn child, the mother rarely died, and her fees were not exorbitant. Depending upon her whim—or the needs of the household—she charged between fifteen and thirty-five dollars. Occasionally, in an attempt to attract a better class of client than

the prostitutes and petty thieves who were her mainstay,
Daisy advertised her service in the daily papers:

> MADAME SHANKS, Professor of Midwifery,
> over 10 years successful practice in this city,
> promises and guarantees certain relief to ladies,
> with or without medicine, at one interview. The
> unfortunate are encouraged to apply for sure re-
> lief. Please write Box 445.

Her results, for the most part, were procured by the
use of powerful purgative drugs, which was certainly
safer than the more prevalent expedient of sharp instruments. Though these drugs sometimes resulted in the
dilapidation of the pregnant woman's nervous system,
the collapse would not occur for several days, long after
the client had safely returned home. The drugs produced fewer corpses than the forceps, and for that reason
Daisy preferred them.

At one time, Daisy had sold these purgative drugs
through an advertisement also. It read:

> Madame Shanks' female antidote. The only relia-
> able medicine that can be procured; certain to
> have desired effects within 24 hours, without in-
> struments or injurious results.

Since the medicine sold for $7.50 a bottle, and the in-
gredients cost only thirty cents, Daisy could realize a fine
profit. But when her mother pointed out that some women
who purchased the medicine might otherwise have come
to her for a much more lucrative abortion, Daisy left off
distribution of the home remedy.

The nature of Daisy's service was of course known to
the police, whose headquarters was but a few streets distant, but officers happily took bribes. Lena Shanks was
also a steadfast contributor to the coffers of the Democratic Party. The politicians did not consider it inconsistent to beg financial support of a household that had no
voting members, and Lena had never drawn attention to
this inequity. The contributions to Tammany Hall, and
the double eagles that were dropped into the cops' pockets, she considered simply to be in lieu of municipal li-

censing. Abortion was adjudged by the state of New York to be manslaughter in the first degree, punishable by an imprisonment of between four and seven years but Daisy had never associated the appearance of a policeman with the possibility of arrest. There was carefully no mention made of the West Houston Street address in the advertisements that were published in the *Herald*, and Daisy and her mother considered this circumspection enough.

Daisy picked a piece of work from her mother's basket, and sat in a chair on the other side of the hearth.

"Where's Louisa?" demanded Lena.

"Gone to see 'Lotta."

Lena jerked her head upward. "What about that one? She dead too? Don't want to send boy and girl out again tonight."

Daisy giggled. "Course not, Ma! Quiet now. Gave her laudanum with the medicine."

"Shouldn't mix," said her mother harshly, and tossed a handful of threads into the fire.

"Oh, Ma, you didn't see her! Never saw anyone so nervy! If I hadn't given her laudanum, I'd have been up there all night!"

"Watch out, Daisy, she'll end up like the other. Too much medicine for the other and she's dead," complained Lena.

"No," laughed Daisy, "Dollie'll be back on the stage tomorrow night. I can tell when the medicine's going to take. It was that waiter-girl that caused me the trouble tonight. Waiter-girl looked strong as the Female Amazon in the Dime Museum. Gave her a dose that would have aborted the Rock of Ages. Five hours, and all she wanted was a plate of hot corn. She could as well have swallowed rose water. I wanted to send her away, but said she wanted the forceps." Daisy shrugged. "Rob runs out of the room when he sees that blood, but Ella's 'cute, and claps a pillow over the girl's head, prevent her from screaming—girl had lungs fit to make a bellows out of. Don't know if she died of the bleeding or the pillow."

"Always Ella knows what to do," said her grandmother.

"Yes," said Daisy, "but won't never make a physician. Once Rob gets so he don't mind the blood, he'll be the one to have by me when I'm working. His heart's in it and the ladies like him. If I could have had him by me tonight, with the actress, I maybe could have saved the laudanum."

"Boy is fine with the ladies," said Lena, "just like you, Daisy. But girl belongs to me. Already she knows about gold and silk and sew secret pockets. Girl's good to have by me all day."

When she had given over her active practice in abortions, Lena Shanks had quickly established herself as a fence; this was a transition that was accomplished easily and with speed. Many of her former customers were thieves, and known to Lena as such. She let it casually be known among these women that she was in the market to purchase whatever merchandise they might come in the way of, promising to give two-fifths of the value in cash; this was appreciably higher than the usual one-third that was offered. The female thieves came gladly to Lena then, and even when she lowered her rates to the customary percentage, they remained with her.

To front her business as a fence, Lena Shanks operated a small pawnshop in the adjoining house, which she also owned. These two buildings were ingeniously connected by two well-concealed doors on the second and third floors, and their common basement was a warren of tiny locked cupboards and rooms for the storing of stolen merchandise. All day long, with Ella at her side, Lena sat behind the grimy counter of the pawnshop, examining, appraising, and purchasing stolen goods. The subterfuge of the pawnshop was of only the most perfunctory nature. The few items displayed for sale in her shop were cracked, filthy, and useless, and the array was never changed.

Daisy Shanks pulled her chair closer to the fire and began to detach the silk fringe from a shawl that had been taken from a house on West Nineteenth Street that morning. The gold clock on the mantel ticked loudly and the coals shifted themselves in the gilded grate. From outside came the occasional shouts and drunken songs of those passing along West Houston Street.

At a quarter past one, Rob and Ella suddenly appeared in the doorway, quite clean and neatly dressed again.

"Come here," said their mother, smiling. The twins

stepped forward and Rob handed his mother seven dollars in gold and silver.

"Were you stopped?" asked Lena.

"No," replied Rob, "no one even looked at us, except to tell us to move to the side of the street, and a man in a black coat asked if my soul was saved."

"Did the man on Bleecker Street quarrel over the price?" asked their mother.

Rob shook his head. "I told him seven dollars and he said was it a man or a woman, and I said a woman and he gave me seven dollars."

"Hold out your hand," said Daisy. The children thrust out their palms, and their mother dropped a silver dollar into each. "Tomorrow we go out. Spend it how you like. To bed now," she said, leaning forward to kiss each.

Ella then turned to go, but Rob lingered a moment, glancing at his mother. "The lady upstairs, could I see her? Very beautiful, ain't she?"

"Lovelier than wax," said Daisy. "Creep up. Creep up and see her, then come down here again, tell me how she sleeps. Ella, go 'long too."

The two children hurried up the stairs of the darkened room next to that in which the actress turned feverishly upon the bed. This was a small chamber, fiercely cold, directly beneath the roof, with one window that looked out over the houses in back. Ella stooped down near the baseboard and pushed aside a panel in the connecting wall. The twins crawled through, Ella first, and crouched behind a screen, listening to the drugged woman's breathing.

Rob peered around the edge of the screen and then stepped from behind, motioning his sister forward. They crept to the edge of the little iron bed and stood with their hands clasped, looking down at the actress. Her fine black hair was disheveled and her complexion of chalk and rouge had been ruined by hot tears and the coarse pillow beneath her head. The rubies in her ears were like spots of thick blood. The small watch on her breast ticked more loudly than her uneven breath came. Her features had become drawn and sharp under the influence of the drugs she had been given and the flickering failing light of the fire in the grate made them even more grotesque.

So lightly that she did not stir, Rob touched two fingers

to the sleeping woman's braceleted wrist and felt her pulse. He nodded to his sister and they retreated behind the screen, slipped through the wall, replaced the panel, and stood erect in the dark frigid room behind.

They smiled at one another, and whispered liltingly: " 'Rings and watch and jew-la-ry . . .'"

Chapter 3

∞∞∞∞∞∞∞∞∞∞∞∞∞∞∞∞∞∞∞∞∞∞∞∞∞∞∞∞∞∞∞∞∞

For several weeks before New Year's, every house in New York with any pretension to fashion is in an uproar of cleaning and cosmetic improvement. It is at this time that new furniture is purchased, new draperies sewn, new paper put up, and new carpets laid down. The families of immigrant Italian artisans have happy Christmases because of the trade in painting and gilding. The only new ornament that will not appear in this season is a portrait, for no one will sit still long enough for the likeness to be taken.

In these weeks, men sit quietly out of the way, behind the locked doors of their studies. Servants are overworked and mistresses are exhausted and short-tempered. Cellars and larders are restocked to make one think the island will be shortly under siege. The farmyard population of New Jersey is decimated, and the ferries across the Hudson River are laden with the carcasses of slaughtered cattle, swine, and fowl. The bakeries and breweries hire on extra help, and the younger sisters of maids and cooks obtain their first experience in service at this time. The stoves never cool down and dressmakers give over sleep as an impossible luxury.

The custom of paying calls on New Year's Day was instituted among the Dutch in the seventeenth century, and though two hundred years have passed, the city increased in size many hundredfold, and Dutch manners, dress, and accents are now contemptuously parodied on the variety stage, New Year remains the unavoidable, frenzied, garrulous, overwhelming crux of the social season.

New Year always dawns bright—no matter what the weather. Calls begin at ten o'clock, or a few hours later when the holiday falls upon a Sunday. The social work of the day is evenly divided: it is the men who pay calls and the women who receive them. The city from morning till sometime after dark is a monstrous winter beehive of increasingly drunken drones paying their respects to increasingly weary queens.

Gentlemen boast of having swallowed a glass of champagne or punch in more than sixty houses. Women more discreetly display the large basket of visiting cards that have been collected in the course of the day. The hallways are filled with cold air, because the outside door is never closed for long, and hostesses pray for dry weather so that their new carpets will not be completely spoilt with mud. Platters of food are constantly brought up from the kitchen by harried servants, who themselves become ever more sodden with expropriated wines and delicacies— perks of the day.

When the food gives out, or the sun goes down, or the callers become obstreperous and unintelligible, the draperies are drawn and a basket is hung upon the closed street door. The ladies of the house are no longer receiving.

They stand about, bemoan the wreckage, wonder briefly if their husbands and sons have met with the accidents that are so common on this day, direct the servants to begin cleaning up, and retire to quiet darkened rooms on the upper floors.

On the next morning, fortunate men lie abed and wonder if they will die. The unfortunate find themselves in jail for some act they cannot remember committing. No one wants to think how many ladies he may have offended in the course of the day.

The ladies put on their heaviest veils to hide their red eyes and go out on quiet calls to their friends, trading

stories of excesses committed by gentlemen and giving
careful inventories of how much was eaten and drunk.

For servants, New Year of 1882 was to be a doubly
wearying day, for it fell upon Sunday. Their Sabbath holiday must be forgone, and they worked all the harder for
the deprivation. Days on either side of New Year's would
be hardly less busy than the holiday itself, what with Saturday taken up with preparations and Monday consumed
clearing the debris. In a spirit of retaliation, servants the
entire city over determined to eat and drink until they
were sickened or rendered insensible.

Late on New Year's afternoon, when the sun had just
sunk behind the Gramercy Park Hotel, leaving a vivid
pink haze over the city, a well-dressed young matron
could be seen standing in the long window of her parlor,
looking out over desolate Gramercy Park and watching
as her last two guests descended the steps of her home.
She smiled, raised her hand, and waved prettily to the
stumbling gentlemen as they passed on the walk.

As soon as they were out of sight Marian Phair stepped
back, slammed the louvered shutters shut, and cried,
"Thank Heaven! It's done with!"

She whirled about and strode into the dining room,
where the servants had already begun to clear the tables.
"Amy," she demanded of a pretty Irish housemaid,
"where's my niece?"

"With the children, I think, ma'am."

"Go and get her then!"

Though Amy carried two large trays and with one foot
was pushing open the door that led to the kitchen stairs,
she came back without protest, knowing the danger of
crossing her mistress. Handing the trays to Peter Wish,
the family's only manservant, Amy Amyst hurried upstairs to fetch down Helen Stallworth.

Marian returned to the parlor and drew the dining
room doors closed. She stood in the middle of the room
and turned before the mantel mirror, critically examining the mauve silk dress that had been sewn specially for
this day. She turned her head this way and that to observe her hair, which was still perfect though her hairdresser, M. Deldalle, had left her at one o'clock the night

before. Marian had not dared sleep in her bed for fear of destroying his exquisite craftsmanship, and had only managed to doze in a chair before the cold grate. She had begged him to come to her at a later hour, but M. Deldalle had declared that he was engaged straight through till noon, and that he must come at midnight or not at all. Marian had begun the day sore and insufficiently rested, but there had been no help for it.

Marian was almost thirty, a woman of medium stature with small hips and a handsome bust. Her small hips were effectively disguised by the mode in dress, and the same dress happily emphasized her fine bust. She was not by nature a graceful woman, but she moved always slowly and carefully, and so gave the appearance of sustained languor, which to most eyes was indistinguishable from grace. Her face was thin and triangular, her skin pale; her eyes were blue and bright. Her physiognomy was not so much pleasing as it was fashionable, and she dreaded the time when another cast of features should come into style and she be left behind with a face that was not only out of currency but aging as well.

When Marian Phair turned before the mirror trying to see if her eyes betrayed her weariness, her niece slipped silently into the room. Helen Stallworth was only a few years younger than her aunt; though sufficiently pretty for most purposes, she did nothing to point or enhance her good features. She was of medium height, with a graceful carriage that was the envy of Marian Phair. Her face was a white oval, and her regular features were delicately placed together in the middle, leaving expanses of white forehead, high white cheeks, and a round soft white chin. Her eyes, like those of all the Stallworths, were quite incandescently blue.

After a time, and without appearing to have taken any notice of her niece's presence, Marian remarked, "Oh, I'm happy that you could be persuaded to come down at last, Helen—now that the guests have all gone. I don't believe you were in this room for a full hour together this afternoon. And you needn't bother to improvise a migraine or tell me that you nursed Edwin and Edith through *cholera infantum,* for I simply won't believe it! You ought to have been in this parlor, at my side."

"I'm sorry," said Helen. "It's just that I'm not . . . not at ease—with so many gentlemen. I think I might have been more comfortable perhaps if you had not served so much champagne."

"I almost wish I hadn't," sighed Marian. "It's so expensive, and by the time most of those men arrived here this afternoon, we could have served them vitriol, laudanum, and indigo dye, called it Plantation Punch and had them go away singing our hospitality!"

"Well," cried Helen vehemently, "it's a disgrace for so many men to be . . . to be *inebriated* on the Sabbath!"

"It's not just any Sabbath, Helen, it's New Year, and it has always been the custom for gentlemen to stupefy themselves with drink on this day. Every gentleman in town is *inebriate* by three o'clock, and says things and does things he would not say or do on any other day of the year. Ladies must simply ignore the things that they do and forget the things that they say. This is the one day of the year when the standards do not apply. I am certain that God does not regard the sins that are committed on New Year."

"Marian!" cried Helen at this casuistry.

"Besides," said Marian with a shrug, "If anyone deserves punishment today, I think it's probably yourself—for wearing that dress." Helen was attired simply, in a dress that was not strictly new and by no means fashionable. It was not that there was not money for a new outfit, but rather that her religious spirit rose against the custom of the day, and it was only with great discipline that she had brought herself to participate in it at all. "And please to straighten the neck and shoulder, Helen, you wear your clothes like an epileptic fit." Helen adjusted the bodice of her dress and waited for her aunt's approval.

"That's a little better," said Marian grudgingly, "at least you don't look as if you had just been pulled from a burning building. And I meant to ask you: who was it arranged your hair this morning? Your coachman?"

"No," said Helen, "after service this morning, I walked over and Amy arranged it for me."

"What! That flannel-mouth! What do the Irish know about hair? Perhaps if you had taken a pig with you this morning Amy could have helped you to dress that, but you ought not to have allowed her to touch your head! Well, at any rate you weren't here long enough to be much observed, and those that did see you would probably be hard put now to say whether you'd a head or not."

Helen, who began to fear that her aunt might continue some time in this vein, looked for something to distract her attention. "Shall I count the cards?" Helen begged. A basket quite filled with the visiting cards of that day's guests stood on a small inlaid table just outside the parlor door.

Marian nodded, and Helen fetched the basket.

"Helen," said her aunt, "I don't mean to seem so angry"—she had seated herself at the end of a couch, leaning into the corner, with several soft pillows behind her—"but I was very much disappointed in you today."

Helen dropped unhappily into a low-seated embroidered chair near the front windows. She emptied the basket of cards into her lap, and methodically arranged them in stacks of twenty-five.

"Now," said Marian, whose eyes were quite shut, "I realize that you didn't care to be here today. I know that you would rather have remained at the manse and read religious tracts on the problem of the Elect, but your father desired you to be here and help me. That is, you had an obligation to be here and you ought to have resigned yourself to it in a Christian manner and not continually suggested ways in which you might remove yourself to a different part of the house. The kitchen could have got along quite well without your assistance, as could the nursery, the attic, the linen closet, and wherever else it was you chose to hide yourself."

"I—"

Marian rode over Helen's interruption remorselessly. "The year my mother died, I began to receive for my father in the house on Washington Square. I was only sixteen, but I didn't shrink! And Helen, I see no reason why you, at twenty-two years of age, shouldn't open the manse to Edward's parishioners."

Helen's father, Edward Stallworth, was the pastor of the Presbyterian church that was located on the eastern side of Madison Square. In a small house farther east on

Twenty-fifth Street, Helen lived with her father and her brother Benjamin; Helen's mother had died of consumption on the day that Abraham Lincoln was assassinated.

"After all," Marian went on, "it's not as if we had asked you to stage an International Exhibition of Mechanical Progress. All you had to do was stand about for a few hours in your own parlor and make conversation with a few dozen well-dressed gentlemen. And of course it's not as if you weren't acquainted with these gentlemen already—they would have been the same gentlemen you see and speak to every Sunday after church. You didn't have to worry about drunkenness, for gentlemen always go to the minister's house first. No one would have insulted you. The worst that could have happened is that some twenty-year-old who's never made the rounds before would have fallen sick behind the divan."

"I had other reasons for not wanting to open the house," said Helen timidly. "Reasons . . . of conscience."

"Conscience?" repeated her aunt dubiously.

"New Year," said Helen hesitantly, "as you probably know, is essentially a pagan holiday. It's not part of the Christian calendar, at least not part of the Presbyterian church calendar, and I would have been very uneasy about opening a minister's house in celebration of a pagan holiday."

"Helen," said her aunt, eyes wide in wonder, "don't you think you ought to let Edward make the decision in such a matter? He's not only your father, he's an ordained minister in the Presbyterian church."

"Yes," whispered Helen, "I've decided that next year, if he wants to open the house, I will be there to receive the guests."

"Good," said Marian, "no more of this nonsense then." She closed her eyes once more. "How many of those cards have you counted?"

"Sixty-three," said Helen. "But there are a good many more."

Marian nodded her satisfaction.

It had grown dark in the room as the two women talked, but neither had suggested that the gas be turned There was comfort in the quiet and the dimness after ng hours of strangers and volubility and movement. The muffled rattle of dishes and crystal and plate behind the dining room doors was a low, almost musical accompaniment to their discourse.

In a lengthy silence, while Helen was counting the cards, Marian Phair fell asleep in the corner of the sofa, and her coiffure was crushed against the upholstery.

Chapter 4

SEVERAL times in the gathering dusk, while Marian Phair dozed in the corner of the sofa, Helen Stallworth heard the approach on the front steps of gentlemen who dropped their visiting cards into the basket hung upon the street door and then hurried away to make the last of their New Year calls.

At last, however, they were disturbed by a sharp knocking and Marian rose in some confusion. Helen would have liked to get up also, but the visiting cards lay in neat piles in her lap and she could not move without tumbling them all together again. Peter Wish entered the hallway from the dining room and in another moment had admitted those without.

Two men appeared in the parlor door, one of them quite old and looking it; one of them only middle-aged but appearing rather younger. Yet because both possessed the same general cast of features, the same transparent skin, and the same brilliant light-blue eyes, they were obviously father and son. Their cheeks were bright pink from the sharp wind, but that little color faded quickly in the warmth of the parlor and they became white again as hothouse lilies.

Judge James Stallworth was seventy-two. He had al-

ways been a large man, but in the past few years, inflicted
with an intestinal disorder that had killed his appetite, he
had lost much of his bulk. He still carried himself, however, as a much heavier man, and the difference between
his carriage and his form made him appear almost gaunt.
He wore his hair fairly long, but combed back over his
ears; his face was smooth shaven.

Judge Stallworth's son Edward was a refined, almost
delicate, specimen of his father's type. The ladies of his
congregation thought his hands very finely formed and
much admired his erect, elegant, easeful posture. His skin,
without wrinkle or blemish, made him seem almost ten
years younger than his actual age of fifty. His hair was
light brown and soft and straight, and though thinning,
did not much recede over his forehead, which was high
anyway. It was cut short to display the fine shape of his
head. His beard was light and wiry, cut into large triangular whiskers that curved around to meet his large
straight moustache, leaving his chin and lower jaw de-
nuded of hair.

Father and son both, with their white skin, their shining
eyes of the lightest, most liquid blue, their light-colored
hair, seemed faded water-color portraits of gentlemen
much more robustly tinted. But what made the father
seem most like the son—and the son most like the father
—was a certain reserved coldness that permeated every
word they spoke, that slowed their limbs and made every
gesture deliberate and meaningful.

"I hope your speech is not slurred," said Marian to her
father and her brother. Edward Stallworth was actually
only Marian's half brother, for the judge, their father, had
been married and widowed twice; there was nearly twenty
years difference in the ages of Marian and Edward and
they maintained rather a distant familiarity.

"Certainly not," the judge replied crisply.

"Good," said Marian, with her eyes closed, "then sit
and talk to me. I've not heard an intelligible word all
afternoon."

Father and son sat and told how they had come upon
one another quite by chance, in a house on Stuyvesant
Square.

"I called upon all the elders and deacons and upon all
those who had contributed—a certain amount—to the

church funds this last year, but I'm afraid there simply wasn't time to get around to everyone in the congregation," said Edward. "I fear some one or two will be offended, but that of course need not have been the case, Helen, if you had consented to open the house."

Helen did not venture to reply to her father's criticism.

"Did you see Duncan, Father?" asked Marian.

"I have seen Duncan twice since breakfast. He showed me a list of eighty-five houses where he planned to call."

"Eighty-five!" exclaimed Helen.

"In 1855," remarked Judge Stallworth, "I made one hundred and seventeen calls. Now it is true that the city was somewhat smaller then, and one hadn't so far to travel—one needn't go above Fourteenth Street then for instance—yet I stopped at each of those houses, paid my respects to every lady in sight, consumed a tumbler of punch and ate whatever was nearest me on the table, went home and prepared a speech for the following morning's session in court. I was the prosecution, and the man was hanged. Though I'm pleased to find Duncan so industrious, I don't believe he will make even those eighty-five calls. New Year has fallen off of late, fallen off shamefully. I think that Fifth Avenue hardly observes it at all. New money does not observe the New Year. New money evidently has other pleasures. I could almost be surprised if Duncan found eighty-five houses that were receiving today."

"Perhaps the custom will die out entirely," said Helen with such eager hopefulness that the others looked at her curiously.

"Helen," said her grandfather, "if the world were formed according to your taste, it would be but a mousy, gray, pinched place. Doubtless you would eliminate criminals and constabularies, harsh laws and harsher prisons. I for one would have no place in such a world as that."

Peter Wish came in to raise the gas in the room. When he had retired, Judge Stallworth rose and warmed his cold slender hands at the fire.

"I have had so many disappointments in my life," said Judge Stallworth, "that I would not be surprised if the custom did die out. It would be but one disappointment more. Twenty years ago, this parlor would have been filled with guests at this time of the afternoon. Even ten years ago. What is the time now?"

"Half past five," said Marian.

"Services are at half past seven," said Edward Stallworth. "I hope we are all to be there."

"Yes, of course," said Judge Stallworth, "we shall all certainly come. It is the New Year."

"Duncan promised to return by six o'clock," said Marian. "I hope that he has not been waylaid or forgot the time. It would be—"

"Did you see Benjamin?" asked Helen Stallworth of her grandfather anxiously.

"No," the old man replied coldly, "I did not, but it may be that Benjamin and I do not make the same social circuit."

Benjamin's father laughed sharply, and Helen Stallworth glanced away in pain, more hurt by her family's disparagement of her brother than by the sarcasm that had been directed at herself.

At that moment, the dining room doors were drawn open by Amy Amyst and Peter Wish. The table had been cleared and placed again in the center of the room, with the chairs set around. A cooler with two bottles of champagne was set on the sideboard, with two large plates of cold meat and sweet pastries to the side.

"Papa," said Marian, "I hope you haven't had so much to drink today that you can't take a glass with us to toast the New Year."

"Marian," replied her father, "in every house I accepted a glass of whatever was offered to me first: claret or sherry or coffee or mulled wine or champagne, and I held it gratefully in my hands and then I set it aside. I've had nothing all day."

"I hope Duncan can say the same when he arrives."

"He cannot," said Judge Stallworth, "I know that."

There was another knock at the front door. This time Helen, who had placed the visiting cards upon the mantel and announced their number as two hundred and seventeen, ran to the door in hope that it was her brother. In just a moment she returned, saying, "It's Benjamin *and* Duncan."

If Judge Stallworth and his son Edward, when they stood together in the doorway, had borne resemblance to one another amply displaying that they were near kin, then the dissimilarity in appearance of Duncan Phair and Benjamin Stallworth was so pronounced that one could scarcely be brought to believe that they were related at all—even by marriage.

Marian's husband, Duncan Phair, was a handsome man, a couple of inches under six feet, with a well-formed body; he was pleasantly fleshly, but by no means corpulent. He had a noble square-shaped head, and his dark hair was parted just left of center. His beard was worn much thicker and longer than the hair on the top of his head and a full moustache covered his mouth completely.

In decided, almost ludicrous contrast, his wife's nephew, Benjamin Stallworth, was neither tall nor particularly well formed. His shoulders sloped markedly into thin rickety arms; his hands were absurdly large and looked like stuffed white gloves tied to the ends of sticks. His head was egg shaped and massive, much larger at the top than at the bottom. His chin and jaw might be called such only because chins and jaws appeared on other men in the place where Benjamin had a single expanse of soft bone and curving flesh. His hair was lank and thin and was combed down over his forehead. His ears were small and lay flat against his head, heightening the overall likeness to a comically painted Easter egg.

Duncan Phair, with smiling playfulness, pushed Benjamin into the room. "I found him wandering up Madison Avenue, having no idea that he was even in New York, stumbling into strange houses and offering proposals of marriage to three hundred-pound widows."

"No," stammered Benjamin, "I was not. We ran into one another near Madison Square. We were both on our way here. I've had very little today. Champagne gives me a sick headache, and hot wine makes me dizzy." He sat nervously in a chair that was apart from the others, and turned his face away, complaining of the heat in the room.

"I'm glad you abstained, Benjamin," said his sister kindly.

After Duncan had briefly described his afternoon and warmed himself by the fire, as host he invited the family into the dining room to toast the New Year with champagne. This was their usual ceremony and without being asked, Helen hurried out to fetch little Edwin and Edith who were to be allowed to press the rim of an empty glass against their lips.

Edwin Phair was four years old and his sister Edith three. They had been allowed in the drawing room for an hour during the time that their mother was receiving. Dressed very much alike in new blue frocks that showed off the piercing blue Stallworth eyes, both had sat primly on an ottoman before the fire, impressed into silence and immobility by their mother's threats of irrevocable banishment to the nursery if they either spoke or raised a finger out of turn. Edwin, who had a distressing propensity to acrobatics, marvelous in themselves but unbecoming to one who was an heir in the Stallworth family, had been hard put to remain still so long, and once returned to the nursery he had promptly executed half a dozen flips over his sister's head in relief.

When Helen returned, the two handsome children having rushed in a little ahead of her, all the family was gathered around the table and Duncan Phair was pouring out champagne into a set of eight glasses. Each solemnly took a glass and raised it. The two children raised theirs high, and had they been full, would have spilled out every drop.

"May we prosper in eighty-two," said Duncan.

"Prosperity," nodded James Stallworth, "and confusion to the Democrats." He beckoned to his grandson Edwin, and tousled his thick hair in gruff affection.

"Continued favor in the sight of God," said Edward Stallworth, with eyes closed briefly.

"May we prove ourselves worthy of the blessings already bestowed upon us," said Helen.

Benjamin grinned doltishly as he raised his glass higher, but said nothing.

"To the Stallworths," concluded Marian.

They drank, only Helen not finishing hers. She placed her glass upon the table, leaned down and took those of Edwin and Edith as well. All the others held their glasses out for replenishment.

"Helen," said Duncan Phair, "please take the children upstairs again. You may wish to stay with them for a while." His tone of voice made her agree, though with some apprehensive puzzlement, that she might do just that.

Helen gathered the children, speaking to them softly and unintelligibly, and ushered them out of the room. As she cast a troubled backward glance at her brother he turned uneasily away.

For the next few moments Duncan Phair was occupied in pouring out more champagne.

"Benjamin was precise," he said smiling, as he handed his father-in-law a glass. "I met him at the southwestern corner of Madison Square, just where Broadway crosses Fifth Avenue, is that not correct, Benjamin?" Now that Benjamin's sister was out of the room, a definite sharpness entered Duncan's voice.

Benjamin had moved skulking to the doors into the parlor, but he paused now to nod sullenly to Duncan's question.

"Don't go away," said his grandfather, but there was no kindness in his voice. "Drink your champagne with us, Benjamin. You don't seem to have overdone it today."

"No," said Duncan Phair, "he didn't. How many houses did you visit today, Benjamin?"

"I'm not certain," stammered Benjamin.

"Three?" said Duncan icily. "As many as five?"

"Five houses!" cried Marian. "Where have you been, Benjamin?"

"Where did you spend the day, Benjamin?" asked his father quietly, noting with distaste the manner in which his son slouched against the papered wall.

"Benjamin, I am sure we are all happy to hear, refused to become inebriated on the New Year. Instead," Duncan went on carelessly, "he hid himself in a brownstone on Twenty-fourth Street—I saw him coming out of it—where he drank hardly at all. Is that not right, Benjamin?"

Benjamin nodded, his features twisted and wry on his eggshaped head.

"Whose house was that, Benjamin?" demanded his father. "At Twenty-fourth Street and Fifth Avenue. I visited the Hettingers early in the afternoon and their home is near there. Were you at the Hettingers' all afternoon, Benjamin?" It was apparent that Edward Stallworth believed that his son might have been anywhere on earth but at the Hettingers'.

"Benjamin spent the afternoon with the Morrisseys," said Duncan Phair lightly.

"I believe," said Edward Stallworth, "that we are not acquainted with any Morrisseys. We have a servant by that name, but I think that the sixteen dollars a week that I pay her is insufficient for the purchase of a house on Twenty-fourth Street. Who are the Morrisseys, Benjamin, and what had you to do with them?"

Benjamin stared into the hallway, hoping vainly that his sister would appear.

"There is only one Morrissey, Edward," said Judge Stallworth, "and I do not know his given name. He runs a gambling establishment. You may know the place by the yellow shades on the windows, and by the negro servants at the doorway, also in yellow, and by the number of well-to-do gentlemen who go in—and by the number of impoverished gentlemen who come out."

"I see," said Edward Stallworth, and tugged at his whiskers. "Benjamin has made a professional acquaintanceship with this gentleman, I take it. It was not a social call, Benjamin?"

Miserably, Benjamin shook his head no.

"Let me ask you, Benjamin," said his father coldly, "did you leave Mr. Morrissey any token of your fraternal esteem? Such as a bank draught, or a promise of payment?"

Beyond misery now, Benjamin nodded his head yes.

Edward Stallworth stalked past his son into the parlor, and sat in a chair that faced the front shuttered windows.

"You're an imbecile, Benjamin," said his aunt. "How much money did you lose?"

"Eight hundred and fifty-six dollars," said Benjamin in a low shaking voice.

"Had you so much money at the beginning of the New Year?" asked his grandfather with feigned surprise.

"I owe most of it," Benjamin mumbled.

"You'll never go back, I hope," said Marian.

"He can't go back," said Duncan Phair easily. It was impossible to tell that his mouth moved at all behind his thick beard. "He won't be allowed in by the negro gentlemen in the yellow coats. He played and lost what he had, and continued to play—"

"I thought I might recover—" began Benjamin.

"—but Benjamin did not recover," said Duncan Phair, "and hadn't the money to make up his further losses. It's too fashionable an establishment to take his watch and his coat and his three little diamond studs, so it took his I.O.U. and simply wrote his name off its lists. It reflects on the family in the first place that he would be found in such a house, but it is a disaster that he should be turned out of it."

"How much of the loss was not paid, Benjamin?" said his grandfather in a light, almost conversational tone.

"About seven hun—"

"Six hundred and eighty-three dollars had to be paid. Of course I went back with him immediately, and left a draught with the banker there. It was accepted without question, and they did not need to be asked by me to have the doors barred against him in the future."

"There is no way to win money at such places," said Marian. "I can't believe you didn't know that."

"No!" protested Benjamin. "There's never cheating at Morrissey's—"

"There's no need for cheating," said Judge Stallworth, "when they have such as you clamoring at the doors."

Defeated, Benjamin reeled into the parlor, threw himself into a chair near his father, and leaned forward in earnest entreaty. "Father, I—"

Edward Stallworth stood abruptly. "Duncan," he said, "after services this evening, if you will return to the manse with me I will be happy to reimburse you for the draught you wrote. And I would like to thank you for taking this in hand. It is an embarrassment enough without the minister of the Madison Avenue Presbyterian Church having to enter Mr. Morrissey's establishment to pay off his son's gambling debts. . . ." He returned to the dining room. "I think I might have another glass of champagne, though I must say that the New Year has begun ill enough."

"You have paralyzed us with shame, Benjamin," said Marian hotly.

"Benjamin," said his grandfather in a deceptively cool voice, "I refuse to believe that you will learn a lesson from this. I have believed so in other instances and have always been proved wrong. From stubbornness or stupidity, I don't know which, you never learn. I only hope that the next time something like this happens you have the decency not to return to us to be forgiven and have your criminal debts paid off by Duncan or your father or myself; but I trust that you will go down to the Battery and drown yourself, so that we'll not be troubled by you any longer."

When Helen Stallworth came downstairs again to announce that the children had been dressed for church, her father, her grandfather, and her aunt and uncle were stiffly seated in the parlor, speaking not at all. She looked about for Benjamin and found him at last in a dark corner of the dining room, sitting on the edge of a chair that had been pulled far back from the table. His lank hair was disarranged and he was sobbing into his cupped hands.

Helen anxiously pulled the doors of the room shut. A quarter of an hour later, Marian rapped sharply and announced that the carriages had been brought around and it was time that they were off to the church. Helen opened the doors and drew puffy-eyed Benjamin after her.

Chapter 5

~~~~~~

As a family, the Stallworths kept their private faces turned away from the world. Though Benjamin's conduct had soured for them the inceptive hopefulness of the new year, neither their expression nor their conversation betrayed their discomfiture to strangers or to friends.

Only Benjamin appeared troubled, even more anxious than usual, with red teary eyes and sweating giddy hands. Before the group departed Gramercy Park, Judge Stallworth demanded that he be sent directly home so that his apparent agitation might not disgrace the family in their prominently situated pew. Helen's low-voiced protest to this banishment was ignored and Benjamin was dropped at a corner. The two carriages rolled onward toward the church without anyone but Helen bothering to say good-evening to the young man.

Cold, but also feverish and clammy beneath his rumpled clothing, Benjamin Stallworth stumbled home to the Presbyterian manse on Twenty-fifth Street. It was not the first time that he had been made to feel that he had dishonored the family. His father often remarked that Benjamin gave substance to the adage that a minister's son was ungovernable, and his grandfather noted coldly that Benjamin hadn't even the stamina or the stomach to be a proper black sheep. Benjamin was little better than a feebleminded child who inspired not a respectable horror but only contempt.

Benjamin had been enrolled in the freshman class of Columbia College but hadn't had the aptitude to finish out a single year of courses. He had been given to understand that he would be asked to leave if he did not withdraw of his own volition. After that he had been employed as a kind of superior clerk in the firm of Phair & Peerce, not because he was suited to the work—for he certainly wasn't—but so that Duncan might keep a close eye upon him. The job had a certain titular respectability, but the fact was, Benjamin did little but run the simplest errands and occasionally copy out a letter that was of no importance whatsoever. He arrived late, left early, and was an object of derision to the other clerks in the office who were, to a man, competent, ambitious, and prepossessing.

Benjamin Stallworth understood his shortcomings and was rendered unhappy by that understanding. He was upright enough to wish for correction but too weak to enforce it upon himself. At times, when he had particularly annoyed his father and his family, Benjamin would retire, fold up—never smile and never speak but under compulsion. This abnegating contrition always disturbed his sister. Helen interceded for him, made his promises for future improved conduct, and undertook to see that nothing else befell him. But Helen's surveillance was limited and Benjamin always stumbled once more.

Benjamin knew that he would be alone in the manse on Twenty-fifth Street, for the servants had the afternoon and evening off and would not return before the morning. Benjamin also knew that Helen kept a certain amount of cash, usually about fifty dollars or so, in a little tooled box behind certain books in the case in her room. Helen's overbred propriety assured Benjamin that he would find the money secreted behind secular not religious volumes. This small horde was kept for emergencies, and Helen's life was such that emergencies arose only rarely, and for half-years at a time she never touched the box. On previous occasions, Benjamin had taken the money there and replaced it as much as a month later without his sister ever being the wiser. If he had been so unlucky at the tables today, it stood to reason that he would have

good fortune tonight, especially, he considered, if he
played in a different place, at a different game, surrounded by different players, and taking different odds.
Benjamin constructed a fervid little fantasy in which, on
the next morning, he presented Duncan Phair with the
eight hundred dollars that had been paid to Morrissey's.
He imagined apologies forthcoming from Duncan, his
father, his grandfather, and his aunt. They all would look
on him with increased respect, and having once won, he
would never lose at the gaming tables again.

Benjamin entered the manse and climbed the stairs
directly to his sister's room. He easily found the box. Not
wanting to turn up the gas, he stood at the window and
counted out sixty-five dollars in small gold pieces. He
would have liked to leave the last five-dollar gold piece,
but after several moments' hesitation he pocketed this too,
to cover the incidental expenses of the evening. Then he
went to his own room and changed into a suit of clothing
that was neither new nor flashy. Benjamin's apprehension
that his absence from the house would be discovered was
only habit. There was little danger, in fact, for on those
occasions when he had disgraced himself, his father would
have nothing to do with him and would even try to discourage Helen from administering comfort. It was possible that Helen might knock softly at the locked door,
but if there were no response, she would assume that he
was asleep or too depressed even for consolation and
would silently retreat.

He left by the back door of the house, taking with him
a key so that he might regain entrance that way. It would
be necessary to remain out well past midnight, so that
he might reenter the house confident that his sister and
his father slept.

Benjamin struck out south along Fourth Avenue, avoiding Madison Square altogether. Although his family were
all in church, he didn't want to risk running into any
latecomers to the service, who might mention later that
they had seen him.

At the corner of Gramercy Park he turned west onto
Twenty-first Street, and continued until he came to Sixth
Avenue. Several times in his short journey Benjamin had
been accosted by reeling pairs and groups of well-dressed
men who, having finished their visits some hours before,

had settled down to the more serious business of sampling
the liquors of different saloons in town. But Benjamin,
glowing with a fever quite different from that produced
by inebriation, had easily avoided them.

Benjamin took the Sixth Avenue el and twenty minutes
later was deposited at the corner of West Houston Street
and Broadway. He was unfamiliar with the neighborhood, of which his first impression was one of danger
underlying strident gaiety, of garishly lighted corners al-
ternating with alleys that were desperately dark—it
seemed a crowded urban forest of predator and prey. He
hurried along West Houston Street in search of Harry
Hill's place, lately recommended to him for the fights that
took place in a back room, but which he had never visited. His fist, thrust deep into his pocket, held tight his
sister's gold, for he was fearful that it should chink
loudly enough to draw the attention of thieves.

He stopped at a large frame house where an enormous
red and blue lantern was suspended between two doors.
Three women, whom Benjamin considered might just as
well have been carrying sandwich boards that read
"Whore" on the front and "For Sale" on the back, stumbled through the smaller of these entrances in a tumult
of coarse laughter and obscene banter. At the larger door,
Benjamin was stopped by a burly porter who wore a
large pearl in the place of his left eye; but the half dollar
that Benjamin placed in the man's grimy palm allowed
him entrance.

After passing down a constricted unlighted evil-smelling
passageway, rather like what Benjamin imagined a coal
mine to be, he emerged into a wooden-floored room
where fifty or so dancing couples flew about with obstreperous inebriated spirits. It was apparent that parti-
tioning walls had been removed to provide so large a
space, for the ceiling consisted of squares and rectangles
of different heights and different textures, some wooden,
some painted plaster, some with lights, some badly sag-
ging. There was no bar, but five men stood behind a
long wooden counter all along one side of the room,
dispensing liquor that was brought up from the cellar.

Benjamin was thrilled by the waiter-girls in their short
skirts and their tiny polished boots, for he had never seen
a woman in tights off the variety stage. One of these

smirking young women came immediately up to Benjamin, opened wide her painted mouth, and screamed at him to know his pleasure—screamed, for it was otherwise impossible to be heard over the five-piece orchestra that played on a tiny platform just to their right. Considering that abstinence would only draw attention to himself in such a place, Benjamin ordered a schooner of beer.

Skirting the dancers, Benjamin moved around the room. Beneath a large Punch and Judy booth in a far corner, he spoke to a man who stood guard over a green-curtained doorway just to the side.

"Fights tonight, aren't there?" remarked Benjamin deferentially.

"Nine o'clock. Cost you a quarter to get in."

It was half past eight. Benjamin ordered another schooner of beer, and stood as far out of the way as was possible in that crowded cramped place. He thought he had never seen a place more economically inhabited— there was not a board, not a corner, not a recess where one wasn't likely to be jostled and jabbed. He gazed at the dancers who whirled before him and was so flustered with the strangeness and the shocking license of the place that he made no reply to—and often did not even understand—the unflattering remarks that were directed at him by the passing dancers, some because of his rude open-mouthed staring and some simply on account of his risible appearance. He had come so far afield this evening because he wanted to make certain that he would not meet anyone who knew him; and as he looked about, he realized that indeed, if nothing else, he was at least safe from discovery.

Benjamin Stallworth was not a young man of wide experience, and he had never been in the same room with a prostitute before. Here, directly before him, assignations were openly made, and the woman who had entered free of charge at one door exited through the other in the company of a man whom she had never seen before that night. It was one thing to see such a woman on the street, quite another to find himself in-of-doors in her company, where a different etiquette must prevail. He wondered distressfully if he would be required to dance with one of these fallen women if she had the effrontery to ask. Benjamin anxiously considered whether his presence in such a place was tantamount to purchasing the feminine favors that were so openly declared for sale. He felt at once exhilarated and soiled, and might have remained rooted beneath the Punch and Judy box all evening, gaping at the gaudy dancers: the women in violet skirts and orange jackets, the men in tight striped trousers with rings in their ears.

At last, however, the curtains across the way into the back room were pulled aside and the doorkeeper took the half dollar that Benjamin proffered, but gave no change. Deciding against making an issue of the overcharging, Benjamin was the first inside; but immediately after came a great rush of men from the dance floor, and some number of women as well. This room was much smaller than the other, no more than thirty feet square with an eight-foot ceiling. Two odd windows were boarded across from the outside. In the middle of the floor was a wooden platform no more than a foot high, with wooden posts at each corner upholding a double cordon of thick sea-rope. Benjamin hurried to the far side of the ring, and secured a place right against the platform; in a few minutes more he was hemmed in by other spectators and bettors, to the extent that any decision to leave now could have been implemented only with difficulty. The gas-lit room quickly filled with cigar smoke, and Benjamin had to order more beer just to keep from choking—despite the fact that he didn't like the taste of it, that it was almost twice as expensive as any beer he had ever bought, and that he was already feeling the effects of having drunk too much. Only for the waiter-girls did the crowd momentarily make room.

While waiting for something more to happen, and as he sipped at his beer, Benjamin looked over the tightly packed expectant crowd. He was pushed so hard against the platform that splinters from the end of a rough-hewn board punctured his trousers and shin. He still held his gold feverishly in one fist inside his trousers, for he had already felt light prying fingers in a couple of his other pockets. He dared not turn around, for he knew that he hadn't the courage to confront a thief in a territory where thieves were the common citizens and he the suffered immigrant. He directed his curious attention rather to the persons crowded against the other three sides of the ring, as snugly trapped into their places as himself.

Passing quickly over several gentlemen in plug hats whose faces were obscured by the smoke that billowed in brown clouds from their cigars, and pausing only with horror at a physical impropriety initiated by a young woman with a cabbage rose on her hat upon a young man in a shimmering green waistcoat, Benjamin observed an old coarse-featured woman who stood just opposite him on the far side of the ring. To Benjamin's discomfort she returned his gaze. The expression on the old woman's face he could interpret only as hate, but he could posit no cause for such malevolence. The woman was fat; she wore a black jacket with black lace trimming, and a wide necklace of jet around her throat. To one side of her stood a boy and a girl, and just behind them were two young women, one a delicious flaxen-haired woman in a bottle-green satin frock, and the other a stern heavy-eyed woman with crimped black hair in a hideous orange dress.

After his initial surprise, Benjamin averted his gaze, but irresistibly his eyes turned back to the fat woman. She stared at him still, and with a disconcerting fixity. Benjamin glanced furtively to either side, hoping to find that she was actually directing her attention to another, but then her slowly gathered menacing smile confirmed that he alone was her study.

His discomfort was allayed by a great commotion in the room. The crowd between the curtained doorway and the ring was wedged apart by the approach of several persons.

A fat bald smooth-shaven man pushed up to the platform first. He struggled for a few seconds with the ropes, but at last with the help of some facetiously violent shoves by the spectators, he was propelled into the center of the ring. He was followed immediately by two young women who were rather small—not what Benjamin had had in mind when he had first heard of the girl-fighters that might be found on West Houston Street. It was the prospect of this novelty that had lured him to Harry Hill's, rather than to some other lower-class establishment.

Both women wore white boots, black tights that exposed the entirety of their heavily sinewed legs, short tunics of black velvet with trimming of gold and green fringe. Little lace collars rose high upon their thick necks, but the women's arms were entirely bare. Their long hair was knotted like a Chinaman's queue and hung down their backs. Neither of the women was handsome in the face and one was particularly disfigured by a broken nose.

The introduction of the woman with the broken nose —the Indomitable and Puissant Annie Leech—provoked such a cheer from the crowd that it was immediately apparent that she was their favorite. Her opponent— Charlotta Kegoe, the Sapphic Pugilist—was greeted with less enthusiasm. However, Benjamin was fascinated by this second lady, not only because of her title and her legs —hard pillars of muscle that nearly burst their black stockings—but because of the nature of her jewelry. Since it would be imprudent in the extreme for a female fighter to wear any sort of ornament in the ring, Miss Kegoe had had numerous necklaces, bracelets, and rings tattooed onto the skin of her neck, wrists, and fingers. They comprised an eccentricity exciting to Benjamin.

The two women paced restlessly around the ring, calling out to their friends in the crowd of spectators, shaking hands over the ropes in a strangely masculine fashion, and giving insult for insult back to their detractors. They smacked the palms of their hands loudly against the low ceiling for emphasis and ignored one another completely.

The fat gentleman in the center of the ring—Harry Hill himself, Benjamin heard it whispered—explained that the first fight would take place as soon as all the bets were made. Four apprentices would circulate through the crowd, two holding red slips of paper and two holding blue. Those wishing to back Charlotta Kegoe purchased red slips for any desired amount, and those wishing to bet upon Annie Leech should go with the blue. Odds would be calculated immediately, and announced before the beginning of the fight.

The four apprentices, who were distinguished by the large blue or red feathers that sprouted from their caps, were immediately mobbed by those wishing to place bets, but so efficient were they at their task that in very little time all the wagers were taken. Benjamin, who at first had determined to back the favorite, changed his mind. He had watched the baleful woman in the black jacket, and she and her companions had each placed a bet on Charlotta Kegoe, the lady of the tattooed jewels. So Benjamin, in a vague effort to circumvent the evil effect of the old woman's gaze, placed sixty dollars on the head of the Sapphic Pugilist. The red slip, with the figure sixty scrawled on it, he folded and thrust deep into his waistcoat pocket, which he then plugged with his thumb. If he won, and the odds proved substantial, he might go a long way toward repaying his uncle. And if he lost, he would have—if nothing else—adequate excuse for departing Harry Hill's establishment, where he found himself very uncomfortable.

The announcement that the odds were four to one in favor of Annie Leech over Charlotta Kegoe brought up a cheer and a surge forward in the crowd. Harry Hill withdrew from the ring and a great bell, struck by a man perched on a high stool in the corner of the room, marked the beginning of the match. Annie Leech and Charlotta Kegoe suddenly turned and fell upon one another in a growling fury. A series of vicious fisted blows left their bare skin first red, then blue with bruising. They cracked one another's jaws and pulled one another's queues; they screamed inarticulately and pushed one another painfully against the ropes.

The crowd from the beginning cheered vociferously, and their noses rose yet higher when the first blood appeared—as Charlotta Kegoe was injured just below the right eye by a well-timed poke from Annie Leech. Another terrible blow stunned Charlotta, and as she reeled against the ropes Annie did a little savage dance of triumph while three-quarters of the crowd urged her on to greater mayhem; the other fourth began to groan loudly, mourning the loss of its stakes.

For these five minutes, Benjamin worried for the fate of his sister's sixty dollars, five dollars of the sum he had borrowed being already consumed; and losing concentration on the fight that was taking place sometimes no more than inches from his face, tried to think of a way to replace that money before his sister discovered that it was missing. He realized suddenly that he had been foolish in taking the gold: his family thought badly enough of his indiscretion at Morrissey's, but that at least had not been outright theft. Benjamin's sole hope now was that Charlotta Kegoe would win after all and that, at the least, Helen's money could be replaced.

The Sapphic Pugilist however was taking a dangerous pummeling from her adversary. The lowest row of fringe on her tunic had been ripped loose and dangled about her knees as she staggered back into a corner of the ring. The cut on her face, and another on the back of her hand, oozed blood. The groans of her supporters were almost as loud as the cheers that egged Annie Leech on in hopes of a quick victory.

When the two antagonists moved suddenly from the center of the ring well to one side, Benjamin had a view of the old lady in the black jacket and the two young women and the two children who accompanied her. All five remained stock still before the agitated shouting mass of spectators. All held aloft their red tickets—for even the children had placed bets—in this manner showing support of their favorite. But not one moved, not one spoke.

Charlotta Kegoe doubled over in apparent pain and Annie Leech moved in close. But then Charlotta drew up in a flash, her hands clasped rigidly in front of her. Her broad bruised forearm, with all her strength pressed into its service, smashed against Annie Leech's neck.

Annie staggered backward, and a great vexed cry went up from the crowd, surmounted by a sharp cheer from Charlotta's supporters. Benjamin, because so much depended upon the outcome of the fight, remained breathlessly silent.

Charlotta pursued her temporary advantage and punched Annie repeatedly in the same spot just below the center of the breast. Annie spat up blood onto her black velvet tunic and collapsed in a heap.

The man on the high stool in the corner rang the bell three times and the fight was over. The dazed Annie Leech was taken up from the platform by her supporters and carefully passed over the heads of the crowd by raised tender hands. Charlotta Kegoe, who had stood by, arms akimbo, watching the ignominious departure of her opponent, suddenly swung over the ropes and landed in the midst of the group directly across from Benjamin. The twins ecstatically embraced her legs, the old fat lady squeezed her hand, and the severe-faced woman with the

crimped black hair kissed her quickly but quite passion-
ately upon the mouth. The pretty young woman in the
bottle-green frock had disappeared, but returned now,
laughingly to distribute the money that they had won. As
a group they all pushed away toward the curtained doorway, the children and two young women ahead, then
Charlotta Kegoe in dignified triumph, ignoring the derog-
atory calls of the disappointed. The old fat woman in
black lagged behind to cast a glance so hostile toward
Benjamin that he was almost unmanned by it.

Benjamin determined that he would leave that place
when he had collected his money. It would certainly be
the first time in memory that he had departed a gambling
house with more money in his pocket than he had had
upon arrival, but he realized that the most important thing
now was to return his sister's gold. Even if he were to
remain and recover the eight hundred dollars that he had
lost during the afternoon's play, his family would know
that he must have got it all by gambling somewhere—and
there would certainly be no gain to him in such a situation
as that.

Benjamin cashed in his red slip, and though he was
anxious over the prospect of traversing the dance floor
again, and dreaded still more the journey down West
Houston Street to the Sixth Avenue el, he pushed his way
determinedly toward the curtained door. The crowd
surged around the bet-takers for the next bout, whose con-
testants had just been announced in the ring, and his
progress was easier than he had anticipated.

He was stopped by the burly guardian of the curtained
doorway who contentiously informed him that if he
wanted to go out now he would have to pay for his entrance again later. Benjamin nodded distractedly, but he
had hardly heard the words that the doorman spoke, for
just beside him leaning against the wall was the Sapphic
Pugilist herself, Charlotta Kegoe. The young woman with
crimped black hair was tenderly washing her cuts with a
damp cloth, while the pretty young woman knelt at Charlotta's feet, sewing the fringe back on her tunic. The old
fat woman, with one hand on the shoulder of each of the
children, was not a yard away from Benjamin; her gaze
was menacing and pitiless. She said nothing, but the
breath through her open mouth was short and noisy.

Benjamin plunged through the curtain, and as he skirted the busy dance floor almost running toward the exit, did not dare look back. He did not hear the laughter that had followed him out.

"Ha!" snorted Charlotta Kegoe, "who was that, Lena? You stared at that boy like you had seen him set fire to the Colored Orphan Asylum."

"Oh!" cried Daisy, still at Charlotta's feet, "he was on the other side of the ring there from us. Bet on you, you know, but maybe it got too strong for him."

Rob had seized one of Charlotta's hands and was minutely examining her tattoos, whispering to his sister that when he was grown he would have just such rings on all his fingers. Ella was more concerned with her grandmother's cane, which she had been allowed to hold for a time.

Louisa Shanks turned and made a brief sign to her mother. *Who was he?*

"Don't know," replied Lena to this silent question. "But when I saw him, it was like a piece of ice stuck between my shoulders."

"That one?" laughed Daisy. "Oh, Ma! You stared at him, and his drawers just about drooped to the floor!"

"Daisy," said Lena seriously, "it was the eyes. Those eyes I know. . . ."

Chapter 6

Just as Benjamin Stallworth stumbled out of Harry Hill's establishment he collided with a woman who stood directly beneath the red and blue lantern. Benjamin was surprised by her appearance, for she was almost certainly a lady. There was nothing of coarseness in her face or her fashion; and her expression, as she listened with averted eyes to his stammered apology, was exactly that he had seen on his aunt's face when she had herself been the victim of one of his clumsinesses. But as he passed on he reflected that he was surely mistaken, for no lady appeared unaccompanied at such an hour in such a neighborhood.

As Benjamin pushed through the dawdling crowds on the sidewalk—dawdling, he was sure, so as to watch for opportunities to pick pockets or expedite other mischiefs—he glanced back at the clapboard front of Harry Hill's. The sham lady no longer stood beneath the red and blue lantern and he could not identify her retreating figure—so he must suppose that she had entered the place.

The woman who had passed beneath Benjamin Stallworth's startled scrutiny was in fact fully a lady in the matters of deportment and dress, and fell short only in the matter of birth. She was an octoroon, her father's mother having been a slave on one of the Georgia sea islands. Under all but the very closest inspection, Maggie Kizer was a white woman, and bore but two telltale traces of her mixed blood: a thin blue line under her thumbnail and a fleck of black pigment in each of her green eyes. Obsessed with these betraying blemishes, Maggie never appeared on the street or in strange company without a pair of the finest white gloves, so close-fitting that she put on her beautiful diamond and emerald rings over them; and in all but blackest night she wore a pair of round spectacles with smoked-amber lenses.

Tonight, Maggie Kizer wore a light-blue dress beneath a long dark-blue cloak that was fastened with a gleaming silver chain across her neck. Her veiled hat was of blue velvet with black trim and her gloved hands were encased in a fur muff. She paused nervously in the passage of Harry Hill's place to put on her amber spectacles, then quickly circling the dancers, Maggie made her way to the curtained door that led to the back. She withdrew one white-gloved hand from her muff and pressed a quarter dollar into the palm of the man standing guard there. Her manner, which had exhibited a certain haste and uneasiness of mind, suddenly altered when she stepped into the back room. Her countenance then was one of dignity and repose, her movement cautious but full of grace.

Standing at the edge of the crowd, she beckoned to one of Harry Hill's apprentices, who now wore a cap with a green feather, and purchased from him a slip of green paper for five dollars.

"Don't even know who you've bet on——" laughed a coarse female voice behind her.

"No I don't," replied Maggie Kizer in a low melodious accent, and quite before she knew to whom she had spoken. Her parted lips warmed into a smile as she turned.

Charlotta Kegoe, still leaning against the wall, sipped at a schooner of beer. Beside her stood all the Shanks family.

"Maggie," said Lena Shanks, "you don't play this way with money."

"No," replied Maggie, "I don't. I've been searching for you these two hours at least." She came up close to the group. Rob stared at the young woman in unreserved admiration; Ella surreptitiously lifted a corner of the blue cloak and peered beneath it. Maggie touched each of the children's heads affectionately.

"We've talking to do, Lena," said Maggie quietly, "talking that wants doing tonight."

Maggie Kizer was married to Lena's younger brother Alick, a hotel thief serving a nine-year sentence at Sing Sing.

Lena nodded, took her cane from Ella, and slowly hobbled through the curtain. Maggie Kizer nodded to Louisa and Daisy, and presented Rob with her ticket. Then, with Ella at her side, she followed Lena out.

Charlotta Kegoe rolled her eyes at what she imagined were Maggie Kizer's pretensions to gentility, and then grabbed Louisa Shanks around the waist. Louisa fell back against the wall and her head knocked smartly against the plaster there; but if she suffered pain, she did not betray it, and only smiled as Charlotta inclined her head and began to whisper hotly in her ear. Rob and his mother Daisy pushed their way a little nearer the ring, for they possessed not only their own yellow tickets but also the green ticket that had been purchased by Maggie Kizer—so they were sure to win.

Once outside Harry Hill's, Lena Shanks, her granddaughter Ella, and Maggie Kizer proceeded slowly along West Houston Street in the direction of the North River. After they had traveled a couple of squares the fidgeting crowds thinned and the way became darker. Those moving along this part of the street were furtive and shy of notice. Noise and light exploded from every tenth doorway, but all in between was closed, black, and silent. As they walked, Maggie talked to Lena in a low, quick voice that was meant only for the old woman's ear; so discreetly was Maggie's information imparted to her sister-in-law that Ella, close beside, could hear nothing of it at all, though she strained.

The metal tip of Lena's cane struck sparks upon the cobblestones, and Ella knew that Maggie Kizer's news was not of the best. "Where is he now?" the little girl heard her grandmother demand, but the octoroon only shrugged her handsome shoulders.

When they had come within sight of the house, Lena paused, drew a key from the pocket of her skirt, and entrusted it to Ella. The little girl ran ahead and opened the door of the pawnshop. She struck one of the matches that she always carried in her pocket and lighted a candle that stood on the sill of the street window.

The front of the shop was about ten feet square. The two windows to the side of the door were shuttered from the inside; but the glass on them was so grimy that they scarcely admitted more light when the shutters were opened during the day. A square deal table and a couple of red-painted chairs were pushed against one wall; and rickety shelving had been raised against the other. Here were displayed dented tarnished copper pots, guitars with broken strings, a row of mildewed books, a pile of music, cracked and badly painted shades for lamps, a couple of frames of moldy butterflies, an array of rusty surgical instruments, some broken filigree boxes wrought by Confederate prisoners, half a dozen chipped figures of painted chalk, and a stack of men's hats with the nap all worn off. These same items had been on the same shelves since the shop was opened and no one ever inquired about their prices.

At the back of the room was a long counter with a closed bottom. Behind this were two high stools, one for Lena Shanks and one for Ella. On a platform in the corner stood a combination-lock safe, large and shining black but whimsically painted with scrolls of flowers along its edges. A wide curtained door led into the back of the house and to the stairs that descended to the cellar.

The floor of the shop was rough and uneven, and in places sank beneath the lightest step. The walls, wholly without ornament, were covered in a much-discolored and water-damaged striped paper of green and black. Nothing in the room was new or even of recent date, and nothing was overly clean; yet half a million dollars in merchandise passed over that long counter in the course of a year.

Breathing noisily and with some difficulty, Lena Shanks mounted the steps and came into the shop. Maggie Kizer followed immediately behind and took the liberty of closing the door after her. The slow walk from Harry Hill's had brought back the tension in her face, and her fur muff was held tightly against her breast.

"What do you have?" said Lena, seating herself at the red deal table.

Maggie moved over by the shelving, where it was quite dark, and stood with her back to Lena Shanks and Ella. In a couple of moments she turned around, holding in her hands a small green canvas bag, drawn closed with a thick white string. She came over to the table, pulled the string loose, and emptied out a dozen pieces of heavy jewelry: three gold rings set with diamonds, a thick gold wedding band, a gold watch, chain and seals, five shirt studs with sapphires in them, and a sapphire stickpin. All the stones were of more than moderate size.

In the gentle light of the oil lamp that Ella had lighted and set upon the table, Lena examined each piece carefully and without haste. Ella sat opposite her and looked at the jewels with almost as critical an eye as her grandmother's but she touched nothing. Maggie Kizer paced the room with a light springy tread, her cloak wrapped closely about her, for the unheated room was cold.

After three minutes had passed Lena Shanks, without looking up, and as she fingered one of the sapphire shirt studs, said: "Three hundred."

"Yes," said the octoroon without hesitation, "just be sure we're quickly rid of it."

Lena brushed all the jewels back into the green canvas bag, and said to her granddaughter: "Bring the lamp." Ella lifted the lamp from the table and carried it behind the counter. She held it up before the safe as her grandmother turned the combination dial. In a few moments the safe was opened and a stack of ten-dollar bank notes extracted. Ella counted out three hundred dollars and handed the bills to Maggie.

"Thank you, Lena," said the octoroon. "It was important that this be done tonight. . . ."

Lena nodded, and leaned forward heavily on her cane. "You'll send the money?"

"Tomorrow morning. But I'll say to you, Lena: I hope never to see him again!"

"*Das versteh' ich,*" replied Lena gravely.

"The watch has an inscription in the case——"

"Melted down tonight——" Lena assured her. "*Wiederseh'n,* Maggie.*"

After the octoroon had turned her back on them once

more in order to secrete the money she had received, she nodded briefly and swept out the door with a sure and determined step.

While Ella bolted the door after Maggie Kizer, Lena Shanks lumbered around to the back of the counter, heaved herself up onto the higher stool, and spread out a large sheet of brown paper. Upon this she emptied the bag of masculine jewelry.

From a drawer in the counter, Lena took out a jeweler's pick, and pried the sapphires from their gold settings. As these were removed, Ella placed them into an envelope taken from the open safe, which contained other stones indistinguishable from them. All the diamonds went into another envelope, and the gold settings were pushed aside into a little gleaming heap.

Only the watch remained. It was a valuable piece—of Swiss manufacture—and on the inside of the case was engraved CYRUS WESTON BUTTERFIELD, FROM HIS DE-VOTED WIFE, TEMPUS FUGIT, 1871.

Lena wound the watch with its key, turned its hands to the hour, and listened to the sweet melodic chimes. She smiled slightly, reset the watch, and played the chimes again, holding the watch close to Ella's ear. Then she put the watch down upon the counter, and with a small iron mallet smashed the workings to bits. She pried the case loose and gave it, with the chain and seals and fob, to Ella. All the broken workings were swept into a brown envelope which she flung into a crate of trash in the corner.

Ella assisted her grandmother down from her perch, and with the tiny horde of gold cupped in their hands, descended to the cellar. Here, from a bar that had been driven into the stonework of the large hearth hung two crucibles over a steadily burning coal fire. With tongs, Lena lifted the lid of the small one and Ella poured in the broken gold jewelry.

Lena smiled, drew a key from her pocket and handing it to Ella, said, "Fetch me the silver box."

Ella disappeared around a jerry-built wall into the dark maze of rooms, closets, and cupboards that lay beneath Lena Shanks's two houses. In a couple of minutes, shivering from the cold, she returned with a heavy wooden box that was a foot deep in plate: small vases, trays, ornaments, and much tableware.

"Some pieces, girl," said Lena, "and throw them in."

Melting the silver was always a treat for Ella. She took up half a dozen forks from the box, of different patterns but all bearing monograms, and dropped them into the crucible. Her grandmother replaced the lid and then sat in a straight-backed chair near the fire. Ella knelt at the side of the box and rummaged through the silver, picking out the pieces she thought prettiest and setting them aside to be melted down. Every few minutes she took the tongs and lifted the lids of the crucibles to check the progress of liquefaction.

Rob and Ella had been carefully brought up. The children of most criminals in New York ran wild about the streets in gangs sycophantic of older ruffian groups, calling themselves, for instance, "The Little Dead Rabbits" and "The Forty Little Thieves." They learned to rob dead men on the street, and attack drunken revelers, and set up distractions in crowds so that pickpockets might work more easily. But Rob and Ella were being trained in their family's occupations. Rob, well versed in the secrets of the female anatomy, was continually delighted with the succession of ladies in and out of the tiny room on the fourth floor of the house. Ella spent most of her day in the pawnshop, close at her grandmother's hand. At eight years of age, she could tell silver plate from real silver at a glance, grade silks to a nicety, swiftly knot a new fringe for a stolen cambric shawl, and make fair appraisals of glass, plate, jewelry, and feminine clothing.

For companions, Rob and Ella had only one another, but they never seemed to want to know other children; the thousands of Arabs and urchins who enjoyed the freedom of the street were frivolous, doomed creatures in the critical eyes of the young twins. In a part of the city full of want and misery and sickness they appreciated the superfluities of their existence, the health and prosperity of their own family: their mother, their aunt, and their grandmother. Louisa and Lena's occasional harshness toward them was nothing compared to what they glimpsed on the street, in cellar dives, and in tenement rooms. They had been made to understand that their well-being was due to their family's diligence; and to avoid the misery that moaned on every side of the two buildings on West Houston Street, Rob and Ella early settled into little lives of strange industriousness. They never, however, gained any sense that what they did might be considered wrong—their understanding of the law was imperfect. Judgments and jails, though certainly they knew of them, seemed afflictions as arbitrary as disease and death. It was the fortunate and the hard-working, not the good, who survived these vicissitudes.

After Ella had set two small salvers chased with patterns of twining grapevines into the crucible, she brought a blanket from the corner of the small bare room in which they sat, spread it at her grandmother's feet, and lay down upon it. The noise of the fire and the gentle sound of the bubbling silver soon sent her off to sleep.

Lena Shanks, however, sat bolt upright in her chair, staring into the fire; though she was close to the bright flames, she neither felt their heat nor traced their dancing patterns. The news that Maggie Kizer had brought that evening had been of a serious and unfortunate nature; but it was not upon this trouble that Lena's thoughts were fixed. She was cold, quite cold, because her mind irresistibly pictured a pair of brilliant light-blue eyes. They had seemed out of place in the sallow face of the weak young man at Harry Hill's, for Lena remembered those eyes as belonging to another—to one whom she hated more than any other man upon earth, the man responsible for her husband's death.

Chapter 7

W<small>HEN</small> she left Lena Shanks's pawnshop, Maggie Kizer
went back along West Houston in the direction of Harry
Hill's place. She paid no attention to the insults that were
directed at her by the gaudily dressed women who
lounged in the ground floor windows of the whorehouses
along the way. These prostitutes might direct a remark
at anyone who came within their sight, but they seemed
to take particular umbrage at this well-dressed, well-
deported woman, who could pass for a lady but for the
very fact of her being on such a street at such a time.

Her amber spectacles had been removed and her white-
gloved hands with the numerous rings she kept tight
within her muff, to deflect attention from herself, but her
carriage and her habit stood forth plainly in that street of
license and dishabille. She was spoken to by several gentlemen, but their flattering remarks she ignored as studiously as she had the insults. One tall, drunken, bearded
gentleman in a long fur coat placed his hand on her arm
and wondered thickly if she were in need of protection
for the remainder of her journey home—he would be
honored to serve as her escort.

"Pardon me," replied Maggie, in a voice that charmed him when it was meant only to discourage. She broke away and continued down the street, but he lurched after, undaunted. She did not hurry her pace, but a few numbers down, turned suddenly into a small drugstore, which was placed between two of the cheapest whorehouses on the street—a favorable location since the bulk of the apothecary's business was with the prostitutes. Women who could not afford Daisy Shanks came to him for remedies for unwanted pregnancies, and he dealt in substantial quantities of opium, chloroform, and morphia.

The gentleman hard upon Maggie's heels did not follow her in, for he was not so drunk that he forgot the danger often attendant upon a gentleman's entering a store alone. He crossed the street, walked a space, crossed the street again, and then lounged outside the door, waiting for Maggie to emerge. But standing there, he was so much taunted by the women hanging out the windows of the neighboring establishment that he gave over the game and stumbled away, out of reach of their shrill abuse.

In the drugstore, which was neither larger nor brighter nor appreciably cleaner than Lena Shanks's pawnshop, three fat, gaudy whores, whose vermilion lay half a dollar deep upon their cheeks, huddled at a small low table, on which stood three large glasses of absinthe. There was a short candle jammed in the mouth of a bottle and its guttering flame shining through the liquid in their glasses cast green shadows onto their pallid, pudgy hands. Their gossip hushed when Maggie entered and they watched her closely and with evident mistrust.

The shop was run by a young man whose hair had fallen out, whose skin was scarred with the smallpox, and whose eyes worked at cross purposes.

"Yes, ma'am," he said slyly to Maggie, "what can I get for you?"

"Powdered opiate," replied Maggie. "Three ounces."

"Twelve dollars," the druggist replied and, plucking out of a little wooden box his one- and two-ounce weights, dropped them onto one side of his scales. Then from a large jar filled with white powder he measured the opium, slipped it into a pink envelope, and slid it across the counter to Maggie. "Can't sleep?" he inquired in an oily

voice. "Bad dreams? Pain in the tooth?" Mischievously
he had listed the common lies of the addict.

"No," replied Maggie, coolly, handing him the money
in notes and silver, "it's for my aged mother who is dying
of a cancer of the breast." There was some sharpness in
her voice, as though she expected him to disbelieve her
and did not care what he thought. The druggist's leer
abandoned him as he stared at the jewels on her white-
gloved hands. But almost immediately the red and green
jewels, the white hand, and the pink envelope disappeared
beneath the blue cloak. Maggie plunged out of the shop,
not even hesitating at the door to see whether the gentleman in the fur coat lay in wait for her.

The whispers of the three fat whores at the very small
table rose suddenly in pitch and volume and they loudly
debated who she was, and what she was doing on West
Houston Street, and whether she really imagined that
she had gouged anyone into believing that she was a real
lady. Their admiration for her clothing, however, was
genuine if grudging, and they listened intently when the
druggist, coming over with the bottle of absinthe—Death's
Green Wine—and replenishing their tall glasses, smirk-
ingly described the jeweled rings on her white-gloved
hands.

"She'd best be careful!" cried one whore.

"She'd best stay away!" cried another.

"If she takes her dainty hands out of her muff on this
street," cried the third, "someone'll do her the favor of
chopping 'em off!"

Maggie followed the route that the twins had taken
when they carried the corpse of the young girl to the
medical students the night before. But she went up
Bleecker in the other direction, all the way to Downing
Street, where a latchkey let her into a small, well-kept
brick house. She walked up a single flight of the blue-
carpeted steps and with another key unlocked a large
set of double doors. These she opened quietly and just
enough to pass through. She slipped inside and pulled
them shut behind her.

Light from the streetlamp shining through the front
windows was sufficient for her to move about without

stumbling and she did not turn up the gas. Laying aside her muff, she unfastened the silver chain at her throat and folded the cloak over the back of a chair. She unpinned her hat and placed it carefully atop the cloak. The money she had got that night she slipped into the drawer of an ornamental table beside the door.

Holding the pink envelope, she was just about to move toward her bedroom, when she detected a slight movement at the far end of the room—a rustle of cloth, the fall of a foot against the double-laid carpets. Without saying anything, Maggie turned the key of the gas and brought the lights of the brass chandelier up just enough to dispel the obscurity.

The small chamber was fashionably decorated in deep rose and dark blue. The furniture was quite expensive and the fabrics and the upholstery and the papering were all sumptuous and soft and deep. At the far side of the room, on a high-backed couch covered in a heavily napped blue velvet, sat a handsome gentleman with short brown hair and a thick brown beard. He was modestly but quite elegantly dressed in a brown-checked suit.

"Hello, Maggie," he said easily, "Mrs. Weale let me in."

"I told her she might," said Maggie, slipping the pink envelope beneath the lid of her desk.

"I've brought you something—my New Year's gift. Look on the mantel."

The octoroon glided to the hearth, which was of a deeply veined pink marble, and there beside the blood-red Bavarian vase which held a mass of blue campanulas, was a small red box tied up with a blue ribbon. She untied the ribbon and opened the box; it contained a gold ring set with a circle of small but brilliant rubies.

"Do you like it?" said the man, who rose from the couch and came near the cold hearth.

Maggie, with voluptuous weariness, threw her arms about his neck, kissed him, and then rubbed her cheek tenderly against his beard.

"Oh yes, Duncan, very much." She clasped her white-gloved hands behind his neck. "I've a weakness for rubies, such a weakness."

When Maggie turned her head beneath the chandelier, Duncan Phair searched out the slight flaw of blackness in each of her fine green eyes. "You seem very tired tonight," he said.

"Oh no," she protested, "no no, earlier I was tired, but you're here now, and I feel that everything's come right." She pulled back, and smiled with a ravishing tenderness. "Everything's come right," she whispered.

Chapter 8

∞∞

JUDGE James Stallworth lived alone now in his large, old-fashioned mansion on Washington Square, at the southern extremity of Fifth Avenue. This had been one of the most fashionable addresses in New York when he had built the house in 1840; but the well-to-do of New York, always restlessly pushing northward, had paused only a couple of decades in Greenwich Village and around Washington Square. By the time of Judge Stallworth's second marriage, to Marian's mother, the rich had built up Fifth Avenue as far as Thirty-Fifth Street, and created for themselves the exclusivities of Madison Square and Gramercy Park. Washington Square, whose well-groomed acres had once been the burying ground for the city's paupers and criminals, and covered the moldering bones of a hundred thousand and more of the socially insignificant, now entombed the city's unfashionable rich.

The Stallworth family was known to be "well-fixed," but in fact they were much more than that. During the Civil War, when he was already a well-established lawyer, James Stallworth got a great deal of money by the selling of commodities: dried meat and flour mostly, with occasional large transactions in captured cotton. At that time he was already twice widowed: his first wife had died in giving birth to their son Edward, and his second wife had succumbed to influenza when their daughter Marian was only six, in 1859.

Now a little more than seventy years of age, Judge James Stallworth was the best-known Republican judge in a city completely controlled by Democrats. He did not take bribes, and was known for his severity in sentencing. He had never become important in the politics of the city as much because of his unyielding temperament as his political affiliation—for places were sometimes found for obliging members of the opposition—but that same inflexibility had probably also saved him from being removed from office.

Judge James Stallworth had possibly a single weakness, and that was the affection he bore his dogs—or rather, his dog, for he never had more than one at a time. This was invariably a black-and-tan, and whether male or female, it was invariably called Pompey. The first of this long succession of animals the judge had possessed when he was a law student at Columbia, and he had grieved severely when that dog had been run down in the street by a vegetable wagon. Ashamed of the depth of the feeling that had been drawn out of him, as it were by surprise, he determined never to allow himself to be so touched again. He purchased another black-and-tan as near to like the first as he could find, called it Pompey and pretended that the first had not died. This little self-deception he had carried on now for five decades, and Pompeys came and went. But whether Pompey lived three weeks or thirteen years, the judge never lamented his death, for he was certain another could be got to take his place on the morrow. Something of this feeling probably carried over into his acceptance of the death of both his wives, and the very guarantee of Pompey's immortality made it possible for him to forgo the pleasure of a third helpmeet after Marian's mother died.

It had been a disappointment to the judge that his son Edward has chosen the ministry as his life's work, for he had designed for Edward a career in the law and politics. But his ambitious hopes had been fanned to life again when Marian married Duncan Phair, a young lawyer who had assisted in the prosecution at Tweed's second trial. Judge Stallworth had encouraged this liaison, and when

Marian was told of the generous settlement that her father would provide if she married Duncan Phair, she was easily persuaded to accept the man's proposal. Judge Stallworth was too old to aspire to much higher place or greater prestige and had decided to expend his energies toward the aggrandizement of his son-in-law, who was not yet much above thirty. James Stallworth wanted to insure that, by the turn of the century, Duncan Phair would be mayor of a Republican city, perhaps even governor of a Republican state.

Judge Stallworth never felt that his trust in Duncan Phair had been proffered foolishly. The man was eager for advancement and in constant consultation with his father-in-law. As often as they dared, the two men prodded Tammany Hall with staves of law and litigation. They had no illusion however that they did more than irritate this lumbering Gulliver with their legal toothpicks, but they still must do what they could, for no Republican would advance far in New York until Tammany was razed.

When he had married Marian, Duncan Phair was perfectly willing to be subsumed into the Stallworth clan. His own family was obscure, and he had left parents, siblings, and more distant relations to shift for themselves in Baltimore. Marian and her father had never troubled themselves with Duncan's relatives, and Duncan neither mentioned them nor appeared to be uneasy about their condition. So far as anyone knew he did not communicate at all with Baltimore. Some had suggested that Duncan Phair would have taken his wife's name upon marriage if it could have been accomplished without ridicule.

James Stallworth had found a partner for Duncan Phair, a plodding capable lawyer called George Peerce, who handled all the workaday business that came the partnership's way, business on which no glory was likely to redound. Anything that entailed exposure to the public or to the society of lawyers in general, Duncan Phair managed himself, with his father-in-law's detailed advice. In this manner he received both honor and increase of reputation while enjoying the greater financial security that the less exciting work provided.

Phair and his father-in-law often took luncheon together, or spent evenings in one another's company in the house on Washington Square or in the lawyers' club, where in low voices they talked over projects and strategies for the overthrow of the Democrats and the promotion of the Republicans—themselves in particular.

For more than a week now, the father- and son-in-law had worked on a plan suggested to the judge by the editor of the *Tribune*—a man who also took solace in the company of black-and-tans. The *Tribune*, Judge Stallworth learned, was soon to begin a series of articles on the depravity of certain New York neighborhoods. The Guiteau trial would eventually be concluded and Oscar Wilde would soon move on to other cities—and something must be found to engage the interest of the *Tribune*'s readership. Subscribers would therefore, in the coming months, be provided with exact descriptions of the crimes and the criminals that existed in dark profusion in lower New York, through the sufferance—if not the actual assistance of—the police and the Democratic politicians.

Judge Stallworth and Duncan realized that it would be well to work with the *Tribune* in this enterprise, for it seemed certain to attract much attention. The Democrats would be hard put to defend the accusation—perfectly true, of course—that they fostered crime because of pecuniary recompense. Judge Stallworth duly introduced Duncan to the editor of the *Tribune*, and the three men had dinner together at the house on Washington Square on the evening of January 2, 1882. At that time it was decided that Duncan would be the legal advisor of the paper in these matters, and would accompany Simeon Lightner—the reporter who was in charge of the investigation—down into the "purlieus of putrescent corruption" that had raised themselves thickest and rankest around police headquarters itself.

The editor of the *Tribune* noted that Simeon Lightner had only just begun his researches, was spending his evenings moving from saloon to dance hall to low theater throughout the area, only surveying that wicked country, and that Duncan might join him at any time. "The presence and corroboration of a well-known and -respected lawyer," said the editor, "will lend substance and gravity to the undertaking, and we shall be better protected against the verbal shafts of the Democrats who will claim that we exaggerate, that we monger scandal, and that we have held up a Republican magnification glass and shown two pickpockets and three whores to be an entire population of cut-throats and bank-thieves."

"It's a good chance," said Duncan to his father-in-law when the editor had taken his leave. "I think I might even persuade Lightner to allow me to append 'A Lawyer's Judgement' to the end of each article that he writes, explaining points of the law, lamenting the present state of the Democratically run courts, and so forth. I'll sign myself pseudonymously—'The Republican Advocate,' or some such—and then have it come out later that I was the author. What do you think, Father?"

Judge Stallworth nodded sagaciously, and stroked Pompey's back. "You be certain that you're in control of this, Duncan. I think it would be wise if you went to talk to that reporter tomorrow. Let him know that you're willing to assist him in anything, committing time, resources, and so forth, and then just make sure that *you* guide it through. Now, what I would suggest is that you concentrate upon a single area within the city, a single criminal neighborhood. You can say: 'Here is a single square, a single street, and see what the Democrats have done: they've set up five houses of ill repute, five pawnbrokers who are in reality receivers of stolen property, two gambling halls, five saloons that remain open all the night through and even upon the Sabbath. Here are thirty-five prostitutes in residence, seventy-five thieves, and these ten houses have produced seventeen murderers and twenty-one victims of murder . . . And so on, you see."

"Yes," said Duncan.

"Then," said Judge Stallworth, "we draw on what influence we have with the police and have them close down the gambling halls, shut up the whorehouses, drag the pickpockets to the Tombs, and in fact, relocate the entire street to Blackwell's Island. Then we set up some charity in one of the vacated houses—an 'Asylum for Infantile Prostitutes' or some such, and then get the credit for having brushed clean the entire city. If you concentrate on the one area, Duncan, you can accomplish something. Expose the bribe-taking schemes, that's very important, show the ways that every criminal business is indissolubly linked to Tammany."

"But which area is best do you think, Father?"

"Well," said Judge Stallworth, and rubbed his thin parchment fingers together, "not the Sixth Ward of course, that's *too* depraved, and that's the Tammany stronghold besides. It's all right to report on it, of course—say how dreadful the tenements are, how many corpses are discovered each night in the gutter, and so forth—but the hard work should be concentrated in a single area. And I have no influence over the Tenth Ward either, for the Democrats make sure that they're in control of the courts there, but I do have a little space that lies west of MacDougal, between say Canal and Bleecker Streets. We're not so very far away from it as we sit here now. The judge—you wouldn't remember him, Duncan—who had it before me, called it the 'Black Triangle' because of its shape and the amount of crime there."

"The area's not improved of late," remarked Duncan.

"No!" laughed the old man, "and a good thing for us. You can make the point that all this horror festers within half an hour's walk of the most fashionable houses in the city. Frighten 'em. Nobody today remembers the Draft Riots, they might as well never have taken place. Have remembrances of the trouble during the war, when houses were burnt and the niggers were hanged within sight of these very windows, when the shops were looted and gentlewomen violated. Make 'em think it could happen tomorrow if this isn't all cleaned up by the Republicans. The Democrats are fomenting a revolution, tell 'em that!"

"Well," said Duncan, with raised eyebrows, "don't you think that's a bit far to take it?"

"No," replied Judge Stallworth, "it's not. This is a good issue and deserves our best attention. I shouldn't worry about other business just now—Peerce can take up your slack. It would be of considerable help if I could try the cases that came up as a result of this series of articles so you might do very well to confine your researches to the Black Triangle. Remember: west of MacDougal, south of Bleecker, north of Canal. Anyone arrested there will come up before me. You know, now I think on it I can remember: along about the time of the war there was a family there, called I don't remember what. Husband, wife, wife's brother, children, and the like—whole family involved in crime up to their blackened teeth. I hanged the husband and shut up the mother at the Island, sent the children away—and was applauded for it in every journal in the city. They lived in the Black Triangle, and I'm certain there are others like them today, ripe for the quashing. Listen to me, Duncan, you be on the lookout —be particularly on the lookout—for a family of criminals. Nothing goes over so well as the destruction of a whole gang—it's as good as exterminating brigands."

"This is a good chance for us," said Duncan mildly.

"Yes, but particularly for you! And remember: this is not the time for half measures. First concentrate on the Black Triangle, paint it blacker than it is. Then find a family, some clan steeped in sin there, and drive 'em into the river. Hold 'em under till they drown! There'll be a crowd a hundred thousand strong on the shore to sing your praises and crown your brow!"

Duncan scratched Pompey's head, and though he nodded acquiescence to all that Judge Stallworth had suggested, his thoughts were of the modest brick house on the edge of the Black Triangle where there lived a beautiful young woman with a blue line under her thumbnail and a black fleck in her bright green eye.

Chapter 9

WHEN he returned home that Monday evening, Duncan Phair explained to his wife Judge Stallworth's plan for the advancement of the entire family, and as he expected she fell excitedly into line with it. Marian was disappointed only that Duncan and the judge had not seen fit to confide in her before, and that the designs had not originated with her.

"Now of course," said Duncan, "this will necessitate my being frequently absent from home—"

"Oh of course," exclaimed Marian absently, as if that were the lowest in an entire course of hurdles to be got over. "Now it seems to me," she went on, "that I might be of some considerable assistance to you and Father in this matter."

"How?" said Duncan, with some slight misgiving. Marian oftentimes schemed for the interests of the family, but her stratagems were of the meddlesome and impractical variety. It was often a difficulty to explain to Marian why her suggestions were not to be taken up.

"I see no reason that I could not, say, organize a committee of ladies whose husbands are of some social or political importance—perhaps with Helen to assist me—to protest the moral degeneracy of the city. We could accomplish all manner of things. We could distribute tracts to fallen women or provide starving newsboys with apples—whatever came to mind, and could be accomplished with least bother. And of course a letter-writing campaign on the newspapers and religious journals would be worthwhile. And all the letters would be signed, 'Mrs. Duncan Phair, Chairman of the Such-and-So Committee.' "

Duncan, rather to his surprise, was able to approve the idea wholeheartedly and encouraged his wife to begin as quickly as possible. But she already had—and was scribbling on the back of an envelope the names of a dozen women it was imperative she visit the following day.

The next morning, Tuesday, January 3, 1882, Marian Phair went early to the manse to gather up Helen Stallworth; she would count on her niece's assistance in these endeavors. At the same hour, Duncan Phair went to the offices of the *Tribune* and called upon Simeon Lightner.

The reporter was a sardonic sort of young man, as newspapers reporters generally were, twenty-eight years of age with wiry red hair, grizzled red whiskers, and a complexion that was alternately florid and pale, depending on whether he were drunk or sober, placid or angered. He had already been told of the collaboration of Duncan Phair on this project and begrudged this division of the labors and honors. He was surprised to find the lawyer ameliorative and diffident, and was won by Duncan's knowledgeable, prudent questioning, and his assurance that he would be no more than an extra, a spectator, an appendage. Duncan fulsomely declared that all his sources, all his industry, all his time were entirely at Lightner's disposal.

"Of course," smiled Duncan, "my motives in this are not entirely altruistic, and I imagine that you understand . . ."

"Oh certainly," exclaimed Simeon Lightner with an urbane wagging of his frizzled red head. He spoke as if disinterested public-spiritedness were a laughable chimera and had nothing to do with such clever fellows as themselves.

Duncan waved his hand blithely: "Of course, the main body of the articles will appear under your name alone, Lightner, and I desire no part of the credit either for the writing or for the exhaustive inquiries I've no doubt that you plan upon. But I shall prepare bolstering columns dealing with the problem of bribes, the difficulties of law enforcement in such areas, the way that trials are misconducted, the shortcomings and insufficiencies of the law which make it impossible to deal with many of the very worst cases, and so forth. My articles will not be signed with my name, and it will never be known officially that it was I who accompanied and assisted you; unofficially, however, I am afraid that my identity may be whispered where it will be profitable for my name to be heard. . . ." Duncan smiled conspiratorially and Simeon Lightner grinned back.

"You've begun your researches, I think," said Duncan.

"Yes," replied Lightner, "I was at McGrory's last night, and what I saw is a bit thick to tell. A pale description of what I witnessed would be judged filth by three-quarters of the city," he said loftily, and then added: "So we must be sure to return there soon."

Smiling, Duncan then made the suggestion that they might do well to confine themselves to a single area, a few streets, no more than a few acres of the island, and simply list and describe the depravities and criminal excesses that could be found therein. "I've made a small walking tour of the area myself," said Duncan Phair, "and felt that perhaps the area from MacDougal Street to the North River, bounded on the south by Canal Street and on the north by Bleecker, would be of great interest. It has a conveniently picturesque name, you know, it's called the Black Triangle, and in that sector of the city may be found criminals of all description, but criminals—if I may use such a term—criminals of a better class than one finds farther east. There will not be the difficulty of excluding so much because of disgusting poverty. It is unquestionably a better area for our purposes than Five Points, where all vice is dressed in rags. Readers of the *Tribune* may be intrigued by vice but never by squalor. What do you think, Lightner?"

Mr. Lightner thought that the easy Mr. Phair, despite his protestations of subservience, had very definite ideas on how this project was to be conducted. However, the reporter only said, "I suppose that you and I might look the area over tonight, if you're not averse to beginning immediately. . . ."

"Certainly," Duncan replied, "everything at your convenience and direction."

"Well," said Simeon Lightner with growing discomfort, "there is in fact a gambling house in Leroy Street that I had intended to visit, where the games are notoriously rigged, and the cheating is blatant."

"If I might make a suggestion—" began Duncan deferentially.

"Yes?"

"I have a nephew—a strange, ill-formed sort of boy, a kind of perpetual victim. No one, I think, is simpler than Benjamin, and his appearance unmistakably suggests that very quality. He also has the distinction of having lost at most of the gaming tables of this city. He is the ideal dupe to have with us."

"Bring him then," said Simeon Lightner with some little enthusiasm. "We could have no better disguise."

"Very good then," said Duncan Phair. "I might add too that I saw a notice in the columns this morning that Cyrus Butterfield, a colleague and acquaintance of mine, was found murdered last night—robbed, stripped, and stabbed in an alleyway very near Leroy Street. That might possibly be a good place to begin your articles, the very danger to life in the Black Triangle." Then, in a loud declamatory voice, Duncan Phair intoned: " 'Behind the brick and mortar, underneath the garish colored lights, crouches inestimable danger. The shrill cry of the shameful, shameless woman who barters her body covers the rattle in the blood-filled throat—' "

"Well," said Simeon Lightner, nonplussed by Duncan's lurid oratory, "I don't know whether I oughtn't turn the whole thing over to you, Mr. Phair. I suppose that all your clients are let off?"

After agreeing to meet Simeon Lightner at ten o'clock at the southwest corner of Washington Square, Duncan took a streetcar uptown to the Madison Square Presbyterian Church, and was pleased to find Edward Stallworth in his study there. They conferred for half an hour, while the weak winter sun shone through the stained-glass windows, painting their faces in strange pale maps of yellow, green, and blue.

"Of course," said Duncan, when he had outlined his and Judge Stallworth's plan in some detail, "we are not soliciting your help in any direct fashion. Your father simply asked me to inform you of our designs so that you might, if you wished, take advantage of them and employ them to your own advancement."

"I see," said the minister politely. Edward Stallworth had listened to all Duncan's speech with perfectly undisturbed gravity, and Duncan Phair had watched in vain for the single word or movement, the slight change of expression—too sudden a blinking of the eyes, for instance—that would have told him what side of the issue his brother-in-law had decided to take.

"We imagine," Duncan went on, a little anxiously, "we hope that in the next few months a great deal of attention will be directed to that area over which your father holds jurisdiction, the crime-ridden streets south of Bleecker, the infamous Black Triangle, encompassing hundreds and perhaps thousands of buildings which house evil, foster shame, and countenance corruption."

"Yes," replied Edward Stallworth blandly to Duncan's eloquence, "we are in the midst of great iniquities."

"Now, I know that you write articles, editorial articles for the *Christian Dawning* and the *Presbyterian Advocate* on occasion, and it would possibly not be amiss if you composed a short essay supporting our work in this area or simply pointed out the value of the *Tribune* articles."

"Yes," said Edward reflectively, "perhaps I could." He paused, then went on in a manner which suggested that these plans had been the moral center toward which all his thoughts for the past year had irresistibly tended. "The financial support of the African missions is, of course, a worthwhile ideal," said Edward Stallworth, "and one which has been treated much of late in the *Advocate*, and the congregation here has raised several substantial special collections, but it might be well to turn now to a cause which is closer to our homes. Such a cause might draw considerable attention to . . . to . . ." He tried to think of a word other than *myself* but could not.

"Yes," said Duncan quietly, "it certainly would. Now," he continued, in a voice that was no longer eloquently persuasive, but businesslike with a casual fraternity: "Marian is to form a committee as well, a ladies' Committee for the Suppression of Urban Vice, or some such, and will enlist all her friends. You might urge certain ladies of your congregation to join as well—those whose husbands have some sort of power within the city government, or influence in other spheres. Or who, for that matter, are simply rich."

"What is this committee's purpose?" asked Edward with a little ironic smile of satisfied conspiracy. "Does Marian intend to nail boards across the doors of houses of ill-fame? Will she smash pipes in the opium dens of Mott Street?"

"No," laughed Duncan Phair, "the committee won't really do much of anything, but noise themselves about and write letters and cry out their indignation against the vicious Democrats who permit and promote vice in this city."

"Well," said Edward, "so long as I can assure the ladies that they won't have to see any of the objects of their charitable work, I think I might manage to persuade several or more into Marian's committee. That is, if she can guarantee at least one afternoon a week for the ladies to gather and knit little woolen caps and boots for the babies who are nightly abandoned in the district. Perhaps, if Helen became part of such an organization," he mused wryly, "it would take her mind off the inconsistencies in the Gospels." Edward Stallworth's dry tone of voice was with him always, except for the couple of hours a week when he actually stood in the pulpit. Then he was quite boomingly sincere.

"Thank you, Edward," said Duncan, "I was certain that you would prove invaluable in these tasks."

"Yes," said Edward, "we shall all do what we can. Helen will assist Marian, and Benjamin, as you say, will doubtless play the part of the gull to perfection. And I assure you *I* shall not be behindhand either. On Sunday, when I see Father, I will talk to him myself of these plans. It was not necessary for you to act as intermediary, Duncan, I—"

"Oh," cried Duncan deprecatingly, "that is certainly not the case. Your father is in court today, and he has asked that for the time being I devote my energies to this. He'd like to see me up for the city councillor race in '83. He was much disappointed by my showing last year, but of course only blames it on the Democrats. He doesn't intend for me to be beaten again."

"I trust that you won't be. I pray that you won't be," said Edward Stallworth, "but be that as it may, I will do what I can to further these laudable schemes. I trust that the entire family will find profit in them. Spiritual profit, I mean, of course."

That afternoon Duncan Phair spent on Bleecker Street, on the second story of a certain small, well-kept brick house. Mrs. Lady Weale, an old woman with a flat, sour gray face and a yellow kerchief tied around her head, had opened the door to him, and allowed him entrance without question. She preceded him upstairs and unlocked the double doors. Inside, he found Maggie Kizer, in elegant dishabille, seated by the window, with a book of Jean Ingelow's poetry open in her lap.

"I hadn't expected you," said Maggie with a smile, "but I'm glad that you've come." She held out her hand to him. It was bare but for the single ring of rubies on it.

Duncan Phair came forward and gallantly kissed the proffered hand, turning the blemished thumbnail sweetly beneath his bearded lips.

"I've come for more than one reason," he said.

"Yes?"

"I've come to warn you . . ."

Maggie's smile faded altogether. "To warn me concerning what?"

He held up his hands reassuringly. "Nothing in particular, nothing that need really concern you. I want only to warn you to be careful, to carry yourself with even more discretion than is usual with you, for the time being."

"I am always discreet," replied Maggie. She motioned him to take the chair near her.

"Yes," said Duncan, sitting, "but this area, the area in which this house stands, will shortly come under scrutiny."

"The police? I have no business with the police, Duncan." A woman with less polish than Maggie would have shrugged her shoulders in irritation.

"Not the police. The papers, other interested groups. It won't be safe for . . . those who are indiscreet."

Maggie looked at her lover closely. Maggie Kizer, though she had been intimate with Duncan Phair for more than a year and saw him three times a week or oftener, knew neither his surname nor his occupation. He had not offered to tell and she had not troubled herself to ask.

Maggie's deportment as a lady was in fact unflawed, and she asked no explanations of him now.

"I just want you to remember, Maggie," he said soothingly, "that this house stands on the edge of a very dangerous neighborhood. Saturday night a gentleman was murdered within a single street of here. He was a lawyer whose offices were directly around the corner from Trinity Church. A knife of some sort was stuck up under his ribs and pierced his heart. He was left naked in an alleyway off Leroy Street, and identified by a policeman who knew him by sight."

"Were you acquainted with him?" asked Maggie, with something of harshness or a slight choking in her throat.

"I had met him only. We knew one another only to speak in passing."

"Because a man is murdered and left naked in an alley is no reason I should be confined to these rooms," cried Maggie. "There have been murders before. A woman was hacked to death in the house directly across the way and the pieces packed into a china crate. And a newsgirl was struck down in the street by a carriage-and-four which did not even halt for her. But such things have nothing to do with me, Duncan."

"No," said Duncan, shaking his head, "I suppose they do not. But circumspection is a virtue in us all, Maggie, and I wish only to advise you toward maintenance of that circumspection in yourself. *There*," he cried, reaching his arms around her waist and abandoning the pompous solemnity in his voice, "I'll say no more of it—not a single word more, not a syllable, not a letter. . . ."

Chapter 10

$\mathbf{A}$LTHOUGH the *Tribune* had already reported the vicious murder of Cyrus Butterfield under the headline FIRST CRIME OF THE NEW YEAR, and told who the victim was and how he had died, Simeon Lightner decided to take Duncan Phair's advice and exploit the story. A few days after the lawyer's corpse was found near the North River docks, the paper provided a highly colored account of the man's last day upon earth. It followed him to work on the morning of Saturday, December 31, threading with him his legal way among associates and clients, watched him at luncheon at a small eatery on Murray Street—even providing the menu—and spoke of his last appointment at a quarter of six in the afternoon with the representative of a firearms factory in Connecticut. The testimony of a minor clerk in his law office provided the last sight of Mr. Butterfield alive, as he climbed into a cab just outside his building. Eighteen hours later the article picked up again with the report, quoted at length, of a policeman on beat near Dock 42, who found the naked corpse of Cyrus Butterfield wedged up between two barrels, a small but deep wound in his left breast.

No member of Mr. Butterfield's family—his wife nor his sister nor his brother-in-law nor his children—could

80

account for his being anywhere near the West Street
docks, when his home was far up in the country on East
Eighty-fifth Street. They could not have been more surprised if his corpse had turned up in Singapore or Liver-
pool. No one denied that the portion of New York
demarcated by Canal Street, MacDougal Street, and slanting Bleecker Street was dangerous, but no one could say
what had taken Mr. Butterfield to the Black Triangle on
the last evening of the year—this was the first time that
memorably and sinisterly descriptive designation had
been brought before the public.

Cyrus Butterfield's practice was exclusively given over
to the legal concerns of large New England manufacturies,
and certainly none of his clients was of the common criminal class. Thus, there was some mystery attached to his
presence there, and Simeon Lightner—writing anony-
mously—stated that the *Tribune* meant to find out what it
was; the *Tribune* meant to bring those responsible for the
bereavement of so estimable a family as the Butterfields
to summary justice; the *Tribune* meant to show that the
lassitude of the Democratically controlled police force was
in some measure responsible for this gifted man's shocking
and sudden demise. And Duncan Phair, writing as "A Bereaved Colleague" of Mr. Butterfield, quoted alarming figures on the number of murders committed in the same
precinct over the most recent year, the number of unidentified corpses that had been taken from those streets to the
city morgue, and—in appalling contrast—the infrequent
arrests and even rarer convictions for those crimes.

The article excited much notice, and the following day
Simeon Lightner came back with a description of the murdered man's clothing and jewelry. This was provided by
Mrs. Butterfield, who was a meticulously observant lady.
Her grief had not caused her to forget that her husband
had worn his sapphire studs and stickpin on the day he
left the house never to return. The *Tribune* announced
that all its sources would be thrown into the task of
searching out every second-hand dealer in the length and
breadth of the city, to trace these items that had been
stripped from Cyrus Butterfield, possibly even while he
was still struggling for life in the cold black alley between
barrels that had been packed with salted cod.

On the third day, the paper carried a full half-page account of the funeral of Cyrus Butterfield at the Madison Square Presbyterian Church, where the family had worshipped before moving so far north of the city. Edward Stallworth's stern sermon was printed at length. A circumstantial account of the progress of the funeral procession and Edward Stallworth's quiet remarks at the graveside closed with an affecting comparison of the quiet rural charm of Greenwood Cemetery and the shrill wretchedness of the Black Triangle. "Here," said the minister, spreading wide his arms to encompass the bleak winter beauty of the graveyard, "in the garden of graves, death is made to seem gentle, almost enviable; while *there*, in those unfortunate streets which collectively we may call 'The Black Triangle,' life its very self is hideous and insupportable. Here, Cyrus Westen Butterfield, surrounded by the happy dead, will be forever at rest; and there, those responsible for the death of our beloved brother, will never cease from trouble."

By the fifth day, when a reward of fifteen hundred dollars was offered for information leading to the capture and arrest of those responsible for this infamous crime, the entire city knew of the death of the lawyer. The police, who at first had seen no reason to distinguish this homicide from any of the several dozen murders of respectable persons that occurred in the city every year, doubled their efforts under the pressure exerted by the excited public. They examined the stock of the second-hand dealers (saving the *Tribune* the trouble), grilled pawnbrokers, called in their informants, delved into hellholes to question proprietors and known criminals, stopped persons in the street all but at random—but no one could tell anything of the circumstances of the death of Cyrus Butterfield.

At the height of this clamor, after printing a large selection of outraged letters which demanded to know why such things were allowed to happen in the greatest city in the country, the *Tribune* announced that it was instituting a series, to appear twice weekly, which would expose that very Triangle of corruption and crime in which Cyrus Butterfield had lost his life. It warned that the revelations would be shocking, but guaranteed the truthfulness and impartiality of their reporters in recording the vice that slunk and caroused within a pistol shot of Washington Square. Simeon Lightner looked on Duncan Phair now with some respect, for his suggestions on how to exercise the Butterfield murder to best advantage had been astute.

Every night now forays were made into the Black Triangle by three men banded together for protection: Simeon Lightner, Duncan Phair, and Benjamin Stallworth. They could not, of course, disguise themselves as denizens of the place, for their bearing and their speech would have betrayed them immediately; but it was not difficult to pretend that they were only three boon companions, intent on gaming away their funds, filling their heads with liquor, and searching out the best places in which to give way to temptation. Benjamin, if he were good for nothing else, at least lent the group an air of bumbling inconsequence.

This common recreation of gentlemen amusing themselves in the haunts of the lower classes was called "shooting the elephant." Criminals never disapproved of it, for such men became easy marks; they rarely failed to become drunk, and so were easy to rob or cheat or dupe. They were, in fact, the easiest money to be had, for there was no need for the criminal to sneak uptown and crawl through the cellar windows of fine houses, when the masters of those houses themselves were so obliging as to take a cab down to West Houston Street and present themselves as ambulatory victims. And men who were victimized did not always complain to the police, for shame was attendant not only upon admitting that one had been tricked, set upon, or robbed, but that one had been in such a place to begin with.

The *Tribune,* which was the principal voice for Republican sentiment not only in New York but across the country, had decided to conduct its researches without the help of the police. It was feared that the strong connections between Police Headquarters and Tammany Hall might cast doubt upon the integrity of the investigation. Therefore, until the greatest part of the series had appeared, Simeon Lightner had decided to remain anonymous, so that he might not be observed or subverted by the department. The three men disported themselves in one low hall after another, night after night. They roamed the streets, stopped to talk with prostitutes, and hired girls to dance with them at Harry Hill's and Bill McGrory's. Benjamin was even allowed, within strict limits, to exercise his gambling vice at one crooked table after another. He never won, of course, but all his wagers were subsidized by Duncan Phair.

The first article appeared on Monday, January 16, when for a week the *Tribune* had had no new information with which to fan public furor over the murder of Mr. Butterfield. It was a description of a panel house on Hudson Street where gentlemen, who resorted there with street prostitutes, were surreptitiously robbed. While the young woman kept the gentleman's attention with some amorous play, a confederate crept through a panel in the wall and purloined the wallet from the gentleman's coat— which the prostitute had placed on a chair conveniently near the panel.

The *Tribune* stated that it could confirm the existence of over twenty-five such houses in the Black Triangle alone, each building housing an average of seven prostitutes who not only afflicted their partners with disease— and charged them for it—but robbed their pockets as well. The gentleman thus robbed did not dare protest for fear it would become known that he had lain the night in the arms of such a woman; and if in dismay of the sudden discovery of the theft he did raise a cry, it might well be stifled with a knife below the ribs. Mrs. Butterfield did not take kindly to this last inference, which sneakingly suggested that her husband had met his death in such a manner, and she did not cooperate further with Simeon Lightner or any other representative of the *Tribune*.

At the end of the article, Duncan Phair gave the police department's estimates of the number of prostitutes in that area, the number of houses of ill fame—both lower than the *Tribune*'s own figures—and compared these numbers with the records of arrests and convictions. The police department's performance was distressingly poor.

Many of the letters the *Tribune* received commenting on this article it printed over the following two days. Then came time for the second article, which described the depravities of Harry Hill's place: the wild, inebriate dancing, the assignations engineered with scandalous forwardness, the obscene Punch and Judy shows, the illegal and bloody fights in the back rooms. And thus the *Tribune* kept up: an article on Mondays and letters the next two days, another article on Thursday, and letters on

Friday and Saturday. Fashionable New York was fascinated by this information, which for the first time appeared in a well-respected journal and had been written in a tone of voice that declared, "No one has ever plumbed these depths of iniquity before. . . ." The *National Police Gazette* printed a sarcastic editorial article which pointed out that it had been writing of the Black Triangle for many years and had presented the same information that the *Tribune* was now claiming for its own. But the gentlemen and ladies who had never seen the articles in the *Police Gazette* did not see the editorial either and imagined that the *Tribune* was breaking new ground, tearing apart the sidewalks to expose the hot-walled red-lighted hell that, swarming with repulsive shrieking monsters, surged beneath their feet.

Chapter 11

L ENA Shanks was clever in limiting her business to female criminals, refusing to purchase even a single yard of stolen lace from a male thief. Although she thereby forwent much rewarding custom, she also, in effect, protected herself against arrest. To convict a fence, the state of New York must prove that the receiver of stolen property had knowledge that the goods had been illegally appropriated. But this was so difficult a task for the law that the police rarely undertook to gather evidence except upon the most notorious, the most indiscreet, and the most successful fences of the city. Lena's very financial mediocrity protected her from persecution.

She had won the trust of female criminals by her scrupulous dealings and by frequent acts of charity. She was known to have advanced money to women who were incapacitated by bodily injury, to have sent baskets of food to the Tombs on the arm of her daughter Louisa, and even to have constructed a special dress for a woman who was intent on stealing whole bolts of silk from H. B. Claflin and Company. Lena rarely smiled, she rarely had a kind word, but her careful upright respectful dealings with these women—many of whom were used to gross mistreatment and abuse at the hands of men—was a far more welcome thing than smiles and kind words which might, after all, be only feigned.

Lena did not trade at all with male thieves, nor with the wives or consorts of thieves, for she knew of too many fences betrayed by the criminals they supported. Resentment would be got up and allowed to fester over the price paid for some large haul and the fence would be turned over to the police in such a way as to prove his complicity. Women working on their own did not fall into such evil ways, and though Lena realized that she could do a much greater volume of business if only she would accept merchandise appropriated by men, she preferred to conduct herself in a manner that did not endanger her family or her trade.

It happened once that an unruly male pickpocket tried to force Lena to accept seventeen gold watches that he had taken during President Grant's funeral procession down Fifth Avenue. It was not that there weren't other fences in the immediate neighborhood who would have been pleased to accommodate him, or that he might not get a better price elsewhere, but it rankled with the thief that this saturnine fat woman would have nothing to do with men. At last, enraged by Lena's adamant refusals, the pickpocket screeched out a series of wild threats, and pulled a knife from his pocket to show that he was in earnest. With a surprising swiftness, Lena Shanks raised her cane and brought it down so hard upon the man's wrist that the bones were fractured. At the same time, Louisa rushed from behind the curtain and kicked the thief out the door into the path of an oncoming water cart. He was trampled beneath the hooves of the horses, but lived; however, his wrist healed awry and he had to train himself to pick pockets with his left hand. He never regained his former proficiency, and died penniless in New Jersey a year after. This incident did not go unreported in the neighborhood, and no more men came to Lena Shanks's pawnshop.

There were in 1882 many hundreds of female criminals in New York, and this number certainly did not incorporate prostitutes, of whom there were many thousands. Each female had a specialty. She was a shoplifter, or a blackmailer, or she stole from gentlemen sleeping in the

Central Park, or she lifted watches in gambling halls, or she lured drunken men into alleyways to be set upon, or she practiced any of a large array of confidence games upon the credulous of all description. But most common were the thieves, of one description or another, devoted to one method or another for the acquisition of one sort of plunder or another. These women, with daily mounds of ill-got clothing, jewelry, and fine stuffs, must resort to a fence to have that spoil turned to cash.

A young girl called Evvie O'Shea operated a single effective ruse. Answering advertisements in the papers, she went to be interviewed for the position of a servant. Her references were false, as were her name, her antecedents, and even her hair. She was respectful to the mistress of the house and was sometimes offered the place. However, her purpose was not to secure a salaried position, but only to steal whatever could be pocketed during her brief minutes in the house of her prospective employer. Say she got three rings from a dressing table when a lady of Eighteenth Street made the mistake of receiving the applicant in her dressing room. An hour later, the rings were exchanged on West Houston Street for thirty-five dollars, and Evvie O'Shea went her way. By the time that the unfortunate woman on Eighteenth Street had applied to the police for the recovery of her jewelry, providing exact descriptions of the stolen rings, the property existed no more. Clothing and linen too could be altered quickly and easily, but with so drastic a change in appearance, that the owner herself would not know it, displayed upon a rack in the street.

On this small scale, women were more successful as thieves than men. In shoplifting, pickpocketing, and petty confidence games, they excelled because of the lightness of their touch, because of their gentle address, because potential victims were less likely to suspect a female of perpetrating a crime. It was the men who succeeded in robbing banks, purloining enormous fortunes in negotiable securities, engineering fabulous swindles, denuding mansions of their contents. However, it was also men who were most frequently caught, because after a great haul in the way of profits they became reckless and extravagant, boasted drunkenly of their exploits to boon—

but not entirely trustworthy—companions. Frequently they were betrayed by informers. Women were closer, more apt to hide their gain and remain mute concerning the state of their fortunes, displaying equable behavior in adversity and prosperity alike.

Lena Shanks had no difficulty in selling precious metals and gems, for even the most respectable jewelers in the city paid well and without asking questions. Altered clothing, bolts of cloth, and items taken directly from shops were sold in lots to the second-hand dealers around Chatham Square and along Catherine Street, who with their faked auctions and their persuasiveness with the country visitors to the city, usually managed to sell an item at a price far above what they paid, or its actual worth.

Furniture and objets d'art, which could not be disguised without substantially diminishing their value, were purchased only at a discount from the normal rate of one-third. These were more difficult to dispose of because of the chance that an object might be identified and traced. Lena Shanks was fortunate in having relatives in Philadelphia, who every couple of months drove a hearse up to New York, loaded it with stolen goods, and returned home again. The horses wore black plumes, and the father and two sons, dressed as undertakers, were never stopped or questioned.

Bonds, securities, stolen cheques and money orders Lena refused altogether, as dangerous to those unversed in the intricacies of modern finance.

With Louisa helping either her mother or her sister as was required, and keeping books—she was a competent forger as well, and often found little ways of exploiting this talent—the Shanks women made just about fifty thousand dollars a year. This would have been a fortune to many New York families living with every trapping of respectability and good breeding.

The greater part of these receipts was kept undisturbed in half a dozen banks along Sixth and Seventh avenues and had accumulated a great amount of interest through the years. Lena Shanks considered that avarice was no virtue among criminals, for greed led one into danger, and such hazards might compel one to take rooms in Centre Street—at the Tombs. "Be like Louisa," cautioned

Lena, "always we should be like Louisa, quiet . . . quiet. . . ."

Monday, January 9, was chill and raw in New York. The snow that had briefly turned the Black Triangle white on the previous Tuesday had long disappeared—trampled by men in search of liquor or marks, soaked into the skirts of women who trod the streets, lapped up by urchins to assuage their hunger, and even in a few places swept away by the municipal authorities who were paid millions of dollars a year to do so. In the middle of this short bleak afternoon, the Sapphic Pugilist, wearing thick boots and a plain gray-checked dress, strode briskly and with purpose along West Houston Street. Finding the pawnshop open, Charlotta Kegoe turned in there, rather than knocking at the private door of the second Shanks building.

Lena Shanks sat behind the counter, sewing black frogs onto a red silk jacket, where before there had been round ebony buttons. Ella Shanks sat at the deal table building a house of cards, which promptly collapsed when Charlotta's heavy tread set all the room to shaking.

" 'Lotta," nodded Lena, in brief greeting.

Charlotta Kegoe returned the nod and stepped forward to the counter.

After sending her granddaughter to fetch Louisa, Lena asked, as she pinned a frog to the edge of the jacket, "News, 'Lotta?"

Charlotta nodded. "Anyone show you the papers this week?"

"Someone writing about us, about our street, *nicht?*"

"Yes," replied Lotta, and drew a folded *Tribune* from beneath her arm. "Brought you one in case you hadn't seen today's. Offering a reward and vowing to check all the pawnshops in all the streets around here, looking for the jewelry of this man who was murdered."

"Where?" demanded Lena, "where does it say so?"

Charlotta opened the newspaper and pointed out the article. At that moment Louisa Shanks parted the curtain in the back of the shop and smiled at her friend. Ella slithered past her aunt and hopped onto a stool beside her grandmother.

" 'Lotta," said Lena, *"danke schön."*

Charlotta passed into the back with Louisa Shanks.

Lena continued to sew and listened to Charlotta's re-
sounding footfalls up to Louisa's room on the third story.
Ella stared out into the street, counting the passersby
aloud. Some peered curiously into the shop but none ventured inside. Most of Lena's business was conducted in
the early morning or the very late afternoon, and the
hours between were quiet.

"Ella," said her grandmother, "read to me." She pointed
to the article written by Simeon Lightner. Ella, who was
nearsighted, leaned forward precipitously, with her elbows on the paper and her eyes only inches from the text.
She stumbled through the article, skipping over the
difficult words altogether and making rather a jumble
of some sentences. Her grandmother, a poor reader herself in English, did not object to the lesions in comprehension and, in truth, was not much interested in the *Tribune*'s
indignation over Cyrus Butterfield's death, and the newspaper's call for swift vengenace. But when Ella came to
the paragraphs that talked of reward, Lena had the child
read slowly and repeat each sentence before going on to
the next.

"Verstehst?"

Ella nodded: "They'll give money to anyone who'll
say who killed the man by the docks. Nana, do we know
who killed him?"

"Go on," said Lena, and Ella continued. The next paragraph contained the description of the clothing and jewelry
of which the dead man had been stripped. Ella looked
up at her grandmother at the end of this recitation, but so
discreet was the child that she did not say aloud what she
knew very well—that Maggie Kizer had received three
hundred dollars for the very items of jewelry there enu-
merated.

"Again," said Lena, but just as Ella had begun the
paragraph for the second time, they were interrupted
by the arrival in the pawnshop of a short, slender snub-
nosed woman dressed in widow's weeds. It was Weeping
Mary, one of Lena's most frequent customers, who always appeared as if she had just got over a crying jag
and was desperately trying to prevent another from over-
taking her.

Weeping Mary was a pickpocket who plied her trade
exclusively in churches. Each Sunday she attended divine

services at some fashionable church in New York or Brooklyn, sitting with the servants in the loft and pretending to be of their number, mingling with the crowd outside, and sometimes managing to pick the pockets of gentlemen, but more often satisfying herself with pocket handkerchiefs or bits of lace and trim from the dresses of ladies. During the week she went to funeral services, where her morose appearance stood her in good stead, and she often passed as a bereaved devoted servant of the deceased. Funerals were easy, Weeping Mary said, for the mourners were frequently quite distracted with their grief and unlikely to feel the slight tug at their pockets or to hear the single snip of the fine scissors that cut away part of their dress.

Though Weeping Mary rarely came away with anything really valuable, she did a great volume of business. She was not lazy, within the scope of her profession, and had developed quite an ear for sermons. She knew the hymns of half a dozen different denominations, could recite all the Catholic prayers and all the Protestant creeds; and though it might be dangerous to return too often to one church, she was sometimes drawn back by the eloquence or the fine appearance of one preacher or another. One of these was the handsome Presbyterian minister whose church was at Madison Square, and when Weeping Mary saw the open *Tribune* on the counter in Lena's shop, she cried dolorously: "These handkerchiefs I brought you today, took 'em right off the widow and her two girls when they was getting into their carriage, took 'em at the funeral of the lawyer got himself killed down at the docks on New Year. Thought there might be a turnout for that one, and 'deed there was. Church was full, been there of course myself before that, but never saw so many there before. Hardly knew where to turn first. Don't think they was all his friends, people wanting to see if they'd have the coffin open, as if they were going to have a little opening in his coat so you could see where the knife went in. Well the coffin was closed, and everybody thought that they was going away with a disappointment, but I tell you how it happened, Lena, nobody went away with a disappointment then, because that preacher—such a fine-looking man—climbed up into the pulpit and prayed a little prayer, and we sang a little hymn, and then he

prayed another little prayer and spoke of the deceased
like he was his own brother, and then just when everybody thinks that the coffin's going to be taken away, this
preacher suddenly starts in on railing against *us!*"

"Us?" questioned Lena.

"Yes," nodded Weeping Mary mournfully, "you and
me, and everybody who lives around here. He talked of
Bleecker Street and he spoke of West Houston and the
depravity of their inhabitants and mentioned the Cities
of the Plain, and he spoke how we should all be swept
into the North River. A lawyer wasn't safe walking the
streets of New York, a clergyman wasn't safe, a lady had
best stay within her own doors. He said a family of respectability might go to the top of their house—to one
of the maid's rooms or the nursery—and with a pair of
field glasses gaze down on the streets of Sodom and
see things they never knew existed, moral corruption that
stank and burned like hell itself. Looking over the congregation, you could see 'em all getting ready to ride home
post and take out their glasses and hang out the windows
to see what all was going on. It was monstrous exciting,
Lena, but not much of a comfort to the widow."

"*Nee,*" said Lena.

"She looked terrible shocked, the widow," said Weeping Mary, "just terrible shocked, I should say, and wouldn't
speak to the minister after. Went right to the carriage,
and that's when I come up behind her and pluck the
handkerchief right out of her sleeve. I think I could have
got her hat and her stockings too, if there hadn't been so
many by just then."

Weeping Mary received three dollars for the handkerchiefs and scraps of lace that she had brought—rather
more than she had anticipated—and was about to leave
when Lena stopped her with a question:

"This preacher? *Wie heisst er?*"

"Stallworth," replied Weeping Mary: "Edward Stallworth."

Lena Shanks beat an angry tattoo on the counter with
her stubby fingers.

Chapter 12

IN 1853, when she was no more than sixteen, Lena Kaiser and her younger brother Aleksander came penniless to New York, from Bremen. At the pier they attracted the notice of a dishonest loafer called Cornelius Shanks who, when he was not involved in schemes to defraud assurance companies, practiced smaller deceptions upon immigrants and visitors from the country. However, it proved that he had met his match in Lena Kaiser—and he shortly thereafter married her. Between that time and the Civil War, Lena bore Cornelius Shanks four children: two girls, Louisa and Daisy, and twin boys, who perished of diphtheria in their second year.

Lena Shanks did not attempt to reform her husband, but rather asked that she be instructed in some skill that would increase the family revenues. Cornelius Shanks looked at his wife, saw that she was too slow in her movements ever to achieve greatness as a pickpocket, and that her English was too halting for her ever to succeed as a confidence trickster; but the fact that she was stout and wore voluminous skirts and capacious jackets suggested that she would do well as a shoplifter—and she did. At the same time, Lena's brother, whose name had been amended to *Alick Kizer*, was apprenticed to a house thief, with equally happy results.

All went well with the Shanks family, and in a modest way they prospered in the apartments that they occupied on Vandam Street. Then, in the last year of the Civil War, Cornelius Shanks unluckily became involved in the infamous Confederate plot to burn the six major hotels of New York. He and his five hired companions had tried the efficacy of their scheme by razing a lodging house on Twenty-third Street in which fire three unmarried women had perished. The six conspirators were apprehended the day before the Albemarle was to have been torched.

In March of 1865, Lena Shanks attended the trial of her husband in the Incendiary Plot, as it was generally known. It was a brief trial, really, considering the magnitude of the crimes and the half dozen defendants. Shanks was judged not only an arsonist and murderer, but a traitor as well. That he maintained that all had been done for pecuniary reward—he had no political beliefs—did nothing to mitigate the severity of his sentencing. All six men were found guilty, but only two were sentenced to death: the youngest because he had killed a policeman who was attempting arrest, and Cornelius Shanks, because the presiding judge—James Stallworth, only that year elevated to the bench—had discovered that the man had also taken large part in the Draft Riots the year before.

Although Lena Shanks had been long in this country, she knew English only faultily and had with difficulty followed the proceedings. When someone explained to her in a whisper that her husband was to die as a result of the sentence that had been passed on him by the stolid, imposing, hard-visaged man in flowing black robes, Judge Stallworth had already retreated into his chamber.

Afterward, she could remember only his eyes, infernally blue and shining, and his skin, white as the starched wimple of a nun. It was those eyes and that parchment skin that she saw again when she was herself brought to trial two months later on a charge of shoplifting from the charity bazaar at Madison Square Garden. Because she had testified briefly in Cornelius's trial, only to establish identities, her English being too rough to bear up under more detailed examinations, Lena trembled lest the judge remember her.

Two witnesses were called, the young fashionable girl

whose hand-worked scarves Lena had stolen and the officer who had arrested Lena and found the goods secreted upon her person. There was no witness called for the defense. The jury, not even bothering to move from the box, debated for scarcely two minutes and returned a verdict of guilty. Some substantial portion of the twenty-minute trial had been consumed in getting the young fashionable girl into and out of the witness box, a difficult operation because of the immense circumference of her hoopskirt.

Lena's lawyer, a seedy man who made fifteen thousand a year by defending criminals with pointedly little enthusiasm, whispered to Lena that she was probably out of luck and pointed up to Judge Stallworth, who turned his candescent blue eyes upon her full.

"Lena Shanks," said Judge James Stallworth in a quiet rolling voice, "you have been charged with the crime of shoplifting, and a jury of twelve peers has convicted you. It is my duty now to sentence you for that crime. Now before I designate the length of your servitude, I think that I ought to address some remarks to the court at large, and of course request that such remarks be entered into the record of this trial."

He paused and looked around the court with a slight smile. His burning blue eyes fell upon Lena again and held her gaze until she was frozen as by the Gorgon; this although she could understand but a part of what the man said.

"The court has seen you before. The court has heard you give testimony in the trial of your husband, Cornelius Shanks, who lies now under sentence of death on Blackwell's Island for the infamous crimes of murder, incendiarism and plotting to incendiarism and murder. The court had no doubt at the time, and has no doubt now, that you were part of that plot, though never charged. Your devotion to your husband in his black hours would have been perhaps touching were it not for the criminal perversity of your lives—a marriage whose foundations were laid in the quicksand of iniquity. You have played a devilish burlesque on respectable marriage; you have made a vicious joke of the blessed and holy institution of the family—the family which alone will be the salvation of the Union in these troubled times. I doubt not but that the United States, which long ago should have won this internecine struggle against the rebellious states of the Confederacy, should now be at peace were it not for the likes of you and your husband and your unhappy unfortunate children, who have been nurtured upon the pestilent milk of crime."

Daisy and Louisa sat in the row of seats behind their mother, and the children cowered beneath Judge Stallworth's stern gaze.

"As an official of this city and as a staunch upholder of the laws governing this state and this country, as a firm believer in the principles on which this nation was founded, I deem it a solemn duty in myself, to see destroyed all such depraved families as your own. This city will not be blessed with domestic security, will never attain its full stature as the greatest city in the world, until crime is rooted out—until the boggy breeding ground of virulent godless vice is drained.

"Your husband, Lena Shanks, will soon die, and in the snapping of the bones of his neck, you will be deprived of your mainstay in crime. However, I am not convinced that this will be sufficient to lead you out of the morass of vice and therefore sentence you to seven years in the female's prison on Blackwell's Island. You will have the comfort of knowing that you are near your husband during his last days upon the earth that he made unhappier and meaner for his existence."

The judge paused and eyed with satisfaction the reporter from the *Tribune*, who was taking down his remarks in detail.

"The court is not so insensible that it does not see the plight of your children, your worse-than-orphans, who, having been deprived of their father already in effect, and very soon in fact—though the deprivation of such a father can only be to their improvement—now must see their mother taken from them as well. From this bench, the court observes that the two children do not appear to be hopelessly mired in corruption and they are hereby declared wards of the court. They will be well provided for in an orphanage far removed from the pestilential streets where they would quickly have learnt all the reprehensible lessons that arrant depravity can teach."

Lena had understood none of this address, until her lawyer leaned over and whispered: "Seven years on the Island, girls taken away."

Lena sat stupefied, with her hands pressed against her breast in agony.

"The court has little hope that your seven-year sojourn in the female penitentiary will do you lasting good, Lena Shanks," said Judge Stallworth, "and the court would have you there longer, but the laws of the state unfortunately limit the number of years you may be sequestered for the commission of your particular crime—though the court has little doubt you've committed others which, if proved against you, would have laid you beneath a sentence far heavier than the one the court imposes now. The court will enjoy, however, the satisfaction of knowing it has uprooted and broken apart a black tree which would have borne no fruit but that of corruption."

Judge Stallworth, after blinking his glowing blue eyes several times, rose and left the court. A policeman stepped forward to lead the stunned Lena away, but suddenly recollecting herself she wrenched herself loose from his grasp. She turned and spoke rapidly in German to her brother, who had accompanied her to the trial. She begged Alick to take the girls away with him so that the court could not get at them; and she would fetch them back when she was out of prison.

Lena stared at Daisy and Louisa, who had understood perhaps less of what had happened in the court than their mother, and whispered *"Vergisse mich nicht."* Their uncle hurried the girls out before any of the court officials thought to stop him.

Lena and Cornelius Shanks were at Blackwell's Island together during May and June of 1865 but no communication, other than a single interview on the day before his death, was allowed her. Lena was not permitted to witness her husband's execution, though it took place only fifty yards from her cell on the other side of a high wall, but with a substantial bribe conveyed to the hangman, she secured the rope that had been wrapped around Cornelius's throat. It was brought to her with the noose tied and the skin of her husband's neck adhering in shreds to the coarse fiber. Lena kept that rope still, in a locked chest beneath her bed.

For a great while, as she languished on the stony island, Lena Shanks was utterly cast down by the loss of her husband. Their final meeting had been brief, laconic, and tearless; but her grief over his death was genuine and intense. Her two little girls were being kept by relatives in Philadelphia but, the entire family being illiterate, Lena had no communication with them and had no idea whether her daughters were alive or dead, in health or sickness. Alick, suspected of a series of robberies that had plagued the inhabitants of Twelfth Street, had temporarily removed himself to Boston. Lena was alone.

Gradually, however, she gave over her grief, vowing in the midst of her misery that when she got out of prison, she would be leaving never to return. She of necessity had formed an attachment to her cell mate, a murderess who acted as the midwife to the women of the prison. Lena became her assistant and received instruction in the delivering of infants, as well as training in the equally practical trade of inducing abortions. When the murderess died, deliberately choking herself on a shredded prayer book, Lena took over her duties. She had, in effect, the run of the women's prison. From other prisoners she heard of all the various dodges and schemes that were practiced upon the simple and credulous, and listened to all the stories of thieves and pickpockets and adventuresses; and what she had not known of criminal New York when she was rowed from the shore of Manhattan to Blackwell's Island, she knew when she made the return journey on Good Friday, 1872.

At that time, Lena had nothing to her name but the clothes she had worn upon entering the place and the rope which had hanged her husband, but she was fortunate in that she left the prison under the protective wing of a young woman who operated a bordello on West Houston Street. This enterprising soul, who had been sentenced to a brief three months for the unintentional killing of a Negro laundress, had suddenly conceived the notion of setting Lena up as the resident abortionist and general physician to the entire neighborhood of prostitutes. Lena was given a room at the top of one of these houses and on a retaining fee she treated all the ladies in that area. A couple of years later, when her protectress decided to move to Montreal, Lena bought the house for a nominal sum and set up an expanded operation—though the little room at the top of the house remained the site for almost all her trade. Now secure in her own mind, Lena one afternoon took the cars to Philadelphia, made inquiries into the whereabouts of her relatives, and found them after a couple of days' intensive search.

Louisa and Daisy did not remember their mother well, but they had been so ill-treated by their relatives that they made no objection when Lena announced that she was taking them back to New York. Daisy at this time was fourteen, her sister Louisa two years older. Louisa, as the result of some illness that her relatives had not thought worth the expense of treating, had been deprived of her voice and been left wholly mute. Her hard aspect and general intractability alone had saved her from being set out on the streets as a prostitute, but Daisy had already been about her occupation for three years, since she was eleven. Her mother promised her, however, that she would be trained in the gentler and more lucrative employment of abortion.

Lena Shanks lived close within the building on West Houston Street and rarely ventured out. The safe house and her discreet trade were her protection against future imprisonment. She grew sullen and fat from her sedentary existence, but had never really lost the fear that next week she might find herself once more between the gray stone walls of the prison on Blackwell's Island. Daisy Shanks had been instructed that, in that dire event, she should prepare and administer a generous cup of poison to her mother; and Daisy had agreed.

Judge James Stallworth, Lena knew, still presided over a court; and the one thing that Lena would not do for her ladies in trouble was testify in their behalf at trials. Though she had not seen him in fifteen years, the lacquered blue eyes of Judge James Stallworth still troubled Black Lena's dreams. She had an almost superstitious dread of him, and had been greatly disturbed when she had seen those very eyes fixed in the egg-shaped head of the young man in Harry Hill's place. And so soon after to have the dreaded name brought to her attention by Weeping Mary! It seemed as though the man had effected a wizard's transformations and was creeping up on her in different disguises. Lena realized that now she must be doubly vigilant: the old man had slept for almost twenty years, but now was rising again, with awesome strength, and confederates who reproduced his burning eyes, or his hated name!

Chapter 13

~~~~~~

TAMMANY Hall and Police Headquarters both felt the stings of the *Tribune* articles. The paragraphs written by Simeon Lightner and Duncan Phair were talked of in every saloon, every drawing room, every club, and on every street corner in town. Daring young men who before had confined their pleasure-seeking to the Central Park and long excursions to Coney Island now walked the streets south of Bleecker in thick bands, exquisitely fearful, and imagining that murderous prostitutes would swing upon them out of every doorway. Timorous ladies, when their husbands had left the house for their offices, would ascend to the attic and, wiping clean a grimy pane, train their opera glasses shudderingly on the red-brick maze of the Black Triangle.

Other papers in the city at first deprecated the *Tribune*'s obvious strategy, but quickly, when they saw what commotion the articles and the letters stirred, took up the cause themselves. The *Herald* began an investigation of the tenements that still existed around Five Points, and the *Sun* gave daily and detailed instances of violence among the Jews, the Italians, the Cubans, and the Chinese.

The police department's defense was ineffectual, for it

was by their own statistics that they were most sorely trounced; so Mulberry Street launched a campaign against the Black Triangle in hope of bettering its position with the clamorous public.

On Thursday, January 19, the gambling hall that Duncan Phair and Simeon Lightner had visited on their first night out together was invaded by the police. Though protesting vehemently that they were quite up-to-date in the matter of bribes, the proprietors were arrested. Gentlemen gamblers were politely escorted to the street, where they quickly availed themselves of the convenience of an uptown car, but players of lower or criminal class were taken away to the Tombs for a couple of nights. All the machinery of gambling was broken up. The tables and chairs were hacked to pieces with hatchets borrowed from the fire department and piled in the middle of King Street. The heap was garnished with cards, dice, counters, script, and printed advertisements—and then doused with kerosene and set alight. It was a symbolic and picturesque action meant to mollify the public, but unfortunately also a dangerous one—for a strong wind blew a handful of burning court cards from a pinochle deck through the open doorway of a tenement house, where they ignited a quantity of oily rags. Simeon Lightner and Duncan Phair, who were in the next street, came by for the commotion and were able to report another piece of police negligence and ineptitude in next morning's *Tribune*. The police countered lamely that the building had been vermin infested and the infant that had perished in the blaze was already consumptive, but it was another point made against them.

Though somewhat daunted, the chief of police ordered that on the following Sunday some saloon be shut down, and a large place on Perry Street was chosen because it was the most ornate and nearly respectable in all the Black Triangle—not because it was forward in the matter of excise violations. Justified by the New York State law decreeing that no establishment selling liquor might be open during any hour of the Sabbath, seventy-three police invaded the place an hour before noon, dragged away the owners and bartenders, kicked the patrons out, broke every glass and bottle and mirror in the place, and smashed all the chairs and tables against the mahogany bar. Representatives from all the sympathetic press were there, and this was rather more of a successful engagement for the Democratic administration.

Thereafter, almost every other day some business in that part of the city was touched: seventeen prostitutes arrested in one house, a fence dragged away from King Street, a stale-beer dive emptied of all its human and potable refuse, a meeting place of thieves boarded up and condemned.

It would have gone harder with the Black Triangle had it not been for the other newspapers taking up the cause and celebrating, as it were, other criminal neighborhoods. The police were forced, to some extent, to deploy their forces to other sectors and show that they were intent on freeing all parts of the city from the dominion of corruption and depravity. But still, since the *Tribune* articles were the most virulent and powerfully antagonistic to the police, it was that area bordered by MacDougal, Canal and Bleecker streets that received the most frequent and meticulous attentions of the police department.

On many counts, the police were unhappy in setting up this systematic persecution. It was a troublesome and dangerous undertaking, for the thieves and criminals of New York were entrenched, and most of them had the idea that they were somehow an essential, if unsavory, arm of the community, and had as much right as any cotton-factor or dressmaker or bookseller to exist and ply their trades. They took umbrage at the incursions of the police into places the police had never dared go before. Already three men had been killed resisting arrest, and one policeman escaped death only at the price of a severe knock on the head, which had taken him out of commission. And quite beyond this it was an expensive affair, for many of the police department, on all levels—but especially the very highest and the very lowest—were used to taking bribes in return for ignoring crime when crime could be quietly ignored. When men and women were arrested, the bribes of course dried up and the criminal classes lost faith in the word of the police.

Those high in the police department and the city government who received substantial bribes from the larger criminals of the city and the politicians who depended on

the wiles of petty malefactors to secure their offices year
after year in election-day frauds, were necessarily made
uneasy by this call for a wholesale sweep of the city's criminal population. This was fortunately only January and
the next election many months away; the politicians considered that, if all this were got through quickly, there
would be time to recoup their losses or with large favors,
win back the confidence of those on whom their positions
and their fortunes depended.

Lena Shanks watched these developments with increasing concern, and in her business was even more discreet
than usual; for the first time in many a year, she actually
gave out pawn tickets—printed up by Louisa on the small
press that she kept in her bedchamber—in exchange for
the merchandise that she received from her women. Her
clients were fewer, and those who continued to come came
less often, for all in the Black Triangle were fearful, and
ever wary of the police.

Lena had a standing order with Crook-Back Bob, the
ragged newsboy who haunted West Houston Street, and
each morning and afternoon the little cripple brought to
the shop all the journals that carried the sensational stories
of New York crime and New York criminals. Ella read
the articles aloud, and in a few weeks her reading was
substantially improved, though her eyesight had deteri-
orated.

Lena was distressed by the frequency with which the
Stallworth name cropped up, particularly in the pages of
the *Tribune*. Every Monday the journal printed Edward
Stallworth's sermon enumerating and condemning the
enormities of the Black Triangle. This minister, Lena discovered from Weeping Mary, was the son of the hated
Judge James Stallworth, whose cursory trials, lengthy con-
cluding remarks, and harsh sentencings appeared in the
Tribune's columns from Tuesday through Sunday. Many
of those sent to Blackwell's Island and Sing Sing Lena was
acquainted with, and three of Lena's women had already
come up before the judge. Two received four-year sentences for prostitution and the third eight years for oper-
ating an illegal gambling establishment. There was even a
female Stallworth—called Helen—who had signed her
name, among those of many other ladies, to a letter that

expressed horrified indignation at the number of abortionists—euphemistically called "angel-makers" in the epistle—allowed to practice within the precincts of the Black Triangle. Lena began to feel that the Stallworths had risen in a body against her and her family, threatening not only their livelihood but their very freedom.

Chapter 14

⊕⊕⊕

Edward Stallworth stood at the door of his church and greeted the Sunday morning congregation as it filed out. He modestly accepted his parishioners' murmured applause for his powerful and affecting address, the fifth of his sermons dilating upon the dangers and iniquities of the Black Triangle. He was pleased with the compliment of a pretty young woman, reputed to be an heiress, who said, "Oh, Mr. Stallworth, with that voice of yours, and those hands of yours, you could talk me into rope dancing or arson."

He and Helen and Benjamin were expected at one o'clock at Gramercy Park for luncheon, but that was half an hour away and Edward felt the need of a little rest and liquid to massage his throat. Helen, according to her custom, had come to his church study directly after the postlude and prepared tea, and now Edward Stallworth sat comfortably back in a deep leather chair before the fire burning in the glazed-brick hearth. Helen sat opposite him with a saucer perched on the narrow arm of her narrow hard chair.

"Helen," said her father with a kindness prompted by the success of the sermon, "I suppose that tomorrow there will be another meeting of Marian's committee."

Helen nodded hesitantly. "Yes, just at two o'clock, at Marian's again."

"I hope it will be as successful as the last!"

Helen said nothing.

Her father looked at her with an exhausted wariness. "You do not feel, Helen, after two full meetings, that the Committee for the Suppression of Urban Vice has been a success?"

"I suppose," said Helen with downcast eyes, "it would depend on how one defined success, or perhaps on what one interpreted the aims of the committee to be."

"Go on please," said her father blandly, but no longer with a smile. "With me, Helen, your words need not be chosen with so much care."

"All the ladies come dressed very fine," said Helen meekly, "and they talk of the articles that appear in the *Tribune* and the *Sun*. Marian praises the articles highest of all, though of course she doesn't say that it's Duncan who helps to write them, so I wish that she wouldn't—I think she should say as little as possible, for it's sure to be found out sooner or later that it's Duncan behind it, and then what will everyone think of Marian's praise?"

"They'll think that she's proud of her husband, as well she should be," said Edward Stallworth. "Duncan's exertions in this matter are entirely commendable, and I see nothing objectionable in Marian's praise. But what did you object to, Helen? You seem to have disapproved of something more than Marian's fulsomeness, which you ought to be used to by this time anyway."

"I . . . I do not concur with the ladies' views on—the unfortunate people who live in the poorer sections of the city. They look on the whole matter rather lightly, as if it were nothing more than a new kind of scandal to amuse them. They talk about vice, and how the police ought to stop it, and how all those people ought to be put into the jails, and the houses burnt to the ground, and opera houses and restaurants and theaters set up there instead. They have"—she paused before making so stern a judgment—"little compassion. . . ."

"You do not believe that to raze the Black Triangle and all other such areas would be a species of improvement to this city, Helen?"

"Father," cried Helen with earnest intensity, "I believe that our purpose ought to be to alleviate the misery and poverty of these people. If we could only insure them enough to eat and give them proper medical care; if we found jobs for the men and educated and clothed their children—why then there wouldn't be any need for them to engage in criminal activity."

"It's a novel idea, Helen, but I think that it ignores the basic disagreeableness of the human character. You've memorized your catechism, I believe, so you must know the definition of Original Sin, even if you haven't applied its precept to the machinations of human society."

Helen was silent.

"You don't wish to argue?" said her father with raised eyebrows, holding out his cup to be replenished.

"No," said Helen, taking the cup, "you are an ordained minister of the Presbyterian Church in the United States and my theology I know is faulty. I only wish," said she softly, turning her back momentarily to fill his cup again, but more so that she would not have to face him while she voiced a criticism, "that you concentrated more on matters of doctrine and interpretation in your sermons. I was very sorry when you abandoned the exegesis of *Isaiah*. I hope it will not be long before you return to it." Her voice was plaintive.

Edward Stallworth paused a moment before answering, and when he did speak his voice was sharp and ironical: "There are fifty-two Sundays in the year, with which fact I suppose that you are acquainted, Helen. And I suppose that you also are well enough informed on matters of church procedure to know that I preach two sermons each Sunday. Considering that I am generally absent on two Sundays in June taking rest at the seashore, I preach one hundred sermons a year. I have thus far delivered five sermons on the wickedness of the city of New York, I may prepare a dozen more. That is less than twenty percent of the number of sermons I shall preach in the course of 1882. It is insignificant when compared to the number of sermons I have preached in my sixteen years as shepherd to my Madison Avenue flock. I hope that you do not imagine that I do this for my own aggrandizement—"

He paused for a denial from his daughter who, in truth, had feared just that, but she only weakly shook her head no.

"You are correct, Helen, I do not. I have seen the opportunity to do some good in this city by drawing the attention of members of our congregation to the vice and criminality—and, as you say, to the poverty and wretchedness—that lie upon our doorstep. I do not do it toward the social or political or financial uplifting of myself or any members of my family, I hope you understand."

Helen nodded tremulously, for her father's stern and cold voice made her now, as always, unhappy, and she was sorry that she had said anything.

"You did not object last year when I preached on the African mission, I believe. In fact, I believe that you yourself composed prayers for the continued safety and health of our Presbyterian missionaries in the Congo. I see no reason to distinguish the natives of Africa from the denizens of the Black Triangle, which peoples are equally ignorant, equally vicious, equally unhappy, and equally in danger of eternal damnation."

"No," agreed Helen.

"*No*," repeated her father, "and I do not know why you set yourself up against the ladies of Marian's committee either, whose only purpose is to do good by eradicating evil. If the evil is brushed away, Helen, why then the good is sure to shine through. I do not understand why you cannot grasp this really very simple concept, which a child of three years would unquestionably embrace as a tenet for the operation of all the societies of mankind, past and present and to come.

"So," concluded Edward Stallworth, "I hope that you will go to the meeting of the Committee for the Suppression of Urban Vice with a different cast of mind; with an eagerness, I may say, to do what you can for this desperately wicked place we call the Black Triangle."

Helen nodded obediently, having allowed herself to be defeated, not by her father's arguments so much as merely by his will to conquer; for Helen felt that she would be remiss in filial obedience if she did not prostrate herself before her father's inclinations.

"Yes, Father," said Helen, after a moment's sad reflection, "of course I shall go to Marian's tomorrow and take the minutes of the meeting and do all that I can to further the committee's laudable schemes."

And, true to her word, on the following day Helen was at her aunt's house ensconced in a corner with a small tablet and a sharpened pencil. At the end of two hours she had noted only the observation of the fifteen ladies in attendance that "vice was a bad thing and ought to be suppressed" and the resolution that four carriages ought to be hired to drive them through the Black Triangle on the following afternoon. Fully half an hour was taken up in discussion of what sort of dress was most appropriate for viewing misery and crime, and nothing was of consensus but that each lady ought to be equipped with a heavy black veil, smelling salts, and plenty of pennies to distribute to children. Recalling her father's injunction, Helen went along with this scheme without protest, but with inward misgiving.

At three o'clock on the next afternoon, four closed black carriages made their way south from Gramercy Park to MacDougal Street, and began a small tour of the Black Triangle. Some of the streets were too narrow to admit the carriages, being blocked with evil-smelling refuse, the carts of vendors of rotten merchandise, heaps of burning rubbish which warmed the itinerant beggars, or simply with milling crowds of the poor who had nowhere to live but the back streets themselves. The progress of the vehicles was slow, being constantly interrupted by wagons that would not move and crowds that would not get out of the way and idlers who seemed to take some delight in annoying this caravan of overdressed ladies from uptown. More than two hours were required to make a circuit around the scant two hundred acres of the Black Triangle.

The ladies, for their part, were almost immediately sorry that they had come. The odors were so noxious and powerful that they kept their handkerchiefs before their faces for the duration of the trip. The cries and shouts directed at them were profane and obscene. Nothing was colorful and nothing was picturesque and nothing was quaint; all was black grimy wretchedness and foul stinking misery. The children that they had thought they would toss pennies to ran up against the carriages with sticks which they broke off in the spokes of the wheels, or they tossed missiles of hard mud—and worse—against the sides of the vehicles. The sixteen ladies saw men sitting against the sides of buildings, in frozen puddles of their own sickness, and they saw babies—little bundles of filthy rag and bloodshot gristle—lined up in rows on the stone steps of a house while their mothers reeled in and out of a saloon hard by. They saw dogs tortured by laughing children, and a man's skull broken open with a brickbat. And their drivers assured them that they had not seen the worst; but when the sun fell behind the houses along MacDougal Street, the ladies grew anxious, for the unfriendly faces in the street began to look positively fiendish. The caravan turned onto Broadway and made as swift a journey back to Gramercy Park as possible.

The ladies gratefully accepted tea at Marian's table and sat stonily silent in the parlor as they drank it. No one talked of what she had seen, and no one suggested any method to effect the suppression of vice in the streets they had driven through. The ladies, even Marian Phair herself, who knew more than the rest, had expected something else, had imagined a world that was more or less like their own, except only dingy and tawdry and dull. No one had expected that crime and violence, destitution and horribly degrading poverty would stare back at them with grinning toothless mouths and infernal gleaming eyes, like fantastical medieval emblems. The suppression of vice in a place where vice seemed the very foundation of life suddenly seemed to be too much of an undertaking for sixteen women who had nearly fainted from the effluvia of the streets alone.

At last, when most had had two cups of strong bolstering tea, one lady mentioned having seen a trained dog performing on a board held across the arms of its owner and another declared that she was sure she heard someone playing "In the Garden" on an untuned piano; and they felt better for these remembrances. Then Marian suggested that all meet again the following Monday and that everyone should bring a list of three things that might be done toward the suppression of vice in such a place as they had just seen. The ladies, a little recovered, took their leave; and Helen Stallworth, who on any other occasion would have remained behind with her aunt a while longer, departed also.

Helen walked home alone. Though it was dark, the manse was only two squares away and she was known in most of the houses she passed. She had been appalled, frightened, and struck dumb by what she had seen that afternoon and she had come away with the conviction that she had been right and her father and all the rest had been wrong. There was no way to suppress vice in a place of such poverty and wretchedness. Crime was a material not a spiritual evil, and the only hope for the Black Triangle lay in the alleviation of its material misery.

She had done her duty by her father and attended Marian's meeting. She would continue to attend and take the scanty minutes of the gathering, but she had no hope that anything would come of the Committee for the Suppression of Urban Vice—certainly no more than a few indignant letters directed to the daily and the religious journals and perhaps a nominal subscription to help fund some charity for the improvement of redeemed Magdalens. Helen's heart was punctured and bled for those who lived in the Black Triangle. And she knew that if she wanted to do any good for that unhappy place she would have to return there alone, but not protected by a carriage, a heavy black veil, and a bottle of smelling salts.

Chapter 15

●●

MANY citizens of New York were outraged by the *Tribune*'s having brought to their attention the existence of the Black Triangle, although they may for twenty years have lived within less than a mile of those ungoverned, ungovernable streets. Marian Phair's Committee for the Suppression of Urban Vice was only the first of many such small, earnest, ineffectual organizations that knew more or less what they were against, but had no conception of how to scourge iniquity from the metropolis.

A couple of days after the *Tribune* had set up the reward for information leading to the arrest of those responsible for Cyrus Butterfield's death, an anonymous correspondent sent to the paper a ten-dollar note, which he requested be added to the sum. The *Tribune* printed the short accompanying letter in a black-bordered square on the front page as a laudable example of public-spiritedness, and within three weeks the reward was swollen to over three thousand dollars and rose with the arrival of every mail.

On the morning of Tuesday, February 21, when the reward was at $3,340, Simeon Lightner received a note directed to the "Blak Tryangele Genntleman" at his desk on the seventh floor of the Tribune Building. The letter inside the soiled envelope was scrawled in a thick-leaded pencil, composed without much regard to the usual proprieties of spelling and punctuation:

Dear Sire Ive envormashune fore yue abowwt Misster Butterfeld meete mee 2day at hungree Charlys place in Washingetonn Streete at 2 Ime a ladye and yue can tele me bye mye yalowe kercheefe I wante the monye

It was not the first such note that Simeon had received, and although he had appeared at all the places named and precisely at the times mentioned, he had learned nothing of value. Mostly, he had found, it was petty criminals who had written the notes in hope that he would show up with the money in his pocket and that he might be robbed or diddled out of it. But Simeon made these expeditions always in the company of either Duncan Phair or Benjamin Stallworth, and made it clear that he was armed. Then the informant either slunk away or else proffered information that was pointless or patently fabricated.

This meeting did not promise to be any different, but Hungry Charley's was a semi-respectable establishment on the river edge of the Black Triangle and not the sort of place in which he would be set upon. And since he was only going to meet "a lady with a yellow kerchief," the reporter decided to dispense with escort.

Simeon Lightner was not entirely pleased with the manner in which the *Tribune*'s undertaking had proceeded. Although he couldn't object to its sterling success, nor to the increase in prestige and salary he had gained by it, he had the uneasy unpleasant feeling that he was being led about by Duncan Phair. The articles appeared in what order and with what emphases Duncan thought best, and were of rather a different consistency and tone than what Simeon would have produced had he been on his own. But since everyone else seemed pleased and since the credit redounded on him and Duncan took none of it for himself, Simeon felt he had not the right of objection. Besides, Duncan Phair, who was at all events a pleasurable companion, never made suggestions that were not well considered or that did not tend toward the improvement of the articles. Simeon tugged at his wiry red whiskers in exasperation over the fact that he could find no real reason for the distrust he felt for the handsome young lawyer.

Simeon arrived at Hungry Charley's half an hour before his appointed time. The restaurant was long and narrow, with walls and floor of red-veined marble. Twenty long narrow tables, sitting six on a side, were set with one end against the wall, leaving only a pinched walk space. The high ceiling was of white tile and a single lamp was suspended over every table. In the middle of Tuesday afternoon there were no more than fifteen persons dining, and Simeon had no trouble in getting a place that commanded a view of the entrance. He ordered a chop and lager and fell to his luncheon without any nervous hope that by the coming interview he would discover the murderer of Cyrus Butterfield.

He had finished his chop and beer, ordered coffee, finished that, and been served another beer, before the "lady" came in, some minutes late. She was short, thin, with a sallow mean-spirited face, and had—as promised —a yellow kerchief tied around her head, as if she were suffering from a toothache.

The woman looked around her uncertainly, and it was only when she appeared in imminent danger of being shown the sidewalk by a waiter, that Simeon stood and motioned her over. The woman with the yellow kerchief nervously pointed Simeon out to the waiter who, receiving a nod from the reporter, allowed her to pass.

Simeon directed her to a seat at the end of the table, against the marble wall. He moved himself, and they were then some distance removed from any other diners.

"What will you have?" Simeon asked.

"Lager," replied the woman.

Simeon ordered two lagers from the waiter and in a few moments they were brought, with a plate of cheese and bread.

"Bring the money?" asked the woman.

"What's your name?" demanded Simeon Lightner.

"Lady Weale," the woman replied mistrustfully.

"Lady Weale?" . .

"That's my name, that's the name **my** ma give me, 'cause I was born a girl: Lady."

"Well, M'Lady, tell me what you know and then we'll speak of money."

"You bring the money?" she demanded again.

"M'Lady, you are speaking to the personification of the New York *Tribune*. If you're deserving of the money that is offered in reward, you will receive the money that is offered in reward."

Lady Weale looked sourly away, and sipped at her lager.

"Now," said Simeon Lightner, "what do you know of the murder of Cyrus Butterfield?" He spoke the question as if he had no idea of receiving any answer that might be of use or interest.

"I know who did it."

"Who did it?"

"Maggie Kizer and her husband Alick."

"Well," said Simeon, "is Maggie Kizer a duchess that I'm supposed to know of her?"

"What?"

"Who is Maggie Kizer, I said?"

"Maggie Kizer is the lady who lodges in my house. I live on the ground floor, Maggie Kizer lives on the second story."

"And one evening, I suppose, Maggie Kizer and her husband strolled out, passed Mr. Butterfield on the street, who perhaps asked them for directions, and so, taking the question as an insult, they forced him to strip to the skin and then stabbed him through the heart?"

"No," said Lady Weale, who had not understood the ironic intent of Simeon's imagination, "that's not how it happened."

"How did it happen then?"

"Maggie is a lady who receives gentlemen, you see what I mean?"

Simeon nodded and Lady Weale went on: "And her husband was in jail—up at Sing Sing—and Maggie was entertaining Mr. Butterfield one night. I let him in the house myself, and she was entertaining him in the bedroom—if you see what I mean—and her husband, who was being let out of Sing Sing, came in and found 'em. . . ."

"Yes?" prompted Simeon, who already found the tale more interesting than he had anticipated.

"Entertaining one another in the bedroom, if you see what I mean."

"I do, M'Lady. Go on please. Madame Kizer then, I take it, didn't know to expect her husband back from his extended visit in the northern provinces?"

"She didn't know he was to get out, if that's what you mean, and perhaps he wasn't, perhaps he 'scaped, if you see what I mean, so he comes a-knocking at the door, and I open the door to tell him that Maggie's not receiving, for that's what I'm 'bliged to say when she's entertaining, but he pushed right on past me and goes up the stairs taking 'em three at the time and goes right through the door and I'm using my lungs, if you see what I mean, and Maggie I suppose jumps up, but Mr. Butterfield's not quick enough and Maggie's husband comes in—"

"And stabs Mr. Butterfield to the heart in a fit of jealousy!"

"No," said Lady Weale, "not at the first. First he's just going in, sly-like, and talks about duties of a wife and rights of a husband—"

"You were by?" questioned Simeon, with a wry smile. "You were by for these edifying remarks?"

"I was in the next room, it was my duty as landlady to see nothing fractious come of it."

"Commendable, M'Lady, go on."

"So," said Lady Weale, knocking on the marble wall of the restaurant with her red knuckles, "then Maggie's husband Alick talks about outraged honor and recompensivities and the like—"

"Recompensivities?" repeated Simeon.

"If you see what I mean," nodded Lady Weale and went on: "And then he goes over to the dressing table, where all Mr. Butterfield's clothing is hanging over the back of the chair and all his jewelry is on top of the little bench there, and Maggie's husband Alick picks it up—all the time he's talking about recompensivities—and he puts it in his pocket, and then Mr. Butterfield gets up out of the bed, ranting how he won't stand for such recompensivities and he can't take my watch and so on, but Maggie's husband just laughs, because Mr. Butterfield doesn't have on a thread."

"You saw all this?"

"Every word."

By this time, though his voice when he questioned the lady in the yellow kerchief was one of bemusement, Simeon Lightner was taking quick notes in a small tablet he had pulled from his coat pocket.

"So Mr. Butterfield—I didn't know his name then, you understand, but I learned it from the papers—comes forward, and reaches out for Maggie's husband, and has him by the throat, and he's red in the face, and he starts choking Maggie's husband—"

"What's Madame Kizer about all this time?"

"She's making sure that the curtains are drawn tight."

"No nonsense there," remarked Simeon.

"Maggie's 'cute," said Mrs. Weale, "but Mr. Butterfield's choking on Maggie's husband and Maggie's husband picks up this needle and stabs Mr. Butterfield in the chest, and he dies."

"A *needle?*"

"A kind of needle," shrugged Lady Weale. "A Chinaman's needle, if you see what I mean. It was gold."

"Opium?"

Lady Weale nodded.

Simeon Lightner whistled and begged the landlady to continue.

"Maggie calls me in—she's seen me in the next room—and she pulls a sheet off the bed, lays it out on the floor, and we roll Mr. Butterfield onto it so he won't bleed on the carpet, but there's not enough blood to fill a teacup. Then she turns to her husband, who's got all that jewelry in his pocket, and she says: 'Take it out, sir!' and he don't, and she turns and pulls a hair-trigger pistol out from under the pillow and says, 'Take it out, sir!' and he takes it out and puts it back on the dresser."

"A cool 'un," remarked Simeon Lightner admiringly.

"Then she says—Maggie talks like a lady—she says, 'We must take him out of here. Put his clothes back on.' So Maggie's husband and me gets down on the floor and we put Mr. Butterfield's clothes back on him, then Maggie says to her husband, 'You take him out of here and don't you come back,' and he says how he don't have any money and he'll starve, and she might as well shoot him and have done with it, and Maggie says she'll sell the jewelry and then send the money to General Delivery in Washington and he can get it there—tells him what name it'll be under—"

"You're right," said Simeon, "Madame Kizer is certainly 'cute.'"

"So then Maggie tells her husband what to do. Mr. Butterfield is dressed as best we can, though it's a bad job to put shoes on a dead man, and we take him downstairs, and Maggie's husband, with ten dollars in his pocket that she give him, takes Mr. Butterfield outside, holding him up like he was falling-down drunk—nobody notices, so many people on the street, most of 'em drunk too, New Year's Eve—and Maggie's husband Alick walks Mr. Butterfield down the street a bit and is about to leave him in an alley right around the corner, but Maggie's sent me out after him, and I tell him he has to take Mr. Butterfield farther away, all the way down to the docks, and he says it's too dangerous, and I tell him if he don't, Maggie won't send the money to Washington. So he curses me, and he curses Maggie, and he curses the dead man he's got his arm around, but then he goes on toward the docks, and I'm watching him cross West Street, trying to stick to the dark parts, and then I get back to the house."

"But when he was found, Mr. Butterfield was naked."

"Scavengers. Ragpickers. 'Round there, they won't leave a dead rat with its fur on."

"Maggie do as she promised? She sell the jewelry?"

"Black Lena on West Houston took it, paid her a good sum for it I would think, considering how Alick Kizer is her very own brother. Maggie took the money and posted it to Washington. He's got it by now."

"This all?" said Simeon Lightner, grinning for his good fortune. When Lady Weale signified yes, he went over the story once more, garnering more detail, demanding descriptions of the rooms in the history, wanting to know what Maggie's husband looked like, asking whether Cyrus Butterfield had died with a rattle in his throat. After once ascertaining that she would almost certainly receive the reward money, Lady Weale answered all Simeon's questions.

They were on their third pints of lager, and Simeon's tablets were close to being used up, when he asked, "Tell me, M'Lady, why do you tell me all this? Wasn't Madame Kizer your friend?"

Lady Weale shrugged uneasily: "I know she's thinking of moving away. I heard her tell it one of her gentlemen, wanted to take a place up on Thirtieth Street. She was a good girl, and I didn't know where I'd find the like to replace her. And if she was going away, then this reward was going to serve for my recompensivities, if you see what I mean."

Simeon told Mrs. Weale that when she returned home there was no need to say anything yet to Maggie Kizer, that it would be much better in fact if she were not warned. The way that Lady Weale glanced at Simeon made him realize that the old sour-faced woman had probably eased her conscience over this betrayal by promising herself that she would give Maggie Kizer enough time to escape. "You see," Simeon smiled, "you won't get your reward unless there's an arrest. Of course, we'd like the police to arrest the man who actually killed Mr. Butterfield, but who knows where he is now, there's no way of tracing him any longer, since you can't remember under what name he had received the money in Washington. Unless Maggie Kizer is arrested and convicted, you won't receive a penny—" He smiled, for it pleased him to prick Lady Weale, who for money had betrayed a woman who had been—by the landlady's own admission—kind to her.

"You—" Lady Weale tipped over the pint of lager she had just received in an effort to destroy the markings on Simeon's tablets, but he snatched them out of the way, and hastily stood. The beer poured over his vacated chair.

"I'll take care of the reckoning," he smiled. "And remember," he said, "just as soon as Madame Kizer permanently changes her address from Bleecker Street to the Tombs, you'll have your money. And tomorrow morning, all the Black Triangle can read about your part in her arrest."

At Police Headquarters, Simeon Lightner checked to see whether there were indeed, at Sing Sing, a criminal called Alick Kizer, and was pleased to learn that Alexander Keezer, with two fellow inmates, had broken out of the prison two days after Christmas. The reporter considered that any further investigation into the veracity of Lady Weale's statement would be superfluous and possibly harmful, in that it provided Maggie Kizer with time to flee the city. After alerting the police to the name and address of the beautiful conspirator in the crime, Simeon Lightner returned to his desk in the Tribune Building and wrote the story out. It was finished by eight o'clock, and received immediate approval from the editor on duty, who decided it would appear on the front page of the morning edition.

Simeon Lightner had not only the satisfaction of solving the case of the death of Cyrus Butterfield, when the police had been able to accomplish nothing at all, but also of just having written the most exciting article in a series that was by its nature sensational—and all had been accomplished without the assistance or knowledge of Duncan Phair. Simeon declared to himself again and again that he would pay twenty-five dollars to see the expression on Duncan Phair's face when he heard that the woman responsible for the death of Cyrus Butterfield had been found out.

Chapter 16

SHORTLY after she heard the outer door of the house slam and saw Mrs. Weale's yellow kerchief headed off on some errand, Maggie Kizer went into her bedroom. She put on a dress of dark green silk with black trim, an old sealskin sacque and a green hat with a heavy black veil. She wore black gloves and but the single ruby ring that Duncan had given her on the New Year. When she emerged from the house she turned her steps southward on Bleecker.

It was Lady Weale and not Maggie who avidly read the articles that had appeared in the *Tribune* on the subject of Cyrus Butterfield's murder. The octoroon did not trouble herself to be fearful of discovery. And once Maggie had explained carefully to Lady Weale that by her assistance in the disposal of the corpse on New Year's Eve she had implicated herself in the crime, Maggie had rested assured of the landlady's discretion in the matter. It had not occurred to her to offer Lady Weale money for her silence or to employ her sister-in-law, Lena Shanks, as a threat. For her help, Maggie had given Lady Weale several pieces of the jewelry that Cyrus Butterfield had presented her in the little time that she had known him.

Maggie Kizer was not a common prostitute and actually refused to receive cash for her favors. Rather, she let it be known—though in a perfectly ladylike manner—that she would be pleased to accept gifts of clothing, of furnishings, and especially of jewelry. These items she kept and displayed for as long as she remained on good terms with the donor, but when, for whatever reason, he no longer kept company with her, those gifts were taken to Lena Shanks and sold. It was this money that paid Mrs. Weale, the dressmaker, and the tavern that sent up her meals three times a day.

Maggie's liaisons, which were invariably discreet, were carried through two and only occasionally three at the time. These multiple attachments assured that she would be well provided with gifts. She could not be expected to languish on Bleecker Street alone and unfunded if her sole protector were suddenly called away to his family on the shore of New Jersey in the summer or on business to England in the winter.

Until recently, her primary benefactor had been a philanthropist, quiet-living but enormously wealthy, whose principal contributions were to charities staffed by or run for the purpose of alleviating the sorrow and discomforts of young unmarried females, whether they be mill workers, or streetwalkers, or the daughters of impoverished Confederate gentry. He had courted Maggie for somewhat more than four years, but since October he had been in Scotland, attending at the bedside of his dying father. This gentleman, shortly before sailing, had introduced Maggie to Cyrus Butterfield, as a man of probity and charm, who would protect her in his perhaps protracted absence.

Duncan she had met at a select after-theater gathering at a restaurant on Fifth Avenue; Maggie was quite beautiful that night and had been so vain as not to wear her dark spectacles. In that carousing group of drunken overdressed women, giggling and accepting all sorts of amorous advances from the gentlemen present, Maggie had stood apart, not in a disapproving manner by any means, nor with the attitude that she had never witnessed such goings-on before, but simply with indifference. Duncan had offered her champagne, conversed with her, and accompanied her back to Bleecker Street.

Since that time, in the summer of 1880, Duncan had visited Maggie two or three times a week and had rarely failed to bring her some trinket; and when he did not, Maggie knew to expect a gift-bearing messenger on the following day. In addition, Duncan had paid for the new parlor draperies and Maggie's tavern bill for the second half of the year.

Duncan knew that Maggie had other attachments, though of their identities he was ignorant. That he was not her sole support was rather a boon to him—he forwent the febrile pleasure of jealousy but was untroubled by the tiresome burden of Maggie's complete dependence on him. So far as Duncan was concerned, Maggie Kizer was the ideal of womanhood: quiet, intelligent, undemanding, beautiful, kind, pleasant, and desirable—not the less either for her bearing the telltale marks of the racially impure.

Maggie Kizer's father had been a mulatto, a slave brought up as a superior servant in a fine house in Virginia. Some years before the Civil War, he had escaped to the North and, passing for white in society, had married the only woman who knew the secret of his birth—a girl from Maine who was heiress to the fortune of an Abolitionist family. The young couple lived in Kennebunkport and Maggie was raised with her two brothers in the city's finest house. A tutor lived in the attic and a dancing master was around the corner; Maggie learned the pianoforte, recitation, and painting on velvet. But in her third year in a ladies' seminary in Portsmouth, New Hampshire, when she was sixteen, it was made public by her father's chance meeting on the street with the brother-in-law of his old master, that Joseph Conway was half Negro. Immediately after, Maggie's mother was disinherited by her family, and the grandchildren disavowed. Maggie was removed from the school in ignominy and went to live with her parents in a village in Vermont. Her two brothers went to sea at that time and she had never heard from them since. After a year of penury in Vermont, Maggie's parents died in the explosion of a paddleboat on Lake Champlain, where they had been employed as maid and waiter, and a gentleman of the town took Maggie under his care. Soon, Maggie became pregnant, and was ejected from the village. She made her way to New York in the back of a cart carrying large blocks of marble for the students at the National Academy of Fine Arts, and shortly after her arrival made a visit to Daisy Shanks in her professional capacity as abortionist.

Maggie became addicted to opium during her period of wandering indigence in New York. It was not only that the drug-induced dreams mercifully occluded the misery of her destitution, but that opium killed the appetite—and it was cheaper than food. If one got a very little money somewhere, the piecemeal purchase of the sticky globes gave one the right to remain all the day upon the bunks in the joint; and on those soft pallets in the darkened rooms of a blind cellar, days collapsed into hours and whole weeks passed as if they had been no more than a few sulfurous days. Once, she had trekked to the joint through foot-deep snow, and when she came out again it was to find that spring was full-blown in Washington Square and Battery Park.

But one day, in that place that did not know time, a man on the neighboring mattress shared a sandwich and coffee with Maggie—food that had been ordered in from a nearby saloon—and asked if he might not take her back to his apartments. Maggie, grateful for his offer, accepted and accompanied the man to his flat on First Street. She remained with him for two months and they indulged their habit in the bedchamber rather than in the unhealthful cellar on Mott Street. But then he was arrested for the robbery of a clergyman who was doing charitable work in Five Points and sentenced to seven years at Sing Sing. Maggie once more was alone, and supported herself and her opium habit by selling off the gifts that the thief, who had been enchanted with her, had stolen for her sake. On one of her expeditions to Lena's pawnshop, Maggie was introduced to Alick Kizer. She soon removed to his apartments in the house let by Lady Weale, and sometime later was married to him.

Her opium habit had abated over the years, for she was no longer a miserable woman. She had no wish any longer to be respectable, for she had learned at great expense that respectability was a bubble easily pricked. She wanted only a modicum of comfort, security, and ease—and those she had achieved. But the poppy dreams were delicious, and her system still craved the drug. She smoked at home now, but occasionally had to make trips to the drugstore or to her old joint for more opium, though she purchased the drug in such quantity that these errands were infrequent. But now she must also replace her *yen hock*, the sharp length of steel with which the gumlike opium is prepared for burning in the pipe. The flattened darning needle she had employed for the past few weeks was imperfect and she liked to have the proper article; her fine *yen hock* of gilded steel, which had served her for eight years, was the metal finger that had pressed the catch of Cyrus Butterfield's life; and in her haste to be rid of the corpse, Maggie had not thought to extract it from his body. She rather wondered at the rapaciousness of the scavengers that had taken the murdered man's clothes, that they had even discovered the golden nail hidden in the lawyer's breast.

Maggie walked down Bleecker Street to Mott and then turned south. After only a couple of streets, the number of Chinamen to be seen was marked. They all wore long queues sticking out beneath round-crowned hats with cartwheel brims, wide shapeless breeches, and blue blouses beneath colorful quilted jackets. None appeared to take notice of Maggie as she approached, though she stood out easily enough on that poor street. However, when she stopped beside a group of four, lounging before a small wooden house and talking Chinese in low voices, one of them said sharply, "Who?"

"*En she quay,*" Maggie replied, words which meant "opium smoker."

"Who *en she quay?*"

"Dark Glass," she said, and lifted her black veil so that the Chinaman might see the spectacles beneath. The Chinaman nodded to a slatternly Irishwoman with motheaten eyebrows who blocked the doorway of the house, and the Chinaman's wife moved aside to allow Maggie entrance.

At the end of a dark hallway whose walls were papered with letters that had been received from relations in China, Maggie knocked at a rickety door. A panel flew open, and a flat yellow face peered out at her. "*En she quay,*" she repeated, and the door opened. Maggie stepped through onto a little platform raised high above the cellar, which was

filled with drowsy layers of acrid blue smoke, palpable and
—at least to the devotees of opium—delicious. The Chinaman who had allowed her entrance stood obsequiously
out of the way and Maggie looked over the room. It was
about thirty feet long and fifteen wide, illuminated by a
single lantern suspended from the ceiling; the glass in the
lantern was of blue and green, and the place was but
dimly lighted. On either side of an aisle running down the
center of the room was a low platform, just wide enough
for a man to lie at full length. It was roughly covered with
a motley collection of bolsters, pillows, blankets, cushions,
and mattresses. About six feet above this platform, and
reached by short attached ladders, was another platform
just like it, similarly cushioned. At the far end of the aisle
was a doorway, boarded up on the bottom and barred at
the top. The small room behind was better lighted and two
Chinamen sat in there, playing a game with many ivory
counters. In a large pottery jar between them were two
dozen or so long narrow pipes and on shelves behind them
were sets of the opium lay-outs—the apparatus required
by addicts.

Only a few of the two dozen persons in the room were
Chinamen. In the dimness, Maggie could see that some of
the addicts lay sleeping with their pipes resting lightly
upon an outstretched hand, some were propped on an
elbow patiently working the opium over the little green-
glass lamps, some smoked their pipes in contented stupefaction. A couple of men shared a plate of food and a
single cup of coffee. A prosperous Chinaman, his handsome Irish wife, and their ten-year-old son lay in a reposeful triangle, passing a single pipe between them. A
three hundred-pound woman from a Bowery freak show
was propped in a corner with her legs spread wide, trying
to make her sausage-fat arthritic fingers do their business
properly with the delicate *yen hock* and the tiny black
boluses of opium. And a young man—evidently a novice
—staggered down the length of one platform, reeling and
convulsive. Though he bumped over others' lay-outs and
kicked others in the legs or their stomachs, no one called
out or appeared to take any notice of him. Besides the
Bowery fat lady there were several women in the room—
none of them so well-dressed as Maggie—who were in-
differently placed among the men.

But despite these pockets of shifting light and movement, there prevailed in the smoky blue cellar an absolute and stupefying silence. It seemed as if in that place, the sense of smell had subsumed all of hearing and much of sight. One heard nothing, saw little, but the smell of burning opium pervaded one's entire consciousness.

Although the scant, colored illumination, the fearful noiselessness, the pervasive sharp odor, the torpidity of all the inhabitants of that room could not fail to make a sinister impression on the casual observer, those who frequented the place knew it to be perfectly safe. No woman was ever molested, no man injured in a fight; harsh words rarely spoken were never attended. And though the place was the frequent resort of thieves, there was honor among them here if there was honor nowhere else. No one was ever robbed, though the jeweled hand of the actress dropped insensible across the breast of the pickpocket.

Maggie descended the short flight of steps into the room and walked slowly to the back. The head of a reclining female figure swayed languorously, and a featureless voice from an invisible mouth whispered, "Dark Glass . . ." Maggie paused and raised her gloved hand in salutation.

"What's it like, Dark Glass?" cried the voice, a little louder, but with no more urgency than there was curiosity in the gleaming liquid eyes that were turned on Maggie. "What's it like out there? Are they still burying the dead?"

Out there meant all the world except this one room, and *out there* was an insignificant space by comparison.

"Yes, Dollie," replied Maggie quietly, "wait a bit, wait a bit. . . ."

Dollie was an actress who, when not in work, had always retreated to the dens of Mott Street. Here she had made her acquaintance with Maggie and helped the octoroon when she was in greatest need of assistance. When however, in the first days of the year, it was found out at the National Theatre that Dollie had become pregnant by a member of the house orchestra and obtained an abortion of that child in the Black Triangle, the stage manager had refused to allow her to rehearse for the next production. Dollie had fled to Mott Street and had scarcely ventured out at all in over a month now.

At the barred window, Maggie purchased a tin of

highest-grade opium, five ounces in a small oblong brass box that was painted with red Chinese characters, the best *yen hock* that was to be had, and a dollar's worth of the second-best opium as a gift for Dollie. She paid a little more than ten dollars altogether.

When Maggie returned to Dollie, she was greeted vacantly—for Maggie's presence had already faded from the hopeless addict's mind. Dollie had got that name from her pink dimpled cheeks and her bright blue eyes that made her resemble a fine China doll. But now her cheek was faded and her eye grown cloudy; her face had fallen slack and her luxuriant black hair was hid beneath a greasy bonnet.

Maggie lay down beside her old friend and, taking out her newly purchased *yen hock*, began to heat a small pellet of the opium she had bought over Dollie's green lamp.

Dollie leaned over and sniffed it. "Good dope," she breathed. Despite scant illumination in the room, the pupils of Dollie's eyes were contracted into points and Maggie knew that Dollie probably could see nothing but the flame of the candle in the lamp. Her only other light was the mixed flowing color of her dreaming. It was a wonder she had found out Maggie's presence in the room.

The opium was placed in Dollie's pipe and the two women smoked. Maggie fell quickly into a slow soft reverie, a reverie that was untroubled by remembrance of distresses past or present, reverie untouched by anxious dreaming, reverie that was nothing but solace for the care that burdens all. She stretched herself softly in her fine green dress upon the stained ticking of an old mattress and thought, when she thought at all, of this small but sufficient world of contentment and security that lay in the dark cellar of an old house at the lower end of Mott Street on the lower end of Manhattan Island. No statesman inspired by a gleaming Utopia, no cleric convinced of the possibility of heaven upon earth, no philanthropist with expansive heart and unlimited funds could have created, or even imagined, so fine an existence as this one. It was no wonder that *out there* was a sordid, deceptive, cold place. *Out there* was that other room, the rest of Mott Street, the rest of Manhattan Island, the rest of the planet—where the light glared and blinded, where the wicked and the weary beat upon the walls and cried out their misery.

Sometime later, Maggie Kizer rose and made her way out of that place, leaving the packet of opium beside her friend. As she slowly ascended the steps to the platform at the end of the room, the obsequious Chinaman bowed continuously, but did not venture to assist her. He opened the door and pointed down the letter-papered hallway. At the other end stood the Irishwoman who moved aside again to allow her passage. Maggie paused a moment and drew her fingers over the ideograms drawn in red ink like blood. Two ragged little girls with slanted eyes and red hair huddled just inside the door, chattering to one another in a mixture of Chinese-patois and heavily brogued English—their speech as mixed as their parentage. Maggie noted only that it was now dark outside.

Slowly, through the Mott Street that was hardly less crowded at two o'clock in the morning—by a skeleton clock that stood in the window of a jewelry shop—than at any hour of daylight, Maggie Kizer made her dreamy, careless way.

Near the intersection with Spring Street, Maggie came upon a cab that was discharging a passenger and she requisitioned it to take her the remainder of the way home. She climbed in and then, without having the notion that any time passed at all, she found that the cab had halted before her own house. Maggie paid the driver and climbed the steps of her building.

"Mrs. Kizer," said a voice behind her. She turned slowly, her latchkey in hand.

"Mrs. Kizer," repeated another voice, from a slightly different direction.

Maggie lifted her veil and raised her dark spectacles. Two men in frock coats had come together at the foot of the steps. In one motion, they pulled back the lapels of their coats and revealed battered tin shields the size of saucers. Behind them stood a young man in a beaver hat whose hair and whiskers were like fire. They all stared hard at Maggie and she lowered her spectacles with a fatigued hand.

"Come along now," said one of the men with the saucerlike shield.

"Why?" said Maggie. "Where?"

"We know that your husband killed Cyrus Butterfield, and that you were a witness and an accessory. Come along now," said the other.

The latchkey fell from Maggie's hand and clattered on Mrs. Weale's front steps.

Chapter 17

HELEN Stallworth, on the morning after her visit to the Black Triangle with Marian's Committee for the Suppression of Urban Vice, did not attend breakfast in the manse, but rather sent word down to her father and brother that she was indisposed. Benjamin of late had developed the habit of detailing at breakfast all that he had done and witnessed in the Black Triangle the night before. Edward Stallworth encouraged these revelations, for from them he garnered material for his sermons. Helen was grieved by Benjamin's amused voice, by her father's satisfied reception of the anecdotes of crime and destitution; and she rarely read Simeon Lightner's articles now without irrepressible shuddering.

On the front page of Wednesday morning's *Tribune*, as she examined it alone in her bedroom over a cup of strong black tea, Helen found a story of particular horror. The facts of the case, as reported by Simeon Lightner, were quite beyond her conception. The jumbled talk of streetwalkers with amber spectacles, opium addiction, escaped convicts, blackmail, murder, and corpse-plundering was like a gothic romance. Yet even after learning the miserable circumstances under which Cyrus Butterfield had been deprived of his life, and contemplating the hard-faced malignity of the courtesan Maggie Kizer, Helen did not waver in her resolve to assist the unfortunates who were forced by happenstance and poverty to inhabit that sink of depravity and misery called the Black Triangle; and she had not lost the conviction either that membership on Marian's committee would do nothing in that direction. Assuring the concerned servants that she was wholly recovered, Helen Stallworth departed the manse and went to visit an acquaintance whose small but fine house was located on Eighteenth Street near Second Avenue.

Mrs. General Taunton was the widow of a Union officer who had died in the Battle of the Wilderness, and though this melancholy event was long past, Mrs. General Taunton remained in deep mourning for her husband. In fact, though she attended all services at the Madison Square Presbyterian Church, Helen Stallworth knew the lady only by her figure and unvarying dress—a stocky short woman in finest bombazine, with large bracelets, necklaces, and earrings of gleaming jet. A large pendant on her breast contained a coil of her husband's hair, tied into a lovers' knot. The veil that covered the face of Mrs. General Taunton was so heavy and so black that Helen Stallworth was not certain that she would know the lady if she were to see her without it. A carte de visite that Mrs. General Taunton had made up for herself and distributed to her affectionate acquaintances showed her standing beside a pall-draped pedestal on which rested her dead husband's sword and military cap, while she—in exquisite mourning apparel—stood with bowed head and drooping hand in an attitude of picturesque inconsolable grief.

Edward Stallworth sometimes lightly ridiculed this particular parishioner, but Helen had been attracted by the unflagging fidelity of the lady's costume. Helen found her not lugubrious by any means, but rather of a somberly cheerful disposition. She had enough money to live comfortably in a moderately sized house in a moderately fashionable neighborhood which, to Helen's surprise, when she first visited the modest lady, was staffed by a mob of servants.

Far more startling than their number, however, was the immediately apprehensible fact that each was in some fashion disfigured. The man who opened the door to

Helen was lacking his right arm, though he dextrously managed, with a handsome swirl, to remove her cape. The maid dusting in the front parlor was a hunchback, and the girl who carried a pile of draperies up the stairs bore terrible scars across her face. The servant, crisply attired and with a pretty smile, who brought cakes and tea, had but two fingers on each hand, and the first time that Helen went out in Mrs. General Taunton's carriage she discovered that the two footmen who rode behind had but a single pair of legs distributed evenly between them.

When Helen had formed sufficient acquaintance with Mrs. General Taunton to remark on these peculiarities of her servants, Mrs. General Taunton replied with a sigh, "My husband had but one leg, you know, and our brief life together was so blissful, so pure, that I declared to myself upon his death that I would never marry a man who was whole. The idea of wedding a man who was whole disgusted me, in fact; and I considered at the time that I should have no difficulty in snuffling out another husband, war wounds being so plentiful in the early years of my bereavement. But I never found a man who suited me quite so well as my mourning did, so I have forgone companionship and kept to the dress."

"But the servants. . . ?" prompted Helen softly.

"Oh yes, of course, all my servants are maimed, as you have probably noticed. I would not hire a man or a girl who was not disfigured. Not only do they remind me with unremitting tenderness of my husband's affliction, but I find that they are invariably better workers than others, whose bodies may be whole but whose minds are filled with mischief and ingratitude. And what is the good of employing a girl or a man who might be employed anywhere? These men and girls I have 'round me would have a hard time of it if not in my service, and they quite know it. They are grateful and they are my children. I have adopted as many of them as my modest income will allow, and I hold to the opinion that my money is better spent in this manner than on luxuries that are worse than useless."

"Well," said Helen feelingly, but only after the maid with one eye had departed the room, "it is a wonder that more people do not follow your example."

Helen Stallworth had discovered that Mrs. General

Taunton's charity did not end with the employment of disfigured servants; Mrs. General Taunton confided to Helen that she sometimes, in the company of a maid and a man, made excursions into the poorer sections of the city to nurse the sick and give assistance to the deserving, and when she came across those who were past such small benefits, to comfort their dying beds with religious consolations. By no means did the lady boast of these charities, but told of them only in explanation of her surprising knowledge of the streets described in the *Tribune* articles.

And so, after the day when she visited the Black Triangle and viewed the unhappiness endemic to the place, Helen went to Mrs. General Taunton and at length discussed what she had witnessed.

Mrs. General Taunton's veil nodded slowly in sympathy with the young woman's distress, and at the end of Helen's description she sighed and remarked: "I regret that I must tell you that you did not see the worst of what is to be seen. You did not after all step out of your carriage. On the other side of those brick walls are torments and moral illnesses far worse than anything that parades upon the sidewalks."

"Marian's committee," said Helen softly, "will do little I fear, to alleviate such privations as I witnessed, and it distresses me that I spend my hours in the comfortable parlor on Gramercy Park every week, that I am assigned to make a cap out of blue wool for a child that is perishing of consumption and which he will wear only in his grave, and told to stuff a pincushion for a seamstress in the hope that the gift of it will keep her undefiled."

"I understand," said Mrs. General Taunton, "but there *is* something more that you can do."

"What is that?"

"You can go with me into the Black Triangle. In the autumn I spent some time in the place, for change of air —though foul enough air it is—from my taxing endeavors along East Broadway. I have resumed my visits there since the articles began in the *Tribune*. Sometimes a particularly unfortunate and deserving case is mentioned in the paragraphs—though one must read carefully enough and not allow the descriptions of prevalent vice to overwhelm one's sympathies for the underlying, perhaps causal, privations—and I do what I can to seek the unfortunate out. I'm not always successful, of course, but there's never any lack, I can assure you, of worthy objects of charity."

"Shall we be safe?"

"Not entirely," replied Mrs. General Taunton, "it may be that God will let us slip through His protective fingers."

Helen was silent beneath this gentle rebuke.

"We shall have one of my men with us, and one of my girls for a guide. She lived on Charlton Street at a time, and I took her from a cellar where she slept in a pile of water-soaked rotting straw. She looks whole, but in fact is prone to epileptic seizures."

"When shall we go then?" said Helen with determination. "I must own to a certain nervousness, but I know that I cannot continue in my Madison Square complacency."

"We shall go," said Mrs. General Taunton, "as soon as we've taken a little luncheon."

The servant whose empty left sleeve was pinned across his livery drew open the door of the dining room and Helen and Mrs. General Taunton rose to go in.

Chapter 18

I N the open carriage of Mrs. General Taunton, with the scrofulous driver before, and the epileptic maid carrying in her lap a large basket of wrapped foods, Helen Stallworth and the widow of the Civil War hero drove southward from Eighteenth Street. Helen was anxious about repeating the previous day's journey, but Mrs. General Taunton seemed so much at ease, consulting several lists that she had carefully drawn up sometime before, that the young woman was to some extent reassured.

"Are we going to a particular place?" asked Helen diffidently, trying not to stare at the maid, who with every tremble of the carriage, Helen imagined, was about to precipitate into a shaking fit.

"Oh yes, certainly," replied Mrs. General Taunton, "charity ought not to be gone about in a haphazard or zigzag fashion. It would not do to drive through the streets distributing largess to the most pitiful-looking person one passed. One learns quickly that the real misery remains in-of-doors. In-of-doors one finds those who are too ill to present themselves as objects of pity on the street. In-of-doors are straitened virtue and troubled decency."

"Then," said Helen, schooled, "where is it that we're going?"

138

"A small lodging house on King Street. I've had notice of a young woman, first cousin to my second cook who, though virtuous herself, contracted an improvident marriage. She is ill just now and her child is ill and she is beat by her husband, a brute who, when not insensible with alcohol, is a sleeping-car sneak—"

"I beg your pardon?"

"He robs persons on sleeping cars. Fortunately, he appears to be away most of the week, riding back and forth from New York to Washington, plying his trade."

Helen trembled. "Do you think it likely that we'll meet him there?"

"Possibly," said Mrs. General Taunton, and turned back to her lists. "We shall in any case have the opportunity of visiting other inhabitants of the house and seeing what is wanted there. You must know, of course, the way that these lodging houses are set up. More expensive apartments are on the lower floors, while cheapest lodgings are obtained at the top of the house. The objects of our visit, Mrs. Leed and her child, are camped directly below the roof."

The carriage turned off Broadway onto Third Street and then south on MacDougal Street, with difficulty maneuvered the corner of King Street, and stopped in front of a narrow four-storied brick building. Before it stood a tall, sullen Irishwoman with three babies of slightly varying age, secured in a wheelbarrow with a length of coarse rope.

Martin and Maisie, Mrs. Taunton's driver and maid, preceded the two ladies up the steps of the house, the door of which was not only unsecured but left quite open, allowing the chill wind to bellow from the bottom of the house to the very top. Helen held tightly to the arm of Mrs. General Taunton as they stepped into the grimy, stinking hallway, which was narrow and dark, with long strips of filthy paper hanging down the walls at every height. The stairs were narrow and rotting and gave dangerously beneath the weight of a single person, so that they all were required to proceed Indian-file and very carefully: first the driver, then the maid, then Helen, and last Mrs. General Taunton, mounting with as much ease as if she had been in her own home and were only ascending to her dressing room for a fan she had left behind.

On the first floor was but a single door, that entire space being given out to a single, relatively affluent lodger, but the second and third stories accommodated two flats each. The poor narrow attic was given over wholly to Mr. and Mrs. Leed and their unchristened infant. On the progress upward Helen was assaulted by odors that were strong, unrecognizable, probably unhealthful, and certainly disgusting. Yet the house was quiet, almost preternaturally so, with no voices to be heard distinctly, only muffled whispers and the occasional scrape and bang of furniture to give proof of habitation. Already used to the blasphemous, shrill cries and rantings that prevailed in the street, the quiet in this house touched Helen as sinister.

The last flight of steps, narrower and more rickety than the rest, led directly up into the attic; there was no barrier to shut out the cold drafts that blew up from the street door; but perhaps these were not noticed particularly, for they were no stronger than the breezes that found entrance through the chinks in the wooden rafters. These spaces were wide and frequent enough to provide, along with ventilation, a dim and inexpensive illumination for inhabitants who could afford neither candles nor fuel to feed a lamp.

The four visitors filled that part of the attic's space that admitted of a person remaining entirely upright; for the sharply sloping eaves made it impossible to stand anywhere but in the center. Helen looked around her appalled. The only furnishings to be seen were two black mattresses pushed against the brick chimney and a minuscule iron stove that looked as if it hadn't seen a match all winter long. Three broken pottery cups were neatly arranged before it, in a heartrending imitation of domestic order and sufficiency.

Mrs. Leed sat on one of the mattresses with her back against the chimney. She was a thin pale woman with a quantity of black hair fast turning to gray, with sunken eyes, a drawn broken nose, and a parched mouth. She had a ragged filthy blanket thrown across her lap and a woolen shawl draped over her shoulders. In her arms was a puny year-old baby that twitched like a galvanized frog.

Without hesitation Mrs. General Taunton went over to the woman, gradually stooping so as not to hit her head against the roof, and asked what was wrong with the baby.

"He's infected with the Michigan itch," the woman replied in a choked voice.

"Are you nursing him?"

The woman nodded dully. "When I'm able to give."

"When was he last fed?"

The woman shrugged and glanced over at the hole in the roof. "Night," she replied.

"We've brought you food," said Mrs. General Taunton, and Maisie took over several small neatly tied bundles and set them on the floor beside the stove.

"Thank you, ma'am," said Mrs. Leed numbly.

Mrs. General Taunton backed away and turned to her maid: "Maisie, you stay up here for a space, open the packages and set out the food for her. I think she is too tired to do it for herself now. See if the child will take any milk. Mrs. Leed," said she, turning to the woman on the mattress, "Maisie here will help you with this food, and you may expect the visit of a physician before night." Mrs. General Taunton turned to Helen. "There is a doctor in the neighborhood with whom I've made acquaintance, a drunkard by night but competent during the day. I sometimes employ him to see after the cases which simple wholesome diet will not cure."

Mrs. General Taunton led the way downstairs, followed by Helen and Martin carrying the basket.

"You can tell such things yourself?" questioned Helen softly upon the stairs. "Tell when food will help, and when not?"

"Mrs. Leed will die shortly," said the voice from behind the black veil, "but not before the child."

Helen wrung her hands in distress.

At that moment the nearer door of the third floor landing was thrown wide and in the aperture appeared an immense Negro dressed in a shiny black suit that was old and had been constructed to hang upon a man who was much smaller than the one who wore it now.

"Who you?" he demanded in a booming voice. "What you seek in dis place?"

Helen shrunk away, for the man's upraised hand was as large as a Cincinnati ham, but Mrs. General Taunton replied impassively, "We have come on a charitable mission to your upstairs neighbor, Mrs. Leed, who was sorely in want of medical assistance. Her child also we found in a bad way."

"Oh yea!" cried the Negro vehemently, "po' helpmeet an' offspring o' that chile of wraff and sin! Dat wicked man who alla time use harsh and 'busive words to the light o' his life and the jew'l o' his 'xistence. I t'ink on Judgment Day de Lawd'll call me into 'count for having married dem two together in de only sometime blessed state of holy wedded married matrimony."

Helen's eyes grew wide.

"You are a minister of the gospel then?" said Mrs. General Taunton, unsurprised.

"I am de Reverend Thankful Jones. I am shepherd to a small flock of black sheep what live in de 'mediate 'cinity. I am——"

"Yes," interrupted Mrs. General Taunton. "Being then a minister of the Gospel, and concerned doubtlessly with the state of men upon earth as well as their future in heaven, perhaps you could tell us if there are any others in this house who are in particular want, particular and *deserving* want, I mean."

"Dey all is, ma'am," replied the Reverend Thankful Jones with a melancholy shake of his head; and he was about to go on, when cut off by a shrill angry chattering behind him in a language that Helen did not recognize.

The Reverend Thankful Jones hurriedly excused himself and moved out of the way just enough to close the door—but also enough for Helen to see that in the room behind him, ill-furnished and filled with smoke, sat four Chinamen at a large round table, playing cards, smoking pipes, and crushing walnuts with their teeth. The door was closed, but behind it they heard the black preacher's brief excoriation of "dis game of wraff and sin . . ."

Knocking on the other door of the third floor they were admitted into the room of a large lady with red hair and a flattened nose who was just pinning a blue velvet bonnet with green and yellow feathers to her hair. Her eyes, Mrs. General Taunton later joked, were in mourning—for they had been blackened. "Peeked out," the woman said, "saw you on your way up to the poor lady under the roof."

She was most evidently a prostitute—this was apparent

even to Helen—but Mrs. General Taunton, instead of remonstrating with her, merely asked if she were contented with her way of life.

"Oh cert," replied the woman easily, "and if it's misery you're after, you'd best knock downstairs. Me and the Reverend Thankful is happy as pantomimes."

"Might I not leave this Testament with you at least?" begged Helen, gathering her courage to speak with the young woman, whose good humor astounded her, for surely prostitutes must be the most miserable and cursed of all mankind.

"Oh cert," replied the lady, "do what you please, but for all I can read it, it might as well be writ in Choctaw. It's all I can do to pick out the letters in my own name."

"We should knock downstairs then?" asked Mrs. General Taunton.

The prostitute nodded and her eyes gleamed. "Sure, either door, either door. Misery enough for the whole pack of you."

Helen left the Testament anyway, despite the red-haired woman's illiteracy. At the door, she paused with the suggestion that she might find someone to read aloud to her from it, and then followed Martin and Mrs. General Taunton downstairs.

"My dear," said that lady upon the landing, "I will knock at one door, and you must knock at the other. Martin will stay between, so you need not fear. Simply see what is needed, taking particular care to ask after the health of any children there may be."

The two women stepped to either end of the small landing, knocked at the doors, and received no answer. Mrs. General Taunton knocked again, called softly, turned the knob of the door, and slipped inside. Helen knew that she could do no less, and though trembling for what tableau of unimaginable distress she might witness on the other side—perhaps finding someone starved to death upon his bed or the victim of a bloody and fatal crime, or even another prostitute in the pursuance of her trade —Helen knocked again, called softly, and turned the knob of the door.

The single chamber was much better furnished than she could have hoped, having viewed the three rooms above. There was a red carpet upon the floor and blue curtains across the window, a larger dresser strewn with bottles and boxes of powder and swatches of false hair, two open trunks filled with sumptuous—if gaudy—clothing, a box piled high with smart boots, a row of feathered hats hanging from pegs on the walls, and a green glass lamp with a painted shade. In the corner of the room, half hidden by a green curtain, was a large iron bed piled so high with soft quilts that she could not immediately see who was in it.

The room was filled with a delicate, dusty light filtered through the blue curtains and there was a pervasive scent of *pomade à la rose.*

Emboldened by the relative respectability of the room, Helen cautiously approached the foot of the bed; but when a board beneath the carpet creaked under her weight, two figures rose up suddenly from beneath the quilts—a gentleman about forty years of age with a thick black beard and thick black eyebrows but very little hair on the top of his head, and a young boy, so softly featured and with such long curling hair that had not his chest been bare, Helen would have taken him certainly for a female.

"Who the devil—" cried the older man.

"Get out!" screeched the boy, pulling the sheet up to his neck, "get out of my room!"

Helen fled, and did not even leave a testament.

She ran past Martin and into the other chamber on the floor. In the small comfortless room, she found Mrs. General Taunton standing beside a narrow iron bed on which lay two emaciated persons of advanced age. A thin coverlet was pulled up around their scrawny necks, and their clouded eyes gaped uncomprehendingly up at their visitors. The two persons in the bed were chiefly distinguishable by their gasping mouths, one being yellow from many years of chewing tobacco, and the other quite black with toothless scaly gums. Both were bald, and their wrinkled pock-marked skin was stretched tight across their skulls.

Mrs. General Taunton said that they were man and wife, both just under seventy years of age, and both suffering markedly from cold and hunger. "They must be fed now or I feel they will die. Please call Martin."

Martin was already inside, and held the basket for Mrs.

General Taunton to take out some small packages of soft food that had been prepared against just such a case as this.

"How did you succeed across the way?" she asked Helen.

"Not very well, I fear," blushed Helen. For one thing, it had been the first time she had ever seen a male barechested.

"What happened?"

Helen hung her head, too ashamed to describe what she had seen and fearing to be confirmed in her dismayed interpretation; but Mrs. General Taunton did not press her. "Very well dear, but you must not think that we shall always be received with perfect politeness and very often our only reward will be the knowledge that we have done a little good somewhere. Now, while I sit here"—she was spooning mashed vegetables into the yellow mouth, which was, to Helen, a repellent operation—"please to go downstairs and knock. It is not likely that those living on the first floor will be in tremendous want —for they are the aristocracy of such houses as these— but we should be remiss if we did not at the least inquire."

Helen nodded, and though she feared a repetition of the scene across the hall, she had rather go downstairs than remain to watch the gasping yellow mouth and the ulcerous black mouth receiving food at Mrs. General Taunton's charitable and fearless hand.

Chapter 19

THE Sapphic Pugilist, Charlotta Kegoe, had been ill for
four days, prostrated with a fever that had been contracted when she went too quickly out into the cold night
air after a match in a damp cellar on Broome Street. She
took to her bed and sent for Louisa Shanks, whose ministrations to her friend were ungrudging and ceaseless.
On this particular afternoon, Ella had accompanied her
grandmother on her visit to the ailing Charlotta. Charlotta
was sensible of the honor bestowed upon her in this, for
she knew that Lena had not left the buildings on West
Houston Street at all since the first night of the new
year.

Charlotta's apartments, though by far the best in that
house, were by no means grand. The furnishings of the
room at the front were scanty and poor, a small rickety
round table covered with a threadbare cloth, a couple of
wobbly chairs pulled up to it, a bare floor with knotholes,
a cracked mirror upon the painted wall, two closed and
locked trunks, a basket filled with soiled clothing, and a
stack of hatboxes in a corner. Pasted on the walls were
pages ripped from the yellow journals, representing prominent female fighters. Ella amused herself here with attempting to pick the lock of one of the trunks. A double

door, closed off by a louvered screen, separated this from the back room.

That chamber was smaller and darker and even more poorly furnished, with the single exception that a patched, much-worn flowered carpet covered a portion of the floor. There was a painted washstand with a bowl and pitcher that were tolerably new set upon it, a cedar wardrobe against one wall, and a small iron bedstead with an up-ended crate beside it.

In the iron bed lay Charlotta Kegoe. Her eyes were sunken with illness and she breathed noisily and with difficulty through her mouth. Her nightdress was cut low on the neck and her tattooed arms lay outside the heavy covers.

Louisa Shanks was occupied in pouring a scoopful of coal upon the fire in the grate and Lena sat solidly in a chair that was much too narrow for her ample girth, next to the chamber's only window. The thin dark curtains had been drawn, for the comfort of the invalid.

This was by no means a cheerful sickroom. Lena Shanks was not adept in the administering of comfort, even to those of whom she was fond; Charlotta Kegoe was not constituted to make a happy or resigned patient; and Louisa Shanks, rather a gruff nurse, was of course entirely silent. For some minutes the only sound in the room had been Charlotta's low-pitched groans of discomfort as she attempted to rearrange herself in the bed; all three women were startled by a knock at the door of the front room.

"*Wer ist's?*" demanded Lena.

Louisa shrugged her shoulders and Charlotta, not knowing, did not bother to answer at all.

Louisa slipped past the louvered screen into the front room and motioned Ella to open the door. The girl slowly turned the knob, then suddenly pulled the door open wide. A young woman, simply but expensively dressed, stood there with a decidedly nervous manner and apprehensive eyes.

"Pardon me," she said with trembling diffidence, "but I and a companion of mine were visiting Mrs. Leed in the attic of this house—she is in great distress—and stopped here to see if there were anyone needful of . . . comfort or succor."

Louisa perforce made no reply and Ella, receiving no sign that she should speak, said nothing to the young woman.

"I'm sorry to have troubled you," she faltered, and backed out into the hallway.

"Wer ist's?" cried Lena again.

"She don't talk," said Ella, pointing at Louisa, who had turned and was gesturing to Lena in the darkened room behind.

Louisa turned back around to face the young woman, pushed the screen out of the way, and waved her into the smaller chamber.

The young woman hesitated, but Ella urged her: "Go on! 'Lotta's ill, in back there!"

She crept through the doorway, nervously brushing against the mute woman. When her eyes had accustomed to the dimness, she moved to the bed, drew her fingers softly across the coverlet—she was reluctant to grasp the tattooed hand—and asked if there were anything that might be provided to relieve the intensity of the tedium of her illness and whether, in fact, that illness had yet been treated.

"She'll live," said Lena gruffly.

The young woman looked up startled. She had been so arrested by the strange figure in the bed that she had not seen Lena sitting at the window. "I'm very glad of it," replied the young woman earnestly. "Is it certain that there is nothing I can do to alleviate the discomfort of this unwelcome season?"

No one made reply to this stiff speech.

"Perhaps I ought to go then, and leave you to your rest," she said quietly.

Charlotta raised herself painfully in the bed, gasped "Water!" and fell back again. Louisa hurried forward, poured out some cloudly liquid into a tumbler, and pressed it to the ill woman's lips. She gulped it thirstily and then turned her head aside.

"Tastes like it washed over a corpse," she whispered, and then twitched with a spasm of pain.

"Has . . . has she sufficient funds that a doctor might be called in?" asked the young woman. "One will be sent for Mrs. Leed, ought he be told to look in here as well?"

"We take care of 'Lotta," said Lena.

"Of course," replied the young woman hastily, and moved as if to take her leave, mumbling a farewell and a wish for the speedy recovery of the patient. But evidently thinking better of her fearfulness, she stopped suddenly, turned around and stepped quickly to Lena's side.

"Here," she said, handing Lena a red-letter Testament, "please take this, for *her* benefit," indicating the woman groaning upon the bed, "or for your own."

Lena Shanks looked up at the anxious young woman who proffered the slim volume. She stood just before the window, and in the motion of raising her arm, the sleeve of her dress had caught the hem of the curtain and drawn it aside. A shaft of watery sunlight fell upon her face and illuminated a pair of shining blue eyes in a field of parchment skin.

Lena drew back sharply. *"Wer bist du denn?"* she cried out, and with one hand she knocked the Testament away. It scudded across the floor; but before it had even come to rest, Ella had snatched it up and thrust it into the pocket of her skirt.

The young woman drew back alarmed. The curtain fell into place, the sunlight was extinguished, and the brilliant blue eyes were no more to be seen in their shadowed sockets.

"Wer bist du denn?" Lena demanded again, waving her cane in menace. "What's your name?"

"Helen Stallworth," she trembled.

The cane clattered to the floor.

"Was willst du denn hier?" Lena hissed. "What do you want?"

"I simply came in to see if anyone needed assistance, if anyone here were in want of . . . of . . . anything at all. I'm in the company," she added, in case these persons were contemplating some mischief, "of Mrs. General Taunton and her servants, her several servants, who just now are in the rooms above this one."

Lena nodded to her granddaughter, who skipped out of the room. Helen a moment later heard the door into the hallway opened. She understood that the child had been sent to determine the accuracy of her statement and she was anxious for what this might portend.

"Name again," demanded Lena.

"Helen Stallworth."

Lena jerked aside the curtain and once more the sunlight fell upon Helen, but she had turned her back.

"This way!" shouted Lena. Louisa Shanks had moved closer and was an ominous hovering presence. Very much discomposed, Helen looked down at the old woman, in whose gaze she seemed to discern an admixture of malevolence and fear.

"Cornelius," whispered Lena, "you took away Cornelius and hanged him, and you put me away at the Island. You tried to take my girls. Now Alick is gone too, and Maggie's in the Tombs—"

"Who is it you think I am?" cried Helen. "I know none—"

"Stallworth!"

Helen was held immobile by the basilisk gaze of the old woman, and understood in that terrified moment to what extent her grandfather's reputation as a stern judge must have vilified their family name in the Black Triangle.

"Please—" said Helen, but before she could speak further, the little girl ran back in and nodded shortly.

Lena Shanks jerked the curtain closed. "Get out!" she cried.

Helen all but ran from the chamber and through the poorly furnished parlor. She reached the hallway just as Mrs. General Taunton was coming down the stairs, followed by Maisie and Martin.

"Yes, dear," said the voice behind the black veil, "and were you more fortunate this time?"

Chapter 20

~~~~~~

FOLLOWING her arrest, at the police station Maggie Kizer was quietly recalcitrant. She gave her name and address, but entirely refused to answer any question concerning the death of Cyrus Butterfield. Her apparent unconcern for the gravity of her situation, which partly was the tag end of the opium trance and partly an aggrieved despair over her plight, infuriated the police. She was thrown into a cell without ceremony.

It was a chamber of stone, seven feet by nine, with a single slash barred window in the far wall that looked out on a blank expanse of brick a couple of yards away. The damp floor was strewn with rotted straw and the entire furnishings were a narrow cot with a grubby blanket and a dented pewter chamber pot. A penny candle was stuck onto a crossbar in the narrow door of the cell, but only guards were allowed matches.

When the warder took away the light and disappeared down the long stone passageway, leaving Maggie in the dark, there came whispers from the neighboring cells, low guttural voices demanding her identity and her crime, high cajoling voices that solicited a particular kind of companionship, irrational strident voices that accused her of setting up conspiracies to strangle Irish infants and assassinate the Pope.

151

Alone in the dark cell, Maggie turned and felt out the compass of the walls, frigidly cold and damp. She sat on the edge of the low, vermin-infested cot and removed from her bosom the two packets of luck—a cocaine mixture—that she always carried about with her. Her small bag containing the opium tin and the *yen hock* had been taken from her.

After inhaling the cocaine slowly, she lay upon her back, threw one arm across her face, and listened to the murmuring voices of all the women incarcerated around her. She lay many hours in an untroubled reverie. In the morning she was roused by the guard. Through the metal flap at the bottom of her cell door he pushed a tin tray of cold biscuits swimming in a gelatinous black gravy.

When he returned an hour later to retrieve the untouched tray, the guard told Maggie that she would be arraigned on the following day, in the court of Judge James Stallworth, and ventured his own opinion that she would be very fortunate if she got away with her life.

Maggie made no reply.

A little before noon, several men came to the door of the cell and peered in at her. Among them, Maggie noted the man with hair like fire who had been present at her arrest. She sat demurely on the edge of the cot, quite composed and as neat as she could make herself, but she responded to none of their numerous, increasingly querulous questions. At last, the reporters went away, exclaiming against her silence and demanding of no one in particular that she be forced to talk to them; but their anger could hardly be heard beneath the shrill demands of the other female prisoners, who screamed for assistance, yelled in derision, and shrieked insinuations and invitations so obscene that the reporters stopped to laugh or take up the banter.

When they were gone, Maggie turned a little on her cot so that her back was to the narrow door of the cell and withdrew the second packet of cocaine from her dress.

Her dinner arrived at three o'clock in the afternoon, but this she ignored also. Hope was a commodity Maggie Kizer had entirely given over. She had realized, in the moment of her arrest, that all the slight comforts of her existence that had sustained her in the few years past had melted away and would never be recovered by her. She did not think, "I have been betrayed," and she did not hope, "I shall be rescued." She simply judged that her life was over. At sixteen she had been plunged into a sea of misery and ignominy, and though her head had been raised above those turbulent black waters for a time, she understood that now she was sunk entirely beneath the waves, not to rise again.

If this were her situation, why then there was no reason to eat, no reason to think of escape, no reason to beg for assistance, or mercy or pity; there was no reason to think at all. If Maggie could have devised a way to kill herself at that moment, she would have done so without qualm or hesitation.

Maggie had stared at the blank stone wall at the back of her cell for she knew not how long when she turned, merely for the sake of movement, and saw Daisy Shanks standing at the barred door. The abortionist wore a mauve dress festooned with pink ribbons that was drawn disconcertingly tight across her breast and down her sides. She carried a basket in the crook of her folded arm and grinned at Maggie as if they had just chanced to meet before the mermaid case at Barnum's Museum or strolling upon the beach at Coney Island.

"Daisy!" whispered Maggie Kizer, through parched lips.

The woman blocked the entire narrow doorway of the cell, but suddenly Rob sidled between his mother and the barred door. He stared intently at Maggie, with his little delicate fingers wrapped around the iron bars.

"I've brought your boy to see you, Maggie," laughed Daisy Shanks.

Maggie stared without comprehension.

"Nana says I'm to be your boy so long as you're here," said the child in an earnest whisper.

Maggie looked up at this, a flicker of interest in her eyes.

"I'm your boy," the child repeated, as if it were a lesson that it was important Maggie Kizer learn. "And I've brought you something."

"I don't want food," replied Maggie weakly.

"No food," said Rob.

Daisy Shanks turned her beaming face to the guard at the far end of the corridor while Rob softly lifted the lid of the basket and withdrew a bulky packet done up in yellow paper and yellow string. He pushed it through the panel at the bottom of the door. Maggie automatically reached forward to shove her tin tray of food out of the way.

"It's a lay-out," whispered Rob.

Maggie snatched the package from the floor, nervously untied the string, and found a cheap, but complete lay-out for opium in it, with several dollars of second-grade dope. "Thank you," she breathed.

Rob smiled and said, "Here, keep it hid in this cloth. Also some brandy and sandwiches." He pushed the items through the slot, and Maggie took them gratefully. Daisy watched these transactions with apparent amusement, and though she said nothing, she shielded Rob's actions from the view of the guards.

"Here," said Rob, pulling from his back pocket a folded page of a newspaper, "Nana says you're to read this."

Maggie took the paper, unfolded it, and glanced over it briefly. It was a detailed account of the murder of Cyrus Butterfield, of her part in it, and even of her arrest the previous night. The article was florid and impassioned, but for the most part accurate.

"It was Lady Weale that peached," giggled Daisy.

"Yes," replied Maggie, "I was almost certain. Daisy, tell Lena to send a cart to Bleecker Street and have everything taken away. Mrs. Weale will have already been through everything looking for my jewels, but she won't have found them and she won't have dared to be rid of the furnishings yet. Take everything; even if I'm ever to leave this place, it won't be to return there. You'll find my jewels secreted in closed pockets within the hems of the parlor draperies. Hold them against my release—"

Daisy nodded. "Done today. Maggie, you think harm might come to Lady Weale?" she asked suggestively.

Maggie shook her head. "I don't think it would help me."

"Nana wants to know if we should talk to anybody," said Rob.

"Talk. . . ?"

"Someone who can help you, Maggie," said Daisy.

"Duncan—"

"Front name or back name?" demanded Rob. "Where's he live?"

"I don't know," said Maggie, "Duncan's his Christian name, and that's all I know. I go to court tomorrow. Try to find him for me, I think he may be a lawyer."

Daisy smiled and whispered, "Ma says take care, Ma says don't worry about the jewelry, Ma says you never left anything with her, Ma says that's what she'll say at the trial—"

The guard approached from down the corridor. Daisy Shanks clapped her son on the shoulder and took a step backward. Rob's face immediately changed its expression and character. He suddenly wore the morose aspect of a simpleton. "Oh, ma! Oh, ma!" he bleated, staring through the bars at Maggie. Daisy dragged him out of the way so that the guard might bend and fetch out the untouched tray of food.

"Won't do you no good not to eat," he remarked, " 'cause they'll hang you 'fore you get the 'tunity to starve."

Maggie glared at him and held her hand tight over the packet of opium secreted behind her.

"This her boy?" demanded the guard of Daisy. He glanced critically at Rob, who wrapped his legs around one another in a good imitation of an imbecile.

Daisy Shanks grinned and nodded. "Boy wouldn't bring half a dollar on the open market," she laughed.

"No," agreed the guard, "don't look like he's going to make much of a name for himself as a orphan, does he?"

Rob snuffled and wiped his face energetically against the sleeve of his jacket. The guard walked away, with the remark that they had been there long enough.

Daisy once more moved to the door, filling it, with Rob pushed up against the bars. "Take care" he whispered to Maggie with a wink of his intelligent eye, "we'll be back."

They turned away, and Maggie whispered, "Thank you . . ."

She stood at the door of the cell and watched the strange pair as they moved down the long corridor. Daisy paused at several cells to exchange pleasantries with women she had come across professionally. Rob knocked from one wall to another, poked his bony arms through the barred doors, wept hysterically, and jabbered as if he hadn't an ounce of good sense in his body.

Chapter 21

Early on the evening of February 22, Judge James
Stallworth and Duncan Phair sat alone in the parlor of
the house on Gramercy Park. It was dark and cold
without and the shutters of the parlor, though unclosed,
opened on so black a night that they were as good as
shut. Duncan stood nervously before the fire, fingering a
China ornament on the mantel with such diligence that
the mournful shepherd was in danger of losing, at the
very least, all the blue of his painted pantaloons. For the
most part Duncan avoided the gaze of his father-in-law,
who sat stiffly in an already uncomfortable horsehair
sofa.

"Lightner ought to be reprimanded," said the Judge.
"It is inexcusable that that reporter should print the story
without consulting you. I am incensed, Duncan, and I
wonder that you haven't presented yourself before Lightner and demanded of him an explanation of his reprehensible conduct."

"I'll see him tomorrow. That will be time enough. I
had rather not approach him in anger."

Judge Stallworth glanced at Duncan sharply—his son-
in-law seemed dispirited, unhappy, abstracted. A dozen
different emotional discomforts played across his visage
—but none of them was anger.

"Duncan," said he, "this reporter is attempting to break free of our influence, and we of course shall not allow him to do so. Such an incident must not recur—"

"No."

"—for I see that you are quite broken up over it. . . ." Duncan made no reply.

"Now," continued the judge, "I would suggest that you volunteer your services to the office of the city prosecutor and participate in the state's case against the woman Kizer—"

Duncan's look was so wild and full of horror that Judge Stallworth involuntarily paused.

"Why do you stare so, Duncan? It is not so terrible a thing to take on *one* case without prospect of remuneration, I think. Tell the prosecutor that you were a particular friend of Butterfield—"

"No, Father," interrupted Duncan nervously, who trembled to think how easily his liaison with Maggie might be discovered. "The Democrats will hardly let me share in the glory of this arrest and this conviction. The *Tribune* has been down too hard upon them, and they might actually believe that I volunteered in order to . . . to . . . to get the woman off, and so embarrass them."

"Well," said Judge Stallworth, as he crossed his elegant, bony legs before the fire, "I think then that the least you must do is to attend the trial and write it up for the *Tribune*—don't leave that to Lightner too—show where the Democrats go wrong and so forth. I've sent word to the Tombs that the arraignment is to be tomorrow morning at ten o'clock, so you may be sure to be present. It is not customary for me to act as magistrate, but in this case I think I must. One never knows to what extent the Democrats may bungle, and we certainly have considerable interest in seeing this woman put to trial."

Duncan did not dare refuse his father-in-law, but at the same time that he shortly acquiesced he was attempting to formulate an excuse for his absence from that courtroom. It was imperative that Maggie Kizer not catch sight of him. Ignorant of his surname, she had no way of finding him in the city, could not direct any message to him; and Duncan Phair, despite the real affection with which he had regarded this young unfortunate woman, had determined that they should never, under any circumstances, meet again.

Maggie Kizer was a woman who in normal circumstances would not betray displeasure, or surprise, or even sudden relief by any abrupt movement or alteration of expression; she was too well bred to be easily astonished and too circumspect to show her hand. But who knew what Maggie's reaction might be if, on trial as an accomplice to murder, she were to see Duncan Phair, possibly her only protector, in the courtroom? Surely she would turn and gaze at him with an intensity to draw the wonder of the whole court; surely she would take the opportunity to direct a few words to him. And even if she made no attempt to communicate with him, Maggie would soon learn through discreet questioning of her attendants that her erstwhile paramour was the son-in-law of the judge who would determine her fate.

Duncan Phair could not afford to have it known that he was acquainted with one of the criminals that the *Tribune* had scourged the police department for not being able to find. It was already known in some quarters that Duncan Phair was assisting in the newspaper's investigations and the discovery now that he had visited Bleecker Street in a private capacity would surely discredit the entire scheme, would raise the judge's indomitable ire against him, and would infuriate and humiliate Marian. Just now his ultimate success or failure in life seemed to hinge upon the single question of whether Maggie Kizer ever discovered the surname of the protector she knew only as "Duncan."

Duncan suspected that the judge, much as he loved his daughter, would not be shocked or even particularly displeased to know that Duncan had taken a mistress; and Duncan was not even certain that Marian would be overly distressed herself. But that he had chosen to compromise himself in the bedroom where Cyrus Butterfield had been stabbed to death with an opium needle would be thought to be carrying indiscretion beyond permissible boundaries.

Beyond these fears for his own future, the lawyer was distressed for his mistress's position. There seemed little doubt that she would be indicted, and already James Stallworth had said that the trial, in the interests of publicity, would be a speedy and sharp one—and if the woman was guilty, as she certainly appeared to be, she would be hanged as an accomplice and accessory.

"Hanged?" cried Duncan, "she needn't be hanged, need she, Father? It wasn't she, by the testimony of the landlady, who killed Butterfield?" Duncan had, with wavering vision and clenched teeth, read twice through the article that had appeared in that Sunday morning's *Tribune*; this while locked in his dressing room, that his acute distress might not be viewed by either his wife or the servants. He had been fortunate in being alone when first discovering the dreadful news.

"No," said Judge Stallworth lightly, "but since we don't have the man Kizer—who actually did the killing—we must make do with his accomplice. The wife will stand for the husband. I couldn't let this go by, even if I wanted to—and I certainly don't—for then the Democratic newspapers would come down upon me, saying that the Democrats caught her and the Democrats prosecuted her and a Republican judge let her off. We can hardly lay ourselves open to that sort of charge, Duncan."

"No," said Duncan softly, turning away; ashamed of his own feeling of hope to think that if Maggie were tried, convicted, sentenced, and hanged, he need fear for himself no longer.

Duncan Phair told himself that if Maggie were guilty she deserved the law's punishment, but it was a wrenching difficulty to imagine that fine woman standing on the gallows in a plain blue skirt, having prayers read to her by a greasy priest. And yet there was nothing that he could do to save her, Duncan told himself; his presence might console her a little, his assurances might lessen her fear for an hour; but she would mount the scaffold all the same, and the greasy priest would mumble the same useless prayers. The rope would break the same bones in her graceful neck whether or not he stood beside her in those last moments—so why then destroy his fine crowded future for the sake of a few moments of comfort proffered, perhaps vainly, a dying woman? If Maggie knew his position she would understand and not condemn his reluctant, difficult decision to abandon her.

On the following morning, Duncan sent his father-in-law a message that he was ill in bed; and in bed he remained until shortly after noon, when he received word from Simeon Lightner that Maggie Kizer had been arraigned as an accomplice and accessory in the murder of Cyrus Butterfield. Judge Stallworth had set bail at fifteen thousand dollars, which sum Maggie of course had been unable to raise, and she had been immediately returned to her small stone apartments in the Tombs. Duncan Phair dressed and took the cars down to his offices on Pearl Street.

Chapter 22

❦❦❦❦❦❦❦❦❦❦❦❦❦❦❦❦❦❦❦❦❦❦❦❦❦❦❦❦❦❦❦❦❦❦

ON Thursday afternoon, after Maggie Kizer's arraignment in the morning, Simeon Lightner made his way up to Bleecker Street, there to present Lady Weale with a bank draught for $3,340. The editor of the *Tribune* had authorized the payment—even though Maggie Kizer was not yet convicted—in the interests of publicity.

Simeon was much surprised to find a great cart pulled up before Mrs. Weale's steps, into which three large men of dangerous aspect were loading a substantial amount of fine furniture: chairs, sofas, rolled-up carpets, tables, mirrors, and crates of smaller items. They were not being as careful as they might have been and many pieces were nicked, chipped, stained, or even broken altogether. But what they lacked in delicacy they made up in discretion, and would not answer any of Simeon's inquiries as to who had sent them, by whose authority they were emptying the house, and whither the objects were bound.

Unsatisfied by the three men, who ignored him wholly except once or twice to butt him with the sharp corner of some piece of furniture, Simeon descended the half-dozen steps to Mrs. Weale's kitchen entrance and knocked at her grimy window. Mrs. Weale, stationed just behind the door, motioned him to go away, but when he waved the draught for the reward money before the glass she grudgingly admitted him. Once she had received the draught and signed the receipt for it, she was all for Simeon's removing himself; but Simeon began to question her about the activity outside the house, and persuaded her to ascend out of the kitchen to have a better view of the work in progress.

"Are those the belongings of Madame Kizer?"

"Yes, and everything you see there is mine!" cried Lady Weale. "It's owed me in back rent. It's all owed to me! And half of it was mine anyway, only lent for the duration of her habitude! And they're taking it all away! Taking it all away!"

"Who's taking it away?" said Simeon.

"Don't you see them!"

"Yes," said Simeon, "but where are the things being taken?"

"Don't know, don't know!" moaned Lady Weale. "Everything you see is mine there!" She kicked a dog that was passing on the walk, to send it yelping into the paths of two of the men carrying out Maggie Kizer's bedstead; but one of the men gave the dog another kick, backward, and proceeded without mishap.

"If it's yours, then why don't you have a policeman stop them from doing it? These men, even if they are licensed movers—and I've no reason to suppose that they are, since there's no sign painted upon their cart—have no right to transfer the belongings of a person without her permission."

"They brought a cop with 'em, made me let 'em in, told me to keep out of their way! I went to get another cop, if you see what I mean, but the first cop told him it was all right. It's not all right! Everything you see there is mine and they're carting it away and I'll never see a stick or a shred of it again. Holy Mother of Moses, I'm being robbed!"

While Simeon Lightner comfortably seated himself upon a stone balustrade of the neighboring house, Lady Weale retreated to her kitchen, where she raised the window and tossed out potatoes onto the walk, in hopes of tripping up the three men who were depriving her of Maggie Kizer's belongings. The reporter amused himself then by noting an inventory of the goods that were brought out, and peering over into the cart and making up a list, as best he could, of what had already been loaded. A quarter of an hour later the cart was filled, and two of the men jumped up onto the board.

The third went and stood just above the kitchen window in the cellar of the house, where Mrs. Weale growled at him and hurled another potato.

He caught it, squeezed it to pulp and water in his powerful fist. "We've not done," he said, "so don't try to lock up or we'll just break down the door when we return."

He hopped up beside his compatriots and the two overburdened horses attached to the cart lumbered away.

Traffic on Bleecker Street was heavy and the animals' progress was slow. Simeon sat on the balustrade a few minutes more, then hopped down, tipped his hat to Mrs. Weale who had come out to gather up her potatoes— either for the pot or a repeated assault—and sauntered on after the cart.

"They're going to Houston Street," snapped Lady Weale, and Simeon paused.

"You do know then?"

"No," she said, "not certain, but I'll bet these potatoes they're on their way to Black Lena's."

"What's the number?"

Lady Weale shrugged, and descended the steps to her cellar door.

Simeon considered whether he might not hurry ahead to Houston Street, hunt out Black Lena's, and wait for the cart; but then he considered that Lady Weale might be mistaken, or even deliberately trying to mislead him, and thought it better, on the whole, if he followed the cart at a distance. Piled high with fine furniture, it was distinctive enough a vehicle in that neighborhood that Simeon had no difficulty in keeping it in view from a distance. He did not want to risk the ire of the men driving if they discovered that he were dogging their tracks. So in this easy but discreet fashion, Simeon Lightner followed Maggie Kizer's belongings from Bleecker to West Houston Street and watched, from a little distance, as everything was carried into the shop at number 201.

The next evening, Duncan Phair and Judge James Stallworth dined at the Republican lawyers' club on

Seventeenth Street, and the judge said to his son-in-law: "Well, I hope that you're relieved of your indisposition, Duncan. I can't tell you how disappointed I was that you were unable to attend the arraignment yesterday."

"Oh yes," replied Duncan nervously, "I'm much better now, almost my old self."

"I didn't like seeing Lightner there alone, but I must say that it looks as if he may at last have done us a piece of very good business."

"What's that?" asked Duncan curiously.

"Surely you read the *Tribune* this morning."

Duncan nodded. Simeon had reported on the removal of all the accused woman's belongings from Lady Weale's house to Black Lena Shanks's pawnshop on West Houston Street. He had noted that Black Lena Shanks, "a notorious and long-standing receiver of stolen property whose transactions are almost exclusively with the female element of the criminal population," was the sister of Alick Kizer, the actual murderer of Cyrus Butterfield. He had gone on to describe the rest of the Shanks's ménage: the elder, hard-visaged mute sister who was an adept at paper mischiefs—forgery; the younger pretty sister, who was one of the best-known abortionists in the city; and the two children, identical twins who—raised in such surroundings—could not help but be vicious themselves.

"Yes," said Duncan, "but I don't know how Simeon's account can help us. I saw him today, congratulated him upon a fine piece of research. He had talked to neighbors, talked to Mrs. Weale again, talked to the police. The old woman herself, Black Lena Shanks, chased him out of her shop, but at least he got a glimpse of the whole family. I congratulated him, because it would have been worse than useless to upbraid him for doing these things without my assistance. But how does the account help us?"

"Don't you see, Duncan? It's the family that we wanted, the family of criminals that I postulated at the beginning of this entire affair. I'm just surprised we haven't turned up another before this. We wanted to find out a family mired in vice, raised in criminality, and here at last they are: doubly vicious because they're all female, doubly vicious because they run the race of so many criminal activities: if we include Maggie Kizer, we have a murderer, prostitute, fence, forger, abortionist—and we can always accuse the children of thievery. Everything but blackmail and kidnapping, in fact."

"Yes . . ." said Duncan doubtfully. "And where does that leave us—and them?"

"Oh it's simple," said Judge Stallworth. "We merely have to bear down upon them now. Everything's already set up for it. One of them has absconded, and one in jail already. Alick Kizer is probably at the end of the earth by now, and there doesn't seem to be much possibility of bringing him back, so it might behoove us to implant a rumor that he's dead, killed in an attempt to rob a bank or some such, so that we can have him out of the way. Maggie Kizer's in jail, and I'll make certain—well, I'll take care of that. Her trial will be played up high enough in the papers without our having to prod. And as soon as that's done we'll start in on the others. As a plan, Duncan, it's faultless."

Duncan nodded silent agreement with his father-in-law's estimation.

"Now," said Judge Stallworth, "I did a little research of my own this afternoon, through my own files. Lena Shanks came up before me in 1865—the name had sounded familiar, I was sure of it, when I read it this morning—and I put her on the island for a number of years. The two girls, grown now of course, were made wards of the court, but were taken away directly after the trial and kept hidden. Lena's husband was hanged in the Incendiary Plot, which was before your time, but it was the first important trial that came under me and I recall it vividly—it was just after I was elevated to the bench. So I have all these records, and you should send Lightner over to me tomorrow and he and I'll talk of this."

"The *Tribune* of course will have its own files as well; for surely the trials were covered," said Duncan. Though he did not relish this plan at all, he felt that some contribution was wanted, lest his father-in-law become suspicious of his implied recalcitrance.

"Yes," said Judge Stallworth, smiling, "exactly. For twenty years now, this family has swum beneath the notice of the police and the courts. A calculating, intelligent woman Lena Shanks must be, to have kept out of sight for so long, building herself up, building up her business with all those women. And all to be cut down because her brother picked up an opium needle off his wife's dresser."

Duncan trembled, but the judge only smiled. "We'll have everything in readiness. As soon as Maggie Kizer's out of the way, we'll take up another of 'em, and so on until the entire family is ground down into the dust of the Black Triangle."

"Oh yes," echoed Duncan Phair, "into the dust."

Chapter 23

こそこそこそこそこそこそこそこそこそこそこそこそこそこそこそこそこそこそ

MAGGIE's trial was set for March 6, ten days after her arraignment; Judge Stallworth considered that this would be ample time for Simeon Lightner and his son-in-law to blazon the case in the *Tribune*, but not so long a delay that the public would grow restive. But the judge was vexed that Duncan, always with one excuse or another, would not come near the Tombs while the murderess—or accomplice to murder—lay incarcerated there.

During this unhappy interval Simeon Lightner, who was frequently at the prison, daily provided details to the readers of the *Tribune* of Maggie Kizer's conduct, appearance, and unsociable habits: how she refused to speak to reporters, to priests, to warders, to anyone in fact but a little boy who visited her twice a day with a small basket over his arm. The boy, evidently a simpleton, came from no one knew where, replied to no interrogatory with anything like sensible speech, and seemed to vanish as soon as he stepped out between the fat Egyptian columns of the Tombs. At first it had been assumed that this was Maggie's own child, but Simeon Lightner provided the news that it was rather her nephew, by name, Rob Shanks, resident on West Houston Street.

Early on the Monday morning set for Maggie's trial,

168

Duncan Phair visited Judge Stallworth in his chambers in the Criminal Courts Building, the enormous red brick and terra-cotta structure adjoining the Tombs. The judge's office was an unhappy sort of dark room far removed from his court—the fine apartments were distributed among the Democrats, while the few Republican judges and officials were relegated to the higher floors, to the noisy corridors, to the single-windowed or leaky chambers.

Duncan told his father-in-law that important business necessitated his spending the morning in City Hall. He would be unable to attend the proceedings against Maggie Kizer.

"Why can't Peerce take care of it?" demanded the judge. "That's why you took him into partnership, to handle such matters."

"George has developed a stomach catarrh, Father. It really is necessary that this business be conducted today."

"This trial won't take so much of your time," said Judge Stallworth, obviously displeased with Duncan, "I don't understand why you must rush off."

"Peerce left some very important business undone that must be attended to at once," replied Duncan lamely, and when his father-in-law's silence seemed to demand a better excuse, Duncan went on: ". . . contracts that want the signatures of all the Aldermen, and it's rare enough we can get them all in the city at once, much less in the same room. . . ."

Judge Stallworth eyed his daughter's husband intently. "I don't believe you," he said evenly.

Duncan looked away in confusion.

"You've been deliberately avoiding this place since that woman was arrested. You've refused to have anything to do with this entire business, even though I have pointed out to you time and again the necessity of our being in control of it. Now I'm weary of your excuses and I demand to know why you prevaricate with me. Tell me quickly," he said, adjusting his robes, "for I'm due in the court in a quarter of an hour."

Duncan Phair knew that his lies had only been tolerated by his father-in-law; there was no real deceiving of the old man. For a time, Judge Stallworth had accepted the false excuses, but now his policy was altered, and Duncan had no choice but to submit with the truth.

"Cyrus Butterfield was a lawyer—" began Duncan.

"That is hardly news," said Judge Stallworth.

"But he was not the only lawyer who had the acquaintance of Maggie Kizer."

"Ah," said Judge Stallworth coldly, "she had a weakness for the profession then."

"It was coincidence, I believe. The lawyers were not acquainted with one another—at least not in their identity as . . . as *intimates* of Maggie Kizer."

"And the other lawyer," said Judge Stallworth, with a bitter smile, "was some friend of yours."

"Yes."

"Was a close friend. A very close friend, perhaps. Was yourself, perhaps."

"Yes," replied Duncan.

"For what period of time did the murderess enjoy your acquaintance, Duncan?"

"Eighteen months—about that."

"It has been a fond—a merry acquaintance?"

"Quiet, discreet. She is a remarkable woman."

Judge Stallworth repeated his son-in-law's words, without expression. " 'Quiet, discreet. She is a remarkable woman.' "

Duncan Phair shifted uncomfortably in his chair. "Maggie doesn't know who I am," said Duncan. "That is to say she knows only my first name. She does not know that I am a lawyer—she certainly does not know that I am in any way involved with her prosecution, through you, I mean. She knows only that . . . that I have deserted her."

Judge Stallworth said nothing, and Duncan, however distressed by this forced revelation, had to continue: "Otherwise she would surely have sent word to me. That is why I have so studiously avoided coming near this place. It would have been disastrous if she saw me by chance."

The judge regarded him balefully. "I'm so pleased," he remarked scornfully, "that you have seen fit to honor me with this confession. If all is not yet lost, it's not for your want of blundering. In the first place, Duncan, it is axiomatic that a respectable man should take as his mistress a respectable woman."

"Maggie is above all—"

"Respectable women do not have husbands in Sing

Sing. Respectable women are not addicted to opium. Maggie Kizer may be cheerful, well-mannered, knowledgeable on a hundred subjects; she may execute excellent Berlin-work and possess a fine hand—but she is not, finally, respectable."

"No," Duncan acquiesced.

"Leave," said the judge curtly, "leave this building immediately. The woman will be brought over from the Tombs in a very few minutes. The landlady has been called as a witness and will be arrive shortly. I take it you are known to her as well. It is imperative that you be seen by neither. Therefore, leave." James Stallworth stood, and Duncan, without another word, slipped out of the judge's chambers.

In the corridor outside, Duncan Phair glanced through a grimy window at the incongruous "Bridge of Sighs"—elegant replica of the famous Venetian span—that connected the stolid Criminal Courts Building with the dismal Tombs. At that moment Maggie Kizer was being led across it by two guards. Her erect figure, elegant carriage, and handsome distinguished face seemed very much in keeping with the delicate stone tracery of that unhappy bridge, over which the most dangerous and degenerate criminals of the city had passed; but in contrast, the men that accompanied her were stooped and beetle-browed Hibernians. In another moment, that criminal queen and her cretinous attendants would step through into the same hallway in which Duncan now found himself.

Duncan allowed himself a few seconds to gaze on Maggie Kizer—he knew that it would be the last time that he would ever see her—before he hid himself behind a square column. Maggie would be escorted down a side staircase and introduced into a small airless room behind Judge Stallworth's court where, on a hard wooden bench, she would wait with the other murderers, thieves, and "victims of 'ficial delinquency" whose trials were scheduled for that day.

He waited a few moments to give Maggie and her guards time to descend out of sight; and in that time Judge Stallworth emerged from his chambers. He saw Duncan standing there, leaning against the peeling column, but his glance might have fallen with as little concern and pity upon a scrofulous beggar in the street.

Judge Stallworth's courtroom was the most modestly appointed of the half-dozen within the Criminal Courts Building. It was small, with polished oak furnishings and tall narrow windows looking out on a blank wall of the Tombs. Whitewashed walls were adorned with darkened portraits of men no one could identify.

A quarter of an hour before the court was called, there was much activity in the room. Clerks and minions were setting up for the day's business, three Negroes were washing the floor of the jury box, which was heavily stained with tobacco juice, while the jury impaneled for the week stood about making introductions and exchanging jokes at the expense of every nationality but the Irish. Lawyers talked among themselves and cast sidewise glances at the jurors.

The reporters who were present because of Maggie Kizer talked of circulation and pay and perks and the notorious injustice of editors, while the newspaper artists drew caricatures of the reporters, the lawyers, the jurors, the minions, and one another.

There was a small crowd of idle spectators—those who had come not for gain, or because compelled by law, but only because of their interest in seeing the female dope fiend who was responsible for the death of a man the newspapers called "one of the city's most beloved and respected citizens, as well as one of its foremost legal minds."

Trials in the Criminal Courts Building, and especially those over which Judge James Stallworth presided were known to be speedy affairs, and even cases of the utmost complexity were rarely carried into a second day. Certainly none of the lawyers or reporters had any thought that Maggie Kizer would be cleared of the charges against her. Judge Stallworth was not known for leniency in his treatment of defendants, either in the course of a trial or in sentencing, and the reporters and lawyers were apprised of what was not commonly known: that the judge's son-in-law had assisted the *Tribune* in its exploitation of this crime. The woman had not a chance.

"Well," said one cynic, deliberately within hearing of Simeon Lightner, "it just about amounts to conflict of interest, if you ask me what I think about it. Old man ought to withdraw from the case."

"Won't, though," replied another, and glanced slyly at Simeon, "too good a case, *Tribune*'ll make fine copy of all this. Old Stallworth would probably lead her up to the gallows himself if he wasn't 'fraid of tripping on his own gown."

Simeon, who had no love for Judge Stallworth and suspected his son-in-law's disinterestedness, did not see fit to object to these snide remarks. His interest in this trial was great, but he doubted· whether it would be so cut-and-dried as the other reporters evidently considered it. In the first place, Simeon had been present at the arrest of Maggie Kizer, and knew her for no common prostitute. She would prove a more troublesome defendant that some doltish painted trollop from Hudson Street. Also, her beauty was much in her favor, and juries, despite overwhelming evidence, despite the exhortations of ireful judges, had been known to acquit certain women of outstanding physical attractions.

Simeon's attention was drawn to the entrance into the courtroom of Black Lena Shanks and her granddaughter —Simeon recognized the plainly dressed child as the twin of the boy who visited Maggie Kizer in prison each day. Lena wore a tight black jacket and a red and black plaid skirt. She walked slowly and with the aid of a silver-tipped cane. They moved into the row of seats just behind Simeon. He turned a little to study them.

It was Ella who most drew his attention. She sat perfectly still and composed, though her eyes darted everywhere, and more than once caught and held his gaze. The child was unlike any offspring of the lower classes that Simeon had ever come across. Those young Tartars were pawing, mischievous, braying, grimy devils; but though this young girl might well be a devil, she was so well behaved as to seem, at first sight, coyly demure.

Simeon plucked his tablets from his pocket and read through the notes that he had collected on the Shanks family. Some of what he had learned about the family was too dreadful to appear in the *Tribune*. He looked around and stared at the fat woman on the row behind him; examined her thin black hair, her black beetling brow, her lusterless black eyes, and concluded that he had much rather be closeted with three knife-wielding prostitutes than with an unarmed Lena Shanks.

The clerk of the court announced the entrance of the judge. All the court stood, and Simeon watched as Black Lena Shanks rose tardily and with seeming reluctance, bearing down upon her cane for support. The little girl, standing beside her grandmother, turned, smiled slyly at Simeon, and tugged at her side curls in a suggestive but uninterpretable fashion.

Chapter 24

〰〰〰〰〰〰〰〰〰〰〰〰〰〰〰〰〰〰〰〰〰〰〰〰〰

JUDGE James Stallworth cast his chilling blue gaze over the courtroom, waved the clerk of the court into silence, and seated himself without ado behind the bench. He closed his eyes and waited patiently for all the machinery that was to grind Maggie Kizer into the dust to start itself up.

Before, her conviction had been a thing that was merely of service to the Stallworth family, but now it had become a matter of necessity. Judge Stallworth did not look at the defendant, he remembered her well enough from the arraignment. He had no further curiosity for the woman who had so charmed his son-in-law, and no compunction either.

The case was announced, the prosecution rose on its bandy legs and declared that the state was ready to prove that Maggie Kizer had been an accessory to the crime that had deprived an unexceptionable citizen of his invaluable life. During this brief perfunctory harangue, Maggie Kizer sat immobile and expressionless beside her state-appointed attorney.

Rather than this speech, the jury had made Maggie Kizer its study—a process accompanied by some few whispers, giggles, low-voiced observations, and eyerollings; which all amounted to a cautious solicitude on account of her beauty and bearing.

The judge, seeing that the jury was inattendant to the prosecutor's speech, urged him on sarcastically: "Yes, yes, the man is quite dead, and we are all inconsolable mourners of his inestimable soul."

The defense attorney, whose only conference with his client had been conducted in a little corridor outside the courtroom during the quarter hour prior to their being called inside, stated simply that his client had had nothing to do with the terrible crime, that she was an upstanding if unfortunately circumstanced citizeness of the city, that she ought indeed to be compassionated for having been forced to witness so foul a deed as that one unquestionably committed by the foul escapee from Sing Sing. She had barely escaped with her own breath intact within her precious lungs; she had labored under the infamous calumnies of the disreputable landlady who was doubtless in league with the escaped criminal; and no one could look at her sitting beside him, so innocent, so well-mannered, so soft-spoken, and imagine that she had ever lifted a violent finger in the course of her brief and unblissful existence.

"Doubtless you have judged her character aright," remarked Judge Stallworth, "but it is time for the prosecution's first witness to be called."

A policeman with a wall eye came to the stand, gave his name, address, history of employment within the police department; described how it came to be that he was acquainted with the deceased Cyrus Butterfield; and provided a minute and colorful description of his coming across the body, wedged naked between two barrels of salted cod in an alley off West and Leroy streets on New Year's Day.

The defense attorney asked no questions of the witness.

A pockmarked young man from the city morgue at Bellevue Hospital nervously testified that Cyrus Butterfield had died of the blow of some sharp instrument to the breast which, piercing deep, had punctured the heart. Other bruises and marks on his body had probably been inflicted after death.

While the nervous young man from the morgue remained on the stand, the report of the coroner's jury—

providing no additional information of importance—was entered into evidence.

Next, Lady Weale was called to the stand. That lady, whose testimony and manner of speech had been recorded at length in the *Tribune* by Simeon Lightner, was regarded with some curiosity by the spectators in the courtroom.

She seated herself in the witness chair nervously, and glanced at Lena Shanks with some apprehension. Lena Shanks glared stonily back. All eyes in the courtroom—except those of Maggie Kizer—had turned on the woman who, with agitation, tugged at the corners of her yellow kerchief that were tied beneath her chin.

Lady Weale repeated everything that she had told Simeon Lightner in the chophouse. The recitation was halting, laden with detail that was mostly made up and tended toward the elevation of her own part and motives in the proceedings. Someone had explained to Lady Weale that she had come off badly in the *Tribune* article, and she now thought to employ the trial as a forum in which to whitewash her smudged reputation. She frequently slipped from the point, did much indicating toward Maggie Kizer (who rather to Lady Weale's relief had kept on her dark spectacles and never looked up from her folded hands upon the table), and leveled spurious charges against Simeon Lightner, such as that he had threatened her, first with a knife, and then with amorous advances. She even hinted darkly that the reporter himself had been involved in the murder of Cyrus Butterfield.

The court—judge, prosecution, and defense alike—was wearied by the half-prevaricated circumstantiality of Lady Weale's testimony, but the jury were vastly amused. They whispered among themselves, chuckled, and laughed outright.

"Yes, Mrs. Weale," said the prosecutor, interrupting a description of a party of streetwalkers who had tumbled against her on West Street when she was watching Maggie Kizer's husband supporting the dead lawyer across the way, "and what did you do then?"

"Hurried back to Bleecker. Nothing more for me to do then, if you see what I mean?"

"And what did you find there?"

"Nothing. What should I be finding?"

"Well, surely you saw Mrs. Kizer again, surely you spoke with her. Between you, you had just relieved yourselves of a very embarrassing item, to wit, the corpse of a respectable gentleman who had been murdered in the rooms of your house!"

"Spoke to her, sure."

"And what did she say? What did Mrs. Kizer say upon your return?"

"Said, 'Did Alick get rid of him?' And I said yes. And she said, 'Good,' and then she said, 'Good-night, Mrs. Weale.' What should she be saying?"

"What indeed? But she seemed—in your perspicacious opinion, Mrs. Weale—not distraught, not upset, not grief-stricken, not conscience-struck, not burdened with the guiltiness of the evening's horrible entertainment?"

"We took the lamp and moved it over the carpet to see if there was blood anywhere, and there didn't appear to be, so we went to bed. Maggie came down to lock the doors herself—didn't want Alick coming back in again."

"And you went to sleep then, slept sound, as if nothing had happened. A man was murdered in the room above your bedchamber, perhaps above the very spot where you slept. For all you knew his blood might be dripping down upon you in your slumber, Mrs. Weale. Do you mean to—"

"No blood, I'm saying!"

"What happened the next day?"

"After the excitement, I was sleeping late. Maggie sent me for the papers, and she read 'em to see if there was mention of Mr. Butterfield and there wasn't. It was New Year's, and so many men on the streets that she didn't venture out, but that evening went down to get money for the jewelry she had taken from Mr. Butterfield."

"Where did she go to do this?"

"Houston Street. Black Lena's."

Lady Weale pointed out Lena Shanks in the back of the court. Judge Stallworth peered over the edge of the bench, closely examined the fat woman with the greasy hair, and then glanced away. Maggie Kizer, not realizing before that her sister-in-law was present, turned and nodded to Lena. Ella smiled at Maggie, as if returning that greeting for her grandmother—whose eyes remained fixed on the gaunt man behind the judge's bench.

"And 'Black Lena' gave her money?"

"Yes," replied Lady Weale, "good money. All Maggie's business in that line was done with Black Lena. Black Lena," said Lady Weale, wanting to mollify the old woman for having brought in her name, "was always good to Maggie. Black Lena gives the best returns in the city, I'm told. And besides all that, Alick Kizer is Black Lena's brother."

After the conclusion of the prosecution's examination of Lady Weale, the defense attorney returned to Lady Weale's relation of the murder of Cyrus Butterfield, in the first hour of the new year.

"Did Maggie Kizer say a single word, did she make a single movement, which might have suggested that she wished any harm to come to Cyrus Butterfield?"

"No," said Lady Weale, " 'Course not. Maggie was good to her gentlemen, didn't wish any of 'em harm. Furious when Alick stabbed him, if you see what I mean. Even said to me she wished it was Alick that had been killed instead of Mr. Butterfield."

"So," continued the defense, "in your opinion—and you were there, were you not, Mrs. Weale?—Maggie Kizer had nothing at all to do with the death of Cyrus Butterfield."

"No," said Lady Weale, " 'course not, 'cept that she was the reason he was there in the first place."

The prosecution objected to this last question and Lady Weale's reply to it, and Judge Stallworth struck them from the record.

Brought up in this, the defense attorney then asked a number of garbled questions concerning Lady Weale's antecedents, her housekeeping practices; wanted to know why she had done nothing to stop the murder (she had feared for her own life, she said), asked for a history of her acquaintance with the defendant, and at the end, asked, "Mrs. Weale, have you any substantial charge, any charge at all in fact, to bring against the character of the defendant who, by your own admission, never treated you but with a kindness and respect that—for all the court knows—may have been beyond your deserving?"

"No," replied Lady Weale solemnly, "I can't say a

word against her. She was the best-behaved, most politest, well-mannered lady I have ever come across, even if she was an octoroon. She never—"

The remainder of Lady Weale's adulatory speech was drowned by the clamor that attended this wholly unexpected revelation. The prosecutor grinned, the defense attorney dropped into his chair, the judge closed his blue eyes in ironic solemnity, but their reactions were the only silent ones. The reporters mumbled to one another their delight at this exciting piece of dramatic discovery, the artists called for better views of the defendant, the spectators talked loudly of their astonishment and their previous suspicions, and the jury murmured hotly among themselves.

When at last the judge succeeded in quieting the courtroom, the defense attorney, with the air of a man defeated, asked Lady Weale: "You are certain of this imputation? You have proof of Mrs. Kizer's mixed parentage? Did she tell you this herself for instance?"

"No," said Lady Weale, "she didn't know I knew. Alick told me when he first brought her to live on Bleecker Street."

"What exactly did this convicted felon tell you, Mrs. Weale?"

"That Maggie was an octoroon. That she had a black line beneath the thumbnail that proved it, so she always wore gloves." Mrs. Weale pointed to Maggie's folded gloved hands upon the oaken table. "And she had a fleck of black in her eyes, so she always wore dark spectacles."

Maggie raised her head and a reflection of the courtroom flashed in the amber glass of her spectacles.

"But," said the defense attorney nervously, wishing to high heaven he had never addressed a single word to this woman, "you had no confirmation of these *unjust,* doubtlessly *false* imputations from Mrs. Kizer herself?"

"No," replied Lady Weale, "never talked of it. Maggie Kizer was a prince of tenants, except of course for the murder, and that wasn't her doing. She—"

"Thank you, Mrs. Weale," said the defense attorney, and seated himself.

The prosecutor considered that he had no need to belabor Mrs. Weale's testimony; its effect would not be dissipated by anything the defense attorney could allege or suggest, and so he signified that he had no further questions of the witness.

After Lady Weale had stepped down the prosecution called Lena Shanks to the stand. He had not proposed this before, but seeing that the lady was in the courtroom already he did not think that corroborative testimony could do any harm; and it was surely a mark against the defendant that she had sold the dead man's jewelry.

Lena Shanks was sworn in, but it was immediately apparent that her English was poor and that questions posed to her would have to be simpler than those which had been put to Lady Weale.

Lena Shanks stood in the witness box to the left of the judge's bench, but her head was turned slightly, and she kept Judge Stallworth within her baleful sight all the time that she testified.

The jury made audible facetious comments on her appearance in general and her massive girth in particular. The foreman voiced the opinion that it wasn't a witness in the box, but a ton of coal that had been delivered to the courtroom by mistake.

"Your name?" demanded the prosecutor.

"Lena Shanks."

"Address?"

"201 West Houston Street."

"You own a shop we believe."

She nodded, and was asked to answer the question aloud.

"*Ja.*"

"What kind of shop?"

"Pawnshop."

"What is your shop called?"

Lena made no answer.

"What is your shop called?" the prosecutor asked again.

"No name. People come to Black Lena."

"Did Maggie Kizer come to you on the night of January first?"

"*Ja.*"

"And did she tell you that your brother, her husband, had just brutally murdered the lawyer Cyrus Butterfield?"

"*Nein.*"

"She said nothing of the death of Cyrus Butterfield?"

"Nein."

"Did she inform you that your brother, Alick Kizer, had escaped from prison and come to her?"

"Nein."

"When did you last see your brother, Mrs. Shanks?"

" '78."

"Well," said the prosecutor, "when Maggie Kizer came to you on New Year's night, did she sell you—beg pardon, *pawn* with you—some men's jewelry, which included several gold rings, a gold watch and chain, and several pieces of sapphire jewelry?"

"Nein."

"No?"

"Nein. Maggie came, and I owed her money. Paid her and she went away."

"You owed her money?"

"Ja."

"How much money?"

"Three hundred dollars."

"Why? Under what circumstances had Maggie Kizer lent you money, when rather it is *your* business to lend money?"

"Lent my daughter Daisy money when my daughter Daisy needed it."

The prosecutor, in some consternation, turned the witness over to the defense, who smirking for the unexpected good fortune, repeated: "Maggie Kizer then brought you no jewelry of any sort, neither man's jewelry, nor a woman's jewelry, nor rings with sapphires in them, nor rings without sapphires in them, nor gold watches, nor watches made of quartz, nor watches made of any mineral whatsoever—is that correct?"

"No jewels," said Black Lena, and stared at Judge Stallworth.

"Madam," said the Judge severely, "I must warn you that if you are perjuring yourself in this matter, you will be treated with the utmost severity by the law. There is nothing to be gained by an attempt at protecting this woman. The police will search your premises, and if you are found with anything that remotely resembles the jewelry that was worn by Cyrus Butterfield on the night he was murdered, you will answer for it with your freedom. You will repent of your perjury on an extended visit to one of the islands situated in the East River."

"No jewelry," repeated Lena, for the first time with a sly smile on her face. She turned slowly away from Judge Stallworth, and was dismissed by both attorneys.

This completed the prosecution's case. The only witness called for the defense was Maggie Kizer herself, who approached the stand with a hesitant gait. There, the judge asked that she remove her spectacles, and she did so with a trembling hand. All the courtroom leaned forward to catch the black fleck in her green eye. Maggie Kizer turned a blank face on the jury. She seemed unaware of the intensity of the attention she commanded.

Her attorney asked her to state what had happened on the night of December 31, and in halting but melodious speech, Maggie Kizer told the story of that night, often wandering from the narrative or trailing off altogether, so that she had to be gently prompted. Her tale, if incoherent at times, or beside the point, still left a better impression than could have been expected, for she spoke of Cyrus Butterfield with respect and some affection, spoke with indignation of the intrusion of the escaped convict and described how she had been powerless to stop the altercation that had developed between the two men.

At this point the attorney for the defense thought it best to have his client leave off, and he thanked her. Maggie unfolded her spectacles again, and was raising them to her face, when her motion was interrupted by the prosecutor: "Oh, if I might have a few words, Mrs. Kizer, before you withdraw from the box—just a few words."

Maggie lowered the spectacles and her eye trailed listlessly to the bandy-legged prosecutor. "Yes," she said slowly, "I will answer your questions, sir."

"Your speech was finely wrought, Mrs. Kizer, may I say, and showed you an evilly circumstanced victim, or perhaps, considering your profession, I should say, an evilly circumstanced victimizer. You have nowhere denied, have you, that you get your living by the prostitution of your body, have you? That for you, 'bed' and 'board' are one and the same thing?"

"I am, sir, as you have yourself said, evilly circumstanced. I am an object of charity, and dependent upon the good offices of others for my sustenance."

"And Mr. Butterfield was a kind Christian man who provided you with such sustenance out of the generosity of his heart?"

"Yes, Mr. Butterfield was a good man, as you have said, unexceptionable I think is the word you employed."

Maggie's speech faltered a little, and fell sometimes to an inarticulate softness. Her eyes seemed unable to maintain their focus upon any object or person.

"And you, in your gratitude, accorded Mr. Butterfield certain favors,"

"Sir," said Maggie wearily, "I have not denied that when the convict entered my rooms, unannounced and through violence to the locks on my doors, Mr. Butterfield was lying in my bed in a state of extreme dishabille."

"Yes," said the lawyer, a little abashed, "thank you for that admission again. We will all do well to remember it. You have declared yourself distraught that Mr. Butterfield was murdered—"

"Certainly," replied Maggie, "my regard for Mr. Butterfield was very high."

"—and yet you did not hesitate to relieve yourself of his corpse, you did not hesitate to protect the murderer of this inestimable lawyer, you did not hesitate to deny Mr. Cyrus Butterfield—whom you held in such high regard —to deny him the small comfort of a Christian burial?"

"No," replied Maggie Kizer without hesitation, "I did not. Cyrus Butterfield, much as I had esteemed him, was past my help or comfort. At that time, I became more concerned with my own safety and wished only to protect myself. I was grieved, but I was not foolish."

Her lawyer rose to protest against these damaging admissions of his client, but Judge Stallworth waved him down.

Maggie Kizer was far away from that court in her mind and she heard the prosecutor's questions directed at her as from a great distance. She answered with a throat and tongue that seemed to have understanding and purpose of their own. Only her eyes belonged to the being that was ineluctably herself, and with them she observed everything and everyone with equal disinterestedness. It never occurred to her all the while that she was on the witness stand, all the while that she testified in her own defense, that these words that came out of her own fair throat might bear upon the outcome of her case, or supposing that to be predetermined, the severity of her sentencing. And in one matter only had she deviated from the truth; Cyrus Butterfield's jewelry, she said, had been thrown into the river for fear of its being traced, and the money that she had sent to the convict in Washington had been gold that was freely repaid to her by Lena Shanks. Her sister-in-law, Maggie maintained, had been in no manner involved in the death of Cyrus Butterfield, the flight of Alick Kizer, or the secretion of the dead man's jewelry.

"And lastly," said the prosecutor with a smile, "Mrs. Kizer, are you—as Mrs. Weale has averred—a woman of mixed blood? In short, are you an octoroon?"

"I am," said Maggie Kizer without emotion, and she was allowed to leave the witness box.

The prosecutor cajoled the jury, and the defense attorney wooed it; Judge Stallworth addressed it in his most pleasant, least sarcastic voice. The twelve men, who at first had been swayed by Maggie's beauty and her apparent honesty and inculpability in the crime, had been disaffected by the discovery of her mixed blood. After three minutes of deliberation, carried on in whispers in the jury box itself while the rest of the court tried in vain to hear what they said to one another, Maggie Kizer was convicted as an accessory and accomplice to the murder of Cyrus Butterfield.

Chapter 25

JUDGE James Stallworth postponed the sentencing of Maggie Kizer for one week, until March 13, not because he was in any doubt as to what lawful penalty he would impose upon the octoroon for her crime, but so that Simeon Lightner might make the most of her conviction.

The *Tribune* provided a *verbatim* transcript of the trial on Tuesday morning. On Wednesday, a long piece appeared about Lady Weale, her antecedents, her history, and her character. Simeon Lightner pointed out that this sour woman was almost as reprehensible a factor in the murder of Cyrus Butterfield as Maggie Kizer had been. She had been present in the next room at the moment that the lawyer was murdered, she had helped to dispose of the body, she had not come forward with her information until more than a month had passed—the *Tribune* inferred that the reward money was then her sole motive for betraying Maggie Kizer to the authorities.

On Wednesday afternoon, to the reporter of the *Sun*, Lady Weale retorted with a garbled story of how she had been threatened with death if she told anything of what had happened on New Year's Eve. It was the dictates of conscience that had *forced* her, in the end, to tell her tale, no matter then the promised injury to her person.

186

On Thursday morning, the *Tribune* reported that Lady Weale had left New York, for parts unknown. The man who owned the house on Bleecker Street said that Lady Weale had been fearful for her life, having seen the Shanks twins loitering about before her house at late hours of the night. She had had no intention of presenting an easy mark for Lena Shanks's revenge.

In the same paper, Simeon Lightner prepared a long essay on the methods employed by Lena Shanks in her pawnbroking business, as it was charitably called, which concluded with a list of her customers who were in jail, or had been in jail, or who were now sought by the police for various felonies. It occupied three columns and a half.

On Friday morning there was a suggestive, though not really detailed, description of Daisy Shanks's business on the fourth floor of number 203 West Houston Street. Simeon's imagination was assisted by the memory of a shoplifter whose cell was next to Maggie Kizer's in the Tombs. She had availed herself of Daisy's services twice in the past three years, but after the second essay had been laid up for two weeks with an infection. Simeon Lightner suggested that many young women never recovered at all from the ministrations of the "Laughing Abortionist."

About Louisa Shanks, Rob, and Ella, he had little to say, though he inferred that none of them was up to any good. He gave descriptions of the aunt, the nephew, and the niece, and added what little gossip about them had been gleaned from their near neighbors who were susceptible to meager bribes.

On Saturday morning, the door to Lena's shop, number 201, was not opened at all. Ella hung about on the stoop all day, reading through the Testament that Helen Stallworth had meant for Charlotta Kegoe, and told all who approached that Lena Shanks had left off doing business for the time being. When asked when the operation would resume, Ella shook her curls and said, "When we can, when we can."

A lady in distress who applied at the next door down was also turned away, but when she wandered aside, Rob surreptitiously approached her, led her around the corner, and took her into the house by the back way. Daisy explained this subterfuge: "With the papers going

at it like they are, Ma can't keep her shop open, and I
have to pretend to turn my ladies away—all to take care
against the cops, you know. Those who would have
come to Ma may go elsewhere, but you, and my other
ladies, where would you go? To a butcher with knitting
needles! To a doctor with no more feeling in him than a
carved stiff!"

On Monday morning, the day set for Maggie's sentencing, Simeon Lightner noted in the *Tribune* that Lena
Shanks's shop had been closed on Saturday and Sunday
both, that Daisy Shanks had left off practicing her
abortions; he expressed the hope that these two women,
through publicity, had been permanently stopped in their
dangerous and criminal careers.

To this, Duncan Phair appended a criminal history of
the Shanks family: providing brief *précis* of the trials of
Cornelius Shanks, Lena Shanks, and Alick Kizer. Maggie
Kizer was not the first of this family to be charged with
murder. It was to be hoped that the other two now, the
maleficent daughters Louisa and Daisy, would be brought
before the law for their infamous crimes in the Black
Triangle. Mulberry Street had begun to gather its evidence against Lena; her shop was shut up, and it was
only a matter of time before she was imprisoned on the
Island. The twins, if not already mired in corruption,
ought to be separated, from their family and from one
another, and carried out west to Minnesota or Wisconsin,
where sturdy young children were wanted for farm in-
dentures. The Shanks clan, by their viciousness, cried out
to be broken and scattered.

This was the first of the lawyer's articles to be signed
not with a pseudonym, but with his true name, Duncan
Phair.

"Margaret Kizer," said Judge James Stallworth on
Monday morning, March 13, "you stand before me condemned of the crime of accessory and accomplice to murder, a heinous malefaction committed under the vicious
and degrading circumstances of concupiscence and robbery. Your victim was a gentleman of great worth and
admirable influence within the community; he was husband to a virtuous wife and father to three inestimable
offspring, all of whom are now bereaved and destitute.

You have brought total ruin upon an innocent family. . . ."

Maggie Kizer stood glassy-eyed beside her attorney. By the court's specific direction, her amber spectacles had again been removed and lay folded on the table before her.

"Cyrus Butterfield, by what devious means known best to you and others like you, was inveigled into the indulgence of licentious pleasures; a defect surely in a gentleman striving toward civil and moral perfection, but a defect undeserving of the punishment he received—death."

Behind Maggie Kizer, in the rows of benches reserved for spectators, sat Lena Shanks, stolid and unmoving and expressionless, but never allowing her eyes to drift from the judge's face as he pronounced sentence. Ella sat beside her grandmother and very slowly twisted in her seat, examining carefully every face in the courtroom.

"It was not possible for the jury, not possible for me to believe that you stood idly and helplessly by, unable to interfere, unable to protest, unable to intercede for the life of Cyrus Butterfield. You were a basilisk to pity. The escaped convict, your husband, whose affections you had betrayed with all and sundry, might have succumbed to remorse, but you, Maggie Kizer, without a single kind word to be wasted upon the deceased, ordered the disposal of the corpse and directed the murderer's escape. It is this unfrenzied imagination, this cold ingenuity we find most reprehensible.

"I have seen no reason," continued Judge Stallworth in a slower, softer voice, "to temper my sentence. There is no urgency to compassionate a woman who herself had no compassion. In a woman less obviously educated, in a woman who had not enjoyed your early benefits, I might have attributed such wondrous salamanderlike cold-bloodedness to your mixed heritage; but with every opportunity to overcome the slight noxious tinge of tainted blood, the fact that you sunk to such depravity that crime and disease fell from you like dust from the folds of your skirts, is a proof that you voluntarily gave way to evil, that you opened your arms to wickedness and embraced corruption."

Maggie Kizer, weary on her feet, swayed a little, was

steadied by the hand that her attorney placed atop her wrist. Her eyes moved dully over the court, and only gradually drifted back to the white parchment face with the gleaming blue eyes set in it like the amethyst chips in a Roman bust.

"Maggie Kizer," said the judge, in a light matter-of-fact voice, "it is the will of this court that the full penalty of the law be exacted for your part in the brutal murder of Cyrus Butterfield. As an accessory and accomplice in fact, and as instigator in our moral judgment, I hereby sentence you to be taken to the prison on Blackwell's Island, and in one week's time, to be hanged by the neck until you are dead."

Maggie Kizer glanced vaguely around the court and, for the first time seeing Lena Shanks, nodded to her briefly in dreaming gratitude for the opium that Rob had brought the previous evening.

Chapter 26

ON the morning of March 14, only shortly after the dim sun had touched the tower of the bridge over the East River, Lena Shanks and her grandson appeared at the entrance of the Tombs. A small bribe administered the day before secured them entrance at this early hour, and once inside, Rob led his grandmother to the cell of Maggie Kizer. At nine o'clock the octoroon was to be transported to Blackwell's Island.

Lena Shanks and Rob stood at the barred door of the cell for a few moments, staring into the dim chamber where the condemned woman lay in a black dress upon the gray cot. Their whispers did not rouse her, and it was necessary at last for Rob, taking Lena's cane, to strike smartly the soles of Maggie's boots.

Maggie waked, twisted her head about, stared for a moment at her visitors, and then slowly raised herself on the cot. "Thank you," she whispered in general gratitude for all that Lena Shanks had done for her over the past week.

"We found your Duncan," hissed Rob at a signal from Lena, "we found his name, we found his address, where he works and where he lives."

"Thank you," repeated Maggie Kizer listlessly, fearful of hope. "I'm certain that he won't come."

"Nein," said Lena grimly, *"kommt nicht."*

Maggie looked up for an explanation of the certainty in the old woman's voice.

Rob's eyes grew wide, and he explained: "Won't come, 'cause he's married to the daughter of the judge. The judge that said you're to hang."

"Stallworth!" hissed Lena Shanks.

Maggie Kizer laughed softly, a weary choking laugh, and fell back against the damp stone wall. "So he knew, did he, knew what trouble I was under? So he knew. . . ."

"Stallworth!" hissed Lena Shanks: "all of 'em Stallworths!"

"The judge is his father-in-law," said Maggie to Rob. "He won't come, he won't even send word. He said nothing to the judge, though the judge sentenced me to death. Perhaps," she mused, "it was Duncan suggested the sentence. Duncan, with his wife, the judge's daughter, by his side. Duncan stood before the mantelpiece and suggested to his father-in-law the judge that Maggie Kizer be executed, suggested that Maggie Kizer be hanged by the neck until she was dead, suggested that the tongue of Maggie Kizer be ripped out of her head so that she couldn't tell of him. Perhaps," she smiled at Rob, "perhaps that's what he said to his father-in-law as he stood leaning against the mantelpiece."

Maggie rose slowly from her cot, stood straight and tall and held out her hands to Rob. "Pull off my ring, child."

Rob eagerly thrust his tiny hands between the bars and twisted off the only ring that Maggie Kizer had kept during her imprisonment, the ruby ring that had been Duncan's New Year's gift. She removed her gloves and tossed them into a corner of the cell.

Maggie spoke to her sister-in-law: "My attorney, who was good for nothing else, at least was capable of drawing up a paper for me." From her pocket she took a bulky envelope and slipped it through the bars to Black Lena. "All my things will be yours legally when I'm dead. There will be no difficulties. You've done all in your power to make this time easy for me, and it is little enough that I do in return!"

Lena said nothing at all.

"One more thing though, just one more thing," said Maggie. The double dose of opium she had administered

to herself to get through the sentencing the day before had
finished in an eighteen-hour sleep; just waked from it, her
mind was preternaturally clear. Her feelings, more mercifully, remained withered and unbeating. She smiled, all
the while that she spoke: "Knowing that I am to die for
a crime that was not committed by my connivance, by my
wish, by my abetting, I cannot find it in my heart to forgive the man who sentenced me to it, nor exculpate the
man who would not intercede for me. Duncan might have
spoken a word to his father-in-law, the judge, requesting
lenient sentencing in my case; or, not daring to betray his
interest in a murderous prostitute, he might at least have
vouchsafed me the reasons for his decision to abandon
me. I am not overly bitter, for I would not have wanted
him to sacrifice his life for mine; and I could not wish for
my sentence to be abrogated from death to a term in
prison. Hanging is preferable to the oblivion represented
by these damp walls. . . ."

The women in the cells around them had begun to stir
in the early morning, and Maggie had to speak a little
louder to be heard above their raucous sleepy calls.

"But it is impossible to forgive that Duncan should
have left me without a word, without indication that he
regretted his helplessness, without the kindness of laying
my hopes in the dust. Therefore," she said, stepping forward and gripping the bars in her bare white fingers, and
staring hard at Lena with her black-flecked eyes, "I want
you to avenge me. I don't ask for his death, nor his ruin,
nor his overthrow from whatever position in the world
he has attained—I knew so little about him, really—but
only that he be conscience-pricked about me, that he fall
for a space and know that it was over the corpse of
Margaret Kizer that he stumbled."

Lena Shanks nodded slowly and smiled a ghastly smile.
"*Sicher, sicher,*" she whispered.

Maggie sighed. "Then there is nothing more you can
do for me."

"*Doch,*" said Lena, " *'was mehr.*"

Maggie had retreated to her cot, and sat on the edge
of it, her face composed and peaceful. "More?" she said
lightly, "what more? I'm to die in a week's time and have
dope enough to last me until then. . . ."

Black Lena touched her grandson on the shoulder. He

reached into a pocket of his jacket and retrieved two small blue-glass bottles with cork stoppers. One in each hand, he thrust his slender arms through the barred door. Maggie took the bottles from him.

"The rope is painful," said Rob. "Drink these. No pain in laudanum."

Maggie Kizer stared at the bottles. "Yes of course," she said, glancing up at Lena. "Yes of course," she whispered, plucked out the corks and drank away the contents immediately.

She handed the bottles back to Rob. "How long?" she asked. "I require a powerful dose you know."

"Two hours," replied Lena. "You'll sleep."

"Thank you," she replied. She reached around the cot and took her bag and the small packages she had accumulated in her sojourn in the Tombs. "Take them away with you," she said to Rob, setting them before the slot in the door, "take everything."

Reaching through, Rob gathered up the last of Maggie's possessions.

"Take these also," she said, removing the rings from her ears. "When the warders find me dead, I'll be stripped anyway."

Lena Shanks took the earrings and dropped them into the pocket that held Maggie Kizer's will. "Lie down," said Lena, weeping, *"Schlaf, schlaf, mein Kind."*

Maggie Kizer stretched herself upon the cot. "Remember," she said softly, "make them tumble, make them tumble."

"Ja, ja," said Lena Shanks soothingly. Then she and her grandson walked slowly away from the cell and left Maggie Kizer to her final sleep.

Soon, the rising cacaphonous voices of the women imprisoned along that corridor melted into a harmony in Maggie Kizer's softening, deadening brain. But what she heard was so distant, it became like the mere memory of sound, no more than a dream of voices.

The guards who were to transfer Maggie Kizer from the Tombs to Blackwell's Island had been told of her addiction to opium, and when they came for her they were not surprised to find her in a stupor. She was brought out on her cot, lifted into a carriage, taken to the landing at the eastern end of Fifty-second Street, and set in a small boat to be rowed across.

One of the two officers took the oars, and the other held the drooping woman up. The day was warm, though still early in the morning, and the sunlight glinted on the gentle waters of the East River.

Just as they had come within the shade of the trees that fringed Blackwell's Island, but before the small boat had been tied at the landing, the second officer looked closely at the woman who lay in his arms, examined carefully her face that was painted green by the sunlight that fell through the dense evergreen foliage, and remarked to his friend that the prisoner was stone dead.

Chapter 27

FROM the moment that Duncan Phair learned that Maggie Kizer had been involved in the murder of Cyrus Butterfield, he had begun to put his mistress behind him. The danger she posed to his life forced him to abandon her entirely, and each day that had passed since her arrest drew her further from his affections and his concern. He began actually to think of her as the cold murderess that Simeon Lightner described—the beautiful harpie who had lured the lawyer to his death. The quiet, saddened woman who moved with elegant lassitude room to room in her elegant apartments on Bleecker Street no longer existed.

Duncan had not a moment of regret that he had been forced to reveal his liaison to his father-in-law. There was, to begin with, relief to be got from the very act of confession. It was with great trepidation, however, that Duncan had anticipated his next meeting with the judge; Duncan feared his father-in-law's hot recriminations and cold scorn. The scorn was there, but the recriminations were only perfunctory. Without difficulty Maggie Kizer had been convicted, and this ease of circumstance perhaps made the judge go easier with his son-in-law. "This matter will lie dead between us, Duncan, to be resur-

196

rected only when the woman herself is dead. I am not concerned with you and your feelings; I feel no need to offer instruction and improvement to a man who would have so little care for himself and his family as to engineer a connection between himself and an opium-addicted, murderous prostitute. It is necessary now only that we come through this undetected; there is therefore no question of *confession* to Marian, do you understand?"

It was with only the slightest pang to his heart that Duncan learned from Lightner of Maggie's suicide. He commended her to God and considered that this death was better than hanging. Maggie had always found comfort in opium, and Duncan knew that she would have had no fear of laudanum.

Duncan himself no longer had any fears. Maggie was dead, past his help; Maggie was dead, and he was past her injury. Lady Weale had conveniently left town, no one knew whither. There was no one now to connect him with Maggie Kizer; her relatives the Shanks had never seen him, and so far as he knew had never discovered his identity. And it was quite beyond them now to approach him, for they were themselves in ever-increasing tribulation. The pawnshop had been shut up, the abortion practice quashed, investigations into Louisa Shanks's activities with forged documents and cheques initiated, watches set upon the children. It was with a mind considerably lightened that Duncan Phair went to Judge Stallworth with the news of Maggie Kizer's death.

"Good," replied Judge Stallworth at the reception of this news. "I could tell that the woman had sense; she evidently had some idea of propriety as well. In taking the laudanum, so quickly after the sentencing, she actually did us a decided favor. Mulberry Street asked me to sign a warrant for the arrest of Daisy Shanks—the abortionist—but I told them I wanted to put it off a week, until we could get the Kizer woman out of the way. But now that she's killed herself, I see no reason not to begin with the others."

"Tomorrow," suggested Duncan eagerly. Now that he had got through the difficulty with Maggie Kizer that had threatened to destroy his career, he had no intention of allowing those to remain who might later bring the whole matter to the attention of the world. The Shanks would indeed be ground into the dust of the Black Triangle. "Simeon and Benjamin and I will be there. The Shanks haven't left their house since the trial, we don't even know how they get their food in. We'll see what effect *this* arrest has. Do you think we ought to arrest Black Lena at the same time?"

"You are too eager," said Judge Stallworth disdainfully. "I will sign the warrant for the daughter, but there is not enough evidence against the mother yet. It is notoriously difficult to prosecute a fence. You and Simeon are going to have to dig a little, find someone who thinks she's been cheated by the old woman, bring *her* forward to testify, and then we'll announce that we've arrested Black Lena Shanks, the head of the wickedest family in the Black Triangle. We must put her aside for the moment, but the abortionist is no problem, no problem at all. . . ."

It was arranged with the police that Daisy Shanks should be arrested at six o'clock in the evening of Thursday, March 16, just two days after the death of Maggie Kizer.

A little before the appointed time, Simeon Lightner, Benjamin Stallworth, and Duncan Phair met at the Tribune Building and took a cab to the corner of King and Hudson streets. On a preliminary stroll down West Houston Street, Simeon silently pointed out the house of the abortionist. The three men purchased cigars from a tobacconist's with a faro bank ill-concealed in the back. They gathered round a streetlamp, and tried to make out that they were interested in the painted females who passed them by. Benjamin kept his hand thrust in his jacket pocket, excitedly fingering the small pistol that he had lately taken to carrying about with him—unknown to either Simeon or Duncan. He told himself, proudly, that in some emergency he would prove himself their timely deliverance.

The sun had fallen behind the brick buildings to the west, and the street was suffused with a soft pink light that allowed the dilapidated structures to present not so harsh or uninviting a scape as usual. A little beyond the hour of six, three policemen appeared from around the corner of the street and made their way silently toward number 203. One of them was Lincoln Pane, the officer who had arrested Maggie Kizer and testified at her trial.

The three men dropped their cigars and followed the policemen at a little distance. Simeon Lightner skipped ahead and stood just on the other side of the stone steps; the reporter exchanged a nod of recognition and complicity with Officer Pane, and then drew his tablets and pencil from his pocket.

Benjamin Stallworth and Duncan Phair retreated into the shadowed recess of a doorway directly across the street. Expectantly they watched the three uniformed men mount the pale stone steps of number 203. There was no response to Pane's first knock, but a second sustained rapping at the door resulted in its being pulled open a small space by Rob, who stood silent upon the threshold.

"Daisy Shanks," announced Officer Pane importantly, "we've come for Daisy Shanks!"

Rob answered nothing, and did not appear even alarmed by the appearance of the three policemen or the severity of Pane's voice. He peered over the edge of the balustrade and carefully marked the presence of the reporter.

"Daisy Shanks!" shouted the policeman, and attempted to push past the little boy. Rob scampered out of the way down the steps, slipping between the uniforms; and his place in the door was taken by Louisa. Her face bore an expression even harder than usual, and the fringe of greasy curls was raked so far down over the low forehead that it covered her brows. She wore a blue dress covered in lace-edged ruffles and green bows, that hung as if it had been plunged in a vat of glue just before she had put it on.

"Are you Daisy Shanks?" Pane demanded.

Louisa made no sign, but Simeon Lightner hissed, "No!"

"Is Daisy Shanks within?"

Louisa shook her head no.

"She's lying!" cried Simeon Lightner.

"Well," said Pane, speaking to Louisa with sarcastic ease, "perhaps you've just mislaid her, or perhaps you're mistaken, or perhaps she's just come in the back way. Let us in and we'll make certain."

Louisa did not move. She paid little attention to the

man who stood on the step just below her, but looked carefully over the other two policemen behind him and glanced for a moment at Simeon Lightner scribbling in his tablet. She even peered thoughtfully into the darkness of the recessed doorway across the street.

Duncan Phair felt himself observed, and shrank farther into the shadows.

At that moment, the door of the adjoining house was opened by Ella Shanks. Lena stood just behind her.

Rob ran over to join his sister and grandmother. The three stood on the steps of number 201, and with disconcerting passivity looked on Louisa Shanks as she defended their home and Daisy within it from the three policemen.

Officer Pane placed his hand on Louisa's arm and tried to pull her out of the entrance, but with one swift motion she jerked herself free of his grasp and knocked his cap off. It flew and struck Simeon Lightner in the face.

"Damn you in the teeth!" cried Officer Pane, and attempted to shove her aside. The policemen from behind him jumped up on the narrow stoop, grabbed the woman's arms and dragged her down. She resisted and they fell over backward. But Louisa Shanks was pulled over with them and all three tumbled painfully down the stoop and were sprawled on the sidewalk.

Officer Pane rushed inside the house.

One of the policemen had knocked his head against the sidewalk bricks and lay dazed; his compatriot was tangled in that man's legs. Louisa Shanks was held fast at the waist by the second policeman. She struggled to disengage herself by smashing her elbows into his face. When this proved insufficient, Louisa pulled a small knife from her pocket and sliced the policeman's knuckles open.

With an anguished cry he released her, shouted out in pain, and wrung his bloody hands together. Louisa immediately rose and rushed into the house after Officer Pane.

The policeman whose hands had been cut struggled to his feet and was about to give chase to Louisa when Black Lena, who had made her slow way forward from the stoop next door, thrust her cane between his legs and

tripped him up. He fell at her feet, and she jammed the
cane as hard as she could into his mouth, pushed, and
then drew it out bloody.

These actions had occupied no more than about fifteen
seconds in the quiet street. Not only to have a better view
but to be well out of the way, Simeon Lightner had drawn
back when Louisa and the two policemen were precipitated down the steps. Now he had disappeared, evidently
to fetch other policemen. Duncan and Benjamin were
so shocked by the drawing of the knife and by Black
Lena's vicious attack with her cane, that they had not
the presence of mind to try to interfere in the altercation.

The second policeman writhed on the sidewalk at
Black Lena's feet, his mouth foaming up blood and a
thick gurgle filling his throat. He tried to grab at her
feet, but she jammed her cane into his eye and he twisted
away in screaming pain.

The first policeman, who had been dazed, struggled
into consciousness. But Rob and Ella together had lifted
a loose coping stone from the balustrade of number 201
and brought it over to where he lay. They held it squarely
over his forehead, and just as he flicked open his eye,
they dropped it. The sharp corner smashed directly
against his temple as he instinctively jerked his head out
of the way.

"Oh my God!" cried Benjamin, and rushed forward
into the street, his pistol held out tremulously before him.
Although Benjamin had visited the Black Triangle
nightly for almost three months, this was the most vicious
fighting that he had ever seen. It was not such as he had
witnessed before: hot-blooded quarrels among men who
were momentarily angry with one another, drunken arguments got up over the fall of a card or the price of a drink
or the imputation of theft. The hard-visaged woman who
had rushed back into the house was surely bent on the
suppression of Officer Pane, Benjamin considered—and
his was now the responsibility of preserving that policeman's life.

Benjamin's saw a woman's figure in the open doorway
of number 203 and heard her voice: "No, Ma! No, Ma!"
she cried: "Stop! I'm—"

Benjamin fired the pistol into the black doorway. A
moment later, a young woman staggered out. Her long

blond hair was tied up with blue ribbons; she wore a
voluminous yellow skirt and a short-waisted green bodice
beneath a tight green jacket. She held a red hand against
her throat. Her mouth was frozen in a wide smile. She
turned her head slightly in the direction of Lena Shanks
and the twins and then collapsed at the top of the
stoop. Blood gushed out of the hole in her neck over the
shallow steps.

The twins screamed and—this time in their heedless
grief—once more dropped the coping stone on the head
of the policeman.

"Daisy! Daisy!" cried her bereaved mother.

Grappling with one another, Louisa Shanks and Officer Pane emerged from the doorway of the house together. Both were stopped by the sight of Daisy sprawled
on the steps before them, her blood flowing in a little
murky stream onto the brick sidewalk. Louisa was the
first to recover her surprise—she stooped, grabbed Officer Pane by the waist, and flipped him over the balus-
tade onto the brick pavement. Louisa's mouth opened
wide, but no sound was emitted; her entire face was contracted and distorted with anguish. Her face locked in its
tragic mask, she tenderly lifted Daisy's corpse. Blood
spilled over her dress as she cradled Daisy's head against
her breast. She mounted the steps again and carried
Daisy into the house. The twins followed a moment
after.

Lena Shanks, oblivious to the heap of policemen beside her, slowly mounted the steps after them.

In the street, Benjamin stood aghast—that he had
just shot and killed a woman, and the wrong woman at
that. Duncan had come forward out of the shadowed
doorway and taken the gun from him. Together, and
both unthinking, they had watched the body of the dead
woman carried into the house.

At the door of number 203, Lena Shanks turned to
Duncan and Benjamin, who had stepped forward and
stood now on the brick walk before the house.

"Your name is Phair," Lena said to Duncan, in a voice
that faltered only upon the first word, "but you're a
Stallworth. And you too," she said, pointing her cane at
Benjamin. "You I've seen before. *Noch einer* Stallworth."
She paused, as if expecting either Duncan or Benjamin

to deny his identity, then went on with an astonishing placidity: "Twenty years ago, *Stallworth*—the old man—killed Cornelius, *meinen Mann*. Sent me to the Island. Took away Daisy and Louisa. Put Alick in Sing Sing. I came off the Island, got my girls again. Alick is gone from Sing Sing. And I have the rope that hanged *meinen Mann*. Twenty years ago," she whispered.

Suddenly she raised her cane and swung it violently before her. "Now you come back!" she hissed. *"Stallworths!* Stallworths put Maggie in jail. Stallworths close my shop. Stallworths keep Daisy from her medicine."

She stopped, rubbed one shaking hand over the other on the head of the cane. Then she resumed, in a voice that was barely audible to the two men she addressed: "Now Maggie is dead. Now Daisy is dead."

She bowed her head and wept. She raised her head and then savagely, with the tip of her cane, stirred her daughter's blood that lay in a congealing pool on the stoop, black in the gathering evening.

"Stallworths! You killed Maggie," she said pointing at Duncan, "and that's one. And there's *you*," pointing at Benjamin, "you killed Daisy, and that's two. The old man: three. A wife to you: four. *Ein prediger:* five. *Eine Schwester:* six. Six Stallworths, *und zwei Kinder!"*

Duncan was frightened. Not only had the old woman discovered their family, but she had known of his connection with Maggie as well.

"I had six too," said Lena. "Cornelius and me, Alick and Maggie, Louisa and Daisy. *Und zwei Kinder. Aber:* three of mine are dead. Cornelius is dead. Maggie is dead. Now Daisy is dead."

Lena Shanks smiled a grim and ghastly smile and pointed to the policemen beside the stoop, dead and dying, their groans providing the burden and bass of her curse: "Go hide," she said to Duncan and Benjamin, "and hide your family and your *Kinder*. This is what will come of you," said she, glancing at the policemen, dead and dying. "We'll see it done," she said: *"Vergisse nicht*: there's three of us dead. . . ."

She retreated into the blackness of the doorway through which her dead daughter had just been carried. "We'll see it done," she said again, and the door was pushed silently shut.

Chapter Thirteen

However, as may be expected that he had no further visits

Part II
The Female Gang

Chapter 28

For the *Tribune* of Friday, March 17, 1882, Simeon Lightner prepared an extensive account of the terrible incident that had taken place before the houses belonging to Black Lena Shanks. Considering the sensational nature of the case and the luck of his having been a witness to it, Lightner composed the paragraphs in the first person. He began with the history of the two buildings at numbers 201 and 203 West Houston Street, which had been disreputable for more than two decades; appended biographies of their inhabitants, and reminded readers of Black Lena Shanks's appearance and testimony at the trial of her sister-in-law, Maggie Kizer; told of the events within the Mulberry Street headquarters of the New York police that had led up to the attempted arrest of Daisy Shanks, and then presented a detailed ledger of the altercation on the sidewalk before the house.

Simeon Lightner concluded:

The presence of mind and daring of Mr. Benjamin Stallworth are entirely to be credited. When Daisy Shanks, the 'Laughing Abortionist,' emerged from No. 203, intent on finishing the job begun

207

by her mother and her offspring, he halted her murderous progress with a courageous and well-timed bullet.

By the time that I had returned to that part of West Houston Street, having secured the assistance of two other officers, the injured woman had already been removed into the house and Mr. Phair and Mr. Stallworth had advanced to the succor of the three endangered policemen. Officer Pane, who had been in charge of the expedition, lay in a heap beside the balustrade of No. 203, dazed and inarticulate. The second officer, Thomas Raven of No. 30 East Third Street, jerked convulsively against the bricks. Blood poured from wounds in his mouth and his eye. He was pronounced dead upon his arrival at the Hospital of the City of New York. The third policeman, Richard Scoggins, of No. 77 Second Avenue, lay stone dead, the victim of two nine-year-old children.

Officer Pane owes Mr. Stallworth a large debt of gratitude for his very survival.

Mr. Phair informed us that no movement had been apparent within the house for at least five minutes. While Mr. Stallworth was dispatched to find a doctor in the neighborhood, the two officers cautiously entered the door of No. 203.

The policemen made a thorough search of the premises, but discovered no one. The four malefactors, Lena Shanks, Louisa Shanks, and Rob and Ella Shanks (the twins), murderers all, had gathered their specie and their jewels and walked out the back door of No. 203. They slipped through an alley to King Street, and disappeared from human sight.

The corpse of the abortionist was found on a couch in a magnificently appointed gold parlor on the ground floor of No. 203. Every piece of furniture, every scrap of cloth, and every morsel of decoration in the chamber was gold.

The dead abortionist lay with her hands folded neatly over her breast. Her injured neck and bruised head were draped with a gold lambrequin that had been snatched from the mantelpiece.

All the ornaments that had stood before the great gold-tinted mirror lay in fragments of gold pottery and gold glass upon the hearth of gold tiles. By her side was a purse containing a handful of emeralds, and a note in a fine but hurried hand which read: "These jewels are to be redeemed for cash. The money is intended for burial expenses. The marble marker is to read: DAISY SHANKS, WELL-BELOVED. 1859-1882."

It was the opinion of the doctor who first examined the corpse that, had the absconding family paused to secure medical assistance for Daisy Shanks, she might well have recovered from the bullet wound. The criminal mother, intent only upon her own safety, had abandoned her daughter without compunction and torn the children away from their mother's corpse.

The Commissioner of Police has registered a protest with the Mayor's Office against the raising of a monument to the memory of an abortionist. He wishes rather that the receipts of the sale of the jewels be expended on obsequies intended for the two dead police officers, Thomas Raven and Richard Scoggins.

A close watch will be kept on the two houses, although the police admit that it is unlikely that the murderers will return. Altogether about $15,000 worth of merchandise, almost all certainly stolen, has been recovered from the cellars of the two buildings. This amount does not include the furnishings of the rooms of the houses, which in most cases were splendid and costly. In addition, besides the surgical instruments found in a bedchamber on the fourth story, there was a printing press in one of the rooms on the second floor. Also found were counterfeit plates for the printing of bogus $10-bills, and a supply of paper similar in quality and texture to that employed by the Government Printing Office.

The Police Department has issued descriptions of the four murderers, and declares itself confident that they will soon be brought to justice. Twenty-eight officers have been assigned to the search. In so desperate a case as this, the zeal of the police is laudable, and we must only hope that their sanguine confidence is justified.

Duncan Phair, writing above his own name again, eulogized the dead officers, execrated the Shanks, and concluded:

Yet, even if this strange family of more than incredible wickedness is never found, never brought into a court of law, the citizens of New York may rest assured that they will do no more harm upon this island. Their identities and aspects are too well known to remain undiscovered here, and they dare not revert to their former criminal ways. From these, if not entirely from others like them, we are safe.

Chapter 29

~~~
≈≈≈≈≈≈≈≈≈≈≈≈≈≈≈≈≈≈≈≈≈≈≈≈≈≈≈≈≈≈≈≈≈≈≈≈≈≈
~~~

Lᴇɴᴀ, Louisa, Rob, and Ella, whose descriptions and murderous offenses were tacked up in police courts all across the country, were not to be found. At six P.M. on Thursday, March 16, 1882, they had entered the house at number 203 West Houston Street bearing the corpse of Daisy Shanks—and never been seen again. In succeeding months there came to be rumors of them, such rumors as invariably arise when there is a matter of substantial reward. Lena was known to be running a house of prostitution in Montreal, the twins were picking pockets on a Mississippi steamboat, Louisa was in California, affianced to a state legislator who knew nothing of her past.

Yet the fact was that the Shankses had disappeared quite as effectively as if the door to number 203 West Houston Street had momentarily opened onto Hell and they been swallowed into perdition, as they deserved.

But all of New York knew what had become of the Stallworths in the six months following the death of Daisy Shanks. They had risen—not spectacularly; for too rapid a rise would have been inconsistent with the Stallworth sense of propriety; but with a most respectable sureness and complacency.

The campaign in the *Tribune* had proved a splendid success. After it had been revealed that Duncan Phair was the author of the articles that had been signed "A Republican Counselor" and "A Friend to Virtue," much business of a prestigious and highly remunerative nature had been thrown the way of the firm of Phair & Peerce. Duncan was even commended by the bar for his researches in the Black Triangle.

The Stallworths could point proudly to the Black Triangle as a blasted area now, where vice remained in-of-doors. The most notorious places of gambling, illegal liquors, and prostitution were shut up, and those wishing to dissipate themselves must do it in dark and secret places within the Black Triangle—or else in the numerous other parts of the city where depravity kept an open shop.

The *Tribune* had been the most widely read of the papers detailing the moral corruption of the city; and the police department thought to do itself most good by following up on that paper's discoveries. It seemed at times that the police dogged the footsteps of Simeon Lightner, Benjamin Stallworth, and Duncan Phair through the Black Triangle. Each dusty window those three men peered into was soon boarded over. Every threshold they crossed was sealed the next day. Any rouged lady who spoke to the three men on the street would be forced to remove her lodgings to the Tombs.

Judge Stallworth had not been behindhand either. Trials in the venue of his court were dispatched with a rapidity that astonished even the public prosecutors and public defenders, who had thought themselves calloused to the summary nature of trials within the Criminal Courts Building. Criminals arrested in the Black Triangle paid large bribes to their arresting officers to say that they had been picked up in another street, so that they would not come before Judge Stallworth. Sentencing was harsh, and the *Tribune* faithfully reported his remarks on lengthy prison sentences as undeniable deterrents to crime.

Marian Phair's Committee of the Suppression of Urban Vice had not returned to the Black Triangle, but its strongly worded letters, numerous petitions, frequent subscriptions, and weekly and very fashionable meetings, did not go unnoticed. Membership on the committee was exclusive and sought after. The women of Marian's class begged their friends to take them along or wrote Marian long letters in apparently irresistible adulation of her efforts to render the city safe and decent. Marian was gratified to find that descriptions of her ensemble, worn at Monday's meeting, appeared in Saturday's *Tribune*, article for article, in the column, "Fashion Hints for the Week."

Helen Stallworth had continued at Marian's meetings and took embarrassingly brief minutes of the inconsequential proceedings. But she no longer complained to her father or even to Marian, for she now was convinced that she was doing some real good for the unfortunates condemned to live in the Black Triangle. She went there almost daily, sometimes in the company of Mrs. General Taunton, but of late even by herself, wearing her simplest black dress, with a large basket of foods and necessaries on her arm. She could call a hundred beggars and petty criminals by their cant names.

Her second life—as she thought it—apart, so different, so worthy, wholly unsuspected by her family, brought a smile to Helen's countenance at odd times, so that the others wondered at her happiness. Helen, who before had always considered lying a sin only slightly less reprehensible than "enforced adultery" (what she called rape), now delighted in the panoply of deceit with which she kept her charitable work hidden from her family.

Benjamin, on his part, was happy also. The many months of expeditions into the Black Triangle, the slight but constant attention that was afforded him because of his supplementary endeavors and his unexampled heroism in having shot the Houston Street abortionist before she slit the throats of the three injured policemen, raised him in his own and others' estimation. He was no longer merely tolerated. His grandfather, for instance, now and then spoke a word to him which was not unkind; and Marian, when no one else was by to take her attention, sometimes condescended to converse with him. His father no longer demanded to know the hour of his coming in at night, and had a latchkey fashioned for his use. His presence was no longer required in the offices of Phair & Peerce, and altogether Benjamin's existence was less onerous to him than it had ever been before.

He had not entirely left off gambling, for it was too great a pleasure to him: real excitement in what was still, despite its increased amiability, a fairly dull life. But all his wagering now was justified as investigation, and he never put down on a table more than he could afford to lose. Benjamin's only debt remaining was that owed to Duncan and his father for payment of his losses on New Year's Day; but as neither of them had ever mentioned the circumstance again, Benjamin had begun to assume that it was forgotten or forgiven.

Edward Stallworth's sermons had attracted much attention, and the size of his congregaton and his collections had increased markedly over the past half year. The texts had been reprinted not only in the *Tribune,* but in the *Presbyterian Advocate,* the *Christian Dawning,* and the *Cumberland Spectator* as well. Among his parishioners now were families from Brooklyn and New Jersey, who ferried across to New York every Sunday morning and raised ire against Edward in the hearts of their abandoned clergymen.

The dissension that remained in the clergyman's family was on account of the killing of Daisy Shanks. The incident had been made out by Duncan Phair, the only creditable witness, to have been an act of heroism on Benjamin's part; it had been reported as such in the *Tribune* and never thereafter questioned. Duncan had told the judge the true circumstances, and the judge had replied that he was just as surprised to hear that Benjamin was possessed of luck as of real courage. Edward Stallworth had feared at first that the circumstance of his son having shot a woman dead in the streets of the Black Triangle might tell against him, but when this proved not the case —his parishioners unanimously congratulating him on having raised so stalwart a boy—he came to smile indulgently on the act.

Helen, however, was horrified by the killing, begged Benjamin to tell her that it had been merely a frightful accident. But Benjamin, counseled by his uncle, stood up for his own bravery in the matter, and would not admit his careless culpability. From that moment, Helen became estranged from her brother; and any deception practiced by her upon him and the family that supported him in his shameful pride was a virtuous prevarication. Thereafter,

Helen never abused those in the Black Triangle of the notion that she was the daughter of Mrs. General Taunton; she tried not even to think of herself as a Stallworth.

August had been spent by the family at Saratoga, in the best hotel, and though their expenses were of the most fashionable proportions, the family concluded that they received full value for their money, if not in accommodation, fare and comfort, then at least in the matter of new and fashionable acquaintance. This was of particular use to Marian, who upon her return to the city in September, was besieged with invitations to dinner, late night parties and opera boxes. Only Helen did not enjoy the month; she had pleaded in vain for permission to remain in the city alone—but propriety would not hear of such a course, and Helen must suffer in luxury.

The beginning of autumn was an exhilarating time for the Stallworths, and their Sunday afternoon dinners together were happier—or at least less troubled affairs—than they had been in many years. On Sunday, October 1, the family was still gathered around the table, though Marian's children Edwin and Edith had already been removed to the nursery, when the conversation fell, as it was often wont to fall, to the Black Triangle.

"Lightner says that we've just about exhausted the place," said Duncan, "and I must say, I can't help but agree. We've been on it now for nine months, and to try to take it even as far as the end of the year would be beating a dead horse."

"Oh yes," said Judge Stallworth, who had already discussed this matter with his son-in-law, "and now it is the question of moving on that must be attended to."

"Moving on?" asked Edward Stallworth. This was the first he had heard of the abandonment of the Black Triangle, and it distressed him, for he had expected to continue his sermons with the active support of the *Tribune*'s researches. "Moving on to what, pray?"

"To Pell Street, Mott Street. Lightner thinks, and I agree, that we ought to move on to the Chinese question. The new Chinese immigration law goes into effect next month and will doubtless draw attention to the area. There's bound to be excitement of some sort: murders, bribery, illegal entries into the country. And of course, if there's nothing else, we can always blow open an opium den," laughed Duncan.

"Well," said Edward Stallworth, "I'm not certain that the Black Triangle is exhausted of its vice, and it seems to me that the Chinese population is so alien a group, what with their outlandish appearance and peculiar ways and unknowable habits, that it will be only with the greatest difficulty that you will stir up any interest in them. The Irish are just as objectionable, and far more populous. I think it might be better if you continued with the Triangle, perhaps taking it from a slightly altered point of—"

"Yes!" cried Marian, who was more forthright in her objections than her brother. "What's to become of my committee if you and Mr. Lightner and Benjamin simply walk away from the Black Triangle? My committee is certain to fall apart!"

"Oh," said Helen softly to her aunt, "it need not, I think, Marian. There's still much good to be accomplished in the area, even if it's not to be written up in the *Tribune.*"

Judge Stallworth glanced sharply at his granddaughter, wondering if her mild sarcasm were deliberate. "Marian, certainly not," he said, "Duncan will insure, through Lightner, that the activities of your committee continue to receive notice in the *Tribune.*"

"Oh yes, of course I will," said Duncan lightly, and smiled at his wife.

"Well," said Benjamin, with some of his new-got confidence, "I don't see why this can't be eased into, gone into slowly. We could be into the Chinese question before they know we've left the Triangle. And I don't see any reason why the heathen Chinese can't be used as the subject of a sermon or two. Why, they're in need of salvation, I suppose, as much as the rest of us."

"I think you're right, Benjamin," said his grandfather, and Benjamin blushed for the pleasure of the old man's approbation.

"Well," replied Edward Stallworth, "I suppose that I shall have to make the best of it; but please leave me time to study this question of the Chinese before you throw yourselves into the area completely."

"Of course, Edward," said Duncan in a conciliatory manner. "Your printed sermons have proved enormous capital to us, you know, and we have every intention of continuing to publish them. We sincerely hope that you *will* see fit to assist us."

Edward Stallworth, suffering himself to be persuaded out of the Black Triangle and into the Chinese community to the east, had just declared that he must rise and return to the church to prepare himself for the evening service, when the knocker of the front door was sounded.

The Stallworths glanced at one another in surprise, for late Sunday afternoon was not the time for making calls in New York, except by appointment. Peter Wish was sent to the door and he returned a few moments later bearing, on a silver tray, eight oblong black-bordered envelopes.

Marian Phair took them all from the salver and flipped through them. "How odd!" she exclaimed. "There's one for each of us—Edwin and Edith too. Someone's dead, but who is so stupid as to send out memorial cards to every member of a family? And children *never* receive mourning cards. It's unheard of!"

She took the one directed to her and began to open it. Judge Stallworth took the others, picked out his own, and passed the rest to his granddaughter.

"Who brought these?" asked Edward Stallworth of Peter Wish.

"A child," replied the servant. "A little boy dressed in black."

Helen had taken hers, but before she had lifted the flap she glanced at her aunt on the other side of the table. Marian's hand, holding the envelope, had dropped heavily on the table and she looked about her in pained surprise.

Helen ripped open the envelope that had her name upon it. Inside was a funeral announcement, a small card of waxed glossy paper, machine-cut on the borders, and representing a young girl weeping over a tombstone in a cemetery with willows. But written across the tombstone in a fine copperplate hand was the legend: R.I.P. HELEN STALLWORTH.

"Oh!" cried Helen, and the card fluttered to the floor.

Duncan Phair found an identical card in his, but one which bore the text: ASLEEP IN GOD. DUNCAN PHAIR.

"Peter!" he cried out, "run after the boy!"

Peter Wish rushed out of the room, and in the meantime the Stallworths at the table stared at the mourning cards in their hands, each of which announced his or her own death. Edwin and Edith's cards lay beside their mother's plate, unopened.

"A poor poor joke," said Judge Stallworth, and ripped his card in two.

Chapter 30

⊗⊗⊗⊗⊗⊗⊗⊗⊗⊗⊗⊗⊗⊗⊗⊗⊗⊗⊗⊗⊗⊗⊗⊗⊗⊗⊗⊗⊗⊗⊗⊗⊗⊗

O F the six members of the Stallworth family who sat at the dining room table that first Sunday in October, only Duncan Phair took at all seriously the funeral announcements that had been delivered by a little boy dressed in black. He had by no means forgot Black Lena Shanks's vow to see three of the Stallworths dead. Duncan watched his father-in-law and, inwardly trembling, tried to match the old man's annoyance and suggested the names of several persons who might be suspected of so malicious and pointless a joke.

The others, if they could not entirely dismiss the unpleasant incident, at least did not imagine that the cards had any real import or constituted any actual threat. Edward Stallworth considered that his position as minister of the Madison Avenue Presbyterian Church had been impugned, and was incensed against the perpetrator. Marian was outraged that she should be the victim of someone's morbid witticism and comforted herself with the reflection that someone's jealousy of her rapid social rise had occasioned the hoax. Helen was shocked to think that anyone could be so callous. Benjamin, so obtuse that he did not align these cards with Black Lena's curse (which he had kept so secret that he had forgot it), only laughed in perplexed surprise.

Among themselves, the funeral cards excited much comment and speculation; but outside the family the incident did not become known. Peter Wish alone had seen any of the cards, as he looked over Marian Phair's shoulder. He was enjoined to tell no one, and he told only the other servants.

The unpleasantness of the incident soon passed, to all but Duncan Phair; for the mourning cards suggested that the foundation upon which his recent prosperity rested was perhaps not so much to be relied upon after all. His own life in the past six months had been of particular agreeableness, if only for its contrast with the bedeviling insecurity of the time when he had been in danger of being exposed by Maggie Kizer and Maggie Kizer's friends. His difficulties had ended, he thought, on the day that the two policemen were killed by Black Lena Shanks and her grandchildren.

Duncan had not told his father-in-law of Black Lena's vow of vengeance; he had hopefully assumed that the Shankses—all wanted for murder—would be impotent to implement such a scheme. For some weeks he had gone about his business with as much insouciance as he could muster, and had tried to give the impression that all was right with him. Soon, he was himself convinced; and in the time since then, only one thing had shaken his growing confidence. A family of squatters in the north of the city, just where the northernmost cross streets were now being laid out, said that two men had come in a wagon and dug up several graves in the potter's field. They were not simply resurrectionists, for all the disinterred corpses were discarded except the last, and that one they took away with them. The grave had proved to be that of the West Houston Street abortionist, Daisy Shanks.

However, since nothing had come of the incident, Duncan forced himself to regard it as a puzzling, inexplicable coincidence.

Once he had conquered the cloying fear that had beset him, Duncan began to enjoy the benefits that had accrued from his attachment to the *Tribune*: increased business for the firm, increased respect among his colleagues, and an increasingly amiable homelife. Marian Phair's opinion of her husband was enhanced by society's approbation of him.

Occasionally, of course, Duncan Phair thought of Maggie Kizer; not Maggie as she had been to him, but Maggie where she lay now: moldering in her unmarked grave in the unshaded prisoners' burying ground on Blackwell's Island. She was silent and harmless, and he wished her peace.

Duncan's relationship to his father-in-law had altered since the revelation of his connection with Maggie Kizer, and Duncan understood that it was not the connection itself to which the judge had objection, but rather to Duncan's perfidy in keeping it secret from him. It was apparent that the judge, having this once only been disappointed in Duncan's honesty, had determined never to trust him again.

Judge Stallworth's superficial attitude toward Duncan was unchanged: he conversed with him as usual, he sought out his company and advice on legal matters, he did not fail to advise him in all things—but there was a substantial difference, and one that Duncan felt tremendously. The old man's hopes for advancement had been centered in Duncan, and he had hoped to see his daughter's husband elected mayor of the city before his death. This hope he gave over entirely, and with an ease that was disturbing to Duncan, the judge resettled his hopes upon a different object—his grandson Edwin.

"Edwin," Duncan once overheard Judge Stallworth say to Marian, "is a fine child—I have scarcely noticed him before, but I believe he is a fine child. We may expect fine things from Edwin." Edwin was occasionally brought to Washington Square—itself an unheard-of indulgence—and allowed to play with Pompey. In the past six months Pompey had actually been three dogs, one male and two bitches, and Judge Stallworth was enormously pleased with Edwin that the child had the good sense and taste not to remark on the alterations in Pompey's appearance. After being brought one afternoon into the front parlor of his house by Pompey's bark and discovering Edwin entertaining the dog with a series of elegant handstands executed on the ladder of a flimsy chair, Judge Stallworth began to encourage the child in his athletic and gymnastic prowess. At the child's behest, this was kept secret from his mother.

On the Tuesday afternoon following the delivery of

the funeral cards, Duncan Phair brought Edwin to his grandfather's by special invitation. While the boy was romping with Pompey in Washington Square, watched over by Judge Stallworth from his study window, Duncan Phair told his father-in-law of Black Lena Shanks's curse on the family.

"I wasn't trying to keep it from you, you understand. It wasn't that sort of thing at all. I simply didn't take the matter seriously. How could I? The family was already wanted by the police, and after the killing of the two policemen they became actual renegades. What harm could such persons do us?"

"None," said Judge Stallworth. "Why do you tell me this now?"

"It occurred to me that Lena Shanks, or perhaps the surviving daughter, might have sent the mourning cards on Sunday."

"I think not," said Judge Stallworth. "I'm rather inclined to follow your initial reasoning: the *curse* of that woman—as you call it—was sheer impotent rage. We have nothing to fear from that family—what little there is left of it now. Besides, such persons as that never take revenge on their betters—vengeance they reserve for their own kind. I tend to agree with Marian: the mourning cards were the joke of someone jealous of our recent advancements, and that is all."

The judge smiled and pointed out the window. Edwin and Pompey had drawn a little crowd just below the great marble arch in the Square. When Pompey stood on his hind legs and barked, Edwin would promptly and obediently execute a flip; and if Pompey barked twice, Edwin would double his maneuver. It was an amusing tableau of reversals, and pleased the judge immensely.

Duncan Phair was as busy now as he had ever been in his life. The investigations into the Black Triangle had not left off, and the new business of the firm, not all of which could be relegated to George Peerce, brought him early to Pearl Street and kept him there until late.

On Wednesday, October 4, Duncan did not finish his day's work until half-past seven, at which late hour George Peerce and the four clerks had left for the day, leaving him alone in the office. He extinguished the lamp, locked the chamber door, tried the other doors, and finally passed out into the hallway. From the top of the stairway leading down into the entrance hall he looked down and saw two women, richly if inelegantly attired, standing on either side of the front door. "Scylla and Charybdis," he thought to himself. The small ceiling lamp did nothing to illumine their features, for their faces were covered with veils that were overshadowed anyway by their peaked, feathered hats. Both were dressed with unmodishly large bustles and a multitude of flounces and both carried large fringed reticules in the crooks of their folded arms.

"Yes?" called Duncan from above. "May I help you? All of the offices in this building are closed now, I believe." He began to descend the steps.

"Yes," replied the woman whose dress was dark green. "We're waiting for Mr. Phair."

"I'm he," said Duncan, pausing at the foot of the stairs. "My offices are up one flight. Why didn't you knock there?"

"We've particular business," said the woman whose dress was crimson.

"It must wait then," replied Duncan, "for I'm late for my supper. You must come back tomorrow, during regular hours. Please return tomorrow, or at your convenience, and apply to my clerk for an appointment. You may state your business to him."

"Our business is with you," said the woman in crimson.

Duncan attempted to pass between them, but the two women seized his arms powerfully and flung him toward the staircase. His back struck solidly and painfully against the studded newel post there.

"What!" he exclaimed.

The woman in the green dress, whose hands had been hidden behind her reticule, now held them before her as she advanced on Duncan. The nails were more than two inches long, and glinted in the light of the overhead lamp. They were made of brass and had been filed to a slicing sharpness.

The crimson woman slipped behind Duncan, lifted him from the floor, and held his arms behind him. He struggled to escape, but his thrashings were ineffectual. He had never known so strong a woman before, and the very novelty of being captured by a female deprived him of strength.

The brass nails flicked against his throat in what was almost a playful gesture, but a moment later he felt the warm trickle of blood down his collar. When he raised his hand to protect himself, the brass nails sliced across his knuckles, drawing rivulets of thick blood.

The brass nails were poised together, and then poked clawlike into Duncan's mouth where they gouged with dizzying pain into his gums. His mouth filled with blood.

He gagged, and the nails jabbed again, shredding his lower lip.

The woman in the green dress drew back, and Duncan stared at her with stupefaction. He was lifted higher from behind.

Holding her third finger and forefinger close together before her face to form a prong of bass sharper than a meat fork, the woman smiled.

She advanced slowly and Duncan stood stock-still. Instead of swallowing the blood that gathered in his mouth, he held it in his cheeks.

The woman raised her hand before his face, and with a graceful circular gesture, pointed the brass prong at his right eye.

Duncan lifted his right foot and brought it down with as much force as he could gather onto the foot of the woman who held him. Her grip faltered and he pulled away from her.

The woman in green lunged at him, and the two fingers plunged into his bearded cheek, piercing it through. Duncan gasped in pain and jerked away, tearing the nails from her fingers. She turned on him with a vicious cry, and dug her hands into his shoulders.

He spat a mouthful of blood in her face and she stopped, blinded.

Duncan threw the weight of his body against the double doors. He crashed through, tumbled down the steps, and with the two brass spikes embedded in his cheek, ran as fast as he could down dark, deserted Pearl Street.

The two policemen dispatched to Duncan Phair's offices found no evidence of the struggle but splattered blood about the base of the staircase and a length of fringe that the lawyer identified later as being from the reticule—he thought—of the woman in green. The two brass nails, once they were dug out of Duncan's cheek, were curiously and minutely examined by the police. One old officer, now relegated to desk duty at Mulberry Street, said that he recalled a young woman during the Draft Riots who had affected these long brass nails on both hands and had inflicted great injury. "Don't think it could have been the same one though, she'd be past sixty now, I'd think, had her teeth filed too—incisors like steel drills, plant 'em in your arm and fill her mouth with blood. Maybe it's her daughter. . . ."

None of the injuries Duncan had sustained—on his face, in his mouth, and upon his hands—was of any real seriousness, but all required time and leisure to heal. He was advised to rest in bed at least a week.

Marian Phair had been shocked and indignant when her husband was returned to Gramercy Park in so disreputable a condition. She considered that victims of crime deserved as little sympathy as the perpetrators; there was something in one's physiognomy, she contended, that invited victimization; something, she was certain, that all the Stallworths lacked, and that others—Cyrus Butterfield for instance—possessed in large measure.

"What happened, Duncan?" demanded Marian sternly, sitting at her husband's bedside, just after the physician had left the house.

"I was attacked, Marian, by two women in the hallway of my offices. Just within the front door."

"Why did they attack you? Did they want money?"

"No," said Duncan, turning his face, "evidently not."

"Duncan," she said, "does this have anything to do with the cards that we received on Sunday? Are you keeping this from me? You and Father? Not telling me that we're in danger?" Her voice became increasingly shrill. "May I expect to be set upon in the street by two harpies, dragged from my carriage, and trampled upon in the mud! Is that what you've cut out for me!"

"No, of course not, Marian," he said uneasily. "This is unconnected with the cards that were sent on Sunday. That was a joke, this was serious business, but with the careful descriptions that I gave to the police, those women are likely to find themselves at the Island if they come near me again."

"I don't believe you," snapped Marian, and walked out of the room.

Duncan was anxious to speak to his father-in-law, for despite his protestations to Marian, he was certain that this attack had been initiated by Lena Shanks. To his surprise, Judge Stallworth declined to take that view.

"No," said the judge, standing at the foot of his son-in-law's bed, and holding a docile Edwin by the hand. "Depend upon it, Duncan, these women were after money—"

"No," protested Duncan.

"—*or*," he went on, over Duncan's objection, "they mistook you."

"Father," said Duncan. "they called me by my name. Before they attacked, they made certain of my identity!"

"Well," said Judge Stallworth, unperturbed by Duncan's reasoning, "I will admit that it is possible that the women sought revenge of some sort. You helped to jail their father, or their sons, or their husbands, their lovers —or sent them to jail themselves. You say you didn't recognize them, but you can't remember every petty criminal that passes through the courts and neither can I."

"These wounds I wouldn't call 'petty,'" said Duncan peevishly. "I don't know when I'll be able to take a mouthful of food without discomfort."

"Doubtless, Duncan, this was merely an unfortunate consequence of your researches into the Triangle. We needn't concern ourselves more with it. These women— whatever their motives for their attack were—are satisfied now." Judge Stallworth lifted Edwin onto his shoulder, tenderly rubbed the child's belly with his bony hand and, warning the child not to knock his head against the doorjamb, walked out of the room without another word to Duncan.

Duncan decided that he had done his duty by telling his father-in-law his fears; he had resolved never to be culpable again in a matter of withholding information from the old man. Helen, Benjamin, and Edward Stallworth, each of whom in turn came to visit Duncan, declared themselves disturbed not only by the violence of the attack but by its meaninglessness, its lack of motive.

Duncan Phair eagerly agreed, and resignedly bemoaned his position as an unoffending victim of the harpies dressed in crimson and green.

After a week's careful searching, the police could find no trace of the two women who had assaulted Duncan Phair. It was a mysterious thing, the police considered, and persisted in their belief that it was all a matter of personal vengeance. And, as the days passed and the members of the family remained unmolested, Duncan allowed himself to think that the murderous attack had been intended only for himself, a result of some minor portion of the Black Triangle investigations. This small deception, practiced upon himself, was far preferable to the thought that Lena Shanks might have begun to act on her fearful threat.

Chapter 31

In the second-floor chamber of number 1 King Street, where Mrs. General Taunton had spoon-fed an aged, dying married couple, Black Lena Shanks sat in a scarlet-cushioned wicker chair, and by means of a mirror that was attached to the window casement, observed the traffic that moved constantly between MacDougal and Varick streets. On this pleasantly chill Saturday morning early in October, her daughter Louisa and the pugilist Charlotta Kegoe sat stiffly in chairs a few feet distant. The children reclined on their grandmother's bed, playing cards.

"Bad choice, I think," said Charlotta, "to send those two girls to do it. They're used only to drunken sailors, and when they come upon a lawyer that's sober and strong, they can't take him. Lena, I'm grieved I told you about 'em."

"No matter," replied Lena with a wave of her hand.

Louisa made signs that were readily interpretable. Next time, she and Charlotta would go out on such an errand themselves.

"No," said Lena, "we're not to be involved directly. Don't want you on the street. Don't want you to be seen, Louisa."

"What about Duncan then, Nana?" cried Rob, knowing

the man only by the name Maggie Kizer had called him.

"He'll lie safe for a while," replied Lena, and paused while a heavy water cart rattled noisily by. "Just for a while."

What's to be done now? asked Louisa with her hands.

"Send for Pet Margery."

Ella threw her cards down upon the sheet and hopped off the bed. From a wooden crate in the corner of the room where her clothing was kept, she extracted a ragged red dress and slipped it over her head. She tied a large yellow bonnet over her hair, taking good care to hide her side curls and, barefooted, ran out into the street.

Lena watched her granddaughter's progress down King Street. Ella seemed an aimless hungry beggar-child, moving without purpose, and everywhere pausing. But presently her wandering took her to the unsigned facade of a gambling house on the far side of Varick Street, and she slipped inside without anyone apparently taking notice of her.

In a few minutes she swung out of the door again, munching a crust of bread and waving a beggar's perfunctory thanks—as if she had unexpectedly obtained charity within. Her aimless peregrination then eventually brought her back to the stoop of her own building, where she played upon the lowest step for a while. Then, as if with pointless curiosity, she wandered up to the doorway and noiselessly dropped inside.

"On her way!" cried Ella a moment later, when she appeared in the doorway of Lena's room. Yet it was a quarter of an hour before Lena Shanks saw the slight, pretty figure of Pet Margery advancing up King Street in a white dress a little the worse for mud and damp filth about the hems and cuffs, and twirling a black and white striped parasol over her shoulder. Ella had wakened the young woman from her sleep and she had wanted time to dress.

Pet Margery was a sixteen-year-old whore, whose mercenary sights were set only on those men who had made winnings in the gambling saloons of the Black Triangle. This specialization had been a natural consequence of her having been reared in the faro saloon of her father, Henry Porter, that stood on Varick Street within sight of Lena Shanks's glass. Pet Margery had made herself the familiar mistress of all the gambling halls in the area, from the most respectable—Harry Hill's back room—to the very lowest, where dice were tossed on a blanket laid over the muddy earthen floor. She had been for several years one of Lena Shanks's regular customers; Pet Margery had been on the streets since she was twelve.

Charlotta Kegoe ran downstairs to meet Pet Margery and accompanied her back up to Lena's room. "Hiding out, Lena?" squealed Pet Margery in a voice that was considerably more femininely childish than Ella's.

"For now," replied Lena.

"What can I do for you, then?" said Pet Margery, dropping daintily onto the edge of the bed, twirling her parasol prettily upon its bent point.

"A little work I want done. . . ." said Lena.

"By me!" cried Pet Margery, and giggled. Her hair was dyed red, but so cheaply that the color had come off on the brim of her white hat.

"*Ja,*" replied Lena solemnly, "by you."

Lena Shanks and Charlotta Kegoe in tandem then gave the girl minute descriptions of the three men who had been touring the Black Triangle for the articles in the *Tribune.*

Quickly, Pet Margery identified them. "Always together," she cried, "always together. Don't gamble much except the young ône; don't drink much, always together. So they're the ones who print the articles. Pa'll be glad to hear, I'm sure!"

"No!" hissed Lena, "not yet. Where were they last?"

"Three nights back: Hudson Street. Hibernia Hall cellar, young one losing at schuss."

"Want you to find 'em again, go out looking," said Lena. "Find 'em again, and send word to me."

"If I'm all the time looking, how'm I to work?" cried Pet Margery.

"How much do you make a night?" said Lena.

"Seven," she replied truthfully, then thinking better for herself, added, "sometimes fifteen."

"I give you twenty a night while you're looking. And not a word, Pet, not a word. . . ."

On March 16, directly after fleeing the buildings on West Houston Street, Lena Shanks and her daughter

Louisa and the twins Rob and Ella had secreted themselves in the rooms of Charlotta Kegoe. They might have
felt themselves safe if Lena had not recalled so well the
strange appearance of Helen Stallworth in that out-of-
the-way house. Lena considered it necessary that they
depart the city immediately, and in fact, by the time
Simeon Lightner's account of the incident on West Houston Street had appeared in the *Tribune,* all four of the
family were already to be found in a small house that
they had taken in Mantoloking, New Jersey. They spent
six months in this seaside resort masquerading as a bereaved and reclusive family of prosperous circumstance.

Weeping Mary had accompanied them in the guise of
a superior servant, had secured the house in which they
lived, had dealt with brokers and butchers and dressmakers and inquisitive neighbors. Charlotta Kegoe guarded
the Shanks's interests is New York, and each week was
pleased to report that no progress had been made by the
police or the newspapers toward their finding-out.

Simeon Lightner and Duncan Phair's boast that the
Shanks family, through the closing of Lena's shop, the
death of Daisy, and the suppression of Louisa, had been
reduced to penury, was ungrounded. For despite these
things, and even despite her family's exile from New
York, money was no difficulty for Lena. Louisa had been
a wonder with the family's finances, and their fortune
was all safely invested, deposited, held in banks all over
the city and in Philadelphia too. Of all that was valuable
in the houses, only the account books had been taken
away. After only two weeks of hiding in Mantoloking,
Louisa made a foray back to Manhattan and withdrew
five thousand dollars from a bank on Chambers Street.
This money was for present exigencies, but it also proved
that the family was financially secure; the purblind police
had not discovered the talents that Louisa had buried in
every part of the city, beneath a great and varied list of
feminine Christian and common surnames.

However, it was not lost upon Lena that if not Daisy
but Louisa had died upon the stoop of number 203, all
their funds would have been irretrievably lost. Louisa's
skill as a forger was required to withdraw their funds
from the bank.

Louisa went back to New York once more, in May,

to arrange for the exhumation of her sister's corpse from the potter's field near Eighty-fifth Street. Daisy was reinterred, by stealth and night, on the side of a hill in Greenwood Cemetery. Louisa could find no one who would undertake the removal of Maggie Kizer's body from the graveyard on Blackwell's Island, however, and the octoroon must remain in that desolate place.

The Shankses returned to New York on Saturday, September 16. With funds provided by Lena, Charlotta Kegoe had purchased the two houses, number 1 and number 2, that faced one another across King Street, almost at the corner of MacDougal. The old couple of the second-floor-front had died some weeks before and their chamber had remained vacant. Simple furnishings were moved in here for the use of Lena and the twins. Louisa stayed in Charlotta's chambers and Weeping Mary was installed across the street. The Reverend Thankful Jones, the red-haired prostitute, and the young boy on the second-floor-back room remained as they were, and were scrupulous in their lack of curiosity about what went on in the rooms occupied by the Shankses. As Mrs. General Taunton had predicted to Helen, Mrs. Leed and her baby had not long survived their visit.

During their first week back in New York, the Shankses did not venture out of the house on King Street. Lena sat at the window upstairs and observed all that transpired in the street below. The children took turns at the door downstairs and minutely examined all who passed on the walk. At the end of seven days, Lena declared herself satisfied that their return to the city had been undetected.

Now the children and Louisa began to make expeditions about the city, always in different, concealing dress. Louisa had gone to the young boy in the second-floor-back room and he had supervised certain changes in her attire, the dressing of her hair, and the paint on her face, which made her unrecognizable as the starchily dressed, greasy-fringed Amazon who had tossed Officer Pane over a balustrade. The most anonymous of spies, these three soon discovered all there was to know of the Stallworths: their occupations, habits, habitations, servants, friends, and finances. They became studiously familiar with the chambers on Pearl Street, the Criminal Courts Building, Madison Square, Gramercy Park, and the Presbyterian manse. Lena's former customers were approached, as Lena directed, and these women, who had been only sorry that Lena was forced to leave the city and had been incensed over Daisy's death, promised their assistance to her in any small way that might be thought helpful. They did not have to be told that they would be well rewarded for their loyalty.

As all this was going on, Lena sat in her scarlet wicker chair on the second floor of the house, and from behind the heavy black veil of her bonnet—for she was still in deep and sincere mourning for her daughter—watched the ever-varying and grimy traffic on King Street. At last, on Saturday, September 30, when Louisa indicated to her mother that a certain young woman, of whose many names the most commonly used was "Cyanide" Susan, had been approached and secured, Lena Shanks raised her veil slowly, and said: "They have forgotten us. They think that we're dead. *Die Zeit ist gekommen!* Our time has come."

The eight mourning cards were delivered to Gramercy Park on the following afternoon by Rob in a neat black suit.

Chapter 32

SIMEON Lightner had long since made the rounds of all the well-known establishments in the Black Triangle, and the nights he spent there now he looked on as gleanings. His articles in the *Tribune,* rather than outraged and indignant, tended to be humorous or pathetic. He would relate interesting anecdotes of internecine wars among thieves, provide an amused account of a breakfast in a house of evil ("all oyster juice and aspirin"), or describe the deathbed of a miser.

On the night of Friday, October 13, 1882, Simeon Lightner and Benjamin Stallworth found themselves on West Street. Duncan Phair did not think himself sufficiently recovered from the attack of the two women to venture out at night into the Black Triangle.

West Street, at ten o'clock, was always awash with drunken sailors whose ships had docked only that day or the day before. The grog and gambling shops along this avenue had all been given names designed to entice seamen: The Sea Shanty, The Southern Cross Emporium, The Sailor's Succour, and the like. Most of the buildings were so meager and poor that the sign painters were put to the extremity of their craft to emblazon the entire name across the front.

Just across from where Charlton merged into West Street was a grimy little gambling hall and saloon called the Jolly Tar's Tavern. It was about twenty feet broad, a single story, with no real door, but only a dirty red curtain thrown across a rude opening cut in the clapboard walls. Two women, probably as repulsive in paint as they would have been without it, stood and beckoned sailors in, with promises of cheap plentiful liquor, cheap buxom girls, and tables of faro and pinochle and sancho pedro where no one ever lost.

Other places along the ill-lighted route being little more attractive, the two repellent shills managed to bring in a number of men, desperate for conviviality, who were just in from the sea. For no reason other than that they had not been there before, Simeon and Benjamin pulled their hats down low over their eyes and allowed themselves to be herded through the red curtain.

The entire low-ceilinged room was the color of saffron —the gaslight shining murkily through the palpable tobacco smoke. Just within the door was a large rickety piano, painted yellow, with a yellow-faced man who played with great dexterity but without expression or interest, and between every two songs, sipped at an empty glass that was kept at his side. There was a short bar to the right, presided over by an enormously fat woman wearing a bright blue dress and quantities of gold jewelry. She wore an expression which said: "When I'm sent to hell, the devil will contrive no greater punishment than to keep me behind such a bar in such a place as this. . . ." To the left were a dozen or so long tables, crowded with sailors of a dozen nationalities, all of whose varied clothing was alike stained with liquor and dirt. They growled and sang and yelled insults at one another and swore eternal friendship and made improper suggestions to the waiter-girls. These half-dozen young women, of singular coarseness, wore indecently short skirts, spangled tights, and boots with bells dangling around the high heels. In the back, several tables were set up for gambling: the promised games, plus euchre, seven-up, and sixty-fives as well.

Simeon and Benjamin, though certainly out of place in a saloon entirely given over to the entertainment of seafaring men, purchased from the sullen barkeep schooners of the best beer and took places close to a circle of Dutch sailors who, soberer than the rest of the room, were therefore probably plotting some mischief. With practiced eyes, Simeon and Benjamin observed everything. The reporter had long given over the habit of making immediate notes, for the appearance of tablets and pencils in such places was not looked on with favor.

After a little, when they had finished their beers and ordered more, Benjamin wandered to the back of the room, and for several minutes observed the games in progress there. Merely in the interests of investigation, he placed several small bets and was gratified that he did not lose all his money at once. Simeon had remained behind, and engaged one of the waiter-girls in conversation.

Neither Benjamin, intent upon his game, nor Simeon enthralled by the prevaricated narrative of the waiter-girl into whose hand he dropped a quarter dollar every few minutes, was aware of the entrance into The Jolly Tar's Tavern of Pet Margery Porter. She wore a red jersey and a blue and white polka-dot skirt and showed herself altogether a better quality female than this place was used to entertaining.

Nevertheless, it appeared that she was acquainted with the barkeep, to whom she nodded friendlily, and from whom she accepted a glass of neat whiskey out of a bottle that had never served a sailor. Pet Margery then made a small tour of the place, airily putting off the vociferous advances of the men at the tables. When she came close to Simeon Lightner, she quickly averted her face and scanned the back of the shop.

Her eyes fell upon Benjamin. She glanced quickly around once more, then turned again to the front of the shop. "I'll be back," she whispered to the barkeep, and stepped outside.

She glanced sharply up and down West Street. Ella, who had been dawdling near the door in rags, scurried over and begged a coin. Pet Margery drew a nickel from her reticule, handed it to the child, and whispered: "The dopey one and the red-haired one are inside, handsome one ain't with 'em. Run and tell Lena. Tell her I know what to do!" The child scampered off down West Street.

Pet Margery pushed inside the red curtain once more and sauntered past the bar to the back of the shop.

Benjamin Stallworth sat on the rough bench before

the faro table, a rough affair itself with a much-stained green baize cover, and the playing board decipherable only by those already familiar with its configuration. Benjamin was.

Beside him sprawled a sailor, very drunk, whose sole motive for sitting there was apparently to lose all his money as quickly as possible so that he might return to the safety of his ship. His companion was a shrewd Yankee, not long a sailor, who kept a stack of silver coins in a dried eelskin and extracted them one by one to place upon the board. His goal was to make as much money as possible, but he only lost.

Benjamin had just lost twenty dollars when Pet Margery in a sweet voice, begged room on the bench beside him. He glanced up at her, recognized her immediately for a prostitute, and nervously gave place. In the past six months, Benjamin had seen and heard much of which he had been previously ignorant, and he was often content to declare that he had really seen and done quite everything that there was to see and be done in New York; but the fact was that the noisy breath of one of these women upon his cheek still raised a copious perspiration on the inside of his collar.

"Here," she said, handing Benjamin a five-dollar gold piece, and accompanying the action with a confiding smile, "place it on the jack to win." The next round was about to be dealt.

Benjamin, blushing, did so.

"That's kind of you," she said. "What's your bet then, sweetheart?"

"Trey to win, deuce to lose," stammered Benjamin and placed his bet of ten dollars accordingly.

The other two men at the table scattered their coins across the board, one with as much care as the other carelessness.

"I win," said the young woman, and drew her arm within Benjamin's, "and I'll buy you a sherry cobbler, but if you win you have to buy me one. How's that?"

"Oh!" cried Benjamin, and glanced toward Simeon Lightner. But he was still occupied with the waiter-girl and Benjamin saw no reason not to imitate the reporter's gallantry. "We needn't wait. Order one for both of us now. . . ."

The young woman laughed gaily and nodded one of the waiter-girls over. She gave the order, just as the banker began to deal off his deck of cards.

With intense interest, Benjamin watched the cards turned up, first on the one hand and then on the other. The young woman regarded them hardly at all, though she watched the banker with considerable attention. Once or twice he lowered his eyes in a deliberate fashion in what was possibly the equivalent of a wink.

The sherry cobblers were brought and consumed, and both Benjamin and the young woman lost their bets. The shrewd Yankee sailor alone won, gathered his money, and ambled satisfied out of the saloon.

The drunken sailor took all his remaining cash and placed it atop the ace to win, while Benjamin and the young woman were more sparing in their wagers. All three lost, just as two more sherry cobblers were delivered to the table by the jangling waiter-girl.

"Oh!" said Benjamin with great reluctance, "I suppose I'm about done for tonight," and he smiled wanly at the young woman at his side. He rose, and attempted to disengage her arm from his.

But she rose with him and pulled him over to the side, pointedly out of the hearing of the croupier. "It's terrible!" she cried. "That's a crooked table!"

"No!" exclaimed Benjamin, "I've seen crooked tables! I know crooked tables. I watched him closely—"

"And I watched closer!" cried the young woman. They stood in close conference beneath one of the yellow gas lamps, and turned their faces toward the dark wainscoted corner. "He cheated! Dealt off the bottom of the deck. And I touched one of the cards: marked with pinpricks!"

"Oh!" cried Benjamin with great disappointment.

"You was good to me," purred the young woman, "so I want to give you some advice—"

"Yes?" said Benjamin wonderingly.

"Don't come back in this place. Won't get your money back, won't do no good to make your accusations known. Your money's lost like you had throwed it off the top of the East River bridge."

"Yes," said Benjamin ruefully. "It's not likely I'll be back here soon."

"You like the cards, don't you though?"

Benjamin laughed. "Yes, I suppose that I do a little." The tête-à-tête with this young woman, who was quite pretty, was pleasing to Benjamin. Any other prostitute by this time would have urged him back to her furnished room on Chatham Street and then gone huffy away when he declined—but this young woman had said nothing about that at all.

"Well," she said, "I know of a place where the tables are straight, least *one* of the tables is straight. . . ."

"Around here?"

The young woman nodded.

"Where is it?" demanded Benjamin.

"Nearby, I'll take you there. . . ."

"I'm here with my friend. May I bring him too?"

"No! You come alone. . . ."

"Alone?" said Benjamin, on his guard once more.

"I like you," said the young woman, "just the kind of fellow I'd take up a suburban residence with in New Jersey."

Benjamin laughed. "I'm not so good-looking, you know. I know I'm not so good-looking . . ."

"Well," said the young woman, "I seen all kinds and I been with all kinds, and you find a man who's perfectly paralyzing in the face, and you go up and make love to him and he knocks you in the middle of next week. . . ."

"Well, I don't strike ladies, I can assure you."

"No," said the young woman, "I could tell. What's your name?"

"Benjamin. Benjamin"—he paused—"Ticknor," giving the name of a prominent lawyer and Democrat.

"Well, Benjamin Ticknor, you meet me tomorrow night at the corner of King Street and MacDougal— you know where that is, don't you?—and I'll take you where there's a straight table. There's probably no more than two in the entire city, but I know of one."

"How do you know it's straight?"

"My pa runs it! And if he don't always run it straight, least he runs it straight for me and my friends. . . ."

Benjamin laughed. "All right then, I'll come."

"Fine! Remember: King Street and MacDougal. Ten o'clock. And it's a secret, you know. Scrape up what you can, grub around in all your pockets 'cause you're sure to win!"

"I'll be there," said Benjamin. "What's your name?"

"Margery," replied the young woman, "but everybody calls me 'Pet.' "

"Well, Pet, I'll see what I can do about raising a little money. I've spent the last year looking for a good table, and if you can show me one I'll be beholden to you."

Pet Margery laughed, shook Benjamin's hand as if she meant to pump another promise out of him, and tripped laughing out of the saloon.

"Well," said Simeon Lightner when Benjamin had rejoined him, "you made a conquest, I think. What'd you have to pay for such a smile and laugh as that?"

"Oh," shrugged Benjamin, with ill-concealed pride, "it was nothing. It was just that we both lost at the table. We both lost a couple of dollars, that's all. . . ."

Just outside the red curtain of The Jolly Tar's Tavern, Ella, in rags, sat hunched and apparently sleeping against the clapboards. However, as soon as Pet Margery appeared she jumped up and ran around the corner of the building. Pet Margery followed.

In the darkness of that alley stood a woman in a stiff black dress, with a short black bonnet drawn close down over her face.

"Meeting him tomorrow evening," said Pet Margery, and grinned. "Ten o'clock, corner King and MacDougal, Lena can watch from her window. Then to my father's. Everything'll be set up."

Louisa Shanks gestured impatiently, and the little girl interpreted: "Why not here? Why not now?"

"Because," said Pet Margery, "he's with a friend. And the place is full of sailors—can't count on sailors. Tomorrow'll give us time to have everything set up, time to prepare—and he'll be alone."

Chapter 33

ᴏ⊚⊚⊚⊚⊚⊚⊚⊚⊚⊚⊚⊚⊚⊚⊚⊚⊚⊚⊚⊚⊚⊚⊚⊚⊚⊚⊚⊚⊚⊚⊚⊚⊚ᴏ

Oɴ Saturday morning, October 14, Marian Phair left the house on Gramercy Park in the company of her two children Edwin and Edith and turned northward toward Madison Square. On Saturday mornings as pleasant as this Marian liked to dress the children in clothes even finer than those they wore on Sunday morning and parade them through the neighborhood. Other proud mothers did the same, and chancing to meet such another, Marian always had the ready excuse that Edwin and Edith were being taken "to visit their cousin." True to her word, Marian stopped at Twenty-fifth Street, fetching out Helen, and proceeded to ambulate Madison Square, nodding to all the gentlewomen who passed, and staring in the shop windows.

However, it was not entirely as a matter of fashion that Marian was taking the children out today. Only the day before, as she was on her way to Gramercy Park, the children's nurse—who had been with Marian for three years, since Edith was born—had had both legs broken by a newsgirl. This grubby child of about ten years, apparently taken with sudden insanity, had run after and attacked the nurse with a length of iron pipe. The child had immediately fled down Fourth Avenue and was lost to pursuit, but her apprehension would scarcely have solaced Marian for the loss of Edwin and Edith's nurse.

As soon as she was informed that the unfortunate victim would not be able to work for at least two months (and possible would always be lame), Marian Phair telegraphed to the *Tribune* to insert an advertisement for a nursemaid, but she could not expect any applicants to appear before Monday. One of cook's nieces could be got in as a temporary substitute, but Marian was reluctant to leave her children long in the charge of an uneducated Irish girl. Marian was vexed, and today only the fine weather and the splendid appearance of Edwin and Edith had reconciled her to cheerfulness.

Madison Square was bright and bustling at noon on Saturday, for nursemaids were often given that afternoon off and mothers took the opportunity to meet one another in the fashionable air of this part of the city. Helen always wore her best when she accompanied her aunt to the square, for she knew she would be upbraided if she did not.

Staked to propriety with the admonitions that they should neither soil themselves nor speak to other children who were not at least as well dressed as themselves, Edwin and Edith were allowed to roam among the flower beds and shady groves of the cool square. Helen and Marian commandeered a bench on the northern edge of the square, facing away from the sun. Marian raised her blue parasol and Helen folded her hands in her lap in unconscious imitation of her father.

"Helen," said her aunt, "I think that after Monday we will hold no more regular meetings of the committee."

Helen glanced away, and touched a gloved finger to her lips. "Oh," she said, trying to betray a surprise she did not feel, "why not, Marian?"

"I've done much thinking, and I've come to the conclusion that charity ought to be individually performed. A committee such as ours will necessarily appear formidable and cold to the impoverished objects of our charity, who might respond more warmly to succor that was personally applied."

"I've always thought so," said Helen softly.

"Well, in this instance, I suppose that you were right. I

will speak to the ladies on Monday—no program has been announced anyway—and suggest that they continue their charitable endeavors on their own. I shall of course thank them for their work, which has been efficacious in its way of course, but explain that we must now move on to other fields."

"What if the ladies do not wish to disband?" asked Helen.

"That is their right," said Marian, offended even at the thought. "Of course they may want to continue, but I must explain to them that my house will no longer be available to them as a place of gathering—and I can hardly see another of the ladies taking on the expenses that are attendant upon such responsibility. And of course I would have to insist that the name of the committee be changed, which was formed under my directorship and my aegis. It could not continue in its present form without me—surely they would understand that, Helen."

"I don't believe that they will *mis*understand you, Marian. I only hope that the ladies will see fit to continue with their charities, once the committee is disbanded. In any case," said Helen, "I shall certainly go on."

Marian turned surprised to her niece. *"You?* What will you do, Helen?"

"I only meant . . . I only meant that I hope that I can continue to be of some small service to the inhabitants of the Blighted Triangle. I've come to prefer thinking of it as the 'Blighted' rather than the 'Black' Triangle, you know."

"By all means," said Marian complacently, "only be certain that you don't go near the place yourself. It is far too near as it is. Your father says that a Roman candle ignited in the Black Triangle would explode over our house. It's a fearful thought!"

When the bells of the Presbyterian church steeple struck the hour of one o'clock, Helen asked her aunt if she might be excused, that she had promised to pay a visit to one of her father's parishioners early in the afternoon. Marian, who approved of anything that propelled her niece further into society, graciously assented, and asked upon whom she intended to call.

"Mrs. General Taunton."

Marian did not know her, and asked for a description,

so that she might identify the woman from the church congregation.

Helen was vague, and mentioned neither her mourning garb nor her maimed servants. "She's plump, I think you might say, of middle age, and possessed of a singularly sweet nature."

Marian still could not identify Mrs. General Taunton, but let the matter pass. She kissed Helen on the cheek and waved her off with a smile. Then she withdrew an advertising circular from her reticule and began minutely to examine and contrast the new hats of the season. Occasionally she looked up to nod at women of distant acquaintance who passed by. Now and then one would stop beside her and speak for a few moments.

After half an hour more, Marian felt that she had had quite enough of air. Most women had already returned home to dress for their dinners—most fashionably served at three o'clock—and although Marian would not dine until five, thought she might as well give the impression that she was required home at the more genteel hour.

She stood, turned toward the park, and called out sweetly for Edwin and Edith. There was no response to her summons.

She glanced over the crowd of children playing among the shrubbery on both sides of her and before her, but could make out neither among the roaring infants. She was distressed, for she realized that they had been out of her sight for more than an hour, long enough to involve themselves in any amount of mischief or danger. Marian suddenly recalled mourning cards that had been addressed to Edwin and Edith, and Duncan's earnest entreaty that the children be watched closely at all times.

She moved a little farther into the square and arched her neck inelegantly in trying to descry Edwin and Edith, but her children appeared in none of the swirling groups that she came across. She began to hurry along the shaded paths, taking one or another without thought or system, and lightly touching the trunks of trees with her fine gray kid gloves in continued expectation and disappointment of finding them.

She came out on the southern side of the square, and with mounting disquiet set out—with some real distraction—toward the eastern end, which was clothed in denser greenery and where Edith and Edwin might possibly have hid themselves deliberately from her view. She passed recklessly along, peering into every clump of greenery and behind every thick-trunked tree, pausing without breath only to ask nursemaids if they had seen her children, who could be recognized by their fine blue pinafores.

Marian had reached the eastern edge of the square, and noted with something very close to fear the amount of traffic along Madison Avenue. Children might easily be trampled beneath the horses' hooves there or, crossing safely, would fall prey to kidnappers or worse. On a bench that faced the street, a few dozen yards from Marian, sat a solitary nursemaid with her charges and Marian hurried toward her to ask if she had seen Edwin and Edith.

Very great was Marian's relief when, coming closer, she found the nursemaid's charges were none other than Edwin and Edith themselves, placidly seated on the bench and eating grape ices. The nursemaid very carefully wiped their faces to keep the liquid from splashing their finely starched tunics.

"Oh Edwin! Edith! Where have you been! You've made me frantic! Frantic!"

"Mama!" cried Edith, and attempted to struggle down from the bench, which was high for her stubby little legs.

The nursemaid held her back and snatched the ice from her hands. "Oh no!" she cried with acute dismay. "You'll spoil your nice new outfit! Be careful!" The nursemaid turned to Marian and smiled sadly, "I found them wandering along the sidewalk about to run into the street, so I bought them ices and kept them here till their mother or nurse came along."

"Oh!" cried Marian, "I'm ever so obliged to you! They could have been killed! Edwin! Edith! Pray give your thanks to this young woman for preserving you from the hooves of the horses!"

"Thank you," said Edwin politely. "Oh, Mama, she bought us ices too!"

"Thank you," said Edith, but wistfully, for her own ice had been plucked away.

The young woman looked to be about twenty-five. She was just over five feet in height, with brown hair and a fair, Irish complexion. Her melancholy face was full and round, and her gray eyes were red-lidded, as if she had recently wept, and copiously.

"Are you a nurse?" asked Marian. "I suppose you are here with other children in your charge."

"No, ma'am," she replied with a deep sigh, "that is to say, I'm a nurse, but I've no position just at present. The family I worked for went to San Francisco this Tuesday past and wanted me to come with them, but my mother is here and I could not find it in my heart to desert her."

"Very commendable," said Marian graciously. She and the nursemaid had exchanged places. Marian dabbed a lace handkerchief to her lips and forehead and sought to recover from her excitement. The nursemaid stood respectfully before her.

"I used to come here with little Emma and Jerome every day and grew very fond of the square; and just now, without employment, it seemed very pleasant to return," the nursemaid said sadly. "I saw your children, ma'am, and thought them the most splendid children I had ever come across, superior even to little Emma and Jerome, though Emma and Jerome were splendid children too." She sighed again, then picked up more energetically: "But they hadn't the grace and beauty of yours, if I may say so. . . ."

"Oh, Edwin and Edith *are* very lovely children, are they not?"

"Very," said the nursemaid, kneeling before Edwin and wiping his mouth dry with her own white handkerchief.

"What is your name?" asked Marian.

"Katie Cooley, ma'am."

"And you're looking for a position as a nurse?"

"Oh yes!" cried Katie. "Do you know of any? I've been searching the papers every evening for a place, but places are so quickly taken, and not everyone will employ an Irish girl."

"No," said Marian thoughtfully, "not if she is like the general run of Irish girls, who are coarse and illiterate and whose red hair will invariably clash with all the furnishings of every room of the house. But," she said more kindly, "you do not seem the ordinary Irish girl. You seem considerably more refined."

"Thank you, ma'am," said Katie Cooley, and blushed.

"My mother was an upper servant in Lord Coombe's house in Dublin. She reared me right. I beg your pardon, ma'am, but *do* you perhaps know of a position that wants filling for a nursemaid, in a respectable household?"

"Yes," said Marian, "I do. Mine."

"Ma'am!" she whispered. Tears welled in her eyes.

"Yes. Would you be willing to take on Edwin and Edith for me—supposing of course, that your references are sufficient? You have references, I suppose?"

Katie opened her bag and drew out three carefully folded letters, which she gave to Marian. "Here they are. I always have them with me."

Marian smiled and took the letters. "If you would be willing to walk Edwin and Edith about for a bit, I will sit here and read these through. The business may be concluded then in a matter of moments."

Katie gratefully took the two children by their hands and quietly urged them down the walk. When she returned several minutes later, Marian sat smiling serenely upon the bench.

"These are sufficient for my purposes," said Marian, returning the letters.

"Oh, ma'am! I'm so glad then!"

"Before you agree to take the position, Katie, we must speak of terms—"

"Anything you wish, ma'am. For two such children as these, I think I should almost work for gratis."

Marian smiled. "My husband and I can afford a little better wages than that." She directed the children away from the bench, and when they were out of earshot she said to Katie, "Sixteen dollars a week, half holidays on Sundays, every other Thursday or Saturday off, if you prefer—"

"Oh, at your convenience, ma'am."

"Saturday is my convenience then. You have a room next to the nursery, where Edwin sleeps. Edith will sleep with you. My husband and I are often out very late and occupied during the day, so the children will for the most part be left to your complete charge. The letters that you showed me indicate that you are not averse to such responsibility, and I shall be happy to leave Edwin and Edith in your care."

"When shall I begin, ma'am?"

"Immediately, if you wish."

"Oh, yes, ma'am."

"Good. Then you may accompany us back to Gramercy Park. And your things will be sent for this afternoon."

When she returned home, Marian Phair instructed Peter Wish to inform all applicants who came to the door that the position of nursemaid had already been filled.

Chapter 34

IN Madison Square, Helen had found Edwin and Edith leaning against a tree, watching with envy as half a dozen children played a boisterous game that soiled their clothing. She kissed them farewells, and went back to Twenty-fifth Street again. She changed into the simple black outfit that she had come to call her "visiting dress," and set out for the home of Mrs. General Taunton, carefully avoiding the streets on which she might encounter Marian on her way home. Marian would doubtless upbraid her for wearing so poor and dismal a frock when out visiting—even a widow.

As usual, Mrs. General Taunton received her companion with utmost graciousness, intimacy, and affection. The woman in black had grown very fond of Helen in the past months and much admired her energy in dealing with the poor and the unfortunate. There was now no hesitation, no condescension, no discomfiture in Helen's manner when she ministered to the needs of the Black Triangle.

Yet though Helen had convinced herself that her motives were selfless—and how could she doubt her disinterestedness when no one but Mrs. General Taunton knew of her taxing endeavors?—Helen was full of pride, over that very selflessness. She burst sometimes wanting to tell her

249

family of her work, so that she might show them that theirs was a perverted misunderstanding of the Black Triangle, while hers was the Christian, the good, and the only right view of the place. But knowing that the Stallworths would never conform to her view of charity, she dared say nothing, for fear that her visits would be interfered with or stopped altogether.

Helen was offered and accepted a place at Mrs. General Taunton's table. While waited upon by the one-eyed maid, on whom Helen could now smile without dwelling upon or even really recalling the girl's affliction, she and Mrs. General Taunton discussed the progress of the cases that had occupied them over the past couple of weeks.

"The Fale child that we saw on Monday," said Mrs. General Taunton, "you remember that pretty, pretty infant not yet given a name, has died of the consumption that looks soon to take their father too."

"It has been buried?" asked Helen, cutting into her chop.

"After a fashion. To save burial expense, the mother wrapped it in a blanket, pretended it was asleep, and took the cars up to the Central Park. There she scooped a hole in the earth with her own hands and placed the child in it."

"Oh!" protested Helen, putting down her fork.

"I remonstrated with her of course. 'Mrs. Fale,' I said, 'your daughter deserves burial in consecrated ground.' She said she thought so too, but burials were such an expense, and all their money was wanted to keep her husband supplied with physic. I gave her money for the burial of the child and have sent the carriage to her this morning, to return to the Central Park and show Dick the place she buried it."

"I'm *glad* you did that, Anne, so very glad!"

"I do not believe that the child would have been denied entrance into heaven only because it had been interred in the Central Park, but I think it will make the mother feel better to know that her precious daughter lies within the precincts of a sanctified churchyard."

"Oh doubtless!" cried Helen.

After their dinner, Mrs. General Taunton invited Helen to accompany her on an expedition to visit a boy with one leg whose father had committed suicide with Paris green and whose mother had absconded with a Chinese cigar maker to set up a laundry in Brooklyn. But Helen declined, and asked only that she be allowed to ride so far as Varick Street—there was an indigent seamstress in that neighborhood to whom she had promised a commission of employment, and it was her plan to pass the remainder of the afternoon there.

"I am happy," said Mrs. General Taunton, "that you are going out on your own, dear. Not that I would not have you by me always, of course, but it is good that you appear sometimes without my protection."

"Yes," smiled Helen, and just as she spoke this, the coach turned off MacDougal Street onto King and rolled past the house where Helen had made her first visit to the Black Triangle nine months past.

She pointed it out to Mrs. General Taunton. "I regard that house with affection now, though I was so frightened then, Anne, I don't think I can say just how frightened I was."

"The woman and her baby are dead," sighed Mrs. General Taunton. "And the husband is in Sing Sing. He tried to rob a United States senator. The old couple on the second story are dead too. It's a hard uncertain life that's led in the Black Triangle."

Out of the windowed door of the building, the little slender face of a boy was peering at the carriage as it drove past. Helen smiled and waved, but the child dropped immediately out of sight.

"I should return," mused Helen. "Revisit the scene of my first embarrassments, and prove—only to myself, of course—that now I'm beyond such personal discomfort, where charity is concerned. Those we tried to help now are dead, but perhaps others, equally unfortunate, have acceded to their place."

There was one piece of charitable work that Helen kept secret, even from Mrs. General Taunton. Early in September, on an afternoon when the widow had been indisposed, Helen had gone alone into the Black Triangle and visited, at Mrs. Taunton's suggestion, a ladies' hat maker living in quite a respectable little house on Morton Street. The ladies' hat maker's consumption appeared, even to Helen's inexperienced eye, to be hopeless; but she left a Testament interleaved with the address of a doctor on a scrap of cardboard, and a five-dollar note. In the hallway downstairs she encountered a young woman who wept copiously; and when Helen inquired the reason for her distress, the young woman—a pretty girl called Jemmie—replied that she had just had an argument with her friend. Helen volunteered to listen to the girl's story at greater length, and was accordingly invited into first floor apartments that were furnished with more enthusiasm than taste.

Here Helen attended to a tearful, disjointed tale of imagined jealousy on the part of the girl's friend. "Oh p'rhaps you've seen Annie—she's the best fighting girl in New York! Annie's always been good to me. It's Annie, you see, who pays for my lodging here and it's Annie that buys me things every day, but she gets terrible jealous when she thinks I talk to other girls, and it don't make no matter that even when I'm talking to 'em—and sometimes I gets lonely, you see—I'm all the time thinking only about Annie, but she don't believe it."

Helen tried to assure Jemmie of Annie's affection, and told her that it was certainly only a matter of time before Annie came to see that Jemmie's love was real and undivided. It was in the midst of this lengthy speech that Annie Leech herself appeared in the room, glowering at Jemmie and threatening Helen with grievous bodily harm.

Helen was amazed by the construction that the Amazon in the doorway put upon her presence in the apartments of her friend Jemmie, and was at terrible pains to demonstrate the innocence of her visit. This was accomplished only when she emptied out her reticule of the eight redletter Testaments that it contained and Annie Leech had interrogated the ladies' hat maker upstairs. She returned to Jemmie and Helen mollified, and though Helen at this juncture would happily have taken her leave, Annie Leech insisted that she remain and take a glass of wine in apology.

As she consumed her small glass, it occurred to Helen suddenly that the relationship of these two women might be called by some word less innocent than "friendship." Yet she could have only admiration for the sincere solicitude that Jemmie felt for her friend's feelings, and rested in wonder at the passion of Annie Leech that could excite such terrible jealousy. She was too nervous to say much to the two women, for she feared offending them; but when it was time to take her leave, Helen found herself engineering an excuse to herself to return to Morton Street. Yet no excuse was needed: Annie Leech herself invited Helen to come back the following Saturday—and though Helen could fathom no reason for this invitation, she accepted it with an alacrity she disguised only with difficulty.

She had indeed returned—and every week after that— so that she looked forward eagerly to the Saturday afternoons spent on Morton Street. Helen built up a strange intimacy with the two female friends. She found them anxious for companionship that was of a better sort than either was used to, and Helen was in the novel position of representing polite society. She gently corrected their manners, suggested small improvements in the furnishings of their rooms (suggestions that were always effected by the time of her next visit), and listened with eager ears to all the gossip of their strange society of female pugilists and their female friends.

It was to Morton Street then that Helen Stallworth directed her steps when Mrs. General Taunton's carriage deposited her at the corner of King and Varick streets. There she found Annie Leech and Jemmie, and Jemmie's young niece fearful and wide-eyed between them on the sofa. Helen greeted her new friends with a warmth she had never been able to lavish on anyone in her life. She accepted tea, she questioned Jemmie's niece on the subjects of her occupations and recreations, she wanted to know of all Annie's pugilistic exploits in the past week, and studied carefully Jemmie's account books. She advised Jemmie to visit a butcher who was almost certainly honest, and whose meat was almost certainly unspoiled; and smiling, she listened to Annie's earnest entreaty that she witness but a single bout in Harry Hill's place.

"Oh," cried Annie, "we'll get you up the longest veil you ever did see, we'll get you a veil to sweep the streets with, and we'll put Jemmie on one arm, and we'll put 'Ralda here on the other arm, won't nobody know you, won't nobody touch you, and in that place, in Harry Hill's place, you won't be seeing nothing you haven't seen worse of in a hundred other places in this neighborhood!"

"Do go with me one evening," pleaded Jemmie. "There's nothing that's so exciting as seeing Annie lay one of her friends on the boards and jump up and down on her face!"

"Oh," laughed Helen, "I'm sure there's nothing like it! Not tonight, I couldn't go tonight, but—"

"Saturday next!" cried Annie Leech. "Saturday next! Then I'm taking on Michigan Sally again, and see if I don't tear her heart out of her bosom and toss it to you for keepsake!"

Helen laughed at the extravagance of Annie Leech's speech, but in her heart she was very happy for the affection that prompted it.

Chapter 35

W HEN Helen Stallworth returned home that Saturday afternoon at dusk, she was very much surprised to find her grandfather seated stiffly in the front parlor of the manse.

"Oh!" she exclaimed softly, "is Father not here?"

"Edward is in his study. I have asked him to remain there while I pursue a conversation with you, Helen."

The sternness of his voice alarmed Helen, and she seated herself near him with some trepidation.

"Grandfather," she whispered, "what is it you wish to discuss with me?"

Judge Stallworth fixed a petrifying gaze upon his granddaughter and said, "As head of the Stallworth family, I am desirous to learn in detail of the work that you have performed over the past nine months—in the Black Triangle of all places. Your reputation, Helen, has at last passed beyond the boundaries of those invidious acres and reached the ears of your ignorant family. Please explain to me, Helen, how it is that you have gained so great a name for yourself in that interesting neighborhood." His white, bony hands lay folded in his narrow lap.

Helen turned away amazed. "If I've a . . . a . . . reputation," she stammered, "it is only for charitable work performed always with love, I hope. A reputation—"

"Behind our backs!" shouted Judge Stallworth, erupting into white anger. "For months you've done this! It's no wonder you chafed so at Saratoga! You've become as familiar with the streets and alleys of the place as any common streetwalker, exposing yourself to danger and moral outrage with every step you take! Breathing pestilential atmospheres! Ministering with your own hands to contagion one hour, and the next you're visiting Gramercy Park, fondling Edwin and Edith! It's a wonder that my grandchildren aren't writhing in their beds with boils and blisters brought up from that place on the tips of your fingers! It's a wonder we've not all died of contagion! It's—"

"I have never knowingly exposed myself to contagion," answered Helen. "I have always been careful. I—"

"Careful!" cried Judge Stallworth. "Were you careful of our reputations? Were you careful of the Stallworth name? Helen *Stallworth*, representing the family, wandering the streets of the Black Triangle, followed by a gimlet-eyed coachman and a grotesque old woman who could make her fortune in a Bowery show—is that what you call being *careful?*"

"How did you . . ." began Helen, but could not complete her question for hot tears.

"How did we discover your perfidy?" said Judge Stallworth with scorn. "How did we learn of your months-long devilments? From Simeon Lightner, who once saw you in an open carriage, made inquiries, and now with some glee, has reported to Duncan. It has been only with the greatest difficulty that we have persuaded him not to publish your exploits. Duncan is amazed, Marian is prostrate, your father's head is bowed with horror. I am angry and I am disgusted. There is no defense for your reprehensible conduct, but please tell me what there is to be told, tell me all—we do not wish for further surprises in this matter."

Helen then, weeping the while, told her grandfather of her demoralizing dissatisfactions with Marian's committee, of her talks with Mrs. General Taunton, of her first frightened visit to the Black Triangle, of subsequent easier visits, of her becoming acquainted with the streets, the people, the ways of the place, of her little schemes and devices for the alleviation of want and suffering; and with a little pride, of the growing acceptance of her presence by the people of the Black Triangle. "Oh Grandfather," she cried, with some scant hope that he would be moved by her words, "sometimes now, when we drive through, on our way to and from delivering a basket or visiting the sick, the people call out to us! They call us the widow and her daughter, and have made up fantastic stories of Mrs. General Taunton's husband, supposedly my father, and of the great wealth we're supposed to be possessed of! These trips have come to mean so much to me. They've filled my whole life. I never realized before how much one or two persons acting simply and alone, could accomplish. Not that I'm proud—I have no right to be—but I'm made glad to the core of my being when I see a child playing on the walks who might have died a month before if we had not brought a doctor to his bedside. It was Father's sermons that inspired me! He painted such misery there, such want and such privation, that I felt my heart would break if I didn't do something to help those poor unfortunate people."

"Those poor unfortunate people are full of criminal wickedness," said Judge Stallworth, "and their very breath is tainting."

"No!" protested Helen. "They are made evil only by circumstance. By inclination, they would lead honest, industrious, gentle lives. I have spoken with them, and predilections to goodness fall from the mouths of all. Oh, Grandfather, and I've seen as bad as ever appeared before your bench!"

"Helen, no respectable woman will consent to set foot in the Black Triangle. When you first contemplated these foolish actions, this ludicrous course, did you stop for one moment to think what the repercussions might be —to yourself and, more importantly, to your family?"

"Grandfather, I—"

"Obviously, you did not. Obviously, you had no thought in the world but the gratification of your own vanity, the setting up of your own spirit on an altar of your own building. Helen, you are such a gull, such a gull! Tricked by that insane woman in widow's weeds, that fat silhouette of mourning, whose house no one will go into because it is no better than a lazaretto, with all her servants maimed and deformed! Duped by those you profess to minister unto, the criminal and the vicious, who want only your gifts, your small-change beneficence, whose real pleasure is to sully a lady with their loathsome contact. You're an object of ridicule to them all, Helen! Have you been so purblind as never to have seen that? Certainly when this becomes known—and how you thought you could keep it secret for long I can't imagine!—you will be trussed and spitted above the fires of gossip and opprobrium. And what will be my position, when it is known that I permitted such a thing for my own granddaughter?"

"You didn't permit—"

"Worse and worse!" cried Judge Stallworth. "We didn't permit, we didn't even know of it. It was done behind our backs. My granddaughter absent from the house four or five hours every day parading around the Black Triangle in an open carriage, in the company of a lady of doubtful mental faculties, and we knew nothing of it! Worse and worse!"

"I have never done anything in connection with the Black Triangle of which I need be ashamed."

James Stallworth eyed his granddaughter closely and was silent for a few moments. When he spoke again, it was with a quietness that contrasted strongly with his former vehemence. "No? Then what of your intimacy with Mademoiselle Leech? What of her 'friend?' What of them? Half-women! Would-be men! What of them? Such loathsome creatures would be outcast even from the society of condemned murderers on Blackwell's Island! And yet you have established yourself as their intimate. . . ."

Helen, mortally embarrassed, looked away. "I have never refused those who were in need of assistance—"

Judge Stallworth smiled coldly. "Mademoiselle Leech is not in want. Mademoiselle Leech is amply rewarded for her appearances in the ring. The friend of Mademoiselle Leech does not suffer from the ravages of any physical disease. And if they are possessed of souls completely corrupted, they are at least blessed with sound bodies and pocketbooks, are they not?"

Helen nodded slowly, and dared say no more in her defense.

Judge Stallworth stood, and came near her chair. "You are to go there no more," he said quietly. "Do you understand? No more journeys on what you mistakenly assume to be a charitable mission. No more commerce with Mrs. General Taunton. I need not tell you that you are to make no more pilgrimages to the Sapphic shrine on Morton Street. So do you understand me, Helen? It is a sorry life I lead, my granddaughter exposing her breast to every stray arrow of vicious calumny that could be fired from a thousand drawing room windows throughout the city. If you must be lashed to the bedposts, Helen, you will not be allowed to endanger our reputations again."

Judge James Stallworth stalked out of the room and the manse, and left Helen weeping in the parlor that was now wholly dark.

When Edward Stallworth came downstairs the next day, he was relieved not to find Helen about. The judge had not exaggerated the effect of the news of Helen's charitable endeavors had had upon her father. He was distressed, embarrassed, and angry—but he still had no desire to confront his daughter. He supposed that she remained in her room, awaiting his summons, the reiteration of the family's displeasure, and the announcement of her punishment.

On his desk, he found an unsealed envelope, directed to him in his daughter's hand. He assumed, as a matter of course, it was the abject apology that she was too diffident to present in person. He stood at the window and held the letter stiffly before him so that the sunlight fell directly onto the page. He perused it with a cold condescension that gradually gave way to a mixture of wonder, shame, and rage. It read:

Dearest Father,
   I am sorry for the trouble that I may have caused you and the rest of the family. I certainly regret the necessity for silence over the past several months in regard to my beloved work, a reticence that you perhaps rightly interpret—as certainly Grandfather does—as deception. Yet that silence was I think necessary if I now consider your response to my endeavors in the Blighted Triangle, under the loving direction of Mrs. General Taunton. I cannot find fault with your views in this matter, for then I would surely be wanting in

filial obedience, but I cannot subscribe to them either. It was of course your own sermons, even more than the articles of Duncan and Mr. Lightner, which prompted me to carry succor to those unfortunately circumstanced inhabitants of our city. It is labor that has been blessed to me, exertion that has doubly turned to joy, dear Father, and I would as soon give up my life as relinquish these gladsome toils.

Therefore, and knowing that I am of age and mistress of my own fortune, I have determined to leave the manse. I could not live every day beneath your reproach. My heart would surely break. In this world a woman's lot is small and circumscribed, and I had long resigned myself, and never protested—but what I had never fully understood was that a woman's power to do good was as limited as the opportunity for great evil. I, who have so rarely ventured out of the manse in the entirety of my life, was still not made for domesticity; I have no influence over servants, hospitality is a foreign tongue, the social round is a forest through which I wander with bandaged eyes. My sphere is there, in the Blighted Triangle, and all other places where want and misery are predominant. It is in the service of such poor creatures as burden this city with their groans and wailings that I will spend the portion of my days.

Oh dear Father, if you would accept this resolution in me, I would happily return to you, so happily resume my place in the manse. In this matter alone, however, I must now and forever remain your

> Faithless but loving daughter
> Helen Stallworth

Postscriptum. I may be reached at the home of Mrs. General Taunton, where I am assured of a warm and indefinite welcome.

Chapter 36

O N Saturday night, at ten o'clock, Benjamin Stallworth stood on the corner of King and MacDougal Streets, and had actually to hang on to a lamppost to protect himself from being carried away into the boisterous passing throng. Newsboys sniggered at him, prostitutes detained and solicited him, toughs facetiously threatened his life, and he had nearly made up his mind to leave, when Pet Margery pulled gently on the tail of his coat.

"I'm mightily glad you came," she said with a smile that promised much.

"Oh yes," he replied nervously, "word of a straight table would draw me to the ends of the earth."

"My feet swolled up just thinking about you, Ben."

"What!"

"My ma always said that love was in the feet, and every time she fell in love her feet started to swell up and she had to put on mustard plasters to draw out the infection of love. After I saw you last night, I went out this morning and laid in a supply of plasters, that's just what I did!"

Benjamin blushed beneath the harsh glow of the lamp.

"And you dressed up for me, I can see it!" cried Pet Margery, and playfully jabbed Benjamin in the ribs.

"Dressed to kill, and barberized to resuscitate, that's what you are! You and Pet Margery will have one night tonight, I can tell you!"

Pet Margery slipped her arm through his, and led him down King Street. She carried herself beside him as if proud to be in the company of such a man as he. Benjamin was overcome with a mixture of pride that he had attracted the notice of so pretty a woman, who even if a prostitute, as surely she must be, had made no mention of money; of embarrassment, for she was after all a prostitute; and of excitement, thinking of the promised straight table and other pleasures too that might come to him this same night.

Pet Margery pulled him down King Street, led him across Varick, and then shoved him down a short flight of slippery steps and through a low wooden doorway, kept open despite the chill night air. Benjamin found himself in the heated yellow atmosphere of a groggery of some little pretension—at least in comparison with the rest of the places on that street. It had a mahogany bar with a brass footrail, and mirrors behind; little marble-topped tables and cane chairs for the customers—most of them women; and in the back a red velvet portiere that Pet Margery dramatically lifted to Benjamin.

The room behind—actually the cellar of the adjoining house—was entirely given over to gambling, half a dozen different tables and games, with single gas lights beneath red and green shades hanging over each. The croupiers and bankers were distinguished by their emaciation as much as by their green eyeshades.

"Oh!" cried Benjamin, "I know this area, but had no idea such a place existed. Very very pleasant," he exclaimed, "especially if the tables are straight!"

He made immediately for the schuss table, but Pet Margery guided him instead to the far corner. "That's my pa, running vanty-yune. It's the only table that's straight, and only reason it's straight is that I told Pa I was bringing a friend tonight. You stick with Pa, Ben, and your fortune's made."

Pet Margery's father was a gaunter man than those he hired, with a frame that was scarcely wide enough to hang a suit of clothes on and skin that was hard pressed to stretch bone over bone. His eyes were sunken and his cheek dabbed with a wispy yellow beard.

"Seat yourself, sir," he whispered through a throat gnawed with a cancer, "and my daughter'll change your cash. . . ."

Benjamin drew forty dollars in gold from his pocket and handed it to Pet Margery, who skipped blithely away. After a moment, which Benjamin passed watching Pet Margery's father deal out a game to the three men on the bench beside him, the young woman returned with a stack of white and red chips.

"Red's eight bits, white's a dollar, suppose you know that?" said Pet Margery's father in a hoarse whisper.

"Yes, sir," replied Benjamin, whisper for whisper.

The cards were dealt, Benjamin rested at eighteen, betting two dollars, and won from the bank.

The second and third hands he lost, but in the next three he was a large winner. Pet Margery had brought him a sloe gin sling, and insisted that he drink it quickly in celebration of his increasing pile of chips. The men beside Benjamin, as he continued to play, were of that sort whose livelihood depended upon their anonymity of appearance, and they alternated without his being able to distinguish them one from the other. They were alike too in that they all lost, and different from Benjamin also in that he was a consistent winner at the table.

Finally Benjamin, sipping his third gin sling, found himself embarrassed by the height of the stacks of his red, white—and now blue chips. "Perhaps I ought to try my fortune at one of the other tables. . . ." he suggested.

"No!" cried Pet Margery.

"Oh," Pet Margery's father warned him, "your fortune might not favor you so there."

Benjamin shrugged, though he mightily suspected that even now the table was not straight, but that Pet Margery's father allowed him to win time after time and sent all the others away depleted. He grew nervous as he heard the other players grumble, but Pet Margery's father silenced them with a look.

Benjamin, through his alcoholic haze, tried to reason this out. The only conclusion he could draw however was that Pet Margery had taken a great fancy to him, and had persuaded her father to allow him to win at vingt-etun. There was a pleasant and startling contrariness to this situation—that he was being given money by a prostitute. He must suppose that when her father had decided that he ought win no more, Pet Margery would drag him up to her room. Even if she demanded money of him afterward, for her own good name perhaps, he would be out nothing at all for the experience.

Benjamin Stallworth had never had connection with a woman before, and his suspicion that this was to be the culmination of the evening (as he had hardly dared hope before) grew stronger even than his love of the game. His attention to the jeweled white hand that was gently laid over his became greater than that to the fall of the cards from the gnarled talons of Pet Margery's father. Benjamin grinned suddenly with the notion that the old man must be in certain difficulty to allow him, who was so distracted, to win at so many hands.

"Oh, perhaps I ought to stop now," whispered Benjamin to Pet Margery, "I'm a little dizzy and can't concentrate on the cards. . . ." She had just brought his fifth glass of sloe gin.

"You've won over two hundred dollars," whispered her father. "I couldn't keep long in business if you came very often, mister. No, sir, I swear I couldn't." And he laughed a shrill laugh that echoed in his ribs.

"Oh," cried Pet Margery, "one more glass—"

"No!"

"One more glass," she repeated cajolingly, "and while you're drinking it, I'll change your chips for you."

Benjamin nodded dumbly and slouched back against the wall. He peered oddly at the man who sat beside him until the man took offense and retorted with an obscene epithet.

"No, no," whispered Pet Margery's father, "he'll be leaving soon, just let him finish his glass. He won't be bothering you, let him finish his glass, that's all."

Benjamin swallowed the remainder of the dark liquid and stood woozily. Pet Margery was suddenly there to support him. Gold chinked in her hands and she spilled it into his pocket—so much gold that he was tilted beneath its sudden weight on that side.

"Two hundred thirty-seven dollars," she whispered. "You're beholden to me, Ben. . . ."

"Oh yes," he murmured, and smiled drunkenly. "Oh yes, what . . . what can I do . . . to . . . to discharge that debt, Pet? Tell me, Pet, what can . . . what can I do?"

He turned and clumsily attempted to embrace her in his gratitude and had some confused idea that if he returned to this place every night for the next six months he would emerge from that habitude a rich man.

He slipped on the worn floor, and would certainly have fallen on his face had not Pet Margery caught him up and steadied him.

"I should take you out of this place," she said, "you're not fit for the games anymore."

"Where are we going?" he whispered, with a crooked smile.

"Oh I'll just take you to my place and feed you some tea, that's what I'll do—boil water and feed you some tea."

"Oh," laughed Benjamin, as he was led through the door. "Your place. I'd like to see your place."

"Shhh!" cried Pet Margery. "Act sober," she said, "the ladies are watching."

Benjamin made a valiant but entirely ineffectual attempt to appear uninebriated as they passed through the groggery. The ladies sitting at the little marble-topped tables nodded knowingly at Pet Margery, who returned their greetings with a bland smile.

"Oh! Which way?" cried Benjamin, as they emerged into the much cooler night air. It was nearly midnight. "What way is your room?"

"This way," said Pet Margery, helping him back across Varick Street. "I live just a few houses down there. . . ."

"Oh," cried Benjamin with almost weepy tenderness, "I won two hundred dollars tonight. I never got so much in all my life at the tables! It's because of you, Pet, because . . . all because of you!"

"That's right," said Pet Margery, carefully guiding the drunken young man down the street. "You've a lot to thank me for."

"Oh, Pet!" cried Benjamin, "do you have a bed?"

Chapter 37

━━━━━━━━━━━━━━━━━━━━━━━━━━━━━━━━━━━━━

"**O**H, it's a fine soft bed," replied Pet Margery, "and it's waiting for us right at the very top of the stairs." She pushed him through the doorway of the small brick house at number 2 King Street. "Hush!" she cried, "all the way to the top, Benjamin."

Benjamin stumblingly climbed the three narrow flights of stairs to the attic of the house. Pet Margery opened a door he could scarcely see and pushed him inside. Here darkness prevailed and he wobbled a little, waiting for Pet Margery to light a candle. The lack of light brought dizziness on, and he thrust out his hands to catch his balance; to his surprise they struck the low slanting beams of the room and came away painfully with splinters. "Oh!" he cried.

Pet Margery whispered, "Hush! Not so loudly, Benjamin, not so loudly!"

Benjamin reached out for Pet Margery, trying to drag her into his embrace, but his falling hand only slapped against her cheek. "Oh," she cried sharply, "watch out, will you? It's dark as a stack of black cats in here!"

She struck a match and lit the candle.

Benjamin was momentarily appalled, despite his drunkenness, by the poverty of the chamber. In the middle of the room, a couple of feet from where he stood, was an unpainted iron bed covered with a filthy sheet. Beneath the window, which was masked with a man's shirt pinned up by the sleeves, was a rickety table with a couple of bottles of liquor and a wooden tumbler upon it.

This was all. Neither the roof nor the floor was painted nor improved with ornament.

"You live here?" cried Benjamin.

"No!" laughed Pet Margery. "I live downstairs. Nobody lives up here. Does it look it now?"

"No," stammered Benjamin. "Why are we here then?"

"Don't want anyone breaking in on us, you see?"

Benjamin nodded dully, and attempted a salacious smile.

"You lay on the bed there and I'll bring another something." She moved toward the window.

"Don't need another. Had too many."

"No, you haven't. Just one more—to loosen your collar, Ben, you'll take another with me, won't you?"

"Yes, s'pose so, yes, I will," he murmured, and lay back gratefully on the bed.

"Here," said Pet Margery, slipping the tumbler carefully into his hand, "you sip at this, and you'll feel a deal better."

He propped himself up in the bed a little, sidling up so that his head was pressed against an iron rosette for support and brought the rough tumbler to his lips. Over the rim he smiled at Pet Margery, who sat on the edge of the bed and tenderly patted his knee. The candle on the floor beside the bed was the only illumination in the room, and it cast flattering light over the woman's face.

"Oh," he cried, reaching for her.

She playfully struck away his hand. "The gin first," she laughed, "I won't have naught to do with a sober man!"

Benjamin swallowed off the last of the liquor, which tasted to be of far inferior manufacture to that which he had been served at the gambling hall, which itself had been none of the best. There was a distinct undertaste of impurity in it, but he had swallowed so much he did not think that this much more would harm him. And even

if he had imagined so, he would have drunk anyway
as a requisite to the favors of Pet Margery.

He watched as she moved from the covered window
back toward the bed—watched as her feet seemed to fly
up in the air. "Pet!" he cried—but no more.

Pet Margery's feet had not flown up into the air, but
rather Benjamin himself slumped over into unconscious-
ness on top of the soiled sheet. The gold coins rolled out
of his pocket and formed a little mound in a depres-
sion of the mattress.

Pet Margery shook Benjamin, at first gently, but then
with increasing violence. Finding that he was beyond waking, and listening closely at his stertorous breathing which
told of pressure on the heart, she retrieved the two bottles
of liquor from beneath the window. Taking up the candle, she quietly descended the stairs, leaving Benjamin
Stallworth alone in the dark attic room.

On the second story of the house she knocked at a door,
which was immediately opened by a young hard-faced
woman with dyed hair and wearing a crimson dress with
a black apron. Pet Margery thrust the two bottles into
her hand, nodded once in the direction of the attic, and
hurriedly descended the last flight to the street door.

She peered up and down the street before stepping
out, but at a moment when the attention of the several
passersby seemed occupied elsewhere, she opened the
door and slipped down to the walk. She proceeded with a
measured tread down MacDougal to Spring Street, crossed
over and came back up again. At last, when no one appeared to be watching, she entered the house that was
directly across the way from the one where Benjamin
Stallworth lay insensible.

There was a little girl in the hallway, plainly dressed in
a black frock, and she whispered, "Pet, Pet, come up."

Pet Margery followed Ella to the second floor and
was admitted into the room occupied by Lena Shanks.
The old woman sat in her wicker chair behind the curtain. Her mirror was trained on the house opposite. Louisa
Shanks stood behind her mother in a position which afforded her the same view through the mirror. The
room was dark.

Louisa drew the curtains at the same time that Ella
lighted the lamp beside the bed.

"I saw you carry him in," said Lena, nodding approval.

"Were we seen?" asked Pet Margery.

"No," said Lena, "no one saw." And Louisa shook her head in confirmation.

"It's bad business to be seen going into strange houses with well-dressed gentlemen—especially if something's going to happen to 'em later."

"No one saw. . . ." repeated Lena with a smile. "And you told the girls?"

Pet nodded. "I knocked on their door. They won't have any trouble with that one."

"How much on him?" asked Lena.

"Two hundred and thirty-seven. That's how much Pa 'lowed him to get at the table."

"That's *their* price. . . ." smiled Lena, turning toward Louisa. Louisa noted the figure in her tablets.

Pet Margery patted her powdered cheeks gently in an emotion that was somewhat between amusement and distress.

"Good work," said Lena to Pet Margery. "What's owed to you?"

"Two hundred and thirty-seven to pay back Pa, except for forty that went for his chips at the first, that's one hundred ninety-seven. Four doses of chloral hydrate, one dollar, that's one hundred ninety-eight. And make it two hundred fifty even for my time and the risk."

Lena laughed. "No risk, no risk," but Louisa was already counting out the two hundred fifty in eagles and double eagles. She dropped them one by one into Pet Margery's outstretched hands.

When Pet Margery had pocketed them, Lena called her over, took her hand, and slipped two more double eagles into her palm. "Not a word, Pet, not a word. Tell your pa: not a word."

"Oh no!" cried Pet Margery, " 'course not. Who's to tell, Lena? Who's to tell?"

"That's right, that's right," said Lena.

"What's to tell?" cried Pet Margery. "Young man wins money at Pa's table, asks to take me out for a walk. I go, he 'tices me up to a room, and then falls insensible 'cross the bed—what's to tell? I don't know what happens to him then, I don't know nothing but that he falls insensible 'cross the bed!"

Two teaspoonsful of chloral hydrate had been poured into the glass of sloe gin that Benjamin Stallworth had drunk in the attic room on King Street. He consumed roughly eighty or ninety grains of the medicine, enough to stop the hearts of a small platoon of guardsmen and paralyze the lungs of a brace of trumpeters.

The woman in the crimson dress and black apron sat on the bed beside Benjamin and slapped his face. He did not respond, and she glanced up at her friend in the green gown who held a lamp. She slapped again, harder. Benjamin's shoulder twitched.

He was not quite dead when the woman in the crimson dress and black apron slit his throat from ear to ear with a barber's razor. She and her friend in the dark green gown jumped out of the way of the spurting blood, and when it had subsided, cursed one another for not having first gathered up the gold coins that had spilled from Benjamin's pocket.

The lamp chimney was speckled with sizzling Stallworth blood, and the pile of gold coins upon the mattress lay a gleaming island in that crimson sea.

Chapter 38

∞∞∞∞∞∞∞∞∞∞∞∞∞∞∞∞∞∞∞∞∞∞∞∞∞∞∞∞∞∞∞∞

THE Stallworth pew was curiously underpopulated the
following Sunday morning, with both Helen and Benjamin Stallworth missing. Benjamin's hours had always
been irregular, and Saturday nights in particular he was
often out late in the company of Duncan Phair and
Simeon Lightner, so Edward did not think it strange that
he did not see his son before it was time to leave that
morning for the church. It was probable, Edward Stallworth considered, that Benjamin had overslept, or that he
had had a sick headache—the result of too much lager
beer perhaps. In any case, he would doubtless make his
appearance at the family dinner on Gramercy Park later
in the day.

Although Benjamin's absence was lightly considered,
Helen's was not. The Stallworth in the pulpit and the
Stallworths in the pew looked anxiously throughout the
service for the entrance of Mrs. General Taunton and
her protégée, for they were determined to demand Helen's
return to the manse. And when neither Helen nor Mrs.
General Taunton appeared in the church, Marian, with
grim satisfaction, judged that it was shame over their
inexcusable conduct that kept them away. Helen's sudden
departure from the manse occupied all their minds and

271

the congregation went away disappointed that morning from the Madison Square Presbyterian Church—Edward Stallworth had been distracted, and his sermon decidedly inferior.

It was really only at dinner that afternoon that Benjamin's absence became as marked as his sister's. Judge Stallworth alone remained unperturbed: "I do not intend to allow my digestion to be impaired on Benjamin's account," he said. "No doubt he will sidle through the doorway at the very moment we have given up expecting him."

"Benjamin is probably in the company of Simeon Lightner," said Duncan Phair, "investigating Sunday openings of the gambling houses south of Bleecker." Marian merely thought it tiresome of her nephew that he so disregarded their feelings in remaining away so long without a word.

After dinner, Judge Stallworth and Marian, notwithstanding their pique at Benjamin's failure to present himself in the last twenty-four hours, went to the theater to witness a special performance of the only small-footed Chinese lady in the world who sang coon songs. They told Duncan sternly—as if it were a matter under his jurisdiction—that they expected better news by the time that they returned home.

. In their absence, Duncan visited the lodgings of Simeon Lightner. The reporter had no idea where Benjamin might be—he had neither seen nor heard from him since they parted company at the door of The Jolly Tar's Tavern on Friday night.

Even the desertion of her niece, and the unaccountable disappearance of her nephew had not disturbed the equanimity and good feeling that Marian Phair had gained by the acquisition of Katie Cooley as a nursemaid to Edwin and Edith. Marian had spoken to the nurse a quarter of an hour longer, to strengthen her fine first impression—for Marian realized that to hire a girl in the park, and an Irish one at that, within the course of a five-minute conversation, was hardly the way that responsible society procured its servants. But then Marian reflected that she might boast of Katie Cooley to her friends, and yet tell them only that she had been obtained through the newspaper advertisement.

What Marian did not know about Katie Cooley, however, was that this demure young woman of melancholy aspect actually encouraged Edwin's feats of tumbling and athleticism. These had always been forbidden on Gramercy Park, since Edwin had shown his mother what acrobatics he was capable of by exactly imitating the tricks and pratfalls of the clowns in a pantomine she had taken him to see. Marian had been shocked by Edwin's performance and warned him severely that young boys of his class *could* not do such things with their bodies. Yet Katie Cooley delighted in all his miraculous contortions and strange dexterities. Cautioning Edith to silence, she laid double mats across the nursery floor and allowed him to entertain them to his heart's content.

When Marian and Judge Stallworth returned from the theater on Sunday night, Marian went upstairs to remove her wraps and gloves. She peered into the nursery and, by the light of the third-quarter moon shining through the window, saw Edith warmly enfolded in the arms of Katie Cooley in the nursery bed. Marian nodded her silent approval of Katie's ruffled nightdress and her soft white cap. A girl who dressed so neatly, even in sleep, was a treasure, without doubt.

In the morning, over breakfast, Marian declared to Duncan her intention of restoring Helen to the manse. Marian was fearful that Helen's work in the Black Triangle was already known to half the city. She imagined hotly that her friends and acquaintances must have been at great pains to hide their pity and their laughter in the past months.

"I will visit Edward, and enlist his aid," she said. "The woman who has bewitched Helen is after all a member of his congregation, and doubtless stands in awe of him —or is at least in love with him. If he appears at her door, she will hardly fail to render Helen up. Helen will be back on Twenty-fifth Street in time for dinner."

Duncan Phair made no objection to his wife's plan, and after breakfast, Marian hurried upstairs to dress. A quarter of an hour later, just as she was pinning her hat, there was a soft knock at her dressing room door.

"Yes?" cried Marian impatiently.

Katie Cooley entered, and presented Edwin and Edith for their mother's inspection. "Ma'am," she said, "I've promised the children that if you gave your permission I would take them this morning up to Madison Square to play."

"Why should they not play in Gramercy Park, Katie? It is closer, it is protected, the company is select. Why go to Madison Square?"

"The children want exercise, ma'am," said Katie Cooley, "and if you'll excuse my saying so, there'll be more opportunity of showing 'em off. . . ."

"Yes of course," said Marian, well satisfied, "I'm going that way myself, and if you have given them their breakfasts already I'll be happy to walk with you."

"Oh, yes, ma'am," replied Katie Cooley, "I know Edwin and Edith would relish their mother's company this morning, wouldn't you?"

Both children nodded eagerly. "Thank you, Mama," whispered Edwin politely, and Edith murmured incomprehensibly and with downcast eyes—both children saw that their mother was agitated, and thought it best to remain with their nurse in the doorway.

"Well then, Katie," said Marian, "we shall leave the house immediately. I'm going to Twenty-fifth Street to pay a little visit to my brother."

Marian's visit to the manse was a wasted journey. Edward Stallworth heard patiently his sister's excoriations of Helen's conduct, then refused flatly to have anything more to do with the young woman. "Helen, as she writes in her letter, is her own mistress. I have no more real control over her movements than I do over her fortune. They are both her own. Father forbade her to return again to the Black Triangle. If she will disobey him, why do you hope that she will listen either to you or to me?"

"I have no intention of allowing my niece to reside with that . . . that deranged widow!" cried Marian. "Be waited on by mangled servants, spend her time keeping company with thieves and fallen women and diseased children. You may say that you give her over, but the fact is, Edward, her position reflects on us all!"

Edward did not reply to this speech, but when he was seeing his sister to the door, he said, "When you see

Helen, ask her if she knows where Benjamin might be found. . . ."

Marian shook her head in exasperation. "Edward, if I thought that Edwin and Edith would turn into such troublesome beings as Benjamin and Helen have been to you, I might wish them both at the ends of the earth! Please send word to Gramercy Park as soon as Benjamin has returned; I have no wish to worry myself into an early grave with the difficulties raised by *your* offspring!"

Marian took exasperated leave of her brother. A few minutes later in Madison Square she found Katie Cooley, who proudly pointed to Edwin and Edith who were playing a complicated and demure round game with several other well-dressed children a little way off. "I'm proud to have 'em by me," sighed Katie, "so proud!"

Marian nodded distractedly at the compliment to her children. "Katie, an important matter requires my expedition. In a while, you may return to Gramercy Park alone. I don't want Edith too long exposed to the sun. Her skin is delicate—"

"Beautiful skin! Such beautiful skin! Oh, ma'am!"

Marian did not see her niece at the home of Mrs. General Taunton. The widow politely but firmly refused that interview. "Helen is ill," said Mrs. General Taunton gravely. "The doctor was sent for this morning and has recommended that she have uninterrupted rest and quiet. Helen is suffering from an exhaustion of her faculties. She entrusted herself to my care, and I will not see her out of her bed."

Even a threat of legal action did not deter Mrs. General Taunton's resolution, and Marian Phair hurried away from that house in anger and frustration. She cursed the woman in widow's weeds for Helen's plight. Passing a telegraph office, she stopped in and sent a message to her father at the Criminal Courts Building, asking him to meet her that evening on Gramercy Park, "to discuss the matter of H and Mrs T." Another was sent to the Madison Square Presbyterian Church and read: "Mrs T claims H is ill. Not to be credited. Come to Gramercy Park, six o'clock."

Then, to calm herself, Marian stopped at an ice cream parlor on Fifth Avenue and vindictively consumed a

strawberry ice. Afterward, she took a cab to the home of
the woman who had served second on the Committee for
the Suppression of Urban Vice. At the end of half an
hour's conversation concerning the views and works of
various members of the committee, including her niece,
Marian was satisfied that her companion knew nothing of
Helen's innumerable journeys to the Triangle.

Yet when she had taken her leave, Marian again fell
prey to doubt. She considered that this good friend might
out of courtesy and respect have avoided what she would
have known to be a painful subject. Accordingly, Marian
took a cab to the home of a woman with whom she shared
neither affection nor sympathy, who had been admitted to
the committee only because of her husband's important
position as superintendent of public works of the city. This
second lady was no friend to Marian, and Marian was
sure that if she knew anything of Helen's unchaperoned
visits to the Black Triangle she would not fail to com-
miserate with Marian on the unfortunate adventures to
which Helen must have fallen victim.

Although suspicious of Marian's unannounced calling,
this second lady was very polite. Only her observation
that, "In such changeable weather as we are experiencing
at this time, it is inexpressibly difficult for a lady to maintain the freshness of her appearance for two hours together, do you not agree?" might have been interpreted
as surreptitiously malicious.

Marian plucked nervously at the perspiration-stained
wristbands of her dress and nodded grimly. "Oh yes, I
entirely concur."

Slowly, Marian walked back to Gramercy Park from
West Fifteenth Street at Fifth Avenue, and several passing acquaintances were offended when friendly nods and
soft words to Marian were unreturned.

Marian was thinking with a concentration that came
only with difficulty to her, thinking what she must do in
order to return Helen to the manse. It would be terrible
if it became commonly bruited about that her niece had
left her father's side and joined the establishment of a
second-rate widow of marked eccentricity—this, even if
the world never heard of her visits to the Black Triangle.

During the three-quarters of an hour that Marian had
spent with the lady who was not her friend, great storm

clouds had been flung over the city from the west. Had her mind not so occupied itself with thoughts of Helen's disgrace, Marian surely would have hailed a cab, but the walking soothed her some. She was caught by surprise in a deluge of rain that began without warning but with quite awful intensity. Even after she ran the last square to her house, she arrived at the door sodden and bedraggled.

Peter Wish immediately opened the door to her when she precipitously knocked. Marian stepped into the hallway, with water pouring from her ruined dress.

"Peter, is Mr. Phair in? Has he come in yet?"

"Yes, ma'am," replied Peter Wish hesitantly as Marian in the hallway before the mirror unpinned her hat and untied her veil. The running of the dye in them had left her visage a pale streaked blue.

"Is he in his bedroom?"

"Yes, ma'am," replied Peter, still with hesitation.

"What is it, Peter?" demanded Marian, turning her blue face on him full.

Amy Amyst peeped out of the drawing room door. "Are you alone, ma'am?" she asked, in a distressed whisper.

"Of course, who should be with me? Amy, I want you upstairs this moment to help me out of these clothes!"

Peter Wish clasped his white-knuckled hands tightly before his waistcoat.

"The children, ma'am," said Amy Amyst. "And Katie Cooley. It's almost five o'clock, and they not been home since eleven this morning. We had hoped they'd be with you!"

Chapter 39

Lena Shanks sat in her scarlet wicker chair beside the mirror set in the window frame, and only now and then cast a cursory eye over the crowds in King Street below. Since their return from New Jersey, she and her family had remained undetected, their presence known only to such women as could be trusted absolutely. Pet Margery Porter had not even told her father that it was Lena Shanks who had set up the young forlorn-looking gentleman to be cheated and robbed, and the gaunt old man—since he had received his gambling-table money again—asked no questions of his daughter.

Still, Lena considered, a woman could not be too careful, and not many hours of the day found her away from her position by the window. Gradually she came to know, by appearance and occupation and habit, those who frequented King Street, came to know them almost intimately, though they had no idea that an observer existed in the second-floor room.

Louisa kept constant company with Charlotta Kegoe downstairs, and only now and then, in ample disguise, ventured out to do business at the banks. Gradually, Louisa had converted the family's financial holdings into negotiable securities. Half of these papers were kept locked in a box that rested beneath Lena Shanks's chair, and the other half were sewn into the lining of Louisa's petticoats. After Daisy's sudden, unforeseeable death had demonstrated the frailty of Lena and Louisa both, the mother and surviving daughter had thought it best that access to their wealth ought not be dependent upon Louisa's abilities at forgery.

The twins were as watchful as their aunt and their grandmother. Because they were small, because no one took notice of them—at least when they were not together —they were the ideal messengers and errand runners; and there was no end to the trust that Lena and Louisa Shanks placed in Rob and Ella. The children always performed their parts with expedition and glad hearts. They were equally content to run miles to a distant part of the city simply to copy down a name from a brass plate on the side of a building, or to while away hours late in the night attending Pet Margery on her rounds of the gambling saloons, allowing themselves to be punched and knocked about by the bullying newsboys, to be shooed away by the police, to be lectured by the unctuous. And when not wanted, they sat in their grandmother's dim chamber, cross-legged on the bed, playing at écarté and pinochle. Each had a little chipped red china cup—gifts from Maggie Kizer in a happier time—and pennies that they bet against one another now filled Ella's cup, only a few days later all to be lost to Rob again.

On this Monday afternoon the children had laid aside their cards and crept up to the attic of the house. Through a hole in the roof they could see the North River and the hundred ships that sailed there. A great storm had come up over the Jersey Palisades and whipped down across the gray water. Boats were blown crazily about, and several appeared actually in danger of capsizing. The clouds grew darker and dropped lower and almost at once the rain began falling torrentially. It drenched the children's surprised upturned faces, doused their clothes, and formed shallow pools on the straw-strewn floor of the attic.

Ella drew back quickly, removed her new spectacles and wiped them dry on the hem of her skirt.

Rob and Ella descended to their grandmother's room. The door was locked, but a brief characteristic knock admitted them.

The rain beat so heavily against the glass on the room's two windows that for a moment nothing else could be heard. Before they had stepped far into the room, however, Rob and Ella could distinguish a tiny voice that cried, "Mama! Oh, Mama!"

In a large chair brought up from Charlotta Kegoe's apartments and set directly across from Lena Shanks, two small children were tied with a thick leather strap. The elder child, a boy, wriggled and wept piteously and cried for his mother. The smaller, a girl, stared intently at Lena Shanks. They were dressed in rain-drenched blue pinafores.

Weeping Mary, lately known as Katie Cooley, nodded friendlily to Rob and Ella.

"Piece of cake," she sighed, "piece of cake. Could have stayed for the jewels, but didn't want to hurt Lena's plans. Wouldn't harm Lena's plans for the world. Their mother had beautiful jewels, I tell you, no end of beautiful jewels. Her two beautifullest jewels are sitting right here though," she said mournfully, knocking her head in the direction of the two children strapped into the chair. "I got 'em here, but I tell you what, I tell you they almost drowned, those jewels almost washed away!"

"Go down, Mary," said Lena, "and tell Louisa to bring us tea."

"Oh sure!" cried Weeping Mary, and shook Rob and Ella by the shoulders as she went out.

Lena Shanks briefly broke her attention from the two small children and motioned Rob and Ella over. "Come," she said.

Rob and Ella slowly approached. Ella went around and stood between Lena and the rain-pounded window. Rob placed himself on the other side of his grandmother.

Edwin and Edith Phair regarded Rob and Ella Shanks dismally. They knew that their mother would never allow them to consort with children who were so poorly clothed.

"Mama!" cried Edwin. "Mama wants us home!"

"No, she don't," said Ella with a smile. "You're to live here with us now."

"Here?" said Edith, looking around and wondering at the dim poor chamber.

"No!" cried Edwin. "Mama wants us home! We live on the park, we live—"

"Your mama has sold you to us," said Rob, and Lena Shanks laid a coarse hand atop her grandson's fine slender fingers. "So now you're ours, both of you, that's all. From now on, you'll live here with us."

"No!" cried Edwin and burst into loud tears.

Ella leaned forward, quickly twisted around several of the rings on her fingers, and slapped Edwin hard across the mouth. He broke off suddenly in surprise, and then began to whimper from the pain. He touched his hand to his cheek, and wonderingly gazed at the blood that he brought away on his fingers.

Thoughtfully, Ella licked the child's blood from her rings.

"Now you have to behave," said Rob with a smile, "or we'll have to sell you again. We'll sell you to a pudding maker, and he'll throw you in a great hot vat and melt you down till there's nothing left but your bones and your hair, and we'll sell your bones to a man who'll carve little soldiers out of them for me to play with, and we'll make your hair into a wig to put on my sister's head."

Edwin sat back terrified, and plucked at the leather strap that cut so tightly into his belly.

"My name is Edith," said his sister politely, "and I'm very, very wet."

Edwin and Edith Phair slept that night on a cot placed by the side of Lena Shanks's bed. Edith, despite the unaccustomed coarseness of the shift that Rob had dropped over her head in exchange for her wet clothing, fell asleep immediately, and seemed not to stir the night through. Edwin, however, with a little gleam in his sullen eye, had sought to lengthen the evening, with the confused conviction that he and his sister were more likely to be discovered by their mother if he remained awake. He insisted on displaying for the twins and their grandmother all his nimble tumbling ticks: the way that he could walk upon his hands, and dance around the furniture in a series of graceful flips, and whirl about with a lighted candle balanced upon his nose. Rob and Ella gleefully applauded this performance, and even Lena Shanks smiled a crooked little smile; but at nine o'clock the light clapping subsided, the smile faded in the wrinkled face, and Edwin Phair was strapped into the bed beside his sister. Though he attempted to remain awake behind his closed lids, the strangeness of the day and his predicament had wearied him so that he soon fell unconscious, with his hot weepy eyes pressed into his sister's tangled hair.

Next morning, the children tasted coffee for the first time in their lives, and devoured less than their fill of the sweet rolls that were delivered to the door of the room by a tall, fearful-looking woman, whose jewelry, painted onto her skin, mesmerized Edwin and Edith.

This woman held whispering conference with the great fat woman, and all the while glanced coldly on Marian Phair's unfortunate offspring. After a little, the twins were brought over, and shortly instructed.

"Edith," said Rob then, turning to the little girl with a bright smile, "you're to go out with me today."

"Home?" cried Edith. "The park!?"

"This is your home," smiled Rob. "Your clothes are here, let me help to dress you. Let me show you how."

While Edwin looked on, horrified—for a year older than his sister, his understanding of their situation was infinitely greater than hers—Rob dressed Edith in a thin layer of dun dirty rags, chalked out the roses in her skin with wood ash, and then smudged her all over with soot. Edith laughed, and confusedly told what her mother had once done and said when she had returned from the park looking much the same as now.

When Rob had completed the transformation of the child, Lena Shanks said, "Come," and motioned Edith over. Edith went forward bashfully.

"Turn," said Lena, but Edith stood still. She glanced back to Rob—not her brother—for guidance.

He indicated with his fingers that she ought to turn around, and smiled comfortingly. Edith obeyed.

"Good, good," said Lena Shanks, and waved the child away.

"What about me?" cried Edwin timorously.

No one answered him, and Edith giggled.

Rob, who had effected a similar costume for himself, took Edith's hand and led her from the room. "Good-bye Edwin," she called from the hallway. "Good-bye Edwin!"

Edwin bolted for the door, but Rob slammed it in his

face, and he collapsed crying onto the bare floor of the room.

A few minutes later, Ella came over to his cot and the way of the door, and the woman whose jewelry was painted onto her skin slipped a key into the lock and let herself out of the room. "There'll be someone coming for you later," she whispered to Edwin malignantly.

Edwin turned piteously to Ella and Lena Shanks. "The man with the vat?" he cried. "Is she bringing back the man with the vat?"

"Come here," said Ella, and motioned Edwin over to the window. "Quick," she said, when he hesitated.

Edwin flew to the window, and Ella pointed down into the street.

"What?" cried Edwin. "What should I see?"

"There!" said Ella. "Your sister, with Rob."

Two little beggars skipped happily along the street, dodging carts and goat wagons. As Edwin watched, his sister fell headlong onto the muddy pavement of King Street, and he gasped. Rob dragged the child out of the mire and held her hands at her side when she instinctively tried to brush the filth from her. She struggled for a moment, then submitted, and they proceeded on, out of Edwin's sight.

"Be like your sister," said Ella. "Be very quiet, lie down on the bed and be very still, or I'll toss you out the window and have done with you!"

For several hours then, Edwin sat silent and morose upon the bed. He begged to be allowed to visit the water closet, but Ella merely pointed to the chamber pot beneath the bed. Humiliated, Edwin turned his face away, but after several minutes had passed he found that he must avail himself of it after all.

A few minutes later, Ella came over to his cot and tossed him a pack of cards with which he amused himself for a time in a most worried and desultory fashion.

Ella Shanks sat quite still at her grandmother's side, reading aloud out of a newpaper, one column after another, without respect to subject: the list of bankruptcies in the city of Brooklyn occupying her and her grandmother's attention as fully as the account of the arrival in New York of Lily Langtry.

Lena Shanks, in the shadow of the thick curtains,

watched her mirror continually. At some time, however, she dropped her hand on Ella's shoulder, which signal silenced the child immediately, and she said to Edwin: "You like to do tricks, *nicht?*"

Edwin nodded sullenly.

"Show me again."

Edwin slipped off the cot, and in a lackluster ungainly fashion, walked about in a circle on his hands.

"Better! Better!" cried Lena. "Last night you did better!"

Edwin turned a series of little Catherine wheels, with a kind of aggressive dexterity.

"Oh yes! Yes!" cried Ella, and clapped her hands. "Do it that way!"

There was a brief knock at the door, and Edwin, hoping it was his mother or his father or someone known to him, fell over to the floor in happy expectation of rescue.

In came the woman with painted jewelry, and a thin man with a blue sallow face, sunken eyes, and a colorless frown. He wore a blue suit and a green waistcoat and a green felt hat.

"This is the boy," he said, with cadaverous certainty.

Lena Shanks nodded.

"Somersault," he said to Edwin. "Forward."

Edwin stared at the man.

"Is he deaf?" shouted the man.

Edwin somersaulted.

"Backward!"

Edwin did so.

The man reached into the pocket of his coat, and withdrew a pair of tiny slippers. He tossed them at Edwin's feet. "Put 'em on."

Edwin poked his feet into the slippers.

"They're nailed to the floor," said the man, staring intently at Edwin, "now somersault out of 'em."

Edwin stared down at his feet for a moment, and then did a backward flip out of the slippers, leaving them wholly unmoved.

"Very good," said the gaunt man, his frown abating a little for the first time.

"Girl," he said to Ella, "fetch me half a dozen bottles —beer, wine, empty, filled, don't matter." Ella ran out of the room, and Edwin was commanded to walk on his hands, his knuckles, the tips of three fingers. There was something in the attention of the gaunt man that made Edwin want to do his best, as if success would save him from the vat, and he whirled about with an abandonment he had never dared display in the kitchen of Gramercy Park, or before his grandfather.

When Ella returned with eight brown beer bottles, the gaunt man took them and lined them straight across the center of the room, about a foot and a half apart.

He stood at the end of the line and motioned Edwin over. "Take hold of the neck," he said. Edwin squatted upon the floor and grasped the slender neck of the bottle with both hands.

"Alley-oop!"

Edwin threw his legs up into the air behind him, and his little body rose straight above the bottle. It wobbled just once, then sat perfectly erect and still on the floor, not out of its position.

"Hold!"

Edwin remained perfectly still.

"One hand!"

Edwin drew one hand away.

"Next bottle!"

Without disturbing the first, Edwin reached before him and grasped the neck of the bottle next in line. His body moved faultlessly into the space between and above the two bottles.

"Abandon first bottle!"

Edwin let go and the bottle fell over, but he remained stationary above the second bottle.

"Poor! Poor!" cried the gaunt man, and kicked the first bottle angrily out of the way.

Blushing not only from the blood that poured into his head, but from anger at his clumsiness, Edwin moved to the third bottle without incident and then to the fourth— all the way to the eighth, and then started back again. He progressed with ever-increasing ease, and the bottles, which shook a little at first, then seemed to be glued to the floor.

"Head on bottle!" cried the man.

"Oh!" cried Edwin, thinking to protest against the difficulty of this, but the man's frown, which to Edwin upside down appeared a vicious grin, silenced him. He lowered his head carefully onto the head of one of the bottles, and then slowly released his hands. He flailed, and knocked aside the bottles next in line, but remained erect, poised on the top of the bottle. Catching his balance, he gradually straightened his legs and folded his arms across his chest. And he grinned in triumph.

"Catch!" cried the gaunt man, and tossed Edwin a mouth organ.

Edwin quickly uncrossed his arms, and flipped his hands over to catch the piece. He missed and it fell to the floor. Moving his arms like windmills he lowered one hand to the floor and retrieved it. He put it to his mouth and blew shrilly.

"Ugh!" said the gaunt man. "Can't you play!"

Edwin tumbled to the floor. "No! No!" he cried, "I can't play! Who are you!"

He turned to Lena Shanks and Ella. Both began slowly to applaud his performance.

"Are you the man with the vat?" cried Edwin.

"Vat?" He shook his head.

"Will he do?" said Lena.

"Do fine," replied the man. "How much will you take?"

"My grandfather is rich," cried Edwin, "he'll give you eleven thousand dollars if you'll take me to him."

"Orphan," explained Lena, while Ella administered a brutal little kick to the small of Edwin's back so that he sprawled at the feet of the man who was to purchase him.

"How much will you take for him?" repeated the man.

"Only twenty-five. And he'll work for nothing for five years. But you must take him far away from here. Far away from New York."

"Boy!" cried the gaunt man, with a quivering of his frown. "You ever seen the Mississippi River? You ever seen California, boy?"

Chapter 40

H ER wet hair streaming, her clothing dripping rainwater infused with pale blue dye, Marian Phair ran furiously through every room of the house on Gramercy Park, screaming the names of her children, screaming for Katie Cooley, screaming for the servants, for her husband, for her father, and for the police.

Duncan sat morosely in his study with his hands folded over his eyes and his back to the door through which his wife made a tumultuous entrance and distressed hand-wringing exit every few minutes.

"References, Marian," he ventured to say once to her quietly, as she stood trembling and drawing in great gulps of air. "Did you ask the girl for references?"

"References!" screamed Marian. "Of course she had references! She had all the best references in the world!"

"Who were the references?"

"I don't know! How can I recall a scrawled signature at such a time! Oh great God! Edwin! Edith! Edith!"

The rain beat against the windows, and Marian screamed for someone to make it leave off.

"Poor Edwin! Edith!" Marian shrieked. "They'd be no better off than if we'd slung them both into the back of a passing gypsy wagon!"

Marian Phair had always regarded her children rather

in the light of ornaments to her person. They were fleshly, they were sometimes willful, they required meat and drink and occupation, but as far as their mother was concerned, they were of importance only when they appeared, well-dressed and well-conducted, at her side on public occasions. There had been times when her conscience assailed her for her reluctance to regard Edwin and Edith as creatures with souls or any need for affection or daily attention; but that conscience she had always stifled with the reflection that when the children were older, and had developed a little conversation, she would allow them to be more often with her. Edith, particularly, was a docile thing, and could be trained toward the accomplishments of whatever ends Marian throught proper; and Edwin would of necessity gain stature as he grew older, if not by his accomplishments then at least by his position as heir presumptive of the family. But now they were lost to her, and her conscience would not be put off.

Marian also suspected that there was a plot laid against her by those jealous of her newly acquired position in society; and the conspirators had struck at her through her children. Marian demanded that Duncan fire telegrams at the commissioner of police, at the mayor, at all the newspapers of the city, demanding to know how it was possible for two perfectly well-behaved children to be abducted from a public park. Rewards must be offered for their return; guards must search every public and private conveyance leaving the city; and their descriptions must be circulated throughout the country.

A moment after making one of these basically logical, if ultimately unreasonable, demands upon her husband, Marian would fling open curtains that were closed in hope of seeing Edwin and Edith in the street beyond, beat upon shut doors in hope that they could be found behind, and run from room to room without check, as if the children fled before her and she must weary them out of their flight. In the kitchen, she railed at cook for having shut them in the ovens.

Passing down the stairs to the servants' rooms from the attic where she had searched for the children behind stacks of picture frames and beneath bundles of old clothing at the bottom of musty trunks, Marian glanced out the streaming window and saw her father hurrying toward the house beneath a wide umbrella. She lifted her skirts high and ran down three flights of stairs, smashing a vase of roses that stood on the lower landing. Wild-eyed and disheveled, she jerked open the street door and flew into the arms of stunned James Stallworth.

"Marian!" he cried. "What's the matter?" Her telegram earlier in the day had betrayed no anxiety, and the judge was amazed to find his daughter in this condition.

"Edwin and Edith—" she gasped.

"What?"

"They're dead!" she shrieked.

"Dead!"

"Dead! They're—"

"No, sir," said Peter Wish, who had appeared quietly in the foyer, "but they're missing. They—"

"Not out here," said James Stallworth, and pulled Marian within doors. "Where's Duncan, Marian?"

"Here! He won't go out and look for them! He doesn't care! He won't—"

"Peter," said Judge Stallworth, "help me to carry Mrs. Phair to her bedroom. Send one of the maids to sit with her, then fetch the doctor. Do you understand?"

Marian was helped to her chamber, and there undressed by Amy Amyst, who was amazed by her mistress's accusation: "Oh please, Amy!" Marian wailed, "if you're in league with that girl, Katie Cooley, tell her we'll pay anything to have the children returned safely. We'll pay anything! Have her mention a price, any price at all, and the money will be there! You can take it to her and no one will be notified!"

Judge Stallworth entered Duncan's study without knocking. Slowly Duncan lifted his weary red eyes.

"What has happened, Duncan? Tell me what you know. Marian is hysterical, I've sent for the doctor to sedate her. Where are my grandchildren?"

"We don't know," replied Duncan in a choked voice. "They went out with Marian and the nurse this morning. Marian left them in Madison Square park. At two o'clock, when they were supposed to have come back here for their dinner, Amy went to fetch them, but they were no longer there. We hoped that they had gone with Marian, but she knows nothing."

"Have you informed the police?"

"Of course," said Duncan. "I sent word immediately. Two officers were here and I gave them photographs of the children and descriptions of their dress."

"Has there been any request for ransom?"

"No! We've no idea what's become of them or their nurse."

"Surely your nurse was dependable! She's been here three years—since Edith was born, was it not?"

"That one is in hospital—her legs were broken last week. This girl Marian hired only on Saturday, met her in the park—Madison Square park, in fact. Found her references satisfactory, took her on!"

"Well," said Judge Stallworth, after a substantial pause. "That's the explanation then. The nurse was a female criminal. She's taken the children into hiding, and right now is probably laboring over her demand for ransom. No doubt Edwin and Edith are safe and dry somewhere or other in the city—frightened I'm sure, but safe and dry. Marian was irresponsible in conducting the business of this family in such a fashion as that! I ought to have taken Edwin to live with me. I am sure that Edwin would have preferred Washington Square to Gramercy Park, I am sorry now that I did not! As it is, we must simply sit and wait for the demand for ransom. We can hope at least that this girl is acting on her own and won't make too strenuous demands. We can hope for that surely—"

"We can hope," said Duncan, "that it is not Lena Shanks and her family that are behind it—*that* is what we can hope!"

"You are falling into inanity," said Judge Stallworth coldly. "I have told you, the lower classes do not take revenge upon the upper. This was an action initiated purely for gain."

"The children's nurse was attacked by a ten-year-old girl in the street. The Shank's had a girl that age—why could it not have been she that did it? And then one of their confederates was sent to pose as a nursemaid in order to abduct Edwin and Edith. Is this not possible?"

"No, it is far too complex a plan. The inhabitants of the Black Triangle are capable of murdering police officers with paving stones, they are capable of snatching away lost children on the street, they are capable of robbery in a black alley—but they are certainly not capable of such plots as this. I believe that you are as hysterical as Marian, Duncan."

"Remember, Father," said Duncan, "that a week ago I was attacked in the hallway of my own office building and might well have been murdered there had I not been so lucky as to escape—the motive was certainly not pecuniary. And remember." said Duncan gravely, "please remember that Benjamin too is missing, and we've no more idea where to find him than Edwin and Edith—"

Judge Stallworth's protest was stopped by the unearthly wail that hurtled down from one of the rooms above: a choking maniacal voice that shrieked, "Edwin! Edith! Edith!"

Two hours later, Duncan returned from Mulberry Street where he had visited the Bureau of Lost Children in feeble hope of finding Edwin and Edith among the hundred or so infants, of every class and description, that were swept up from the streets of New York every day. Amy Amyst stood at the foot of the stairs, grasping the banister with white knuckles.

"Oh, sir," she cried, "is there news of the children?"

"None," he said, and paused to listen for his wife's voice. "Mrs. Phair—"

"She's upstairs sleeping, sleeping at last. The doctor came, gave her laudanum, said he'd have a nurse from the agency for Mrs. Phair. And the agency's already sent her over with a paper describing terms. Judge Stallworth accepted her—he's in the parlor with the Reverend Stallworth, awaiting on you for dinner, sir. I've—"

"Thank you, Amy," said Duncan hurriedly, "I'll go upstairs now."

The door to his wife's room was shut, and very cautiously he pushed it open. In the pale lamplight, Marian lay disheveled and restless in her bed. Her hair was damp and tangled upon the starchy mound of pillows. At the side of the bed sat a harsh-featured young woman, dressed in somber bombazine and a starched white cap of lace that concealed her hair entirely. She paused a moment in her knitting, and glanced up at Duncan.

"Is she all right?" whispered Duncan.

The nurse nodded, and resumed her knitting.

"When will she waken?"

The nurse shrugged without looking up.

Duncan backed slowly out of the room.

When he turned, Amy Amyst stood before him. "Sir," she said, "I came up after to tell you: the nurse is the finest there is, but she's mute. She can't speak a word."

Chapter 41

AFTER Marian Phair's visit to him on Monday morning, Edward Stallworth had passed a bleak enough day. That Benjamin had disappeared, and that Helen had deserted him to live with a crazed Civil War widow were events that had scarred and pitted his round smooth life. Of Benjamin he had heard nothing at all, and tried to convince himself that the boy only lay drunk in a jail somewhere and hadn't the wherewithal to free himself or the temerity to communicate his helplessness. And Helen, though ill, persevered in her resolution to be removed from the manse.

It was when he discovered, upon obeying Marian's telegraphic summons to be at Gramercy Park at six o'clock, that Edwin and Edith were missing as well that the minister began to fear for his son's safety almost as much as for his own reputation.

That evening, Judge Stallworth, Edward Stallworth, and Duncan Phair did not compose a happy trio; a hundred plans were suggested for the restoration of the third generation of the family—Edwin and Edith, Benjamin and Helen, within two days all four had been taken from them—and each of the one hundred plans was then judged insufficient. Duncan volunteered to return to Mulberry Street, but Edward Stallworth still would not allow his brother-in-law to report Benjamin as missing. "If I were to return to the manse," he said, "doubtless I would find Benjamin there."

"Send Peter Wish," said Judge Stallworth cruelly, "send Peter Wish to learn if Benjamin has indeed come back. . . ."

"No, no," whispered Edward Stallworth, "we might want Peter here to fetch medicine for Marian or deliver some message. I'm sure when I return home tonight, it will be to find Benjamin asleep in his bed. Perhaps Helen will have come back too. . . ."

Judge Stallworth turned his face away, disgusted. "Then go home, Edward. If you're so hopeful of finding them there, go home and send word to us of your good fortune. We might do with such a word on this day."

But Edward Stallworth, who knew in his heart that neither Benjamin nor Helen would be in the manse, tarried and tarried, and would have slept on Gramercy Park if a bed had been offered him, or if he had not been too ashamed to ask for one.

At last came midnight, however, and Edward Stallworth must return home. The manse was dark, silent, and empty. The minister sat out the night in his study, with his chair drawn up to the window that overlooked Twenty-fifth Street. He held back a corner of the drapery and peered out into the empty street. For all his hectic patience, he saw no more than a single carriage pass, in the last hour before dawn.

The next morning he dressed wearily and made a slow progress back to Gramercy Park. In the night, there had been no news of Edwin and Edith.

"I'm returning to the Bureau of Lost Children," said Duncan. "I would advise you, Edward, to come along and report Benjamin missing."

"Yes," replied Edward softly, "I have brought along a photograph of Benjamin for the purpose."

After ascertaining that neither Edwin nor Edith had been found, Duncan managed for his brother-in-law the terrible business in the Lost Persons Bureau. The cab that the two men then took back uptown was directed neither to Gramercy Park nor to the manse—but to Bellevue Hospital.

Here at the admitting desk they learned that no unidentified children—and no one fitting Benjamin's description—had been brought to the hospital within the past
week. A child had perished of consumption the night
before, but it had been at least ten years old and the
parents had claimed the corpse.

When they emerged from the building, Edward would
have started out for his own home five squares away, but
that Duncan detained him with a word.

Edward turned and Duncan pointed out to him a little
low door in the front of the gray-stone hospital. Over it,
in letters that glinted gold in the bright early morning
sunlight was the single word: MORGUE.

"No," cried Edward. "We mustn't go in there! They're
not there! If . . . if the worst had happened, the police
would surely know. The police would have already sent
descriptions. The police—"

Duncan, without reply, moved toward the small door
in the iron-gray facade and his brother-in-law followed,
his protests growing inarticulate and finally ceasing altogether.

The New York morgue, where unidentified corpses
found within the precincts of the city were left on display
for forty-eight hours in hopes that they might be identified,
was a single room, not larger than twenty feet square.
The forward portion was a corridor five feet in width,
with a scrubbed yellow brick floor. Near the door was a
desk behind which sat a hospital attendant, whose func-
tion was principally to see that the idly curious and the
morbid, who were often drawn to this place, kept proper
respect for the anonymous deceased. A couple of stray
chairs were leaned against the wainscoting in some kind of
mockery of hospitality—as if persons came there by
chance and might want a place to rest or converse before
moving on.

A glass wall divided this narrow viewing corridor from
the remainder of the room. There the slanted floor gradually descended into a metal trough at the base of the
glass wall. On this raked floor stood four stone tables
with ornate wrought-iron bases. Upon these slabs the dead
were laid out, their heads propped upon large bricks, and
their feet pressed against a high metal lip at the base of
each slab to prevent their sliding off. Though separated

by glass, the dead lay not more than a few inches from the spectators.

A fine spray of water pumped from the East River just outside cascaded over the head of each table constantly; and served to preserve the features of the corpses from decay, at least when decay had not already set in. The water flowed over the corpse into the grooves that edged the slabs, spilled down onto the floor through a hole in the slab, and disappeared into the drains at either end of the metal trough. It was the sound of trickling gurgling water rather than the odor of death that was most oppressive there.

As Duncan spoke to the morgue attendant, Edward glanced nervously over the rough dark walls and the uneven brick floor of the place.

"There are no children here," said the attendant. "We've had no dead children for a week, except for a couple of Chinese babies that were left in a flour sack in Shinbone Alley, but—"

Edward Stallworth, unable to restrain himself, moved past the desk and up to the glass. From here his view of the four stone tables on their mockingly ornate wrought-iron frames was unobstructed.

On the first table lay the corpse of a young woman with black hair. Hers was a coarse rubbery visage that seemed to vibrate with muted expression beneath the stream of water that plashed over it.

On the second table lay an old man, the sheet that had modestly covered the woman having been folded over to the waist. The water that poured over the old man's face ran in rivulets through the thick, matted gray hair on his chest and continually—and needlessly—cleansed the two bluish bullet holes in his belly.

The third table was empty, and the water flowed down its length in gray sheets. When he saw the figure on the fourth table, Edward Stallworth cried out inarticulately and fell clawing against the glass.

The attendant rose, his chair clattering onto the bricks. Duncan Phair hurried to the minister and tried to draw him away.

"Benjamin," cried Edward.

He pointed in mute horror. On the fourth table, the

wet sheet tucked about his slashed neck, lay Benjamin Stallworth.

Edward had not at first recognized the strained apoplectic visage of his son, the blue lips parted in a grimace so that the spray splashed off his teeth—those teeth that seemed unnaturally long because his gums had shrunk far back into his mouth. His bulbous eyes popped beneath sutured lids, as if straining to open for the last look at his father. The skin of his cheeks was drawn and green. His lank wet hair was brushed far back from his brow and secured with a black string that had been tied around his head.

"Benjamin!" the minister cried, and pressed his burning forehead against the cool glass that separated him from the dead.

Chapter 42

AFTER he had adjourned his court that unhappy Tuesday afternoon, Judge James Stallworth took a cab directly to the manse of the Madison Square Presbyterian Church. Here he was admitted by a professional mourner, whose long-practiced moroseness did not begin to rival that evinced by the judge himself.

The old man was shown directly into the parlor. The undertaker's assistant went to the window and held back one of the draperies to provide grudging illumination to the dim chamber. The coffin sat pall-draped across mahogany trestles over the central rosette in the dusky carpet. The judge peered perfunctorily into it.

Though he had seen the dying and the dead many times before, Judge James Stallworth quickly withdrew his gaze from his grandson's corpse. No man ever appeared less reposeful in his casket. Already the decay that had been retarded by the running spray of East River water in the Bellevue morgue had set in on Benjamin's countenance. The drawing mouth and popping eyes strained at the sutures that barely held them closed. Benjamin's neck was sadly shrunk inside his high collar so that now, more than ever before, his head resembled a white acorn-gourd mounted on a stick.

"I am Judge James Stallworth," said the old man to the undertaker's assistant, though without looking at him, "where is my son?"

"In his bedchamber, I am given to understand, sir," murmured the assistant, and allowed the drapery to fall into place. "Mr. Duncan Phair is with him, I believe."

Judge Stallworth stalked to the door manfully, but the glass knob rattled in his trembling grasp.

Upstairs, Edward Stallworth had been laid out, almost corpselike himself, in his bed. Sweat beaded around his scalp, and the pillow was damp beneath his burning cheek.

"Well," said Judge Stallworth loudly, "what news then, Duncan? What news of all these troubles?"

"Father," whispered Duncan anxiously, "come downstairs. We mustn't speak before Edward."

"Edward is past hope and past care, Duncan. I don't believe it matters what is said before him now. Are Edwin and Edith yet found?"

"No. But come downstairs, Father. Edward is ill, Marian is sedated, Helen isn't able to come. There's no one but you and I to sit up with Benjamin. It must be done."

Judge Stallworth made no further protest, but followed his son-in-law downstairs. Candles had been set at the head of the coffin, but Benjamin's dead face was so ghastly and so fearful in the flickering light that Duncan drew the candelabrum away toward the front of the room. He placed it between two chairs, so that when he and the judge sat, the coffin was not visible behind them.

"Duncan," said Judge Stallworth when the undertaker's assistant had been dismissed, "I am as ill as Edward upstairs. These are dreadful calamities that have fallen upon us, one after the other. I have come to believe, as do you, that they are not unrelated."

"No," said Duncan, "I fear they are not."

"I doubted for a while," said the judge. "I doubted for as long as I could, but now I find myself burdened with certainty."

"On the day that her daughter died on West Houston Street, Lena Shanks cursed our family," said Duncan. "Three of hers were dead, she said—her husband Cornelius, Maggie Kizer, and her daughter Daisy, the abortionist. The Stallworths were responsible. She said that she'd see three of ours dead."

"Benjamin is one," said the judge, and glanced morosely behind him in the direction of his grandson's casket. "And I fear that Edwin and Edith constitute the complement of that curse."

"Oh," cried Duncan, "we're not certain of that!"

"Now there are three of us dead," said Judge Stallworth ignoring Duncan's interruptions. "Benjamin, Edwin, and Edith, three of my four grandchildren taken from me—and who can know if Helen will recover from her fever? Lena Shanks took her revenge on our three weakest—the two children and simple, silly Benjamin. Would that one of those poor victims had been you instead, Duncan!"

"Father!"

"Would that the guilty had taken the place of the innocent—for all of this must be your responsibility. It was your criminal connection with that harlot that—"

"It was you condemned Maggie to death!" protested Duncan. "And it was you hanged Black Lena's husband, put her on the Island, attempted to take away her children! It was you—"

"Edwin and Edith are surely dead," said Judge Stallworth in a voice that was slurred and awful. "Black Lena is now satisfied. She has murdered three Stallworths. We need no longer be concerned with her. The world may see our misery, but the world will never know that one of our number brought it upon us. I will not now institute a search for Black Lena Shanks, we will not inform the police of the identity of Benjamin's murderer. We will allow the police to continue their search for Edwin and Edith, but we can allow ourselves no hope that they will be found."

"Surely—" began Duncan.

"It's a sorry pass that you've brought us to, Duncan! A sorry pass!"

The funeral and burial of Benjamin Stallworth was very possibly the sternest, quickest, and most secretive burial in New York in all of October 1882. Even Maggie Kizer had been turned into her grave on Blackwell's Island beneath the eyes of a minister, the two required witnesses, and a parcel of gravediggers from the men's prison; a troop of squatters had watched Daisy Shanks slipped under the earth above Eightieth Street. At the bare ceremony in a bare corner of the Stallworth lot in Greenwood Cemetery in Brooklyn, it was only the cemetery chaplain, Judge Stallworth, and Duncan Phair who stood beside the coffin suspended on leather straps above the deep-dug grave. Cemetery gardeners had acted as pallbearers, and had gone away.

The judge wondered bitterly how short a time would pass before five more dollars would have to be expended to dig another hole within the charming cast-iron fence that demarcated the Stallworth plot in this garden of graves. Not very long, he concluded, and the only question was the name on the stone that would be raised above it.

The judge tossed a spoonful of earth across the top of the ebony coffin, flung the spoon into a dense shrubbery where the chaplain had to search half an hour before finding it again, and returned with Duncan to Gramercy Park.

Marian was worse. Her incoherencies had degenerated into ravings. The laudanum had only quieted them to an incessant, barely articulate murmur. At one moment she begged that Duncan be brought to her, and at the next she spoke harsh imprecations against Helen for having taken up with Mrs. General Taunton. In her mind, she readied the children for a walk in the park, and adjured Edwin against acrobatic displays. She feverishly addressed the ladies of the Committee for the Suppression of Urban Vice on the dangers of forged recommendations.

Judge Stallworth stood at the side of the bed and waited for Marian to recognize him. After several minutes her swollen red eyes, casting all about the room, at last lighted on him and she wailed, "Edwin! Edith! Edith!"

Marian Phair clawed at her father's trouser legs with such violence that the cloth was shredded beneath her nails.

Rising instantly from her chair, the nurse clasped Marian's hands—though the insane woman's strength was wild—and crossed them forcibly upon her breast. With a shake of the red fringe of false hair that crossed her brow like a frieze, the nurse motioned for the judge to leave the room.

The judge found Amy Amyst across the hallway in Duncan's bedchamber and questioned her concerning the nurse. Amy had only praise for the young woman. "She's the only one"—here she hesitated to make a criticism of her mistress, but the judge nodded for her to continue— "the only one who can keep Mrs. Phair quiet. She's the one gives her her food, and sees she don't excite herself, and don't hear nothing to cause her worry. She don't leave that room no more than Mrs. Phair do. Sir, meaning no ill of Mrs. Phair, because of course now with all the trouble the whole family is under it's no wonder she's slid a little off her beam, but we were nearly all driven out of our heads with the screaming. . . ."

"It is well," said the judge, "that we were able to find a nurse who is capable of taking care of Mrs. Phair."

"That one's strong as a brace of butchers," remarked Amy admiringly. "And it don't seem to make no difference that she can't speak a word. Don't make no difference at all."

During that and the following two days Marian Phair was lucid only twice, but at those times—during the middle of the night—only the nurse was present. And though Marian asked of her a hundred questions concerning her children, her husband, and her own condition, she received no reply at all. She was too weak to raise herself, her voice too weary to call out; and an increased dose of laudanum, quickly administered by the mute nurse, tripped Marian's rational mind back over into somnolence and quietude.

In these two days all New York talked of the misery of the Stallworths: Benjamin dead, the children missing, Marian thought to be insane, Helen rumored to have eloped with a penniless missionary to Syria. It was Simeon Lightner in the *Tribune* who wrote in most detail —and greatest frequency—of these misfortunes; he felt a shameful delight in enumerating the unhappinesses of the family that had kept him so long under its thumb. They were so distracted, in fact, that they did not even think to protest—and that failure to complain of his treatment of them rather lessened his pleasure.

The city was most interested in the abduction of the

children, Edwin and Edith Phair—pretty creatures surrounded by mystery. Benjamin had foolishly frequented dangerous places, Marian was known for her highhandedness, the elopement of a sheltered clergyman's daughter was hardly news—but two precious and exquisitely innocent children abducted by a bogus nursemaid caused some excitement indeed.

Judge Stallworth had trebled the reward offered for their return, and the police had sought for them with unwonted thoroughness. Their likenesses appeared in the daily papers, and copies of their Easter photographs were made up in the hundreds and outsold even those of Lily Langtry and Oscar Wilde.

The assumption that no one thought to question was that the children were still together. Whether held captive in some attic in Five Points, whether sprawled with mangled limbs at the bottom of a dry well in Connecticut, whether weepily wandering the streets of some sleepy New Jersey township, Edwin and Edith Phair were always imaginatively pictured in one another's company.

Thus it was unlikely that the children would ever be discovered. Edith Phair had been transformed into a careless urchin, utterly devoted to Rob, who was ever so much nicer to her than Edwin had been. Every day she wore a different set of clothes, and was never told to keep herself unsoiled. Every day she saw a different part of the city, and every day she played a different game: sometimes begging money of strangers to whom she told a story of her mother being very, very ill, sometimes doing a little dance in the street to distract the attention of a beautiful young woman whose lacy handkerchief Rob coveted. She often talked of her mother and asked Rob when she would be taken home. Rob always said, "Tomorrow," and Edith always believed him.

Edwin Phair performed three times nightly on a variety stage in Cincinatti, Ohio, walking across a line of empty milk bottles. A newspaper had already written of him, that he "could do things upon a candlestick that are more surprising than pleasant." He vaguely comprehended that he had been stolen, and sometimes felt guilty that he did not attempt to escape and return to his parents. But he had been warned of the inadvisability of this course—the danger of it—and cagily decided that he would learn to read and write so that he might send letters to his grandfather and his mother, telling them what had become of him. He was almost certain that they would have noticed his absence by this time.

Yet the fact was that, in his captivity, he was granted a degree of freedom he had never before enjoyed. He could eat as much as he wanted, and of what he wanted; he wore terribly flashy clothing; he was dandled and darlinged by a host of very pretty ladies who also went out upon the stage, and he was given a little trunk all his own with his name painted in gold letters across the top —from Edwin Phair his name had been economically altered to "The Elfin Fair"—the contents of which were entirely his. He possessed the sole key to this trunk and kept it on a gold chain around his neck. He was not encumbered with lessons or any instruction except that which tended toward the perfection of his gymnastic prowess; and nightly he received the riotous applause of hundreds of men and women and children. Edwin thought rather frequently of his mother and father, but never asked after them. In what he thought was a very cleverly deceptive manner, he only asked each morning of the gaunt man, his master, what town it was they were in, whether they had returned to New York yet. And Edwin was not too badly disappointed that the answer was invariably, "No."

Chapter 43

M<small>RS.</small> General Taunton was certainly correct in assessing that it would be of greatly deleterious effect on Helen if she were to learn of the death of her brother and the abducting of her niece and nephew. Mrs. Taunton's protégée suffered from a high-grade fever, a symptom of what disease the physician could not say, but one which left her at times weak and lucid and at other times lifted her to giddy heights of indomitable delirium.

Mrs. General Taunton understood that Helen's illness was the result of her decision to leave her father's house. For the twenty-three years of her life, Helen had never dared cross her father and grandfather's will, even in her mind. Now to deny their opinion and their authority altogether, was a matter of no small consequence, an act that required no small tariff of courage. The fever brought on by Helen's removal from the manse was complicated by a chill she had contracted in the damp cold air of that Sunday morning's dawn.

Even in moments when Helen's brain was clear, she did not ask after her family, and Mrs. General Taunton understood that this reluctance did not token any diminution of affection, but rather had its foundation in the young woman's strong sense that she had betrayed the

Stallworths, her father in particular. Gramercy Park,
Washington Square, and the manse had never been
closely discussed by Helen and Mrs. General Taunton,
and the widow was not put to the extremity of evasion or
lies, in keeping from Helen all the sorrowful tidings of
the family calamities.

In those hours that she feverishly languished in her
bed and watched the progress of the sun as it cast its
beams first into one corner of the comfortable room and
at last into the opposite, Helen's affectionate heart did not
whelm with thoughts of her family. The Black Triangle
instead occupied her waking thoughts—and her dreams
as well: the dozens, even hundreds of persons whom she
had encountered, spoken to, assisted, prayed for, and
loved. She begged Mrs. General Taunton for news of
these, demanded to know whether a certain newsboy for
whom they had purchased clothing was now making
enough daily cash to send himself to a twenty-five-cent
lodging house each night, whether the gums of a certain
lace maker had healed yet, whether a carpenter for whom
they had secured work on the East River bridge had yet
given over strong drink. When Mrs. General Taunton
could report favorably on these cases, she did so with a
glad heart; and when she could not, she told of the failure
as lightly as possible, and concluded that there was certainly hope in the near future for the unfortunate man,
woman, child, or family. The affectionate messages directed to Annie and Jemmie on Morton Street, Mrs.
General Taunton promised faithfully to deliver.

All the evening long, while her grandfather sat up
with the corpse of her brother at the manse, Helen Stallworth's sleep was disturbed by dreams, not of her family,
but rather of the inhabitants of the house that she had
first visited on King Street.

The young woman and her child in the attic were
perishing of cold and hunger, and the Reverend Thankful
Jones's flesh lay in elephant-folds around his rickety black
skeleton. The prostitute across the hall had lost her
orange hair in disease and was destitute, the young man
in the room below was about to be stabbed to the heart by
a jealous male admirer. The old man and old woman on
the second floor opened and shut their round black
mouths like dying fish in the bottom of a boat, and in

extension of that metaphor in her dream, they flopped out of the bed and twitched in sopping throes all around the room. A murderer had snuck through the window of the first floor and was about to cut out the wrists and throat of the young woman there, intent on stealing her tattooed jewels.

Helen waked sweating in the bed, certain of nothing but that she was required in King Street. All the inhabitants of that house called out for her help. She rose trembling in the darkened room and, having no idea of the time of night and making no attempt to deaden the noise of her movements, she dressed herself hurriedly, took up her bag, made certain that she was well supplied with cash, and fled downstairs, glancing this way and that hoping for sight of some servant who could accompany her to the Black Triangle.

A church bell tolled three, and Helen paused in the hallway, realizing that at so early an hour none of the servants would be about and that she must go on alone. She hurried into the parlor, lighted a candle and penned this note at Mrs. Taunton's writing desk:

> I must return, my dearest Anne. I know that I am needed, and when I have done all that I can —all that is wanted—I will come back to you. Your ever affectionate daughter (I *would* be your daughter),

> Helen Stallworth

> *Postscriptum.* I am quite well now, and am anxious, oh so very anxious! to see my duty done. H.S.

She folded the page once, scrawled *Anne* across it, blew out the candle, and quickly left the house.

No cab was to be had on Eighteenth Street, and none on Fourth Avenue either. Helen, though feverish and exhausted, determined that she would walk to King Street, and so, not even bothering now to watch for some conveyance to carry her thither, she set out through the chill night in a long-striding hectic gait toward the Black Triangle. In a quarter of an hour she passed her grandfather's house on Washingtons Square but did not even glance up at the windows to see if they were lighted.

Helen hurried on, swinging her bonnet by its strings, for her head was too hot to bear even that light covering. Though awake now for an hour and more, she had lost not a whit of the virulent conviction of her dreaming, but was as firmly convinced now as when she had sat bolt upright in the bed, that all the inhabitants of the house in King Street would perish if she did not hasten to their aid.

Helen did not remember that the young woman and her child were dead, that the old man and his wife had perished soon after. Her decreasing strength, shortness of breath, and occluded brain rather urged her toward the Black Triangle than detained her. She must reach the house on King Street before she collapsed. If she allowed herself to falter, or lingered to recoup her faculties, she would arrive to find that the inhabitants had perished of hunger or disease or been killed outright in their beds.

Her pace increased as she came within the precincts of the Black Triangle. Those out so late upon the streets were astonished by this specter of the young gentlewoman hurrying along, ill and disheveled, gasping for her shallow breath, stumbling at every uneven place in the walk, and grabbing at posts to propel her forward.

At last, Helen had reached MacDougal Street, and hurried along its familiar length until she reached King Street. Just at the corner, a melancholy untuned piano on the third floor of a house played "Oh, Bless Me, Mother." And in the last, maudlin stage of a night's debauchery, a cracked drunken duet was made of the final verse:

> I hear soft music on the air,
>   Oh, cool my burning brow!
> The angels beckon from above,
>   I feel so happy now;
> So bless me, mother, ere I die,
>   And fold me to your heart!
> You'll miss me, mother, very much,
>   Oh, kiss me ere we part.

Helen laughed aloud in her relief, for the house on King Street was visible to her, just visible in the darkness that prevailed in this narrow way. Helen's strangled voice joined the cracked chorus of "Oh, Bless Me, Mother," and she staggered toward the house. She stopped for one moment at the foot of the stoop there, pressed one clammy hand against her strangled heart, and mounted the steps.

The door was locked, and she beat wildly upon it. "Oh please!" she cried. "I've come—"

Suddenly the door was jerked open, and in its frame stood the woman whose jewelry was tattooed onto her wrists and neck. Her feet were bare, and she was clothed in a short blue shift.

Helen cried out in joy that the young woman was not dead. "Thank heaven!" she gasped. "I've come—"

Helen collapsed on the threshold. Her head struck the edge of the first step, and her cheek was scraped bloody against the bricks.

Charlotta Kegoe stooped, lifted the insensible girl, and carried her inside the house. A moment later Rob appeared, and gathered up Helen's bag and bonnet. He glanced quickly up and down the deserted street, then backed inside the building and kicked the door shut.

From the house on the corner, the chorus was repeated, in lachrymose duet:

> Oh, bless me, mother,
> Bless me, ere I die;
> Oh, bless me, mother,
> Oh, bless me, ere I die.

Mrs. General Taunton, when she had read the note that Helen Stallworth had left for her on the desk in the parlor, had assumed that her charge had returned home to the manse. Helen had evidently discovered the afflictions that prevailed in her home and departed stealthily, knowing that her friend would attempt to dissuade her from leaving. Mrs. Taunton questioned her servants carefully whether any of them had spoken to Helen of the death of her brother, or even whether they had talked of it among themselves in a place where they might have been overheard by the invalid. None of the servants would admit to such an indiscretion, and Mrs. General Taunton, knowing their loyalty, believed them. If to nothing else then, Mrs. General Taunton must ascribe Helen's flight to the intuition of a sympathetic soul.

The widow tactfully refrained from calling on Helen at this difficult time, and even deprived herself of the pleasure of writing to her protégée. Mrs. General Taunton knew that her intimacy with Helen was ill-regarded by the Stallworths, and she was reluctant to raise any contentious feelings in so sorrowful an hour. She regretted that Helen had left before completely recovered from her fever, but told herself that now Helen was at home, there was no point in dragging her back; she could recuperate as well in the manse as on Second Avenue.

In the papers, Mrs. General Taunton followed the disappointing progress of the search for little Edwin and Edith and the investigation into Benjamin's murder. In the description of the funeral that was printed in the *Herald*—a story that was got from the Greenwood chaplain for an undisclosed amount of gold—Mrs. General Taunton was surprised to find that Helen was not present, though she had left the house early on the morning of the interment. The widow supposed either that Helen was overcome with her own grief, or too attentive to her father's to attend.

Yet the next day, Friday, having no word from Helen, Mrs. General Taunton grew worried, and mistrusting that the fever had come back upon her friend with renewed vigor, sent off a short note by coach to the manse. The bearer was to wait for a reply, but the servant at the door curtly maintained that as Miss Helen was not within, no answer could be returned.

Mrs. General Taunton was disturbed by this, and hoped for the simplest explanation for Helen's absence from her father's home; that she was briefly visiting her aunt and uncle on Gramercy Park or her grandfather on Washington Square. She resigned herself to this hopeful construction for the evening, but the next day waited impatiently for a reply to her letter.

None came. Mrs. General Taunton dispatched another messenger, who received the same reply. Late on Saturday afternoon, Mrs. General Taunton herself stood on the steps of the manse and knocked at the door. In her best mourning habit in honor of Helen's brother she looked, on the whole, rather like the dramatized spirit of a hearse.

The female servant, with almost a surliness of demeanor, denied that Helen was within. When Mrs. General Taunton asked if she might be allowed to speak to the minister, the servant replied that her master was overcome with grief for the death of his son and was fit to speak to no one.

"But please to tell me," said Mrs. General Taunton, "if Miss Stallworth is staying here. Please simply tell me when she will return."

"Ah sure!" cried the servant. "Only she's not in now!" When Helen had first left the manse on Monday morning, the minister had ordered the servants to maintain to all who inquired that Helen was still a member of the household, only "not at home at present."

"I'm greatly relieved to hear it! Then when she does return, please give her this letter, and say that *Anne* anxiously awaits word from her."

"Certainly," smiled the servant, pleased with the success of her deception—and withdrew.

Mrs. General Taunton went away greatly relieved in her mind.

At that moment Helen Stallworth lay on a narrow couch that was pushed up beneath the single window in Charlotta Kegoe's bedchamber. Her flesh lay blotched and loose upon all her extremities, and each day Rob gathered up and braided all the hair that had fallen from her scalp. After three days, in which she had eaten nothing but a few spoonfuls of oyster stew, she was nearly bald; and was so weak that when she rolled off the couch onto the carpetless floor, she had not the strength to turn her face from the dust there.

Fever had destroyed her intellect, and she did not know how or what or where she suffered. She could not hear when Ella read to her the account of her brother's death and funeral, she could not feel when Rob wrote poems on her bony bare feet with a sharp quill pen and violet ink, she could not see when her niece Edith, astonished to find so familiar a face in such unfamiliar surroundings, danced a straw doll before her face and called out, "Play with me, Helen, play with me!"

Chapter 44

DIRECTLY after attending Benjamin's funeral on Wednesday morning, Duncan Phair had inquired at Mulberry Street whether there was any news of the bogus nursemaid or of Benjamin's murderers. This visit, and the visits made on succeeding mornings, were made merely *pro forma*, for Duncan had no doubt that it was Lena Shanks who was behind everything; and he possessed as well a belief in her almost supernatural power to escape detection. She was a black angel, and her family were devils out of a vengeful hell. Duncan had but scant hope he would ever see his children again outside a coffin.

He spent his days on Pearl Street. Although he was little fitted for trial duty, the trivial and commonplace work of the law office soothed him somewhat and made him forget for minutes at a time what had happened to him and to his family. In the evening, it was drink that procured his oblivion. He visited his wife's room each night, but invariably found her in a trancelike sleep, and the mute nurse indicating that she would not come out of it quickly. In the dining room after dinner, he sat and drank wine, and over and again told what was lost to him and recounted by what measures and what means his life had come to so hopeless a pass.

He drank because after a few hours, in those long quiet evenings at home, the wine brought on insensibility, and he longed for sleep despite the nightmares that invariably accompanied his slumber. Terror-filled and irrational as those frightful dreams were, they were never worse than the reality to which they inevitably gave way.

On Saturday afternoon, at his desk on Pearl Street, Duncan received a letter which his clerk said had been pushed under the door, the messenger not presenting himself. The letter read:

Sat. 5 P.M.
Duncan—
I have heard of your recent troubles and sympathize fully. Im happy to say that Ive recv'd information that will lead you direct to Ed & Edith yr children. It will be available to us this eve. at 7 p.m. at the opium den at no 46 Mott St. When the chinaman at the door wants the word to get in just say *Dollie* & youll be let in. Go downstairs and ask again for *Dollie*. She dont want the reward because she dont want it known where shes keeping, but bring $300 or she wont talk. Ill be there too but dont wait for me outside, it wont do to have us seen together.

Yr friend,
S. Lightner

The missive was perplexing but welcome. Merely from the address upon the envelope that was slipped beneath the office door, Duncan had recognized the familiar script. Had he been less pleased with the contents, Duncan might have been more puzzled by the wording of the letter, which was not in Simeon's distinctive style; but such an incongruity was overwhelmed by the familiarity of the handwriting, and even more so by the hopefulness that Duncan attached to the letter.

Smiling for the first time in almost a week, Duncan wrote out a draught for five hundred dollars, and sent one of the clerks to have it turned into cash. With this in his pocket, he went out to a dinner more substantial than any he had consumed in some time. His thoughts then were sanguine.

Three hundred dollars would purchase the information that would bring back Edwin and Edith whom, in truth, Duncan loved very much; and the return of his children, Duncan told himself, would doubtless reconcile Judge Stallworth. Marian would recover, and the Stallworth wagon would once again ride in the ruts of prosperity and felicity. To avoid considering the possible complications that might thwart this simply patterned success, Duncan thought blithely of the years ahead of him, when Judge Stallworth would be dead and Marian would have inherited the greater portion of his wealth; when he would himself be a city commissioner and Marian an arbiter of fashion, when Edith would be a beautiful young woman and he would give her away at the most brilliant wedding that New York had ever seen, when Edwin, the acknowledged Stallworth heir, would be a young man over whom any father might justifiably crow. A palace opposite the park, a cottage at Newport or Saratoga, journeys to Europe and introductions at court—Duncan set out on his way to Mott Street dreaming of fortune past knowing and honor past pride.

He did not stop to consider that if Edwin and Edith were still alive, there were two Stallworth deaths yet promised.

Edward Stallworth dreaded sleep, for since he had been brought back to his bed from his collapse at the Bellevue morgue, all his dreams were of Benjamin—not his son alive, the callow disappointing ill-favored young man that he had grown to be, not Benjamin as a boy, disappointing and ill-favored even then, but Benjamin dead, laid out on a stone slab, his livid head hinged upon a slashed throat, his slashed throat a dull red-black line of congealed blood. In those dreams the tilted slab rose ever higher until Benjamin's corpse was precipitated forward into Edward Stallworth's straining, frightened arms. The lolling head was torn from the shoulders and flew off onto the yellow brick floor of the morgue. On Saturday morning, Edward drew on a quilted black robe and went downstairs, still trembling from that terrifying familiar vision of his slumber.

On his desk, Edward found a great stack of memorial cards, still smelling of ink. On five hundred oblongs of cardboard that bore the embossed delineation of a fallen tree, symbolic of manhood cut off in its prime, was the legend: "In Affectionate Remembrance of Benjamin Stallworth Who died 15th October, 1882, Aged 22 Years. Interred at Greenwood Cemetery, 18th October." Beside these were ten boxes of black-bordered letter paper and envelopes. Edward supposed it was Marian who had troubled herself with these details, and he was grateful to her. He recalled only vaguely now his sister's hysteria over her missing children and assumed that, in the somber light of his own greater grief, she would have recovered herself.

Edward Stallworth picked up one of the memorial cards and examined it carefully; there was something indecently familiar about it. He rang for a maidservant, and just as he was giving her directions to bring him tea, he suddenly recalled the Sunday dinner—actually less than a month before—when all the family had received such cards, each card announcing his own death. Edward broke off in the midst of his direction.

"Aggie," he said, "have my niece and nephew been found yet?"

"No, sir," replied the maid, as if with shame. "No one yet knows what's come of them."

"And my sister?"

"Still took to her bed."

"Has Helen called? Has my daughter been here?"

Aggie shook her head, and Edward dismissed her.

For the remainder of the day, taking luncheon at his desk, Edward Stallworth thoughtlessly, mechanically replied to the letters of condolence. The terrible violence of Benjamin's death and the dramatic discovery of his corpse had been brought forcibly to the attention of all New York, and many of the several hundred letters that the minister had received proved to be from persons unknown to him, or forgotten. He read over the missives briefly and, in truth, with little comprehension. His mind was beset with wondering just what had happened outside the manse in the period of his great, debilitating grief. His father had visited him twice in that time, but had only sat beside his bed, hard-visaged and silent.

Edward had asked no information, and Judge Stallworth had proffered none.

Edward had no idea whether Benjamin's murderer had been discovered, and he had not dared to ask so important a question of the maidservant. He could not know even whether Helen had been informed of her brother's death; he must suppose that in fact she had not, since she had not returned to the manse, not even to compare their grief.

Now, Edward Stallworth's grief for his son was a problematical thing; it was an emotion that he had not anatomized himself. The shock of finding his son in the morgue had caused the first great rift in Edward's brain, and that single shock had incapacitated him for an entire day. Many hours passed before he came to think of his son as dead, removed from earth, lost to him and to Helen. Only then did the needles of grief begin to prick at his extremities, and this while the great arrow of shock was still lodged in his breast. But quickly the discomfort of those needles and that arrow were subsumed in his realization of the *meaning* of Benjamin's death.

Benjamin had been murdered, his throat slit from ear to ear. He had lain twenty-four hours unclaimed in the city morgue. Edward feared that the discovery of the man or men who had done away with Benjamin would expose the fact that his son had been disporting himself in some disreputable part of the city, gambling in Five Points, whoring in the Black Triangle. It would be said that Benjamin Stallworth had got no worse than he deserved, and he would be held up as an unfortunate example of what fell to undisciplined young men let loose in the city. What then would become of Edward Stallworth's reputation as God's champion against depravity? Who would listen to the inveighing against vice of a minister whose only son had been slaughtered in an alley behind a house of evil?

As he worked mechanically at the stack of letters before him, opening each, glancing at the signature without even bothering to read through the sentiments to which that signature was appended, and writing out a brief unemotional unspecific acknowledgment, Edward Stallworth grew more and more restive with wondering just how much was known about the circumstances of Benjamin's death. He realized that he knew only that his son was dead, and that knowledge came solely of having seen him on the stone slab in the morgue. When he had come downstairs that morning he had not even known whether Benjamin was yet buried, and dreaded to think that the burial was a trial still before him. Perhaps Benjamin lay high-collared in the house on Washington Square, and the services had only awaited his recovery. The notation on the memorial card that Benjamin had already been laid to rest at Greenwood was considerably relieving.

Edward was anxious to know who had been in attendance, to what extent the funeral had been covered in the newspapers—Benjamin after all had been a colleague of sorts to Simeon Lightner, and it could not be expected that the ravenous *Tribune* would fail to turn to account the death of one who was, after a fashion, one of their own reporters. He feared to see the columns, feared to be told what was said of Benjamin, and of him—feared to know the extent of his falling. At the same time he became ever more troubled by his ignorance of his situation.

He directed a message to his father, called in the maid, and sent her out to the telegraph office on Madison Square. Judge Stallworth he begged to come to him as quickly as possible; that he was as well as could be expected, but had matters of urgency to discuss with him.

Shortly after the maid departed on this errand, the bell of the house was pulled. Edward Stallworth instinctively rose from the desk and peered out the bay window to see who called. Finding it was only a small child holding a letter prominently before him, Edward allowed himself to go to the door. The child thrust the letter into the minister's hand and was gone before Edward could question him.

Assuming that the letter was merely another message of condolence, Edward returned to his study, resumed his chair, and only after sealing and addressing the letter he had just finished, did he slit open the hand-delivered missive.

He read trembling:

Saturday, 6 P.m.
Dear Rev. Stallworth,
I regret to inform you that your daughter lies very
ill, at no 2 King St. A physician is in attendance,

but she sinks. She asks for your presence continually, please come at once. The doctor advises that you will come alone, as excitement would be hurteful to your daughter. Come at once.

Yrs most sincerely,
Mrs. A. R. (Anne) Taunton

Without giving thought to the puzzling crudeness of the letter, the minister readied himself to go to his daughter. "I've gone to fetch Helen. Return as quickly as possible," was the note that he left for his father on the marble table beside the street door.

Chapter 45

DURING the ride in the hackney cab to the Black Triangle, Edward Stallworth wrung his hands, and beneath his breath swore at all the vehicles that blocked every street and crossing early on a Saturday evening. The minister was certain that he could maintain his sanity only with the help of his daughter Helen. His resentment that she had secretly engineered charitable work in the Black Triangle had disappeared in the days of his sick horror over the death of his son, and now he wanted her quiet presence in the manse again. It was no longer a question of forgiveness, no longer a question of who had been in the right. She should not be upbraided, she should not be denied her endeavors with Mrs. General Taunton, if only she would consent to return to him. Now the poor girl lay ill in some close vile room in the Black Triangle, and he must be her rescue.

Edward Stallworth felt the sleeve of his coat and examined his hat and realized that in dressing himself so quickly, he had come away without any symbol of mourning for his son. He flung his hat toward the wall of the carriage and fell back muttering. The perspiration that poured from his forehead stung and blinded his eyes, yet he did not wipe it away, only murmured to himself the

319

louder, so that at last, the driver leaned down and asked if he meant any change in his directions.

The bells of the city chimed seven o'clock just as the hackney cab was passing within sight of Judge James Stallworth's house on Washington Square. Edward wiped his eyes with his kerchief and leaned out of the window of the hackney, looking for lights in the mansion and wondering if he ought not stop there and ask his father's company. But no lights were visible, and it would not do to postpone the reunion with his daughter.

A few minutes later Edward Stallworth, shaky on his feet, was deposited before a small brick house on King Street. He gave the driver seventy-five cents and asked that he wait; he might be as much as a quarter of an hour within. The driver nodded, and exchanged a wink with a prostitute who, leaning out of a second-floor window of the house adjoining, was within a dozen feet of him.

Edward Stallworth nervously mounted the steps of the building, whose windows were uniformly black and betrayed no trace of occupation. He knocked at the door softly, then immediately more loudly and waited for a few moments, wondering whether he ought not simply go in. Helen was probably in a back room, perhaps on an upper floor; her attendants might not hear his summons.

He turned the knob, and found the door unlocked. But just as he pushed, it was jerked back wide by a little girl wearing a plain gray dress. Her head was a mass of tightly wound side curls.

"My daughter—" whispered the minister. "I'm looking for my daughter Helen."

The little girl nodded, and pointed up a flight of stairs that was so dark Edward had difficulty in making out even its position in the hallway.

"How many flights up? What room? Is she well?"

"Three flights up," said the little girl. She knelt on the floor, struck a match, lighted a candle on a cheap tin stand, and handed it to the minister.

"Three flights up—" she repeated. "Door on the right."

Edward took the candle. The flame trembled in his hand. He waved it before him and uneasily marked the troubled banister and the uncarpeted steps. Slowly he mounted the stairs, slowly although he was desperate to find his daughter in the room above.

At the first landing he turned and saw the little girl's head blackly outlined against the grimy glass of the front door. He went hesitantly on, holding the candle in his left hand and convulsively grasping the banister in his right, never minding the grime that caked upon his moist skin.

At last, even the dim light from the front door had disappeared and Edward Stallworth found himself on what appeared an endless stairway, close and creaking. The air was vile and hot, and only the fact that he was ascending kept his imagination from likening the progress to a journey into Hell. Garishly painted doors, awry in their jambs, stood three on the landing and mocked him to try their handles. Behind one he thought he heard labored breathing, but silence otherwise prevailed in the house.

At last the fourth story was attained and Edward Stallworth turned to the door on his right, which led evidently to the room that was at the back of the house. He paused before it, leaned close so that the candle flame in his hand singed the lapel of his jacket, but still he could hear nothing inside. He cautiously turned the knob and stepped into the back chamber.

The room was empty but for a pine coffin set on high trestles in the center of the floor. Six tall lighted candles were stuck upon the joints of the box.

"Helen!" cried Edward Stallworth, and fell heavily to his knees on the rough deal floor. "Helen," he groaned, and rubbed his soiled hands violently on the legs of his trousers.

He knelt choking and weeping for perhaps half a minute with his head bowed, the muscles of his body taut and straining; and only then became aware of a slight rustling movement in the room.

He looked up quickly. The candle flames wavered and the unpainted coffin trembled on its trestles.

Edward Stallworth tried to jump up, but his constricted posture wouldn't allow the movement, and he fell over at full length upon the floor. "Helen!" he cried out, all but mindless now, with grief and the horror of this place.

Edward Stallworth again cried out his daughter's name, and struggled to his feet. He lurched toward the coffin and grasped its sides, shaking it.

The girl inside sniggered. She was fourteen, with tangled dark hair, yellow teeth and a black tongue. There was a large purple bruise on her belly and she was entirely naked.

Edward Stallworth cried out and fell backward. But his convulsive hands had not released the coffin and it tumbled to the floor. The girl inside was thrown out and knocked her head against one of the upset trestles. The six candles went out, all but one.

Cursing, the young girl flung out her hand and broke the tall candle in half. The last flame was extinguished and the room foundered in darkness.

A few moments after Edward Stallworth had disappeared around the first landing, Ella opened the front door and went out to the hackney cab. She called to get the driver's attention.

"Mister," she said, "the gentleman inside said not to wait. He said you were to have this"—she lifted a half-dollar piece high into the air—"and to drive on."

The driver nodded, took the coin, and with a wink to the whore still in her window, drove his hack on down dark narrow King Street.

Mott Street early on a Saturday evening was a crowded, noisy place, and Duncan Phair was a well-dressed anomaly among so many Chinamen and slatternly Irishwomen. There were other white loiterers, those who had come to try the stuperous embrace of opium, those who had never before seen a real heathen except for the Indians that sold trinkets around Niagara Falls, those inveterate gamblers who had learned enough Chinese to play at fan-tan because they supposed that the Chinese ran honest games. None of these, however, moved with the quickness or the purpose of Duncan Phair, who impatiently counted off the numbers of the buildings until he reached number 46. Two Chinamen of indeterminate age and sallow complexion stood with their crossed arms hidden in their jacket sleeves, smoking long clay pipes of tobacco. Behind them on the stoop two white children were playing an amorphous unintelligible game with marbles, that *would* roll off the stoop.

"Who?" demanded one of the men softly of Duncan,

when he attempted to pass between them on the stoop.

"I've come to see Dollie," replied Duncan in a low voice.

"Who?" repeated the other.

One of the children peered around the green robe of the second Chinaman and cast her glance over Duncan. She tugged slightly at the Chinaman's skirt, and he stood aside.

Duncan stepped between them, but as he did so, the second child rose, took his hand, and placed over his smallest finger a ruby ring. With an exclamation of surprise, Duncan Phair brought the ring close to his face and turned it this way and that in the meager streetlight.

It appeared identical to the ring he had presented Maggie Kizer on the occasion of the New Year.

"Boy," he cried, "how did you come by this?"

"Shhh!" said the child with a smile. "Go inside, ask for Dollie." He opened the door for Duncan, and made a little bow as the lawyer passed inside.

Much wondering at the incomprehensible circumstance of the child having the ring that had belonged to Maggie, the lawyer cautiously treaded the hallway papered with red-inked letters from China, and knocked at the little door at the end of the curious passage.

The slot was pulled open with a bang, and an unseen guardian cried, "Who?"

"Dollie," whispered Duncan.

The door was opened, and Duncan stood silent for a few moments at the top of the platform. The attendant, a short Chinaman with a bandaged eye, waited until Duncan's sight had adjusted to the obscurity, then plucked at his sleeve and led him down among the opium dreamers.

Past slumbrous and slow-moving shadowed forms along the double row of bunks, Duncan Phair moved with silent astonishment. The dim red and blue light from the shaded lamps above made the place unearthly; he had seen much in the Black Triangle, but he had never found anything to match this heady silence, this sinister indolence, this dense atmosphere of smoke and dreams. He had thought to look out for Simeon Lightner, but forms were indistinct, faces hidden.

His attendant paused at last in the farthest, deepest

corner of the place and pointed to a pale white face in a frame of black hair. The opium smoker's form was softly illumined by a tiny candlewick in a green glass lamp. Darkly attired, she lay on her side upon a thin pallet. Smoke exhaled between thin colorless lips veiled the face suddenly, like a spirit at a seance, and the waxen lids drooped over the black expressionless eyes.

"Dollie?" whispered Duncan Phair, and knelt beside the recumbent figure.

"I'm Dollie," she said slowly, and smoke enveloped her face once more.

"I'm Duncan Phair, what do you know of my children? The two—"

The dreamer's eyes had slowly opened. "Dark Glass," she said softly, with a smile.

"Edwin and Edith are my children," he repeated in a rushed whisper. "I've brought money, the money you requested," he said, and took the bills from his pocket. He laid them beside the little lamp, expecting that she would take them up and count them.

"Dark Glass," she said again. "Dark Glass asked to be remembered to you."

"You have information!" Duncan Phair cried, still in the whisper, for his eyes had grown aware that other dreamers lay close around them. Just beyond Dollie, ensconced in even deeper shadow, was another woman— great and fat—whose pudgy hand held the lighted green lamp far from her face. Beside her, in those black shadows, moved the figure of a small child, the most restless thing in that dim, enclosed, slow-moving world. "Dollie—"

"It's not for your children you're here," said Dollie, and smiled. "It's for the sake of Dark Glass."

"Who the devil is Dark Glass?" cried Duncan, in his exasperation.

"Maggie Kizer," whispered a voice behind him.

Duncan turned and saw, not five feet away, the hideous grinning face of Lena Shanks, staring at him just as she had stared on the afternoon that her daughter was killed on West Houston Street.

"Papa!" cried Edith, and he saw—for a moment—her smiling face emerge from the obscurity behind Lena Shanks.

"Edith! You're—"

"Shhh!" cried Lena Shanks, and pushed Edith back into the shadows, "it's for Maggie you're here, not for the girl. . . ."

"No," whispered Duncan, suddenly alarmed. "I'm not to blame for Maggie, I knew nothing, it was Father who—"

"Stallworth!"

"Yes! It was Judge Stallworth who—"

"There's three of us dead," said Lena Shanks grimly, and nodded to Dolly.

"Oh—" cried Duncan, but that single exclamation must do for surprise, and wonder, and fear, and pain, for Dollie had plunged the gilded length of her *yen hock* deep into his throat.

The blood that spurted out of Duncan's neck extinguished Dollie's lamp, and he thrashed in darkness. Those who attended to the gurgling in that black corner of the vast room took it for the common sound of a beginner at the game falling sick from his first pipe.

Lena Shanks placed five more gilded opium needles into Dollie's blood-drenched hand and, patiently feeling out for her victim's invisible mouth and eyes and ears, she plunged them one by one into the writhing man's head, until a few minutes later, in the sweet dimness of the opium den, he had ceased to struggle.

Chapter 46

━━━

As she had sat at the side of Marian Phair's bed and watched over the delirious woman, Louisa Shanks propped a large and well-stocked writing desk upon her lap and was forever busy about it. She wrote constantly with a great variety of pens and inks and papers, and always smoothly hid her work at each knock upon the door of the room. The servants in the Phair household variously assumed that she was writing her mother, her sweetheart, or a sensational novel. Occasionally, a little boy appeared at the kitchen door and asked if he might be allowed to confer with his sister for a few moments; and the servants, rather than taking the trouble of bringing Louisa down to Rob, brought Rob up to Louisa. With their mistress quite out of her head and their master either away or drunk, the servants did much as they pleased in these lax, troubled days.

Rob stood quietly at his aunt's side and conferred with her at length, often producing a letter from his bright vest, sometimes taking a brief message—and always some morsel of lace or trim that belonged to the ill woman—away with him.

On Saturday, October 21, however, Rob was given eight letters, each directed to a person other than his grandmother. And Louisa indicated that the missives were to be delivered in a particular order and at particular hours. Rob nodded his understanding and acquiescence. The first of these letters was slipped under the door of Duncan Phair's offices on Pearl Street; and the second was given directly into the hands of Edward Stallworth. Six more were delivered in the course of that Saturday evening, each to the offices of one of the newspapers in the city: the *Tribune*, the *Times*, the *Sun*, the *World*, *Harper's Weekly*, and the *Police Gazette*. The letters read:

> Sir,
> If you want to unmask a double-dyed deceteful hypocritical clergyman well known for his preaching against the black Triangle you should take yourself tomorrow Sunday morning at 7 a.m. to no. 2 King St in the black Triangle and find a picture well worth the recording.
>
> A sincere well-wisher to the cities press.

All six papers sent representatives, since the story—if true—looked to prove a fine one. Moral turpitude in a high place was at least as interesting as corruption in a low one, and there was no one could not feel satisfaction at the overthrow of a hypocrite, especially one of standing and influence.

Louisa's notation concerning the tableau that was to be presented did not go unheeded, and *Harper's Weekly* and the *Police Gazette* assigned artists to accompany its reporters.

The first reporter to arrive on King Street Sunday morning was Simeon Lightner, his wiry hair positively frizzled in the early morning damp. As he knocked at the door, he was joined by the artist from the *Police Gazette*. They were admitted to the house by a young woman of fierce aspect, shown into a little barren parlor, and instructed to wait quietly until all their number were present. When she returned to her station behind the street door, the artist whispered to Simeon that the young lady was none other than the celebrated lady pugilist, Charlotta Kegoe.

Soon all six reporters and both artists had arrived and

despite the early hour, formed a jolly company. Commanding quiet, Charlotta then led the eight men up the narrow stairs to the fourth-floor landing, where they were hard put to find room to stand, which caused some barely repressed mirth among them. The artists were given the places beside the door of the room to be entered. In case the promised tableau lasted only briefly, it was thought wise to reserve the best view for those able to reproduce it later.

Charlotta placed a finger to her lips and swung the door open wide. The reporters craned over the shoulders of the artists to gaze into the room.

It was a small bedchamber, with a slanting ceiling directly beneath the roof. A single grimy window looked out over King Street and dusty red curtains filtered the hot morning light.

In the iron bed pushed beneath that single window lay a middle-aged man. Unconsciously, in troubled sleep, he pushed aside the bedclothes, and discovered himself entirely naked between the sleazy sheets.

At that moment as well, from behind the recumbent figure, whose back was to the reporters in the doorway, there rose the pale, small, smiling face of a young girl. Her long hair fell discreetly over her breast. With a finger to her lips, she too cautioned the reporters to silence. From her nakedness, and her company, and the inevitable conclusion that must be brought to bear upon such a scene, the girl might well have been more bashful than she was.

But she only smirked, and with scaly fingers turned the heavy head of Edward Stallworth, so that his sleeping countenance fell in full view of the eight men who had eased themselves inside the room.

He was immediately recognized by the reporter of the *Times*, who whispered his name aloud. All the others grinned and turned grinning to the stupefied Simeon Lightner, who had to contemplate the chagrin of the *Tribune* when it became known that the minister whose sermons had been printed week after week in Monday morning's columns had been discovered in a narrow iron bed beside a young girl who could not be more than fourteen.

It was certainly true that Simeon Lightner had not been

behindhand in chronicling the disasters that had characterized the Stallworths' fortunes of late, but still the reporter had no relish for this scene. Thinking to alert the minister, Simeon called out his name, but the *Times* reporter clapped his hand over Simeon's mouth and drew him out into the hallway. "None of that please," he laughed, "he'll wake soon enough. Just let us get our notes and let the artists make their sketches. Then you may have the pleasure of telling the old man that he's been found out. . . ."

With the knowledge that no denial on Edward Stallworth's part would undo the harm already accomplished, Simeon acquiesced, and waited miserably in the hallway. The two artists sat upon the dusty floor, with their tall books laid across their laps, and pencilled in scenes which duplicated each other's work almost line for line, except that one sketched the two figures as they were—Edward Stallworth with his mouth open and snoring, the young girl perched gaily over his shoulder and exchanging winks and other conspiratorial communications with the reporters—and the other placed the sheets a little higher upon their persons, for propriety's sake.

When the artists had completed their work, they stood aside, and the reporters regrouped themselves. One gave the nod to the little girl, and she shook Edward Stallworth into drowsy consciousness.

He choked on his own thick breath, struggled against the sheets and the unfamiliarity of any bed partner at all, opened his eyes, and stared uncomprehendingly at the strange men grouped about the bed.

The little girl turned his head and kissed him with a passion that was not entirely credible, considering the ridicule she had displayed toward his sleeping person.

Edward Stallworth threw the girl off and attempted to rise. Finding himself entirely unclothed, he snatched up the sheets around his neck. He spluttered, but could not find the beginning of coherent speech.

Simeon Lightner came forward. "Reverend Stallworth," he said pitifully, "do you know where you are?"

The article that appeared the following morning in the *World* began, "While the corpse of his murdered son lay scarcely cold in the narrow plot of Greenwood Ceme-

tery . . ." The other papers were not less cutting, and
described in shocking detail the scene in the garret room
of the small house in King Street on Sunday morning,
when Reverend Edward Stallworth was commonly thought
to be so borne down by grief over the death of his murdered son Benjamin that he could not even bear to receive his most important parishioners.

The *Times,* which was generally lenient to ministers,
charitably submitted that the man had been driven insane by the discovery of his son's corpse in the morgue;
and that he was not morally responsible for this fearful
degeneration. Simeon Lightner, following his editor's
commands, timorously submitted that the entire incident
had been manufactured by the enemies of virtue, those
who stood to lose when the Black Triangle was swept
clean. The *Tribune* stood by the righteous minister of the
Madison Square Presbyterian Church, and declared that
the unfortunate incident—they gave no details—had been
altogether fabricated, a vicious plot of the Democrats, of
rival ministers, of a gang of female criminals.

When the reporters left laughing that Sunday morning, Simeon Lightner haltingly explained to Edward Stallworth what had happened; the minister remained dazed
and uncomprehending, and Simeon gave over the attempt.
The young girl had disappeared, with a sheet wrapped
around her body; and not being able to find the minister's
clothing, Simeon wrapped him in the second sheet, and
led him down the stairs to the street door.

The parlor was deserted, and the celebrated pugilist
not to be found.

Simeon sent a passing child to fetch a cab, and then
accompanied Edward back to the manse, where the maid
and Judge Stallworth, who had just arrived, received him
with blank horror.

The *Tribune* worked hard to discredit the story, and
might have succeeded in reducing the strength of the
blow that had fallen upon Edward Stallworth, had it not
been for the two illustrations that appeared on Wednesday in *Harper's Weekly* and in the *Police Gazette.* No
swiveling words dreamt by Simeon Lightner, and not
the most ingenious counter-accusations could deflect the
crushing weight of those two cuts.

Many persons did charitably agree with the *Tribune*

that Edward Stallworth had been set up; how else to explain the invitations to the reporters, the lack of surprise evinced by the young girl herself, the difficulty of rousing the man from his sleep, suggesting that he had been drugged? But those same persons were of Marian Phair's mind exactly: there was something distasteful about victims. *Good* persons were not set upon in the street; *unexceptionable* ministers were not entrapped into garret rooms with prostitutes.

A meeting of the elders of the Madison Square Presbyterian Church that Thursday afternoon relieved Edward Stallworth of all his pastoral and ministerial responsibilities. They also commiserated with him on the troubles that had so recently and with such violence plagued his unfortunate family. At the same time, a committee was appointed to visit certain churches in New Jersey and Connecticut in hopes of finding a minister to take his dishonored place.

On Thursday night, Edward Stallworth went alone to his study in the Madison Square Presbyterian Church. Into half a dozen small crates he began packing his sermons, books, and letters, but before even half this work was accomplished, he gave over the effort and threw himself into a chair beside the cold hearth. For several minutes he gazed at the stained-glass window of the Shepherd and the Lost Sheep, dimly illuminated by a gaslamp outside. Then from the pocket of his coat he took the pistol with which Benjamin had shot Daisy Shanks, placed the barrel between his lips, and blew away the top of his head.

Chapter 47

EDITH Phair had not seen her father die. The gilded *yen hock* needles had been plunged into his neck and head in darkness and later, when they were out of the opium den, Lena Shanks had explained to the little girl that the man who had lain beside Dollie was not her father, but only someone who closely resembled him. Edith was unsure and uneasy, but accepted the explanation.

Lena Shanks, Edith, Rob, Ella, and Charlotta Kegoe remained nearly a week immured in the house on King Street. Directly after Charlotta, on Sunday morning, had shown the reporters to the garret of the house across the way, she had returned to Lena Shanks, and an hour later, they were gratified to see the minister, wrapped in a sheet and supported by the wiry-haired reporter, standing in the doorjamb, pale and disoriented.

With great interest on the following days did they follow the reporting in the newspapers of this incident, and though Simeon Lightner's pronouncement that it was a gang of female criminals that had engineered the destructive escapade caused Lena some alarm when Ella read it aloud to her, the reporter's equally assured assertion the following day that Tammany Hall was behind it restored her ease of mind.

On Friday morning, when Ella read of the suicide of Edward Stallworth, actually within the walls of the Madison Square Presbyterian Church, Lena Shanks smiled, drummed her fingers on the arm of the chair, and whispered, "Three. *Der war der dritte . . .*" She gave orders that all their belongings should be packed. To this purpose, Charlotta Kegoe dragged up two large trunks from the cellar of the house, and everything that was of any value in the possession of Lena Shanks and her entourage was quickly placed inside.

"Are we going back to Jersey?" asked Rob, as Charlotta was snapping the latches and turning the keys in their locks.

Lena Shanks shook her head. "We go back to Germany, boy."

"Edith go too?" begged Rob, who had grown attached to the child.

"Louisa too?" cried Ella, fearing that her aunt, who had kept apart from them for almost two weeks now, would not be accompanying them on so great a journey. At least the child must suppose that Germany was a distance; her grandmother's tone indicated that it was certainly farther from New York than Mantoloking had been.

Lena nodded. *"Ja, ja. Natuerlich, Louisa und Edith auch. Und* new clothes *fuer alles.* Tonight we sail, on a great ship."

Rob and Ella clapped their hands in delight, and Edith clapped in mimicking motion and with a mimicking grin, though understanding nothing but that there was some treat in store.

The remainder of that day was occupied by Rob, Ella, and Charlotta Kegoe in effacing all traces of their habitation from that house on King Street. The mirrors outside the window were smashed with a hammer, and Rob destroyed his grandmother's wicker chair with a hatchet. Ella took the cushions to the attic, ripped them open with a knife that she carried about with her, and showered the feathers out the holes in the roof. The curtains, as well as all their various disguises, were burnt in the grate by Lena, who sat heavily upon a low stool, with Edith now and then diffidently tossing in a rag or two.

The rooms of that house: the attic space, Lena's chamber on the second floor, and Charlotta's suite on the first, were rendered bare and insipid, without a scrap of paper or cloth to tell how recent had been their occupation. In fine new clothes, the three children sat upon a bench in the hallway, Edith imitating the twins' patience and silence as she imitated them in everything else.

One bundle alone was yet to be disposed of, and Charlotta Kegoe and Lena Shanks stood over it in the pugilist's bedchamber. Helen Stallworth lay wasted and near to death of a fever upon a low sofa beneath the single window of the room. The sunlight burned white upon her hairless head. Her parched lips were caked with dried blood, and her unseeing eyes popped from their sockets. Her stained white shift stank of illness.

"What do we do about her?" said Charlotta. "The others—the others we're well rid of, but this one . . ."

A quarter of an hour later, on Morton Street, Annie Leech looked out of the window of her parlor and saw a great black carriage with curtained windows draw up before the house. Annie motioned Jemmie over, and they watched with surprise and curiosity as Charlotta Kegoe, in sumptuous mourning garb, climbed down, holding across her outstretched arms an angular blanket-wrapped bundle.

Annie and Jemmie hurried to the front door, opened it and were about to speak when Charlotta thrust the bundle at them, cried, "She asked for you all the time!" and leapt back into the carriage. It was immediately driven off.

Jemmie, amazed, plucked at the blanket to discover what malodorous gift Charlotta Kegoe had left them, and screamed when a head, bald as a wigmaker's dummy and quite as colorless, fell out upon her breast and breathed up with a noxiousness that she later described as being like "a volcano of sulfur."

Chapter 48

THE Phair household was now greatly reduced in size and consequence. The second maid had been let go, and the cook, whose principal duty lately had been to provide meals for Amy Amyst, Peter Wish, and the mute nurse, left each afternoon by four o'clock. Marian Phair took but scant nourishment, clarified broths and the blandest white breads soaked in milk.

Duncan Phair had been missing since Saturday afternoon. Judge Stallworth learned that he had taken himself off in high spirits after the arrival of a letter of unknown content, but that neither he nor the five hundred dollars that he carried with him had been heard of since. Judge Stallworth kept this information from Marian, and merely told her that Duncan was on important business in Philadelphia and would return as quickly as possible; but the judge's unease over his son-in-law's disappearance was overwhelmed by the revelation of Edward Stallworth's discovery in the bed of an infantile prostitute in the Black Triangle. The Stallworths knew no end of trouble.

So that he could be near his daughter, and because he felt unprotected living alone in Washington Square, Judge Stallworth stayed his nights on Gramercy Park. Peter Wish packed several bags of clothing for him and brought them uptown; and Pompey, now the judge's sole comfort in life, found new quarters in Duncan Phair's bedchamber.

On Friday afternoon at four o'clock, while Edward Stallworth's suicide was being heatedly discussed the city over, the mute nurse in Marian Phair's room rang for Amy Amyst. That sounding bell coincided with the cook's farewell before she departed the house for the day.

Amy came upstairs, and received a short note from Louisa that instructed her to travel to a little shop very near the Battery Park where she was to procure a specified quantity of a certain medicine; she must insist that this powder be pounded on the spot. Amy wondered why she must travel so far when competent apothecaries abounded on Fifth Avenue, but did not presume to question the directive; instead, she said only, "You know you'll be here alone, don't you? Peter is packing the rest of the judge's things on Washington Square. There's no one else in the house."

The nurse nodded her satisfaction, indicating perhaps that despite her speechlessness, she intended to get along quite well. Amy spoke softly to Marian Phair, who responded not at all, and crept softly from the room.

A quarter of an hour after Amy departed the house on her errand, a cart, driven by a little Chinaman's child— half Chinese and half Irish—drew up before the Phair house. Presently and stealthily, two Chinamen with blue quilted caps surmounting the queues that hung down their backs like anchors, jumped out of the peaked tent that was raised upon the back of the vehicle and lowered to the street a great square tea chest. It was painted quaintly over in red, blue, and gold with scenes of domestic life in Peiping and its lid was secured with a large chased brass latch. They carried it up the front steps of the Phair house, but were not put to the trouble of knocking, for Louisa Shanks opened the door and guided the two men to the apartment of Marian Phair.

The sick woman looked up when the Chinamen, nodding eagerly at her and smiling imbecilically, placed the tea chest close beside her bed. It smelt headily of camphor.

"Nurse," cried Marian, for Louisa appeared in the doorway directly after the Chinamen had spasmodically bowed themselves out of the room, "what is this?" Her voice was strained and scarcely audible, and her smile was of the most clouded perplexity, for she was not even certain that she did not dream. When had Chinamen ever visited Gramercy Park on any errand whatsoever?

Louisa crossed to the window, saw the Chinamen spring into the cart, even as the boy was driving it off. She turned to Marian, smiled, and helped to raise her in the bed. Propped against her pillows, Marian gazed with languid expectation at the staid figures that struck indecipherable poses over the surfaces of the mysterious painted chest.

When, late on Thursday night, news had been brought him that his son had committed suicide, Judge James Stallworth evinced no apparent emotion. He thanked the reluctant, apologetic messengers, saw them out himself, and then retreated to Duncan's study that overlooked Gramercy Park. He sat in a chair by the window, shivering with cold for no fire had been lighted. All night long, with Pompey sleeping at his feet, he watched the last of autumn's leaves blow against the amber streetlights.

He decided to give over his judgeship. For future greatness of his family he had now no thought: Benjamin and Edward were dead, Helen was in the keeping of a deranged widow, Duncan was gone who knew where! Edwin and Edith, who might have recouped the Stallworth name and fortunes in a third generation, had been abducted and doubtlessly slain.

Only he and Marian were left, and Marian was perilously close to insanity. If ever she were well again, they would take refuge at Saratoga Springs, far away from New York and its tribulations, and there they would comfort one another.

It was a dismal prospect, and that there was plenty of money to keep them was a meager consolation for all the dreams and golden hopes that had been broken— and all broken within a single month's time. The old man sat at the window until the rising sun had blotted out the illumination of the streetlamps, and only then, as if he had feared that morning would not come if he did not station himself against its arrival, did he lay himself upon

Duncan's canopied bed. Yet even then it was not to sleep.

On that Friday, Judge Stallworth attended to many things: Edward's funeral, to take place on Sunday; his own resignation from the bench, immediately effective; and the closing up of the house on Washington Square. Late in the afternoon he took a hackney cab from the Criminal Courts Building, which deposited him at the end of Twenty-first Street, a weary and hopeless old man.

He walked slowly toward the Phair residence, and marked with some trepidation the large black carriage that was pulled up before it. Stopping abreast of the horses, he tried discreetly to peer into the black-curtained windows, but he could see nothing of those within. The coachman stared straight ahead and did not glance at the judge.

Just then, the mute nurse appeared at the street door of the house with a black veil over her face and a large carpetbag in her hand. She hurried down the steps and the carriage door was flung open to accept her.

Judge Stallworth rushed forward and clutched her arm. "My daughter!" he protested. "Why have you left her?"

Louisa grinned, wrenched her arm free, and climbed into the carriage. Open-mouthed with indignation and astonishment, the judge stared after her into the black interior of the vehicle. There, upon one side, sat two women, both dressed in deepest black, one of them tall and large-boned, the other grossly fat; across from them, also in fine black clothes, were three children, two of them the same size, and one much smaller. All five faces peered out at him calmly and without expression.

Just as the nurse climbed in, to seat herself beside the children, the smallest child giggled convulsively—a tiny laugh that startled the already astonished judge by its familiarity—and the door was slammed shut.

The carriage rolled off, but though the wheels were loud upon the cobblestones, they did not cover the screams of Marian Phair in the bedroom upstairs when, with the little strength that insatiate curiosity had afforded her feeble frame, she had lifted the lid of the painted tea chest and found her missing husband inside, carefully packed in shredded camphor leaves, with a hangman's rope draped loosely around his neck and six gilded needles protruding from the livid wounds in his head.

Epilogue
at Noon

No city has a shorter memory than New York. Two months passed—November with the last vestiges of autumn, December the harbinger of winter—and the Stallworths and the Shanks were forgotten. The newspapers, even the *Tribune,* wrote of other families, other crimes, and other sorrows. Dead or dispersed, the Stallworths and the Shankses were united in their rapidly acquired anonymity.

The buildings that had housed the Shankses knew them and of them no more. West Houston Street had been abandoned for the past eight months to a group of mulatto prostitutes, and Weeping Mary, who went no more by that name and had abandoned her old profession, was now the landlady of numbers 1 and 2 King Street, and made a sufficiency of income by gouging her tenants.

The Stallworths had fared scarcely better. The Twenty-fifth Street manse was given over to the new minister of the Madison Square Presbyterian Church; all of Edward Stallworth's furniture and effects had been sold at an auction a week after his funeral, and the proceeds—Helen Stallworth's whereabouts being then unknown, and the judge and Marian already departed from the city—purchased a handsome carved pulpit for the church. The house on Washington Square had been sold to a philanthropic organization, and each day several dozen crippled children played upon its square flat roof.

Only in the house on Gramercy Park, now owned by a steel industrialist recently moved to New York from Pittsburgh, was there the shadow of remembrance of the Stallworths. On New Year's Day 1883, visitors to the former Phair residence remarked to one another, "We were here last year this time, this house belonged to Duncan Phair. Terrible death, you know, murder never solved. What became of his wife? Handsome, stiff woman. And her father the judge, where is he now?" But no one could say, with any certainty, what had become of Judge Stallworth and the young lawyer's widow. And those who ventured to reply to so idle a question made merest guesses: they were at Saratoga, at the Great Divide, at the bottom of the sea in the latest ship disaster.

New Year's Day, by Marian Phair and her father, was spent in a small frame house in the Carolina mountains, at a hot springs resort that was scarcely habited in the winter. The judge and his daughter sat in a rough little parlor before a blazing oak fire and listened to Marian's canaries singing in their cage. On the table before them stood two large pitchers of the water for which the place was known; and through the windows they could see nothing but the slender trunks of pine, the low spreading green needles of these trees, and the snow that had fallen incessantly since the day before. Pompey curled before the fire, and Marian read to her father out of the Bible: the Lamentations of Jeremiah.

Only a couple of hundred miles away, in a small house in Arlington, Virginia, two young women with their arms around one another's waists stood at the foot of a bed and quietly toasted the new year with tiny glasses of wine. In the bed, Helen Stallworth, with a thick soft white cap covering her head, smiled weakly, and replied, "Thank you, Annie, thank you, Jemmie—I know that we'll all be happy. . . ." Helen's own small fortune, and what she inherited from her father as his sole heir, was more than sufficient to keep her and her two devoted nurses in genteel recuperation and indolence. Annie fought no longer in the ring, nor with her friend Jemmie; and no child was ever more devoted than was Jemmie's niece 'Ralda to the slightest wishes of her benefactors. The only shadow upon this small household was Annie Leech's terrible knowledge, kept both from Helen and Jemmie, that Mrs. General Taunton (who had procured the house for them) had been murdered in a Water Street tenement house on Christmas Day, beat to death with a cooking pot by an Irishman suffering with delirium tremens.

The Elfin Fair that New Year's afternoon was in Sylacauga, Alabama, performing his newest trick, in which he tossed, alternately, five saucers and five cups, from his right foot onto the top of his head; when the astonishing pyramid was complete, he finished off by depositing a teaspoon and a lump of sugar in the topmost cup with an elegant switch of his tiny foot.

The Stallworth family, that had begun the year of 1882 with such arrogant complacency, was scattered to the four winds. Edith was the farthest removed—she was the darling of a small but elegant hotel on the bleak coast of the North Sea at Dagebuell, near the German border with Denmark.

Here Lena Shanks had taken up a residence in two very fine suites of rooms. In one she lived herself, with Rob and Edith; and the other was occupied by Louisa, Charlotta Kegoe, and Ella. Some of the guests wondered how it was that the hotel had been persuaded to accept guests that, although exhibiting quiet, retiring, unexceptionable behavior, were still obviously of an inferior social class. It was only the manager of the hotel and the hotel's lawyer who knew that Lena Shanks had bought the place outright, on the third day of November.

A great New Year's feast was prepared in the vast kitchens of the hotel, and served in the small dining room that was attached to Lena's suite. Here the Shanks family gathered, closed the velvet draperies against the glare of the midday sun upon the gray North sea, and toasted the coming new year. For them was no more labor, and no more trouble.

After their dinner, all the family wrapped themselves in furs and walked out upon the beach. Lena sat in a great wheeled chair and was pushed by Charlotta Kegoe —who now wore real jewelry to hide that which was tattooed onto her skin. Louisa preceded them at a distance, giving a hand to each of the twins. Edith Phair moved at the side of the wheeled chair, searching for perfect shells which, when found, she dropped into a basket Lena Shanks held in her lap.

**AN EXPERIENCE IN HORROR
YOU MAY TRY TO FORGET . . .
AND TRY . . . AND TRY . . .**

COLD MOON OVER BABYLON

BY MICHAEL McDOWELL
AUTHOR OF THE AMULET

Terror grows in Babylon, a typical sleepy Southern town
with its throbbing sun and fog-shrouded swamps.

Margaret Larkin has been robbed of her innocence—
and her life. Her killer is rich and powerful,
beyond the grasp of earthly law.

Now, in the murky depths of the local river,
a shifting, almost human shape slowly takes form.
Night after night it will pursue the murderer.
It will watch him from the trees.
And in the chill waters of the river,
it will claim him in the ultimate embrace.

 AVON 48660/$2.50